Into Dust

JONATHAN LEWIS

arrow books

Published by Arrow 2012

654321

Graham Lewis 2011, 2012

Jonathan Lew   be identified as the author of th   work under the
Copyright, Designs and Patents Act 1988

Carrie-   words and music by Allan Clarke, Graham Nash and   ony Hicks
© Copyri   92 Graham Nash Ltd/Universal Music Publishing   International
Limited. A   l copyright secured. Used by   permission of
Music   s Limited.

First published in Great Britain in 2011 by Preface Publishing
20 Vauxhall Bridge Road
London, SW1V 2SA

An imprint of The Random House Group Limited

www.randomhouse.co.uk

Addresses for companies within The Random House Group Limited
can be found at www.randomhouse.co.uk

The Random House Group Limited Reg. No. 954009

A CIP catalogue record for this book is available from the British Library

ISBN 978 1 84809 260 0

MIX
Paper from
responsible sources
FSC® C016897

The Random House Group Limited supports The Forest Stewardship
Council (FSC®), the leading international forest certification organisation.
Our books carrying the FSC label are printed on FSC® certified paper.
FSC is the only forest certification scheme endorsed by the leading
environmental organisations, including Greenpeace. Our
paper procurement policy can be found at
www.randomhouse.co.uk/environment

Typeset in Times by Palimpsest Book Production Limited,
Falkirk, Stirlingshire

Printed and bound in Great Britain by Clays Ltd, St Ives PLC

For Weasel and Woo

Prologue

Once it was easy.
I lived for myself, in thrall to no one.
Then I met her.
She is beyond words, beyond self.
But behind her – he stands.

It will not be easy, or gentle.
He is as good at his job as I am.
Maybe better.

She is curved and shining.
She is the fish-hook I cannot pull out of me,
Without ripping my own throat.

1

THE MAN LAY MOTIONLESS IN the grass, waiting to kill.

He had been there for hours. It was a little uncomfortable at first
– he'd wanted to stretch his legs, have something to drink. But he
knew that he couldn't. He mustn't move, and he must leave no
traces. It was like hunting. No – this *was* hunting.

He wasn't worried. He wasn't sweating. Everything had been
checked. The gear was battle-tested. The hole was easier to dig
than he'd thought. He just had to stay awake. It had been a long
night. That would be bad, if he fell asleep.

First streaks of dawn over the far ridge. What time was it? Had
he dozed off? Must keep his eyes open, fixed on the little road.
He picked up a jagged rock in his free hand, wondering whether
to try squeezing it to hurt himself. Silly. It wouldn't work. If you
were really exhausted, your hand would relax after a while anyway.
And it would be no good having sore palms for the next bit. Besides,
this was a day for inflicting pain on others, not on himself. No,
there was something that would keep him sharp. He hadn't particularly wanted to use it, but if it would help . . .

He reached into his pocket and pulled out the little packet. He
took care to keep the wrapper. A moment or two later and he knew
he'd be OK for the kill. Better than OK.

* * *

3

For once, amazingly, Ned Bale was on time for a murder.

He usually showed up so late that his colleagues were wondering whether to pack up their bloody gloves and huff off home. They'd long since turned the place into a crime scene: outer cordon of poorly parked cars with blue lights flashing; cat's cradle of 'Police Line' tape stretched everywhere; hearty scrum around the body. It was a bit like royalty thinking the whole world smells of fresh paint – Ned had come to see murder as an event attended by policemen, not killers and their victims.

But this was different. This time, the Detective Chief Inspector was a witness.

He was driving along the foot of a valley on the edge of the Brecon Beacons. Coming off the road at right angles ahead was an ancient humpback bridge carrying a dirt track over a stream and up the side of the valley. And hurtling down that track towards the road was a cloud of dust. A few beats later, and Ned could see the black 4x4 that was stirring up the sand devil. It didn't seem to be slowing down, as if the driver intended to jump Ned's path using the bridge as a springboard – except there was no road on the other side. Just as Ned started to brake, all collision danger vanished – in flame and smoke. The 4x4 leaped into the air, propelled forward by its momentum and both upwards and sideways by an explosion that juddered the ground under Ned's car four hundred yards off and echoed around the valley.

Mid-air, the stricken vehicle's fuel tank extended the firework display by blowing away what remained of the structure. It looked like a photograph taken nanoseconds after Big Bang by one of those miracle space cameras that have somehow mastered the trick of looking back to the start of time. Debris raced tongues of fire in flight from the epicentre, and then Ned realised that some of that debris – the stuff which would have been identified as galaxies in the making – were not heavenly bodies, but human. And they were not being made but blasted apart.

Ned skidded to a halt and jumped out of the car. What the hell had just happened? A bomb, presumably, but what had triggered it? Was it the action of the 4x4, passing over it? Or had someone pressed a button? Someone who was still out there?

Very gingerly, Ned edged along the stream to the humpback bridge. That would give him a bit more cover. He worked his way up the bank on his stomach under the lee of the parapet and scanned the far side of the valley. High on the hills was another road. He wouldn't have noticed it but for a brief stretch of balustrade as the road dodged round a sharp corner. It was about a thousand yards away and perhaps two hundred yards above him. Damn – he had binoculars in the car. No – he still had them in his pocket after looking at those buzzards the day before. He put them to his eyes and panned back, losing the road behind low ridges and then finding it again. Still nothing. Silence.

Go at it another way. Where would he position himself if he wanted to trigger a bomb down here from up there? Dead ahead of him, almost in line with the dirt track itself, the high road jutted out before diving back into the folds of the hills. There seemed to be a barrier of rocks to stop cars flying off the edge. Perfect. Ned was about to shift his position so he could stare at it more comfortably when he saw a flash of light from that very spot. In fact, two flashes of light between grassy boulders. Another pair of binoculars. Another pair of eyes. Another person hiding, watching. The bomber.

Ned dropped his own binoculars. Where was the sun? Behind him, and his were non-reflective. Still, not worth the risk. Stick to the naked eye. Watch. Wait. No more flash. No movement. Murderer up there. Copper down here. Bits of shattered corpse all around. No one coming to help. No gun. Impasse.

Ned lay for an age staring up at the vantage point, kept alert by discomfort, an aching back and fear. It was like a Hitchcock film. Hiding in plain sight with the sun beating down and baddies in the hills. And then he heard a car. It wasn't the bomber's because it didn't suddenly start up. It came from the distance, and it came from behind Ned. From up the dirt road. Not good. Someone was about to drive straight through a crime scene into a huge bomb crater. And maybe there was more than one device. Ned had to take a chance. He had to stop that car. But it would mean breaking cover and turning his back on whoever it was up there. A running, receding target, sure, but the track was narrow. It would take a bloody good shot to get him at that range, but this guy was probably no slouch at that either. Plus Ned couldn't keep an eye on the hillside and stop the oncoming car. Listen. No sound of it slowing. Bugger it. No option.

Ned never liked the phrase 'as if his life depended on it'. It was bollocks. He figured that the trouble with life was you were never given the foggiest clue what it depended on, so you didn't have anything to compare it with. Certainly he had nothing to compare with zigzagging up a dirt track trying not to trample a crime scene to stop someone else doing the same and then getting killed by smashing into a hole or getting blown up, while presenting a rather nifty target to a terrorist with a perfect vantage point. 'As if' didn't really come into it. His life *did* depend on it. Case proven, thought Ned. Absolute bollocks.

On the plus side, no shots rang out behind. In his supercharged imagination, Ned already had the bullets pinging off the rocks around him, but his problems lay ahead. The car – an open-topped Merc – didn't want to stop. He waved. He shouted. Still it came on. It occurred to Ned that his current goals were not easily reconcilable: to be as noticeable as you can in front, and as invisible as possible behind. More windmilling with his arms. Getting hoarse. Nearly at the hole himself. Oh, God! What's that? A forearm? And there? A torso? Ned felt the bile rise, just as the sports car slewed to a halt, enveloped in dust. He slowed his pace and stepped as carefully as he could around the crater towards the car.

The dust cleared, revealing a woman in her late thirties. As he bundled her to the ground, it occurred to him that she seemed faintly familiar. She, for her part, was in complete shock. Not because she had nearly totalled the car and herself. Nor because some stranger had then grabbed her and wrestled her to the ground with him on top of her. No, her problem was that she had seen a smoking chunk of the 4x4, and then the body parts. And she knew exactly whose they were.

While Ned held her tight in his arms and attempted to get a signal on his mobile, he scanned the distant hill, trying to spot the vantage point again, hoping to see a flash or movement. But all he got were wrenching screams and the message 'No Network Coverage'.

It was a local sheep-farmer who saved Ned from being drowned in tears. He had spotted the plume of smoke from the end of the valley and, knowing who his neighbour was, phoned the police and came running himself. The Secretary of State for Defence, the Right Honourable Sir Michael Ridley MP had a weekend cottage up the dirt track. He'd spent the weekend there with his new-ish wife, who was some sort of television presenter. He left in the ministerial 4x4 on Sunday morning with his driver and bodyguard, with Lady Ridley a few minutes behind. So Ned wondered, had the bomber adroitly placed the bomb under the dirt track the previous night, with the Minister's movements for the weekend in his brain?

Within a couple of hours, the bomb crater had become Mecca to every agency in the country with even tangential interest in peacekeeping, felon-apprehending, bomb-disposal and state security. The widow was whipped away, roads cordoned off, helicopter landing sites established with flare paths and air traffic controllers; the three police forces whose boundaries happened to meet in that valley coughed up their chief constables while an outfit more used to films and *eisteddfods* laid on disaster scene catering.

Ned slipped away before the herd of officious jackasses, realising he was the sole witness, could pester him for statements. He wanted to reach the vantage point before the scent went cold. Fat chance finding the bomber hanging around, but there might be traces. Clues. Finding the point wasn't as hard as it might have been. Ned's binoculars had a built-in compass and he had noted the binocular flash's bearing: 357°. All he had to do was drive along the road until the bearing on to the dirt track was the reciprocal of 357°. Unfortunately Ned's grasp of maths was tragically third-rate. He only worked it out by imagining his school protractor in its green cardboard box with the compasses, ruler and well-thumbed photo of Madonna looking impossibly pert. Be fair, thought Ned, this was 1986.

In the event, it was obvious where the bomber had been, because only at one point opposite the dirt track did the high road jut out with a border of stones. He looked down through his binoculars at where he had been lying. 178°. Spot on. He put up cones and tape and then, staying on the tarmac, walked along the edge staring at the rocky verge with a sheer drop beyond. Nothing. There was one place where he fancied the grass was slightly crushed, but it was a dry summer and there wasn't that much grass in the first place. No bits of wire. No sandwich wrappers rich in fingerprints. No Coke bottles dripping with DNA. Nothing to the cursory glance.

The bomb site below looked a lot less messy than it had seemed at ground level. For a while he had worried that the hordes were being allowed to graze at will. Up here, he could see the barriers holding the bulk back, while an orderly line slowly made its sweep across the field, and just two scene-of-crime officers in white jumpsuits knelt in the dust of the crater. Someone must have taken charge down there. Someone with enough authority to boss a load of plods and spooks about. Wonder who that could be?

'Wotcha, cock!'

Who else? Fatso Fullerton. Larger than ever, unlit fag in one fist, half-eaten ham roll in the other. Greasy mat of hair glinting in the sun. Rare – unheard of, these days – for the Porker to pitch up for a dead body, or even three dead bodies. But this was what the Detective Superintendent called a 'giant stiff' and he wasn't about to lose it to the wallies from MoD Police, or the Special Branch tossers, let alone the big girls' blouses from the local constabularies. Fatso had little respect for crime-solvers other than his own, but even if there had been a bunch he half admired, he'd still have kneecapped their grannies to keep the giant stiff for his beloved Ned.

'Sharp timing on your part, Ned. How come you happened to be passing by?'

'I was staying with my sister for a few days. In North Wales. Decided to take the scenic route home.'

Ned saw Fatso's expression and smiled.

'I don't like it much either, sir, but it's pure coincidence.'

Fatso shrugged resignedly, gulped down the last of the ham roll, licked his lips rather ineffectually and gestured Ned closer. Up at the vantage point the air had been clear. Down at the crime scene Ned could smell burned human flesh. He started to feel queasy.

'You look a bit anxious, cock. Don't be. Finders keepers. You found the case – we keep it. There's going to be a meeting in the local boozer at six sharp. We might have to arm-wrestle a few chief constables, but nothing to worry about.'

Fatso lit his cigarette and wandered away towards the catering van. Ned finally lost the struggle and went behind a tree to throw up. Sudden memory of childhood car-sickness. The Cortina pulled onto the verge, with his mother seizing the time for a fag and his sister peering sympathetically out of the back window, while his father stood by his bent-over skinny figure. He used to hold Ned's forehead in his cupped hand while the lad heaved up his Shreddies. Not sure why he did that. It was rather intimate, and little Ned just wanted to be left alone. Plus his forehead was invariably baking by the time he'd wrestled the nausea for an age and lost. The last thing he wanted was Dad's hot palm haltering his retches.

For some reason, Ned always apologised to him. It was a bit like those public school films where the boy has to thank the prefect for beating him. Sorry, Dad. That's all right, son, he'd say, handing Ned a grubby hanky to wipe his mouth. His mother's only concession to maternal responsibility would be to hold out a tin of barley sugars at arm's length – 'to replace the lost energy and take the taste away' – and that, plus the menthol fumes from her Consulate, was often enough to set him off again. Wonder they ever got anywhere.

'Hullo, Bale!'

'Hullo, Wilton!'

Doubled-over, wiping his mouth with a grubby hanky and his

mind thirty years in the past, the old reflexes kicked in regardless. Julia Wilton. His flirt friend from university. The girl with a photographic memory and a superb rump. Flirt friends predated fuck buddies in every sense; as far as he could remember they'd never actually slept together. She'd remember, but now wasn't the time to ask her. Plus she probably outranked him, if the Secret Intelligence Service – MI6 – had ranks.

'You all right?'

He was about to mumble something about having a dicky tummy rather than admit that, oddly, he had zero stomach for his own specialist subject: murder. And then he saw a gleam in the undergrowth, thankfully out of his recent firing line. He reached into his pocket for a forensic bag and tweezers. It was part of a small metal box, jagged at the edges. An electrical connector was riveted to one side with a short length of red and white plastic-covered wire. And, amazingly, still soldered to the ends of the flex was a piece of printed circuit board.

'Thought for one minute you were barfing, but you were finding crucial evidence instead. Clever old Bale. Give us a kiss.'

'Best not,' said Ned, writing on the bag's label. 'I *was* barfing.'

'So what the fuck happened here?'

They found a dry-stone wall clear of clues and human tissue, and sat. Beyond them, a second line of searchers picked over the ground. A reedy, youngish man from the MoD was collecting the Minister's papers which the explosion had scattered. A tent was going up over the crater and a second over the biggest chunk of the 4x4. By morning there would be a canvas village in the adjacent field.

For all the activity, the eye of the storm was almost tranquil compared with what Ned imagined must be going on beyond. There'd be a quarantine zone around and a civilian no-fly over the valley. Then radiating rings of road blocks, barriers at stations, searches on trains. The further from the bomb crater, the greater the disruption. The more people unable to go to work or get home. The longer the tailbacks, the shorter the tempers. Flights grounded, ports shut, the Channel Tunnel sealed. The nation's highest and mightiest locked-down. The press muzzled and drip-fed by turns. Briefings and blackouts, with both sides claiming the national interest.

But all this, it occurred to Ned, would look like slow motion set against what must be happening in Julia Wilton's world. The secret world. They would be as if on speed: the listeners and the watchers. Those who act and those who think. The tappers of phones and the steamers-open of envelopes. The ones who check the passenger lists and follow suspects, and the ones who rock back in their chairs and try to work out in whose interests is it that this has happened? Around the world, over hastily convened drinks or the weekly game of squash, friendly foreign agencies will be asked if they have heard anything. Deeper in the shadows, favours will be called in, and in the darkest corners of all, it will become an excuse to settle old scores. No nation likes to lose its Defence Minister to a terrorist attack in its heartland. Looks bad.

'So why you, Wilton? Not that I'm not delighted to see you.'

She shrugged and stood.

'You know how it is. Phone goes. Half the office is watching the cricket, and the other half the tennis. They can't be bothered to tear themselves away. Plus I was duty muggins. You know about this meeting in the pub?'

He nodded, unenthusiastically. She looked at her watch.

'We'll be late. Nearly six.'

Ned wondered if he really had to be there.

'Well I need a drink. And I'm not walking into that snake-pit alone.'

A bunch of Special Branch bouncers had set up an exclusion zone around the pub to stop the press getting snaps of key spooks. Meanwhile the defenders of the realm had taken over the saloon bar. The three chief constables whose turfs converged at the crime scene pretended to be polite to one another, while keeping their distance from the nondescript representatives of assorted security, intelligence and anti-terrorism agencies. The latter's talk seemed to be not of bombs, but holidays. Flotilla sailing in Turkey seemed to be the favourite; it apparently kept teenage children nicely busy. Fatso sipped his beer and looked utterly unflappable.

Sitting in the corner was an old cove in tweeds whom nobody seemed to know. It occurred to Ned that he might be a local sheep-farmer who'd been dozing in the bar since lunch, and that maybe they should throw him out. The minute Wilton entered the room, he seemed to wake up. Perhaps it was the sudden whiff of her Chanel No. 5 against the overpowering pong of self-important men in sweaty suits that wouldn't see the dry-cleaners till autumn. Anyway, he turned out to be Sir Somebody or Other from the Joint Intelligence Committee, and he was delighted to see dear Julia. He gallantly staggered to his feet, kissed her on both cheeks and made sure she sat next to him. Ned spotted the man who'd been gathering the secret papers at the crime scene and introduced himself. He turned out to be Clive Hawkins, the late Minister's bagman from the MoD. We need to talk, Ned started to say, but before Hawkins could reply the meeting was called to order. Ned found a perch on the wood-basket and the fun began.

It took a while before Ned twigged what was going on. His mistake lay in his preconception that they'd all be fighting to own the case. The chief constables could not agree among themselves which of them had jurisdiction, and so concluded that none of them did. The men in suits seemed to divide into two camps. Those of the intelligence persuasion argued very reasonably that they had no statutory powers of arrest, and that whereas they would give whoever was tasked with solving the crime whatever help and advice they could, they weren't actually in a position to . . . do anything. Meanwhile the counter-terrorism lot had all the necessary powers and mandate, but unfortunately now was a particularly bad time for them. Height of the summer, lots of people away on leave, staff shortages, budget cuts, hands full elsewhere . . .

What about Special Branch? Surely Mr Armitage had to take

this on? He was near retirement age; soft-spoken and engagingly frank. Everyone seemed to like him enormously. All eyes in the room turned to him.

'Here's the thing. Under normal circumstances, we'd grab this with open arms. But as some of you may know, we lost Phil Cousins the other day.'

The room immediately looked down, out of respect. Ned only knew Special Branch's legendary investigator by name, and had no idea if he was dead, retired or simply mislaid, but he gave a sombre little dip of the head as well so as not to seem callous. Nice Mr Armitage went on.

'We've got a couple of chaps off sick, and one or two who'd love to cut their teeth on this, but frankly aren't quite up to it yet. They will be in time, no question,' he added quickly, 'but just not quite yet, if you get my meaning. After all,' he slipped effortlessly into a let's-remember-why-we're-all-here tone of voice, 'we want this thing solved and pronto. I'm sure we're all agreed on that.'

Body language and grunts around the room indicated general concurrence.

'And this is going to be a teensy bit tricky. It's already shaping up that way . . . Best to have someone who can hit the ground running, I always think . . .'

Again, the rumble of assent.

'So there's really only one chap for this . . .'

More nodding.

'So that's settled then,' said the elderly gentleman from the Joint Intelligence Committee. 'I'm seeing the Cabinet Secretary and the PM the minute I get back to town. I'll give them the good news.'

With that, they all started shaking hands, but the person whose hand they seemed to be shaking the hardest was Ned's.

When they'd all gone – Wilton with a tender peck on the cheek for Ned and her mobile number on a beer mat, the others almost tumbling out of the door – he sat in the saloon bar, empty except for Fatso. What, he gingerly asked his boss, was that all about?

The response was appropriate, given that Fatso was staring at the food blackboard.

'Hot potato. There's not one of them could find their own pricks if their flies weren't open. It's all yours, Ned the Yid. Knew it would be. Spoke to Armitage in the bogs earlier, you see. I'll be off. Reckon I'll eat on the way.'

Ned felt more alone now than he had felt in the ditch by the hump-back bridge, pinned down by the invisible bomber.

He had a midnight call from Chief Superintendent Larribee, Fatso's leathery-faced boss. She told him how pleased she was that this vital case was theirs and that many eyes would be on him. 'Future foreshortening' – she loved meaningless buzz phrases – was not an option here. All necessary processes would have to be gone through, arduous though they might be. Cases like this were 'stamina sucks'. And he must be vigilant; in her experience, terrorism had a 'dynamic unpredictability'. There's a surprise, Ned thought. His investigation would need considerable 'granularity', but she had absolute confidence in him. Ned politely mumbled his thanks. And then she said something odd. Maybe not odd, but Ned was so used to her clichés that her last trope rather stood out.

'On this case, Bale, I'd advise thinking big. Good night and good luck.'

He lay in bed, thinking. What did she mean? That the bomber was the Pope? Or perhaps the President of the United States? Ned worried at it for a good ten minutes before deciding that, like everything else the old bat uttered, this was just more senseless drivel. He rolled over in bed on to his stomach in his usual going-to-sleep position, with one leg crooked high and the other kicked out straight behind. Unfortunately the pub's best room had a mattress painstakingly modelled on the surrounding landscape. Ned tried resting his left knee on the vantage point with one foot in the stream and the other in the bomb crater, and went straight to sleep.

* * *

A short and sturdy woman with chiselled features was waiting for Ned when he emerged from breakfast. Detective Sergeant Jan Span had worked very happily with him for four years. She had a sharp, methodical mind and wasted no time on intuitions. Ned was very pleased to see her.

'Right, Jan Span,' said Ned. 'Enough yarzelling about. Let's go for it!'

Hawkins from the MoD was waiting outside the pub. From the packed bag and laced-together walking boots, Ned deduced that Hawkins felt his work there was done.

'Ah,' said Ned, 'sorry if I've kept you waiting . . .'

Hawkins looked a tiny bit uncomfortable. He mumbled something about not knowing the DCI wanted to see him . . . he was hoping to catch the 11.15 back to town.

Blimey, thought Ned. The Minister of Defence is bumped off in broad daylight, with his driver and bodyguard, and the MOD's man on the spot thinks it's OK to wander around the crime scene gathering evidence and then run away without actually talking to anyone, let alone sharing his finds. And having thought it, Ned said it aloud. Hawkins who was already pink from the sun, went a shade towards carmine.

'Look, I don't know that I *can* show you what I've found. The Minister had taken his boxes away for the weekend, and quite a lot of it is secret. Most of it, in fact. There's stuff from the service chiefs, from the force commanders in Afghanistan and Iraq, from the embassies, from SIS, the Security Service . . . You'll appreciate that I can't simply hand it over.'

No point in locking antlers with a jobsworth. Need other stuff from him. Shift tack.

'Why don't we leave it to our bosses to sort out the clearances?'

Hawkins looked relieved. Ned went on. He would like a log of all the documents found, so he could cross them off his list if and when he got a chance to look at them.

'DS Span here will help you draw up the log after we're through.

11.15 train you say? You should make that. Didn't know there was a night sleeper . . . Best leave your bags – thought we'd walk to the crime scene. That way we can make a start on my questions . . .'

Jan Span barely suppressed a smile. More like – so don't try keeping anything from us, Hawkins old son.

By the time they reached the humpbacked bridge, Hawkins was a little drained. He had heard of Detective Chief Inspector Ned Bale. Heard that he was on the bright side. That he thrived on impossible cases. That there had been repeated attempts by various agencies to poach him. When Hawkins had rung the office after Bale was anointed in the pub the previous evening, the late Minister's chief hatchet man had described Bale to him as 'dangerously dogged'. The phrase came back to Hawkins several times that day. It was both falsely reassuring and alarming. Falsely reassuring because it suggested Bale was a tenacious plodder, rather than an inspired unraveller. Alarming, because it suggested he could not be relied on to be on 'our side'.

And then there was this Jan Span person. She looked as if she didn't miss much. She had the odd ability to write notes on the move. Just an aide memoire, she said. A bit of a worry, the pair of them.

Who else, Ned first wanted to know, has the use of the dirt track, other than the Ridleys? He'd had a squint at the Ordnance Survey map on the wall in the bar, and as far as he could make out there was a farm . . .

The track in fact served two farms as well as providing access for the Ridleys. Lesseps Farm had another way out via the next valley, but that was a long way round to get to the main road for markets etc. The Thomases only used the track. They had all been security-cleared, incidentally. The track was shared three ways as far as the tarn, about half a mile beyond the humpback bridge, then there was a fork. Left for the two farms. The turn-off to the Thomases was half a mile further on. Turn right for the Ridleys' place. That's why they'd put the gate and heavyweight surveillance stuff up there, rather than down at the road. It wasn't ideal – the security chaps weren't happy – but there wasn't much choice. It was Lady Ridley's before they met. Had been in her family. She was not about to give it up, and the Minister loved it there. Ideal head clearance zone, was how he described it.

'What was he like, the Minister?'

This was the first time Hawkins had had to think about the Minister since he got the call. Think about him as a man in life, rather than as a problem in death.

'He was a soldier, Chief Inspector. Served in Northern Ireland, First Gulf War, Kosovo. Mentioned in Despatches in all three theatres. He loved the Army, and the Army loved him. He was perhaps the most respected Defence Minister since Denis Healey. Healey could look the Chiefs of Staff in the eye because they knew he had been the beach master at Anzio. Same with Ridley. When he had to sell the cuts to General Sir Mark Collet last November, he was talking to a man he had been with when their column ran slap-bang into a nest of SCUDs on the outskirts of Kuwait City in Operation Desert Sabre. Remember? Pinned down, engine conked out, taking casualties. Who jumped out under fire, stuck his head under the bonnet and jury-rigged the fuel line? Who – in effect – got them out of there?'

They walked on in silence, and then Hawkins spoke again.

'The Chiefs of the Defence Staff have been known to pop a post-election bottle of bubbly when they know they're getting shot of a particularly unhelpful Minister. They might have raised a glass last night, but it won't have been champagne and it won't have been celebration.'

Ned made a sympathetic noise, while privately having severe doubts about the Hawkins hagiography. Ridley may have been fancied rotten by everyone above Brigadier, but there had been a constant rumble of discontent at troop level throughout his tenure of office. Wrong kit, bad kit, not enough kit. Bullets that didn't fit rifles, Land Rovers that crumpled if you sneezed near them, warehouses full of metal detectors and jammers back home, with front-line troops trying to find and disable roadside bombs with their folding knife and fork sets. And it wasn't only angry troops, but wives and girlfriends nursing amputees, and bereaved parents, dadless children and widows.

They were nearing the bridge. The crime scene was alive with activity. Forensics like worker ants criss-crossed the scene without bumping into one another. Ned spotted two familiar figures. Doc Bones was peering at something ghastly in the light outside the refrigerated truck in which he was gathering bits of bodies for the autopsy. And alongside another, smaller vehicle a lanky man with buck teeth and glasses was erecting a tent. Extra Bilge's job was to map the crime scene and coordinate all finds. Ned found the sight of his own colleagues working away decidedly reassuring. Particularly by comparison with the shifty Mr Hawkins.

'Could you give us a brief rundown of the full security arrangements at the Defence Minister's country retreat?'

Hawkins drew breath. He listed the outer and inner rings of surveillance cameras up at the cottage, the various sensors, alarms and floodlights, the emergency buttons and shutters, the converted lambing shed where the personal protection officers monitored the systems and screens 24/7. The HLS – sorry, Helicopter Landing Site – in the adjacent field. Oh, and they'd converted the cellar into a panic room cum bomb shelter.

'And when you say 24/7, does that mean every day of the year?'

There was a little pause. Odd question, thought Span. The boss may live a bit in a world of his own, but he certainly knows the expression. Watch out Mr H. You're about to get Nedded.

The colour now seemed to drain a tad from the Hawkins cheeks.

'Well, every day of the year . . . that the Minister is in residence . . . at the cottage . . .'

Ned looked a little puzzled.

'Security naturally takes the view that our man has to be protected at all times. So whether he is at the Ministry, or the flat in town, or his constituency . . .'

Hawkins ran out of steam. But Ned had tons of it.

'So, Mr Hawkins,' said Ned, pointing up at a telephone pole near the bridge. 'If we were to take a look at the recorded output from that camera up there, we'd see everything and everyone that had gone up the dirt track for the past, what, week? Fortnight? Month?'

Span hadn't noticed any camera, but there it was, sure enough, almost hidden behind the insulators. Hawkins glanced up, and then rubbed his face with both hands.

'You really need to address these questions to the security geeks, but . . . as I understand it . . . not exactly.'

'How do you mean?' Ned asked.

Hawkins looked like what he was – a man wondering whether to tell the truth and feel a fool, or tell a lie and feel a knave. And then get caught out. The fool won.

'When the officers arrive with the Minister – arrived, I should say – they'd have switched the camera surveillance on. And when they left yesterday morning they'd have . . . switched it off.'

Span looked aghast. Ned merely puzzled. Was this an energy-saving move?

'Energy-saving, cuts, modulated threat response . . . whatever you want to call it . . .'

'Bloody foolhardy' came into Ned's mind.

'. . . Plus no one in practice is going to watch thousands of hours of nothing happening.'

'But what about when something *does* happen? Like, say, someone burying an improvised explosive device in the dirt track?'

Hawkins shrugged.

'Security assigns different protection profiles to different scenarios and locales. That's what they mean by "modulated threat response". The stuff at the flat in town is never switched off, but here scores much lower. It's out of the way, he's not here very often, and his movements aren't advertised.'

Ned shook his head.

'Look, Chief Inspector, you can't break into the cottage without the alarms going off at the local police station. Most of it's never switched off. It's only down here by the road that there's a bit of a . . . gap.'

A bit of a gap that a lucky or well-informed bomber had squeezed through.

'So if they remembered to flip the switch, we may be able to see everything down this track from the time the Minister arrived to just before he died?'

Hawkins nodded. All that stuff was up at the cottage. He'd get the tech guys on the case. The detective chief inspector should be able to see it straight away. They walked carefully around the scene towards a police Land Rover standing by beyond the crater. On the way, Ned was cornered by Doc Bones waving a bloody pair of forceps.

'Bit of an odd one here. Do you want to come in and have a look?'

Ned did not want to come in and have a look. Could Doc Bones describe it using as few adjectives as possible?

'Certainly. Not all the torn-asunder flesh round here is from *Homo sapiens*. Some of it is from *Vulpes vulpes*. Red fox.'

Red fox? Was it possible a fox happened past at the exact moment when the IED went off? By the same token, presumably slumbering birds in adjacent trees had also become victims. Ned was about to beat a hasty retreat, when something occurred to him.

'Doc, is there any chance of knowing what the time of death was? For the fox, I mean?'

Doc didn't think he had enough bits to go on. And what he had were little more than smears, but he'd have a stab at it. Ned thanked him and moved quickly on. Funny chap – young Ned, Doc mused as he scanned his chilled compartments, wondering where he'd parked the kit of parts to make a dead fox. Always asking these daft questions that turned out, more often than not, to be rather on the money.

The cottage was straight from a country lifestyle magazine. In fact, the country lifestyle magazine in which it had starred was framed on the lavatory wall. Along with the obligatory self-mocking/ self-regarding ephemera. A typically sharp Steve Bell cartoon showed the Minister of Defence in battle dress, defending himself from his enemies while exposing himself grotesquely to the future Lady Ridley – with a caption about 'private parts'. An aerial view of the cottage was splayed across the front page of the *Sun*, with the headline 'Top[less] Secret – Fiddly Ridley's bonk-nest!'

It all came back to Ned: the noisy affair, the crisp divorce, the snazzy wedding. It had happened so fast that, lucky for him, the Minister didn't have time to lie about it. And given the new wife was rather sexy, the old one was rather grim and the PM was no puritan, there was no talk of the Minister having to resign. That was perhaps a year ago. The attention of the tabloids had switched to other clever-dick girls and dick-led men.

Hanging over the toilet-roll holder was a pair of framed letters: one of terse rejection addressed to a young would-be reporter; the second five years later addressed to Lady Ridley as she now was: begging her to accept a stonking sum to present her own show. The once dismissive programme editor now a fawning channel controller.

Ned pulled the chain, washed his hands with an artisanal bar of cucumber and myrtle soap, dried his hands on a fluffy designer towel and went off to the lambing shed to play Spot the Bomber on the surveillance screens.

The tech guys looked about fourteen. They wore jeans, trainers and the usual sweatshirts from improbably lofty universities, except it turned out she *had* done her masters at MIT and he *did* have a Cambridge doctorate. They were there to gather in the gear that the Widow Ridley would have no need of now: the surveillance stuff, the scrambler phone, the encoding device and the short wave radio in the cellar that could withstand the electromagnetic pulse from a 10-megaton bomb exploding over the cottage. Should you be telling me this? asked Ned, feeling a bit priggish as he did so. It's all on the Internet, they replied, if you know where to look.

'So where do I look to see everything recorded from the camera on the telephone pole down by the humpback bridge?'

Click, and there it was: the camera almost centred on the spot which would later be blown apart by the bomb, tight enough on the track to read a number plate. They started on Saturday afternoon, running at high speed, slowing it down when something happened – which wasn't very often. The Merc sports car went out once, returning a couple of hours later. Various farm vehicles passed through. Some walkers. Apparently they were turned away by Security up at the tarn. That was in another file on the harddrive as well as in the paper log. There was obviously a cycle race through the hills in the afternoon because for about an hour those odd Martian helmets zipped across the bottom of the frame, and then one of the cyclists pulled off the road on to the track and fiddled with the bike chain or gears for a few minutes, before riding off. Nothing seemed to go through on Saturday night. According to the log, the Ridleys were tucked up with pizza and wine. Dawn came up on Sunday morning, and then at 10.41 a.m. the screen went blank. Plug pulled by men in a hurry to whisk the Minister to town, with his wife leaving shortly afterwards. During the previous fifteen hours no one had been seen to dig a hole and then fill it with explosives.

'I didn't notice it, but presumably there's a light on the pole somewhere near the camera?'

The female technician answered Ned.

'There is. It's triggered by a motion detector, but the circuit is only live during the hours of darkness. There's a photo-electric sensor which kicks it in when the light drops below a certain level. And then when the sun comes up, the sensor trips out.'

'Could someone have disabled it?' Ned wanted to know.

'Not without triggering an alarm in here.'

Ned made some notes.

'So the evidence from the recording is that no one came or went on either night?'

She slid over a hardback diary.

'Correct. And that's corroborated by the paper log.'

'Could I see the last few minutes again?'

The geeks obliged, Ned leaning in for a close look. He next asked them for a copy of the file containing the surveillance material they had just seen. Again they obliged, putting it on a memory stick. He then asked – but it wasn't really a question – if he could keep the logbook. Before Hawkins had a chance to think, Span handed him a receipt. Ned thanked them all, and set off to walk back to the crime scene.

'Odd,' said Ned, when he and Jan Span were safely clear of the cottage.

'What's odd, sir?'

'Glad you asked me, Jan Span. It got dark around nine p.m. on Saturday night. By dawn, there was a dead fox lying on the verge.'

'We are in the countryside, sir. There's always roadkill.'

He carefully shut the gate behind them.

'Absolutely. Poor furry beasts. But you saw for yourself: not a single car passed down the track during the night. So how did the fox get there?'

2

'STILL SEE YOU, SIR.'

He drove at a snail's pace along the high road. Every minute the walkie-talkie crackled into life with Jan Span's voice.

'Still see you, sir.'

Ned needed to know how the bomber had got away. Why hadn't Ned seen his car? Was it hidden below the barrier of rocks which bordered the upper road? So he'd got Span to lie on the bank by the humpback bridge in the same position he had been in the day before, looking up at the vantage point. At the bomber.

'Still see you, sir.'

It turned out there wasn't anywhere on the high road along the length of the valley where she couldn't see him.

'Relax, Jan Span. Something we're missing here . . .'

Ned drove back to the vantage point, got out and had a think. The troops below were still working like good 'uns. He could see Forensics bearing down on Doc Bones like dogs retrieving balls. And talking of dogs, he could see one of Large Sarge's vans pulling in behind Extra Bilge's. Couldn't see who it was getting out. For a moment his heart leaped. He pulled out the binoculars. No. Of course it wasn't. How could it be? It was Millie. She opened up the back and let out her dog, which shook itself after the long drive. A big glossy black Labrador, not a small Cocker Spaniel . . .

Ned lowered the binocs. Of course. The bomber's vehicle might have had a lower profile.

'. . . the point at which as little of the car is visible as possible, Jan Span, tell me to stop. Got it?'

The next pass was entirely conducted in radio silence. Ned was starting to wonder if either or both of their walkie-talkies had conked out, when she spoke.

'OK sir, I know where it is. I didn't want to say it was one place when there was an even lower one further on. Could you go back, please, sir, and I'll stop you this time.'

Ned got about six hundred yards beyond the vantage point when she spoke again.

'Stop, sir! Now back up about a car's length . . . Stop! You're right on it. I can just see the bottom edge of your side window and upwards. Nothing below.'

Ned got out and measured the distance from window to tarmac. Thirty-six inches exactly. How many cars are only a yard high?

'Thanks. You can stand down for a bit. I'm going to poke around up here. Oh, by the way – the Army's sending us their champion bomb disposal expert. A Major Butterman. Can you keep an eye out for him? If you find him, let him have a good peer at everything and then be prepared to tell us how it was done.'

He drove back to the vantage point. How the hell *did* they do it – and not be seen? That 4x4 must have been armoured. Would have taken a weight of explosives to toss it into the air. One man's work? Or more? They call them IEDs but this one can't have been that improvised. Loads of questions for the major. Then, once the bomber had dug it all in and maybe tested the circuit – do they do that? – he'd have had to dodge back up here and tuck himself away. Must have been here for hours. Maybe eight hours. He's got to eat. Got to pee. Might have been smart. Thought ahead and brought a bottle. Or peed over the edge. Someone's going to have to go down there. Can't see Extra Bilge abseiling. Must be a

Mountain Rescue outfit in these parts. And let's get that dog up here. Wonder if it does urine as well as explosives?

'You OK, Jan Span?' asked Ned.

DS Span realised that she must still be wearing an aghast expression on her face. A tabloid journalist in the tea queue had just told her – woman to woman – how much she must enjoy working with the detective chief inspector. He was so . . . Jan Span did not let her finish the sentence. She didn't want to know. *She* was DCI Bale's sergeant. Admittedly, so was DS Sam Pick, but he was a guy. Not the same thing. She felt . . . well . . . possessive about the DCI. He was so . . . very, very fanciable. There weren't that many men women stared at, but DCI Bale was one. It annoyed her seeing other females being distracted by him. 'He's got a brain as well, you know . . .' she wanted to shout at them. And as his sergeant, she probably had the right. But the other women would leap to conclusions, wouldn't they? That Jan Span was jealous. Ridiculous!

'Fine, sir. Meet Major Butterman. This is DCI Bale. We got you a tea. They don't do rock cakes, I'm afraid. The major's not been here long; he's had a look at the crater and that's about it . . .'

Major Butterman was around forty, with a pleasing, weather-beaten face. He had a chestful of ribbons and one leg missing. Ned couldn't help but think the abundance of the one and the shortage of the other were connected. They sat on a wall and drank their tea while the major quizzed Ned gently but precisely about what exactly he'd seen of the explosion. Was it a ball of flame? Or a tongue? How high? Straight up or at an angle? Was there any preceding flash? Only one bang? Had any bomb debris turned up? Fuse, trigger, electronic stuff? Ned didn't know if anyone else had got lucky but he had happened on one bit. The major looked interested. They downed their tea and headed off to Extra Bilge.

If there was one kind of place Extra Bilge loved more than anywhere else it was a crime scene. All those messages, all that information, all the questions – hidden in long grass, smeared on mirrors, buried in the rifling of a gun. All waiting to be found, bagged, labelled, mapped, logged, collated, studied, compared. Then decoded, translated, unravelled, stripped of their mystery, brought into the light. Understood. Here a hair, there some DNA. A fingerprint, a voiceprint, handwriting. Blood, semen, saliva. Telltales all. Brimful of facts waiting to spill out across a case, magically transforming questions into proofs.

Next to crime scenes, Extra Bilge loved people who knew things he did not. Ned could see him stiffen in anticipation at the appearance of Major Butterman in his tent. He watched him peering down the trestle tables at the serried ranks of bagged evidence. He took in the medal ribbons. The missing leg. He knew the major trained those very few who made the grade in bomb disposal. He also knew the major had faced the ticking timers and ball-bearing-studded plastic explosive in hot-spots around the globe. He must know TONS! If only there were a helmet you could bang on to someone's head with wires connected to a similar helmet on your own, and then flip a switch and transfer all that glorious information in a trice . . . Ned saw Extra Bilge size up the major's cranium and, knowing him of old, reined him in.

'Show the major the bit I found, Extra Bilge. I assume if it's still the biggest by knocking-off time, I win the box of chocs?'

Extra Bilge, knowing Ned of old, was grateful to be returned to the here and now.

'It's over here, Major, in pride of place.'

On went gloves. Out came forceps and magnifying glasses. Out too, came words like 'claymore', 'graphite', 'chromatography'. Acronyms like 'PE4', 'EOD', 'TPU'. Phrases like 'armour penetrator', 'trigger mechanism' and 'daisy chains'. Bilge and the major were bonding. This could be a long one.

Extra Bilge's mobile laboratory was the most organised and labelled place Ned knew in the whole world. On another level, it was a bit like Dr Frankenstein's garden shed. There was a rack of jars containing the stuff of nightmares. There were reference works on poisons and the trajectories of bullets. There was a copy of

Standing and Aston's *100 Alibis Worth Remembering*. There were test tubes, hypodermic syringes and jagged-bladed knives. There was a testing kit for nuclear isotopes. And it wasn't all high-tech. There was a spade and an axe, and Bilge being Bilge, painted in red on their mounting panel were a full-size spade and axe with the words SPADE and AXE underneath. There were also a number of items that Ned found hard to reconcile with crime-solving. What, for example, did a bound volume of *Bus Route Monthly* for 1961–62 have to do with murder? And why was there a tray of garish cupcakes on the spotless Formica worktop – all but one ominously missing? Ned was just bending over for a closer look, when he heard a generous voice from the adjoining tent.

'Help yourself, Mr Ned sir. It's the remains of my lunch.'

And what was this? Looks interesting. Hanging off the side of the van was a whiteboard, and on it Extra Bilge had mapped the crime scene. The location of every find was marked: the pieces of the 4x4, fragments of bomb and rarer fragments of electronic bits. Key items had *in situ* photos taped round the edge, linked to the places where they were discovered by different coloured lines. The 4x4 was black, the bomb mechanisms seemed to be red; perhaps five other colours were in use. The detail may have passed him by, but the pattern on the map reinforced what Ned had seen: that the vehicle had been blown sideways through the air. It looked as if the bomb had been buried not under the track, but in the bank to the right as Ned had seen it. As the bomber had seen it. Exactly where the fox happened to be lying dead on the surveillance footage.

The major and the Bilge were almost exchanging marriage vows, so Ned wandered out of the tent. He could hear helicopters hovering somewhere over the next valley. Two Mountain Rescuers were dangling off ropes from the vantage point, scouring the hill-side. And then along came DS Sam Pick. Road blocks were drawing a blank, apparently. Nothing yet from those choppers. Further afield, SO15 had been rounding up the usual counter-terrorism suspects, bagging all the best spots for their prayer-rugs at the dodgiest mosques, dressing up as check-in staff at Terminal 3, and talking to their narks and informers. And the result of this mighty expenditure of taxpayers' money and loss of shoe leather was precisely nothing. No one had heard a thing about the Brecon bombing. Or, as the papers were now calling it, The Brecon Bombing.

According to Spick, as he was known, MI5 and SO15 admitted they were surprised. Normally they'd be snowed under with tip-offs and rumours. An operation like this always leaves traces. Someone's cousin gets wind that someone's brother-in-law needs putting up. Or there's a rucksack to move from one railway station locker to another. And naturally, people talk. But not this time. It was for moments like this that people risked their lives going undercover. And yet, so far, their Category X people hadn't heard a whisper. Of course, it was still early days – a couple or three in really deep cover hadn't yet phoned in – but that was how it was looking. Add this to the fact that, according to GCHQ, there hadn't been so much as a breath about it in the ether beforehand and there were only two obvious explanations: either there was a real hellfire and damnation three line whip out calling for total silence, or whoever did this operated without any help from or links to, known extremist networks.

Hmm. Ned had a think. If it was the former, then sooner or later someone would blab. You can't keep a secret. But if it's the latter . . . best way to keep a secret is not to know it.

'And no one's claimed it?'

Spick glanced at his notebook. Apparently Al-Jazeera had had a call from some Jihadist group, but the bloke had given a nonsense security code, and when Al-Jazeera rang the group's front office, they categorically denied involvement. Spick had checked with MI5; they knew about the phone call, and weren't taking it seriously.

'Is it your impression, Spick, that they're all assuming the bomber is from the Middle East?'

Spick reckoned it was.

Ned shook his head a little. Silly. Terrorism wasn't a Muslim extremist monopoly. Not by a long stretch. People were still getting bumped off in Northern Ireland; Basque Separatists, Colombian Revolutionaries, Chechen rebels – they were all still in business. And it was odd how overlapping their interests were. My enemy's enemy is my friend and all that.

'We need to remind our dear colleagues to think laterally. Perhaps it would sound less nannyish if we circulated them a paper outlining the late Minister's points of contact with the world's baddies. Who has he rubbed up the wrong way? Didn't he give evidence to President Obama's Threats Commission? Could you take a look at the paperwork and see whose cages Ridley has rattled over the past decade?'

Sam Pick was the kind of brave-hearted copper who preferred chasing villains down back alleys and the occasional shoot-out, but he knew he had to raise his game in the reading/writing/thinking department.

'Piece of piss, governor.'

And off he zoomed to borrow a pencil from Extra Bilge.

'None of the farmers left their houses on Saturday night, sir.'

Thanks, Jan Span. Useful to know.

'Sir? Didn't we sort of know that already? From the surveillance camera?'

'Not really. All we knew was the tape didn't show any vehicles moving down the track at night. Had one of the farmers gone to pick his daughter up from the Saturday-night disco, then we'd have had easy proof that the tape had been tampered with.'

Where's the wunderkind going with this one? No matter, she reckoned, all grist to the memoirs.

'That's why I quizzed the two geeks up at the cottage about their sweatshirts. Did you check their IDs? No – neither did I. Simply took it on trust that Hawkins was vouching for them. But did he know them? No idea. They may have been a pair of wrong 'uns clearing up after the hit. We all expected geeks, and geeks we got. It was just quicker finding out if the farmers stayed in on Saturday night than to get security to check the geeks' inside leg measurements.'

'Brilliant, sir. It's just that, although the farmers didn't go out, you were spot on about the daughter at the disco. Except they call it clubbing nowadays, sir. And someone did drive her home.'

Bloody hell, thought Ned. Right for the wrong reason again.

'His name is Edward Tamblin, and he drives a beaten-up Toyota. He lives on the far side of the next valley, and the club is back along this road. So he always takes her home up the track here. Apparently Jackie gets a major bollocking if she's in after midnight, so he cuts the engine at the top of the hill, rolls down to Lesseps Farm, she tiptoes in and he coasts the rest of the way, only starting his engine at the bottom. I had to promise Edward I wouldn't tell her dad.'

Still isn't enough, thought Ned. Why hadn't they appeared on the tape?

'What colour Toyota?'

'Dark blue.'

'And are his rear lights working?'

'Never asked, sir. Stupid of me.'

'Doesn't matter, Jan Span. Perhaps they weren't on. Perhaps they go past the security cameras with the lights off. That way if her dad checks with the Security chaps, they can't dob Edward in it for getting the precious Jackie home late.'

Span smiled, but Ned still wasn't happy. Why hadn't the car triggered the floodlight?

'Nothing on this evening, Jan Span? Take a close look at this.'

He handed her the memory stick.

'Have a look at it again, at a slightly less headlong speed. See if you can spot the ghost of a Toyota in the dark. Plus the magic moment when the fox appears. Also, can you get Mr Edward Tamblin to pop down here for a moment? Oh, and we'll need a ladder. Tall enough to get up to the top of that telephone pole. And we'd better get those geeks checked out. Mr Armitage's lot should oblige.'

Delegation – that's a sign of leadership, thought Span, with the selection board for Detective Inspector looming.

*   *   *

The major showed no sign of escaping Extra Bilge's clutches, so Ned decided to winkle him out. He needed to know how this bomb worked. How it was rigged. But he also had a question for the Bilge. Dangerous, he knew, because there was no knowing how long the answer would go on for.

'The 4x4, Mr Ned? Yes, indeed. Vital question. The major and I were just starting to wonder about the size of the charge, weren't we, sir? Essentially what you are asking is not what the bomber needed to get the job done, but rather, what did he use to cause this particular effect?'

He gestured towards the white-board. Ned tried to look as if that was exactly what he was asking.

'Naturally, if we knew the size of the charge, we could estimate the weight of the vehicle by reference to the concentric circles of debris scatter and dispersal – what we call the DS&D – radiused out from ground zero.'

Ned was about to glaze over when Extra Bilge returned to the real world.

'Another starting point might be the spec. of the actual vehicle.'

Extra Bilge produced a sheaf of photographs, cutaway plans and elevations.

'It was an armoured Range Rover, powered by a 4.4 litre V8 engine producing 281bhp. Triple fuel and braking systems giving multiple redundancy in emergencies. Run-flat tyres, allowing escape after puncture. It carried its own oxygen supply in the event of chemical warfare attack. No air bags, of course, so as to keep going after an impact – essential anti-ambush procedure. The floor was reinforced, ditto the sides, though not as heavily. Bulletproof glass all round. Completely revamped suspension system to compensate for the extra weight using a custom set of air dampers. Unfortunately, given this extra weight, the fuel consumption was a meagre 10mpg, although enlarged tanks kept the range up around the 240 mile mark. Price on the road £165,000, though the electronics and comms fit probably added a further £30,000.'

Extra Bilge had nearly finished, but not quite.

'And then there'd be road tax to pay on top.'

Ned wasn't sure whether Extra Bilge had mentioned the bloody car's weight, and he'd dozed off and missed it. Or if he had, as so often, lost sight of the vital question amid the trivia. Luckily, the major had kept awake.

'Fascinating. And the all-up weight?'

'Four tonnes.'

The major started to do some sums on the back of an envelope, while Extra Bilge sat back, baring his teeth at Ned in a satisfied grin. He looked like a mad horse. An annoying, frustrating mad horse. And then Extra Bilge quietly dropped one of those crucial little bombshells that made you want to hug him.

'By the way, Mr Ned sir. You know the bit you found? Turned out to be part of the trigger mechanism. Did I mention there's a fingerprint on it? A nice clear one.'

They walked over to the crater. Major Butterman talked and Ned listened. He explained the origins of IEDs in the guerrilla wars against the Germans by the Resistance in France and the Belarussians: blowing up trains with command wires or delay-action fuses. The techniques were developed by both sides in the Vietnam War. The Viet Cong would hide hand grenades in huts, their pins pulled and the levers held in by thick rubber bands. The American troops would arrive to burn down the village, the rubber bands would melt in the fire and the grenades would explode, killing the US soldiers who'd hung around expecting nothing more than the heat from burning straw. For their part, the Americans would wedge grenades into glass jars with the pins pulled, and then drop them out of helicopters. The glass smashed, allowing the levers to spring open: boom!

The IRA refined the art, placing IEDs in culverts and drains, employing car bombs, developing complex trigger mechanisms and long-delay timers. The 1984 Brighton bomb involved an elapse of weeks between placing the 100lbs of gelignite and the explosion. The IRA used radio transmissions to trigger bombs, the British evolved jammers, the IRA learned how the jammers worked and in turn increased the sophistication of their remote firing techniques. Washing-machine timers, electronic garage-door openers – all those little things that made lives easier also came in handy for terminating them.

Booby traps, anti-tilt and anti-tamper devices rendered the bomb disposers' task even more lethal – nothing really that their forerunners hadn't faced in the Second World War. The chaps who had trained Major Butterman would laugh at the idea that any of this was new. But now add in the growing international dimension: the Libyans supplying the IRA with Semtex, the IRA training the Libyans – and others – in how to use it. Bright, nasty ideas shared and refined. Electronics becoming evermore miniaturised. By the time Coalition forces were steaming into Iraq, IED know-how had been disseminated in training camps and over the Internet between Global Jihadists, bespectacled youths from Kerry, bombers from Medellín, the Balkans, the Middle East, you name it – anywhere where one lot of people wanted another lot of people off their land. Or what they believed was their land.

'Now, about your bomb, Ned. This is my best guess at this stage. I'm Paul, by the way. The explosive charge was PETN. Pentaerythritol tetranitrate. Your man Bilge has found definite traces. It packs a big punch for its weight, which is why it's used in detonating cord and small anti-personnel mines. But it can be mixed with TNT, producing the explosive pentolite, or you can plasticise it, in which form it can be penetrated by a probe without giving the game away. It's very hard to detect. Serious stuff. It's what al-Qaeda made that printer-cartridge bomb with – the one that got past all those airline security checks. Ideal explosive to smuggle into the country, for example, and not too heavy to lug around.'

So how much, Ned asked, are we talking about here to produce this result?

'Could have been as little as a kilo. Nothing, really. And it was dug not under the track but to one side. Remember Extra Bilge's map? The vehicle thrown sideways? Well, you watched it happen yourself. Plus Bilge mentioned that the Range Rover was less heavily armoured at the side than below. And windows are much weaker than lower door panels. More and more we're seeing IEDs placed higher, creating air blasts rather than exploding up through the ground. It was here, in the side of the bank.'

'Could it have been simply placed on the surface? Making the bomber's time on the ground much less?'

Major Butterman screwed up his face.

'Less likely. Given the hardness of the target, he'd have wanted the blast directed sideways, but not dissipated. Best tucked in a bit further down. Not that easy, judging by what's left of these tree roots, but maybe there were hollows under there, or rabbit holes, to make the bomber's task easy. And we aren't talking about digging a huge hole. The bulk of the trees on top would further serve to concentrate the explosion to the side. Bear in mind it didn't have to be put in place this past weekend. The PETN could have been there days, weeks, months. No telling. But I gather you've got a weird and wonderful dead fox that materialised out of nowhere on Saturday night. Correct?'

Ned nodded.

'It's an old trick, the use of dead dogs in the Middle East. Ideal place to put the trigger mechanism. Quick to hook up. And no one thinks twice seeing a dead dog. You don't automatically think, "Must stick my hand into its bloody mangled stomach to see if there's a radio receiver in there or infra-red device or whatever." You drive on. Boom!'

'Boom!' was obviously a Major Paul Butterman figure of speech. He must have heard a lot of things go 'boom!'. It all made sense. For dog read fox. So how was the bomb triggered?

'Number of choices. Simplest option is a pressure pad or trembler, like an old fashioned landmine. OK, but not if there's other traffic on the road and you want to hit a specific target. A timer's no good for that either. Hard-wired? Works fine, but given you saw him lurking all the way up there, then that would have meant a hell of a run of wire. He certainly didn't dive down to clear it all up or you'd have seen him. Unlikely he could have pulled it up without it snagging somewhere, and there's not a trace of it to be seen. That leaves remote. Couldn't be a mobile phone in these hills. No signal to be had. Satellite phone? Maybe. But doesn't make sense with a man on the spot with line of sight. That points to an RCIED.'

Ned looked blank.

'Sorry, Ned; all soldiers love acronyms. It stands for "radio controlled improvised explosive device". The receiver would have been in the dead fox, along with the trigger mechanism. Your man up the hill had the transmitter. He'd have waited till the 4x4 was short of the IED, then pressed the button – on a key fob, most likely. You know, for remotely unlocking your car. Not at all suspicious if one's found on you. Small, neat, simple. Click – lock. Click – unlock.'

Or in this case: click – boom!

Ned imagined the hand holding the key fob. Was it tanned? Clean fingernails? A ring? Trace of blood from pushing the plastic bag full of electronics into the dead fox? Who was he? Or was it a she? A fingerprint. They had a fingerprint. But Extra Bilge said it would take time to secure the image, convert the file, upload it and then await the result. And the Internet connection in the valley was non-existent. No problem: the Bilge had found a good spot in a town eleven miles away. It was simply a matter of time. And whether the owner of the fingerprint was known to the world's fuzz.

'And he was there in person to make absolutely sure of blowing up the Minister of Defence and not some farmer on his way to market?'

Paul Butterman nodded. Ned stretched. Suddenly feeling the stiffness in his lower back reminded him that there was a personal element here. He wondered if the bomber had been armed, and if so, why he hadn't taken a pot-shot at Ned. The probability was the man was unarmed. It wouldn't do to get stopped with an automatic stuffed down his shirt. Besides, Ned wasn't his target. He'd have stayed up there only long enough to make sure Ned was too distracted to see him slip away – and Lady Ridley guaranteed that. Did the bomber know she was about to pop up over the hill in the Merc? Ned hoped not. He hoped he wasn't up against someone as good as this chap would have to be to plan all this. But inside, deep down, he knew he was.

Doc Bones was standing outside his tent having a breather when Ned went by. Did the great man have any wisdom for him? Not about the poor blokes in the car, no. It was as expected. Death was caused by the pressure wave of the primary blast, followed almost simultaneously by violent dismemberment and penetrating wounds from the secondary. Then the fuel tank exploded – the enlarged fuel tank, Ned now knew – which would have ripped what was still intact apart and charred the remains. Next came the injuries bodies typically sustain after being thrown some way through the air. But by then, Doc Bones shook his head sadly, none of them were feeling anything any more. Thank heavens. 'And that brings me, young Ned, to your fox.'

Ned looked up, forcing himself to listen to the Doc after the effort of trying not to hear that morbid catalogue.

'Your fox wasn't killed by the bomb, you'll be interested to hear. We found a goodly chunk of foreleg. Won't bore you with the details: muscle tissues, tendons, rigor mortis and all that stuff. He'd been dead for several days.'

The Doc could tell from Ned's expression that he already knew something of the fox's role.

'What was it? Good place for the bomber to hide the tick-a-tick Timex?'

Ned nodded. Doc Bones was no fool.

'See you for a drink after a wash and scrub-up?'

Ned smiled.

'Good idea, Doc. Only I've still got a tiny bit of poking about to do.'

It was Doc Bones's turn to nod. He filled his lungs with fresh mountain air and dived back into the muck and blood.

Ned's next port of call was the telephone pole. Jan Span was waiting for him, perched on a dry-stone wall. And leaning against the pole was a ladder.

Ned had barely reached the top when, armed with a fine view down the road, he saw a dark blue Toyota pickup hurtling their way. So he climbed back down.

'Mr Tamblin, I wonder if you could answer a simple question?'

Mr Tamblin said he'd certainly have a good try. Only he'd rather nothing got back to old man Lesseps. He had zero sense of humour where his daughter was concerned. Not that he'd . . . DS Span's eyes narrowed a little.

'Exactly how old is Jackie, Mr Tamblin?'

'Let me see . . .'

Ned sensed her reaching for her handcuffs.

'Thirty-five. She'll be thirty-six in November. The twenty-third. But she doesn't look it. She'd pass for thirty any day. Well. Let's be fair. Say thirty-two.'

Ned's made sure he didn't catch Span's eye – he knew he wouldn't be able to stop himself from laughing.

'Now then, Mr Tamblin. We know you have a silent method of dropping off Miss Lesseps at the farm, and then making good your escape. My very simple question is this: when you turned off the road here, did the light come on?'

'No it did not. Which always means His Nibs isn't in residence at the cottage. But Jackie had seen him mowing the paddock on his little tractor and said wasn't it strange and perhaps the bulb had gone.'

Brilliant security, Ned thought as he started up the ladder again. How do you know whether the Minister of Defence is at home? You drive past and if the light goes on, bingo. Or, as Major Butterman would say, boom!

Right, Jackie, let's see just how strange it was.

Ned climbed past an odd ribbed-lens thing which he assumed was the motion sensor. Just above that was the camera. And then – ah!

No wonder there was no light to betray the illicit lovers' return. And no wonder Ned hadn't noticed it from the ground. No, Jackie, the bulb hasn't gone. The light assembly was entirely covered by a piece of black foil, held in place with gaffer tape.

'This over the light anything to do with you, Mr Tamblin?'

Edward Tamblin looked genuinely puzzled and surprised.

'No. Bloody brilliant idea, though. No chance you leaving it up there . . .?'

Ned smiled and climbed a little higher. He could now see the light sensor at the top of the pole. He edged himself round a bit, carefully shifting his weight on the ladder. Holding on with one hand, he reached into a pocket to find tweezers and evidence bag.

'You all right, sir?'

She seemed genuinely anxious.

'Fine, Jan Span. Fine.'

Too much to hope for prints off this as well, thought Ned, as he carefully eased the tape with its foil attached off the pole. This wasn't looking good. The bomber clearly knew enough about the Minister's security arrangements to sabotage surveillance down by the road quickly and easily without triggering any alarms. Ned sealed the bag, but decided to label up on the ground. He didn't want Jan Span to die of worry on the spot.

As he drove back down the valley Ned kept looking up at the high road. He was still mystified as to how the bomber had come and gone in broad daylight without being seen. Perhaps he had climbed over the hill, but that would be a tough haul. The Brecon Beacons afforded very little cover. Just the occasional clump of gorse and heather, and not much of that above a thousand feet.

So how did he do it? The argument against a very low car was that dwarfism often went with performance. Ned would have heard it roar away. Unless the bomber had once courted forbidden fruit up a hill and knew all about coasting silently down to the bottom. Trouble with the bomber doing a Tamblin was that the high road, Ned realised as he turned on to it, was almost level for half a mile on either side of the vantage point. No, he was missing something.

The abseilers, on the other hand, seemed to have missed little. A Coke can – too rusty to be recent. A used condom – unlikely, given the time pressure on the bomber. An unspooled Barry Manilow cassette – even less likely. And a small brown wodge of something. The two lads wondered if it was plastic explosive. Or Jurassic chewing-gum. The DCI didn't need to worry. They'd used gloves and tweezers. Wouldn't want to touch that lot anyway, particularly the Barry Manilow. They even wondered if the first three had all been lobbed over the edge in the one event, so to speak: a romantic evening of music, drink and comic car sex. More than most people got around here. Not sure how the wodge fitted in. Ned wasn't sure either, but he liked the wodge a lot. Then he showed an interest in the rest, so as not to seem churlish.

The lads were from the climbing club of the local police force. They turned out for mountain rescues, and walkers who'd got caught out. Sheep, they'd done a few sheep in their time. For old Lesseps. Pulled his lambs off High Crag only this year. Yes, they knew Jackie. Went to school with her. And Eddie. No, they wouldn't fancy the bomber escaping over the top. The nearest road was ten miles away. No house or shelter in between. It'd take a fit man three hours minimum. No way the choppers would have missed him. It's bare, exposed. So how'd the DCI know he'd been up here, the bomber? Oh, the binoculars. Must be weird, almost seeing him. Yes, said Ned. Just a bit. Thanks lads. Well done.

'So why do you call him Extra Bilge?'

Major Paul Butterman had seen Ned's car approaching and had the publican on a hot stand-by. It was only a matter of minutes before they were sitting with a drink in the garden at the back, not talking about the bomber. Extra Bilge. Ned hadn't really been aware that he had stopped using the Bilge's real name and rank. If he'd ever started. It was a long story. Or rather, it was a story that went a long way back.

'We were at school together. He was the swot. He knew everything. Forgot nothing. Came top in all the sciences. Particularly biology, which we used to call Bilge. He wasn't so hot at arty subjects – he doesn't do ideas much. But facts!'

Ned shook his head in wonderment at Extra Bilge's hunger for information. He had come to assume the Bilge was somewhere on one of those spectrums where you can draw vast buildings in huge detail after only seeing the photo for a second – the down-side of which is you are pants with people, don't like anything to change and are a slave to petty rituals. Except that none of that really fitted.

'He's got a thing about facts. He sees them as caged birds to be freed. He and I ran the school newspaper. I did the bolshie stuff – you know, why do we need all these bloody rules? – and he did the gossip. He was brilliant at finding stuff out, and insistent that it had to be disseminated. Surprising he didn't become a teacher, but then he can't tell the wood from the trees. Or maybe he pretends he can't. Somehow, if you can keep awake and stop yourself from garrotting him, the bit you need is always in there somewhere.'

They sipped their beer, and then Ned asked if he could ask a question.

'The Eiger. Bad smash coming down. Everyone assumes I was parted from it by an Iraqi roadside bomb, but no.'

Ned looked a little taken aback.

'I wasn't going to ask about your leg, Paul. It was about our bomber. You've seen the crater and the bits we've found. You must have an idea what it takes to mount and execute an operation like this. Presumably bombers and terrorists have signatures. Do you recognise anything in all this that points towards someone specific?'

The major laughed.

'What, like those films where they get the gnarled old rogue out of retirement and show him the snaps of the crime scene and the victims, and he says, "Only three men in the whole world could have pulled this off," and it turns out one is dead and the other's serving life and . . .'

'That's exactly what I mean,' said Ned, who loved those bollocks moments.

The major shook his head. It wasn't quite like that.

'Well, I should say, it *is* like that in the sense that a chap will wire the devices up his own particular way – or maybe he's got a roll of Hello Kitty sticky tape, which means you can recognise his work, as long as the tape lasts. And if you survive long enough to see it again. But this is the exception, not the rule. After a while in Basra we started to recognise one joker's handiwork, and it turned out he had taught six other bastards to put IEDs together. These six followed his instructions to the letter. We started to see the joker's creations all over Basra. Couldn't work out how he found enough hours in the day. Then it stopped. Suddenly. Not the number of IEDs but their absolute similarity.

'It turned out he'd twigged that churning out identical devices made it tougher for our intelligence bods to build up a picture of him, but it made our task easier dealing with the IEDs themselves: you hold it horizontal, not vertical . . . unscrew this screw, but not that one . . . you snip the red wire, never the black, etc., etc. No, where your scenario from the movies falls apart completely is the numbers. There aren't just three chaps doing this in the whole world; there are hundreds. Maybe even thousands. There's a constant turnover as they get killed, caught, replaced, supplemented. Not forgetting that the bombers themselves adapt in response to counter-IED techniques.

'So there may well be patterns – briefly identifiable MOs – but they change constantly. Keeping up with them is a full-time job in each conflict zone. Army Intelligence in theatre is really starting to get across this. Building up pictures of the teams – bomb-makers, placers, triggermen. But there's always new stuff coming along. Remember, these are cottage industries churning out roadside bombs, not just in Iraq and Afghanistan but in Iran, Syria, down half the turnings off the Karakorum Highway. Sorry, but I personally can't peer at your crater today and say, "Abdul, you little rascal, you've been at it again." There may be someone somewhere who can, but not me. Wish I could.'

It was getting chilly. They took the glasses and started indoors. And then something occurred to Ned. How did the major know all that? About the joker and the six bastards and why he disrupted their bomb-production methods. That wouldn't be apparent from staring at a cell phone hooked up via a firing circuit to a pair of 107mm rockets under a sack by the side of the road. The major was impressed. Not by the knowledge but the deduction.

'A mole. We had a mole in the cell.'

Extra Bilge's van wasn't hard to find. Ned looked for the closest telecomms mast to a chip shop. He pulled in behind it and knocked on the door. Span opened it without looking round, mouth full of scampi. She had tried to view the surveillance stuff on her laptop, but didn't have the right program. Luckily Extra Bilge did. Ned slid in beside Span and for a while watched nothing much happening down a country track at dusk. No sign of the Toyota. And the fox? Nothing yet. Span kept her eye on the screen. She had started at the beginning and would work through to the end.

'By the way, sir. Special Branch says the geeks are in the clear.'

'Thanks, Jan Span. It was a very long shot.'

Extra Bilge was also glued to a screen, filled with a huge finger-print being slowly uploaded into the ether.

'Purkinje.'

Extra Bilge must have gone a bit heavy on the mushy peas. That was a very odd belch.

'You know, Mr Ned. Jan Evangelista Purkinje. The Professor of Physiology at the University of Breslau in the 1840s.'

Oh, him. Of course. Old Purkinje. How could Ned forget.

'It would be wrong simply to see him as the inventor of the microtome. After all, there are his histological discoveries. Plus his work on eye diseases and the effects of opium. But I'm sure in our heart of hearts, we really just think of him as the father of finger-printing. Should know by morning, Mr Ned. I'll stick something under your door.'

Still no glimpse of Toyota or fox on Span's screen. Only those oily shards of burnt chips left, so Ned thanked them for their hard work, drove back to the pub and turned in. He decided to work the mattress topography slightly differently. This time he tried lying with one leg on the side of the hill which Edward Tamblin drove up, and the other on the side which he coasted down. Once he'd tucked his chin into the pub garden, Ned slept like a top.

He woke when the alarm went at 7.30 a.m., and had clean forgotten about what Extra Bilge had said until he opened the door to go down to breakfast. He picked up the envelope and opened it. Bloody hell. It was – if correct – the most surprising information Ned had ever received in his entire life. He'd always hated Purkinje; now he knew why.

The fingerprint on the casing of the trigger for the bomb which had murdered the Minister of Defence and two others came from the index finger of the right hand of WPC Kate Baker, holder of the George Cross 'for the most conspicuous courage in circumstances of extreme danger.' Kate Baker, the most beautiful woman he had ever clapped eyes on. Kate Baker, the woman he adored. The woman he thought he knew. And the harder he thought about the ramifications both personal and professional, the louder Ned heard in his mind the stentorian bellow of the wild boar Fatso:

'WHERE'S THE DOG TART?'

3

IT HAD ALL BEGUN, AS trouble often does, with a scrap of paper. Experienced sniffer-dog handlers, it read, were needed to go out to trouble spots with their dogs. Volunteers only. Kate went straight from the main noticeboard at the kennels to Large Sarge's office. The head of the Dog Unit was rocking back on his chair, staring at the budget sheets, wondering how he could slash feed costs by 14 per cent without the dogs going on strike. The whole thing looked perilous. To Large Sarge, and to Kate. It was only a matter of time before Large Sarge misjudged his own tipping point. Kate always made sure she came into the room with a good tap on the pane and some hearty doorknob rattling. Didn't want to startle him in a teetering doze.

'Hullo, Sarge. What more do you know about the opportunities to get blown up a long way from home?'

'Blimey, young Kate. You're quick off the mark. That drawing-pin must still be warm from my thumb.'

He pendulumed forward, propelling himself to his feet in one move. He made her the usual mug of green tea while trying to work out if there was any way to put her off. She was the best he had, and he couldn't spare her? Nah. First bit true, second bit bollocks. It was too dangerous? Her job was dangerous full stop. Jiffy was still untried? Inexperienced certainly, but coming on a treat. He was a Spaniel puppy with rare promise and she was an ace talent-spotter. Not for nothing did they call her the Dog Tart. You are special and I love you like a daughter – I don't want you to go? Ah. The truth at last.

'Yeah, looks interesting, doesn't it? If you fancy a change of scenery. Do you?'

Funny you should ask that, thought Kate. I love my job. I'm deep into a crazy, impossible tangle of a case that's all about dogs, and I adore dogs. I'm working with Detective Chief Inspector Ned Bale who's the sexiest, cleverest, funniest, gentlest man. Plus he's unattached. Plus he seems to like me. We get on really well. In fact, if we carry on like this, there's every chance we might . . . fall in love. Of course I don't fancy a change of scenery.

'Yeah. I was wondering about it . . .'

Sarge told her what he knew. That the wild men of Afghanistan were planting more and more improvised explosive devices. They were now the main cause of death for NATO forces. And IEDs were slaughtering civilians. Kids murdered, maimed. The locals don't go around in armoured vehicles. They wear cotton, not Kevlar. You only have to think about the effects of a 200lb bomb in a crowded marketplace. He shook his head and didn't say anything for a bit.

'They're only finding around half the devices planted. So, the MoD needs a load more clever handlers with good dogs. Dogs who can keep going in the heat. Handlers who stay calm.'

Kate nodded. Hmm, thought Large Sarge. She doesn't look fazed. Like a rock under fire, our Kate. Some get flakey near the flame – she just gets cool. Better stick in a government health warning, not that she'll heed a word of it.

He ruffled through the piles on the desk.

'I had a piece from the papers somewhere. Can't find it. Interview with a bomb-disposal hero serving in Afghanistan. Anyway, he reckoned on a six-month tour in Ulster during the fun and games he'd average half a dozen IEDs. Says he's getting that a day in

Helmand Province. Now you and I know that you can get as dead from a bit of villainy over here in the rain as over there in the baking heat. But the thing is, young Kate, the odds. The odds are stacked bleeding high against you over there.'

Kate wondered about saying that someone had to do it and at least she had no dependants. Or that better she and her dog found the nasty little surprise than some lads out on patrol. Lads who'd wind up legless in the totally unfunny sense of the word. Or . . . But it all sounded a bit obvious and priggish, so she thanked Large Sarge for the tea, took the email address and went back to see if Jiffy wanted to play. Ten minutes after she'd left, Large Sarge found the clipping, but the moment had passed. And he'd seen the steel in her eye. Poor odds were what got her up in the morning. Better if he'd told her it was a dosser's paradise out there and don't forget the Factor 40.

She flew on an RAF Tristar from Brize Norton. She and Jiffy and their kitbags. Jiffy travelled in a cage, from which she rescued him during the stop in Cyprus. They then switched to a Hercules, and the journey became even less like a holiday flight. It wasn't simply the stripped-back interior and camouflage colours. Before they took off, several large sacks were hefted on board by two soldiers led by a well-tanned lance-corporal who plonked himself beside her. He was, he assured her, going to spend the next six months making damn sure none of that in them sacks was going to be used on his account. Nor his boys' account neither. Kate looked puzzled. There had been a last-minute request, he said, for grass seed to plant on memorial sites. They fly your body back, but they also mark the spot out there. She thanked the lance-corporal and hoped he was the sort who slept on long flights. He was, helped by the fact that he and the boys had not unreasonably drunk Colchester dry the night before.

The officer on her other side was some sort of medic. He was reading a report on the latest techniques for treating battlefield wounds which, unfortunately, was profusely illustrated with colour photographs. She reckoned the less he told her about how he'd be spending the next few months the better. Anyway, he didn't need to. All she had to do was look sideways and there it all was. Far from drinking anywhere dry, the good doctor had clearly not eaten for a month. He managed to gobble down several hearty meals without missing a beat in his studies. Impressive.

Kate dozed fitfully between going back to check on Jiffy. The vet had suggested a tranquilliser to settle him down for the flight, but she didn't fancy it. He might have to fly in helicopters and planes once they were there, and she couldn't keep drugging him. Anyway, it wasn't as if they could sleep it off by the pool each time they arrived anywhere. They'd have to be alert. She didn't need to worry about Jiffy. He wagged his tail when he saw her, ate a bit and slept. Luckily he didn't have any old dogs of war as travelling companions to scare him witless with their macho chatter.

Things took a decisive turn for the weird and scary about four hours out from Cyprus. The lance corporal woke, sharp and sober, peeked past the window blind into the pitch darkness, checked his watch, then told Kate they were well over Afghanistan. As they started the descent into Kandahar they'd all be told over the tannoy to get their full body armour and helmets on. Just in case. Hmm, thought Kate. That greedy medic might come in handy. Hope he's read as far as the kind of wounds you get when your plane is burned to toast by a ground-to-air-missile. And then the lance corporal found a place in Kate's heart.

''Ere, Miss. Come with me – we've got a few minutes. They generally keep some Kevlar blankets at the back, for putting over stretchers when they fly casualties out. We can tuck 'em round your pooch's cage.'

They were getting back into their seats when the tannoy started up and the lance corporal gave her a knowing wink. Two hundred men and fourteen women struggled into body armour and strapped on helmets. The next sounds were of safety harnesses being clicked home. Then the lights went out, the pitch of the engines changed and everyone fell into an eerie silence. It was one of the longest thirty minutes of Kate's life. Stupid, she thought. All these tough-as-old-boots, petrified people thinking the same thing: be silly if they kill us before we even get there.

Kate got used to camp life surprisingly quickly. There were quite a few working dogs there: a few other sniffers and a fearsome gang of German Shepherds used on guard duties. They didn't look the sort who would share their bones, so Kate steered clear. She found being regimented quite relaxing. She and Jiffy shared an air-conditioned tent with Fran who was in the Royal Artillery. Fran really liked dogs, but Kate didn't see much of her. Fran's patrols took her out at all times of the day and night, after which she seemed to spend hours writing reports, particularly when something happened, which it generally did. Off-duty life revolved around meals, which was a little difficult for Kate. She still had to remind herself from time to time that eating food was OK. But everyone seemed very kind. A few of the men tried to hit on her which was to be expected given the 50–1 sex ratio, never mind the way she looked. Keeping body armour on wasn't an option given the heat, but taking care of Jiffy provided the ideal get-out. In time the guys seemed to realise that Kate wasn't fruit waiting to fall. And when fresh troops pulled in and their jaws dropped at the sight of her exercising her spaniel, the old hands soon put them straight.

The work was something else. She was, after all, doing one of the most dangerous jobs on the planet. It wasn't simply what Large Sarge had said, that the tasks came thick and fast. It was that while you and your dog were minding your own business finding bombs hidden in the dust, unfriendly types with sniper rifles would try to kill you. The first time, Kate didn't realise what was happening. She and Jiffy were working their way down a dirt road outside a village perhaps ten miles from the base. The landscape looked deserted. In fact that's what first alerted the patrol who radioed the shout in. Normally there was plenty of coming and going around a scruffy old garage and workshop with adjoining tea-house. Farmers would bring in a plough or axle to be sharpened or welded, and drink *chai sabz* and chew the fat next door while the work was being done. But this time, the place was empty.

The boys from the Mercian Regiment smelled a rat, slipped off their safety catches and slowed down. The first little roadside treat was obvious: a sussy length of concrete drainpipe that hadn't been there when the patrol passed through two hours before – when the tea-house was crammed and the welder's sparks were flying. Binoculars picked out what looked like disturbed dirt four hundred yards away and at that point they called in the experts. Kate bundled Jiffy into an armoured vehicle and off they roared. She and Jiffy waited while their escort from the RAF Regiment fanned out and took up firing positions along a canal running a couple of hundred yards from the road. Then they got the nod.

Kate and Jiffy went out alone, without escort. That way, if a bomb went up, no one else would get killed. She was used to the lonely walk – not that she ever felt alone with her beloved dog – but not to the ridiculous heat. Luckily there was no wind – Jiffy worked best in still air, preferably in the cool of an early morning. But it was almost midday and Kate could hardly breathe in her body armour. The dog zigzagged ahead, then homed in on the drainpipe. A long sniff at one end, then he sat, tongue out for a second, then mouth closed. A definite! She put down a marker and took a good look at the pipe. It seemed to contain an artillery shell. How was it actuated? She didn't want to step on a buried pressure plate. Wires were visible curling out the far end into the earth. Didn't mean there wasn't also a pressure trigger. What was that little indent in the dust? She gave Jiffy a congratulatory pat – couldn't give him the usual tennis-ball reward yet. She radioed back what she'd found and that she was moving on. She saw the thumbs-up from the driver of the armoured car. The one they called Greasy.

She let Jiffy dart ahead, nose to the ground, and it was as well she did because instead of making for the disturbed ground the Mercian patrol had spotted from afar, the spaniel got interested in an innocent-looking tuft of dead grass just two hundred yards beyond the pipe. Circled it. Then sat, staring at it. He really was an extraordinary dog: 48° centigrade and he was still focussed. Still finding IEDs. Still barely panting.

Kate was six feet from him and about to place the second marker when the firing started. She vaguely heard the distant crackling and registered something was kicking up spurts of sand ahead of her, but didn't make the connection. Greasy shouted something to her. She looked ahead; gunmen on half a dozen village roofs were spitting fire, much of it at her and Jiffy. To her left, the armoured cars were retaliating through a haze of smoke. Behind her the RAF had opened up from their cover along the edge of the canal. Small arms fire, a grenade machine gun and anti-tank missiles argued the toss over her and Jiffy. They were bang in the middle of a firefight, and the kicks in the sand were getting closer. Disobliging people were trying to kill them. The Kevlar suit might have its uses. She dropped to the ground, grabbed Jiffy, tucked him under her and wondered if the next bullet would hit her or the IED.

'It would be best, dear dog,' Kate whispered to Jiffy, 'if we vanished – right now.'

She lobbed a smoke grenade as far as she could between them and the scrappy row of buildings. Then another. Waited till the green and orange pall filled the still air like a garish curtain. Then scrambled to her feet and she and the dog ran, crouching, back to the canal, cheered on arrival by the RAF lads. Kate and Jiffy hurled themselves over the lip to safety as a sniper bullet struck the pressure plate of the IED they had just been nose-to-nose with. The explosion rocked the ground, covering them all in dirt. Kate's response was to laugh, which made a good story even better in the Mess that night.

Can't let Jiffy think this is any kind of worry, she thought, rubbing his tummy.

'This is fun, isn't it, little Jiffy.'

And Jiffy gave her a face a good lick, converting dust into mud.

'What we do has nothing to do with IEDs. We do not clear mines to support military operations. Never. It is very important I say this and you all understand it. We do what UN calls Humanitarian Mine Clearance. I explain. Three days ago, in Paghman eleven miles east of here, young boys had a football game on waste ground behind their house. Normal, happy scene. Suddenly big explosion, two brothers eight and nine years of age killed. Their friend lost both legs. Two more boys they are still operating on to remove fragments. One boy will never see again. Yes. Yes.

'No one knows for sure how many live mines are buried in our country Afghanistan. But it is millions. This land is seeded with death. It is lost to our people for economic use, agriculture, recreation, everything. It is dead, yes, and it kills. Average is ten to twelve mines explode every single day, killing and maiming civilians, from people travelling or tending animals, to children fetching water or playing.

'These mines were placed by the Russian invader and then in the mujahideen time of civil war. Some were even made to look like a child's toy – to say to children: "Play with me." Others were for blowing up army tanks. So far we identified mines from thirty-eight countries under our soil. I could say you the TCE/3.6 anti-tank mine from Technovar of Italy. Or the CBU-58/Bs cluster bombs made in USA. Or the Model 36 fragmentation bomb of Hungary. Or Iranian YM II land-mine. Also we have live grenades, bombs, shells, even missiles. So we said, "Enough!" We train the people, we train the dogs, even if it takes all our lifetimes, all our lives, we will find them . . .'

Jamila was small, slightly rounded and about forty. She wore mostly blacks and browns. Her camel-coloured headscarf framed one of the strongest faces Kate had ever seen. Her mouth was straight, but with the tiniest curl at the corners. Her skin was smooth, her eyes were black, and they danced. High cheek-bones. A long, faint scar across her forehead. Her English was very good, but oddly she'd say difficult things really well and then, with something easy, she'd switch words round. She sounded as if she had spent time in America. She spoke as if nothing else mattered in the world but sweeping her country clean of mines.

She was a widow. Her son Fazl was nine years old. Her husband, Sadhar, whom she had met in Cleveland, had been killed walking across a patch of ground behind some houses. He was a doctor, going to visit a man who had sliced himself with a scythe. Sadhar stepped on a land-mine and died in agony. He was the only doctor in the district. There was morphine in his bag, but that had been blown to smithereens. And anyway, he no longer had any hands to administer it. The people around had no idea there were mines there and no one fancied going to him to help. Not that there was any help they could have given him. He was dead by the time Jamila arrived. She didn't listen when the people standing around shouted warnings to her. She just ran straight across the rubble and loose earth, desperate to reach Sadhar before he died. She carried what was left of his body back herself, not wanting to put anyone else to the risk. Not wanting to ask for help and be refused.

By the time she met Jamila, Kate and Jiffy had been in Afghanistan for nearly six weeks. She hadn't counted the IEDs they had found. She hadn't counted the number of days she'd suffered from Bastion Belly. She hadn't counted the people she'd met, like Fran and Greasy, who had been evacuated out with bits missing courtesy of IEDs, sniper fire, ambushes, road accidents, a helicopter rotor blade slicing into a watch tower. She hadn't counted the people she'd met who had been flown home with a flag draped over their coffin. She didn't need to. There was only one of those she knew in person: a twinkly officer from the Royal Dragoon Guards. He was the Incident Commander on the day Kate and Jiffy had to find a bomb somewhere in a market seething with people and animals – without causing a mass panic stampede. He amazed Kate with his consideration for the safety and feelings of the local people. A week later he and his platoon were on duty at an outlying patrol base when a volley of rocket propelled grenades hit their fort. Here one minute, cheerfully helping a very elderly lady pack up her stall of garlic, herbs and dried chillies. Gone the next.

Kate had been sent to Kabul for a two-day conference on IEDs. She sat next to a nice, rather wooffly looking American scientist from Camp Leatherneck who was researching the odour signals given off by explosives and trying to understand what conditions caused these signals to become too weak for a dog to sense. In the event, a bomb scare at the venue on the second day shut the conference down early, giving them all a free afternoon. The wooffly scientist asked her if she'd like to fill the time seeing some 'civilian' sniffer dogs. They were joined by a man who trained Danish bomb disposal operators and a Belgian expert in fuses and booby-traps. The taxi dropped them near the top of a hill overlooking the city. They walked past kite-flyers towards the sound of barks. Set among trees high on the hill were the HQ and kennels of an organisation dedicated to making Afghanistan mine-free.

After her introduction, Jamila led them to the practice area where an eighteen-month-old German Shepherd on a very long leash was being trained to search in a straight line. The handler, Wahid, was very tall and thin with a bushy black beard. Jamila interpreted for him. He had lost his right arm to a mine as a teenager. He said that the only work he could do then was to herd his family's sheep and goats. He liked animals. He had been scared of dogs as a boy, but after he lost his arm, he grew to love Dosti, the Kuchi dog they used to guard the sheep and scare away wolves. Then he heard about these brave people, these brave dogs. He walked all the way from his village to Kabul and begged them to take him on. He hadn't wanted to leave Dosti behind, but knew he was too old to learn anything new. Wahid had trained many dogs. In the early days they had come from

Thailand, and only responded to orders in Thai. Then they had German and then Dutch dogs. Wahid knew the word for 'Stay' in many languages! Now they were breeding as well as training, the dogs all understood their Afghan language.

The wooffly American asked Wahid some question about whether dogs found it easier to detect the scent of explosives in metal or plastic mines. Then the director led a group of staff members from the offices to meet the visitors. There were tables and chairs in the shade of the trees, and they sat drinking iced lemonade and eating *baklawa*. Except for Kate and Jamila. They walked away from the others and talked. Jamila was the first Afghan woman Kate had met. She had seen them in the streets, and there were some who came into Camp Bastion to work. But Kate had never exchanged a word with any of them. She made up for lost time with Jamila.

Jamila had spent ten years in America, returning after the fall of the Taliban to take this job as a mine awareness educator, particularly among women. Women stood less chance of being injured by mines than men or children because most of their life was spent at home, but they were the key influence on the young. It was the young who went out looking for firewood, or ran errands or took short cuts through the rubble of war-destroyed buildings to get to school. Often uncleared danger areas in towns and villages were marked with signs and red lines, but children are children and think they'll live forever.

Talk of women led to talk about the restrictions on their lives. The Taliban were no longer running the government but their influence was very strong still, particularly in the south. Anyway, many of the warlords who had carved the country up were no less fanatical about keeping Afghan women in the dark ages. A 'good' woman stays indoors, cooking and cleaning. She obeys her husband, his father, his brothers, even her own sons. If the husband wants sex – whenever he wants it, however he wants it – the 'good' woman gives it. And, please, with a look on her face as if she is grateful and loving it. Rape in marriage? There's no such thing. Run away from your in-laws? Chop your nose off. Want an education? You must be a whore. No, you are worse than a whore. At least a whore knows her proper position.

Kate asked why Jamila wasn't wearing a burqa. How risky was it? She said it was OK in Kabul and some places in the north to wear only a veil, though many women couldn't face the frequent catcalls, the spits and even kicks.

'They are killing us with cotton.'

Which was why, on a rare day off, Kate found herself dressed in a burqa being escorted by Jamila's son Fazl through the southern city of Lashkar Gāh, so she could see for a few hours what it was like being an Afghan woman. The answer was: smelly, uncomfortable, scary. She had been briefed by Jamila before she started out. Don't go too fast to be noticed. Nor too slow to get in anyone's way. Never walk down the middle of the street. Keep away from the gutter. Avoid groups of men, time your arrival at intersections to keep moving, don't respond to anyone except Fazl. He would be her *mahram*: the close male family member who accompanied Afghan women when they went out: the brother, son, father prised from study or sleep or gossip to preserve the decency of the family's womenfolk. To be their interface with the outside world.

Kate moved with her eyes down, as if re-learning how to walk. Her feet popped out from the folds, like a cartoon penguin's. 'Shuttlecocks', they called these burqas. Blue shuttlecocks that gave away nothing of the age, shape, status of the woman inside. Mustn't trip. Must look up. Where's Fazl, my lifeline? There he is: a little in front and a little to the side. My *mahram*. Only a kid, but he knows exactly how to stay in my field of vision. Be bad to lose him. If we did get separated, could he tell me from the others? Don't put it to the test.

Men. Men everywhere. Confident men, laughing men, staring men. A man Kate had seen on a bridge over a dried-up river suddenly materialised ahead of her. A man with extraordinary, penetrating eyes. He had stopped by a kebab shop, turned and was looking back in her direction. Why? What did he see? She looked like the rest. Or was it something else? Did she smell different? No anti-perspirant next time, just in case. There were men around the table outside, laughing. Aluminium bowls of *pulao*. Yoghurt. Chilli sauce. Perhaps her deodorant would be lost in the sickly sweet smoke of blackened lamb. Head down, going past the man now. Phew!

It was stifling. She had showered before coming out, but after fifteen minutes she was dripping with sweat. The mesh was hard enough to see through when she had first put the burqa on, but now it was as if there was a heat haze in there, smudging her vision even more. The smell wasn't of betraying ice-fresh roll-on, but of must, mothballs and old mutton fat. Horrible.

They reached a kerb and were about to cross, when Fazl suddenly raised his arm. They stopped. A truck cruised past. It was full of men in black turbans with black beards, scanning the crowds. They seemed to be wearing eyeliner. Why? Who knows. Doesn't matter. Scary. Mustn't look! She could hear her heart beating. Fazl dropped his arm and they moved off. And then they turned down the street of butchers.

The two figures – the serious-faced Afghan boy and the burqa-clad Englishwoman – wove down the street between the backs of the buyers and lookers-on. Beyond them, and so unseen, were the *mahram* – the males in the middle. Modesty buffers in the bargaining zone, hammering down the price of chickens. The butchers were occasionally visible, standing on a box to lower a carcass down from a hook. Sometimes a woman lifted the mesh for a second to see a little better, but only if she thought the butcher wasn't looking. Maybe some of the older women didn't care so much, but they knew the rules, and news of inappropriate behaviour had a way of travelling so fast it sometimes got home before the woman did.

Before Kate left the UK, a friend had sent her a link to a TV ad on YouTube, showing a beautiful woman slipping sinuously into the sexiest black underwear, then popping a burqa over the top to go out. Male fantasy nonsense. It might work if your assignation was an air-conditioned limo ride away. But a ten minute walk through the Afghan heat and you'd knock him dead with the pong when you clambered out of it. And what if you tripped over on the way? What would the humourless men in beards make of the display of basque and thong? Stoning would be too good for you.

Whatever you could get away with in Kabul, down in this battered, repressed southern city it was safest to obey the oppressors' rules. Clothes must not be thin, or adorning, or tight. They must not resemble non-Muslim women's clothes. They must not make a noise. Footwear ornaments must not make a noise. Women must not make it possible to attract the attention of men who might gaze upon them with lust. All in all, it was surprising that it did not suit her.

Baggy clothes used to be her trademark. Overalls four sizes too big for her. Amorphous padding, concealing layers. No one could see her, and she could not see herself. No breasts. No waist. No bottom. Legs like the pillars on a bouncy castle. Perfect. And yet, for all the camouflage, men still used to stare at her. You'd think being encased in cloth from head to foot would be the answer to her prayers, and maybe it would have been a few years ago, but not now. Now it was worn from expediency, not for relief. The burqa-clad young woman following young Fazl down the backstreets had moved on a bit from the teenager who'd stick her fingers down her throat after meals. Who'd stare at herself naked in a mirror for hours at a time, wondering which bit of her was the ugliest. Whose self-hatred became so intense that even her family noticed it. Eventually. Turned out they were – surprise, surprise – part of the problem.

Her condition had a name: body dysmorphic disorder. Some of the experts she was sent to were stupid enough to tell her that there was no need for her to hate her appearance, because she was so very, very . . . beautiful. Oh yeah? Soon fix that. Bit of broken glass was as good as anything for dragging across your skin. She still had a few scars which would serve as useful reminders if ever she forgot what she'd been through – and what she'd overcome. Except she could never forget. Which was why, as she Pingu-walked past the other shuttlecocks, the last thing she thought was: where were burqas when she had needed them? Instead she remembered Jamila's words to her when they first met on that hill in Kabul, with the dogs barking and the men too far away to hear.

'They are killing us with cotton.'

It was a relief to reach the cool sanctuary of Jamila's house. And lovely meeting Jamila's friends. Smelling new smells: that night's noodle, bean and vegetable soup simmering. Tasting new tastes: cardamom tea and the milk custard pudding *firni*. Hearing new sounds: the women talking between themselves in Pashto; someone in the street outside playing the lute-like *rebab*.

It was nice, but very unfamiliar and not just because it was so foreign. Kate was doing something she never did at home: relax with a group of women. Sure, there was the gang of girls in Large Sarge's dog team – Millie, Pauline, Em, Bishakha and the rest – but they were workmates. Kate filled her downtime with dogs, not people. This was different, and it grew on her. There was much laughter, and there was some sadness. They weren't all as feisty as Jamila; some had more liberal husbands, some clearly had bastards. Some were single. Some faced arranged marriages with old men they found revolting, when there were men their own age – maybe a cousin – who had exchanged glances with them at a wedding. Glances that now seemed to promise the most romantic, unattainable love.

The women seemed to like the fact that Kate was there, and that she'd got there the same way they had, scurrying invisibly through the streets with a male escort to ensure decency. Even the least open-minded of them had no doubt that this was hugely insulting. Even the most far-sighted – Jamila's older sister Parween – could not envisage a time when the country's men would remove their heels from the necks of the country's women.

Jamila's brother drove Kate back to the base. Zabiullah worked in the laundry and passed easily through Security, although the guards were surprised when the shuttlecocked woman with him removed her veil and produced an MoD ID card. She got some funny looks walking through the camp in the burqa, but none as odd as the expression on the faces of the clutch of Royal Military Policemen and women who had turned her tent inside out and were now waiting for her. That, from her dress, she had clearly gone native only made them even more tight-lipped.

'WPC Kate Baker?'

'Yes. What is it?'

'Stand absolutely still with your arms stretched out to your side, shoulder-high. We are going to give you a full body search, and then we need you to come with us. To answer some questions about the murder of the Minister of Defence.'

'WHERE'S THE DOG TART?'

The team was sitting around in the main office awaiting morning conference when they heard the distant roar. It took Fatso only seconds to speed-waddle there from his sty – he moved surprisingly nimbly for one so generously shaped. The answer came from Span:

'WPC Baker is in Afghanistan, sir, at Camp Bastion ninety miles east-north-east of Kandahar. It's the main British military base out there.'

Fatso looked impassive. Abroad to him was all the same. Calais, Calcutta, Capri, Canada, Kandahar. Nothing to choose between them.

'She was taken into custody by the RMP yesterday at around 1800 hours local time and was held overnight behind bars by the Military Provost Service. They're four and a half hours ahead of us, sir.'

Different time zones – another nail in abroad's coffin.

'She is being questioned about now, sir, by a Colonel Sillitoe. He's the senior RMP officer out there. The Provost Marshal, they call him. We spoke to him last night and again this morning.'

Fatso nodded.

'How long she been out there . . . in Afghanistan?'

'Four months sir.'

'No sign of her having popped back on Ryanair to blow our bloke up?'

Spick shook his head.

'No sir. Only the RAF flies into Camp Bastion. I've checked with Brize Norton – they've got her going out on the twenty-seventh of March. They've not brought her back yet.'

Ned pulled the wrinkly nose face none of the team liked to see.

'But she could have hitched a lift with the Americans to Kandahar. From there she takes a domestic flight to Kabul, or blags her way on to an aid-agency plane. Once she's in Kabul there are international flights via Dubai, Islamabad, Delhi, Moscow, Frankfurt . . .'

The team had been curious which way the DCI would jump. They'd heard the rumours that the Dog Tart had become a bit more than a colleague to him. But she clearly couldn't expect mate's rates from him now.

'I'll get on to the airlines and customs.'

'We can't,' Span chimed in, 'assume she travelled on her own passport.'

A little pause followed while the team wrapped its head round the possibility that one of their number had gone over to the dark side. Fatso broke the silence.

'Has the Dog Tart ever said anything or done anything at all iffy? Anything to suggest she might not be one hundred per cent with us?'

There was a lot of head-shaking, but a little bit of shifting about as well. Spick put the hesitation into words.

'The short answer's gotta be no, boss. But the thing about Kate is, she's . . . I dunno . . . She does her job brilliantly, right? And then she goes off home. Won't come up the Dog and Vomit for a sharpener after work. She's private. That's how she is. It doesn't make her a terrorist. But it means I can't put my hand on my heart and say, like, "I know her and no way could she be involved in all this . . .'"

Another pause.

'Mind you . . .' added Spick '. . . you can get pissed with your mates every night and still be a total bleeding mystery to them.'

'Tell us about it!' came a voice from the back, followed by a welcome ripple of laughter. Then Fatso turned to Extra Bilge.

'And her dabs are all over the timer?'

'It's the casing round the trigger mechanism, sir, but yes. One clear print.'

Fatso sat for a moment, then rose fast and beat it out of the main office, beckoning Ned to join him. He had barely closed the sty door when Fatso cut to the chase:

'Bad if it turned out you'd been bonking the bomber, old cock.'

Ned reassured his boss that there was no danger of that.

'Because she isn't the bomber, or because you haven't bonked her?'

Ned looked thoughtful.

'She knows a lot about explosives. She's almost impossibly cool under fire. But it doesn't make sense. She's risked her life often enough to stop terrorist attacks on this country. It's quite hard to see Kate Baker as our bomber.'

'How about our bomber's sidekick?'

Fatso sat back, peeling his lower lip over in a long, curved, moist pink sausage. Ned shrugged. The same thing applied.

'You ever met her pals? She got any dodgy ones with big beards? Or those even dodgier ones – with beards and no moustaches? You ever been to her place?'

Ned shook his head. He'd never been inside her flat. Well this might be your chance, Fatso reckoned. If this Colonel Sillitoe smelled a rat, they'd be breaking the door down this afternoon. Probably do it anyway. Oh God, thought Ned, suddenly seeing Kate not as Patty Hearst or Ulrike Meinhof, but remembering her as she was. She's so private. She'd go spare. She couldn't stand it. He'd taken her home several times and she'd never once asked him in. She wouldn't even switch the light on till she'd closed the door, presumably so he couldn't see anything inside. The thought of the mob going through her belongings, her clothes . . .

Right up Spick's street, that kind of thing. He always leaves a place looking raped. Can't insist on Span doing it, though. Can't be seen to be going light on her. What if she is somehow connected to the bomber?

Fatso, as so often, was thinking along similar lines.

'Who'd have ever thought it, eh? Never really know people, do we, Ned?'

Ned agreed that we don't, and that, whatever happened, no personal considerations would get in the way of solving the case.

'What a load of bollocks, Ned. 'Course personal considerations get in the way. No fun if they didn't. It can even be the personal considerations that get them solved. What you've got to do is understand them. Can't see how you can do that without getting your arse over there. Colonel Sillitoe is probably a genius at finding out who got the regimental goat pissed, but anything more'd be a stretch for him.'

Ned nodded and stood. He'd nearly reached the outside world which didn't smell of fungal growth, rancid lard and ancient nicotine, when Fatso remembered something.

'Here, you didn't answer the rest of my question. About bonking her.'

'Give me time sir,' replied Ned ambiguously.

Fatso gave a grunt, and stuck his snout in the *Daily Mail*.

'Much as you need, Ned. Long as you want.'

In the event, they didn't have to break the door down. They had a call from Colonel Sillitoe telling them where the key was. WPC Baker said could they possibly water the plants if they seemed dry. Her neighbour was a bit forgetful. Oh, and if DCI Bale was coming out to Afghanistan, would he mind bringing her chunky blue sweater? Because it got so cold out there at night.

Not exactly the message of the most private person in the world, let alone that of a mad terrorist who'd just had a confession tortured out of her. And, if Ned needed further proof that he didn't know people, Spick sidled up to him as the hit squad was assembling to pull Kate's place apart. He was off to check with customs, immigration, the airlines and that, and leave Span to run the search. Well, he knew he was a bit heavy-handed, and didn't like to think of Kate coming home to find her things all over the shop. It wasn't as if it was likely she'd done anything wrong, was it?

Probably not, Spick, probably not. Right, we'd best be off. Is Extra Bilge coming? He's got a gentle touch with a ransacking. Pauline will meet us there, bringing Jammy over to see if the Dog Tart keeps cordite in with the baking powder – Jammy, legendary finder of bombs on jumbo jets and mother of little Jiffy.

Kate heard his name as Colonel Silly Toes. It seemed appropriate for the ludicrous situation she was in. She wasn't crazy about being strip-searched, and fretted until she knew one of the other sniffer dog handlers would exercise Jiffy. But her cell was clean and she knew she hadn't murdered the Minister. The colonel didn't say anything when she was brought into his office the next morning, but carried on reading a file. A file on her. She could see her name on the outside. When he spoke, it was from behind the papers.

'Who presented you with your gong?'

'The Queen.'

She could see him nod. Then he put the folder down.

'When did you hear that the Minister had been killed?'

Kate thought for a moment. It was at breakfast. On the radio. So that, the colonel replied, would be sixteen hours after it actually happened. And where had she been sixteen hours before? Kate had had all night to think about this, but it hadn't taken her more than a minute to remember. Outside Kariz. A little village on the Helmand

River, two and a bit miles from Lash. She and Jiffy had gone out with the guys to a shout from a Welsh Guards patrol. Their second vehicle had been blown up by an IED. The driver was dead. One of the Javelin guys was in a poor way. Friendly locals said they had seen men digging further on. So, at about the time the Minister was killed, she and her dog were working their way slowly down a dusty road south of Kariz.

They found three devices. Each had double dets, and the middle one had an anti-tamper sensor. They were all non- or minimum-metal, Lieutenant Ellison reckoned. The Vallon metal detector didn't pick them up at all. He used a disruptor on them. Oh, and he said something about the one which destroyed the armoured car being a 'Hezbollah-style claymore'. Apparently when it went up it totally atomised the trigger mechanism and wiring. Ask Lieutenant Ellison. He'd remember.

Hmm, thought Colonel Sillitoe. Not the worst alibi I've heard. And he'd already spoken to Ellison. Couldn't get him off the bally phone for singing her praises.

Hmm, thought Kate. Lieutenant Ellison certainly would remember. When he came back from blowing the third IED, he asked her to marry him. He was also the one who advised her to carry her morphine in her right map pocket. A lot of them kept it there. It meant there was a good chance other people would know where hers was. In case it was needed.

'Now,' said the colonel, who turned out to be rather a nice old stick, 'the sergeant here is going to get us all something cold to drink and maybe some biscuits, and then we're going to work out how your fingerprint came to be on that casing. Oh, and sergeant? I think we could safely remove WPC Baker's handcuffs.'

Ned sat in the car outside Kate's flat, watching the crocodile of searchers, sniffers and violators streaming in. What the hell was this all about? Could she really have had anything to do with a man who had buried a kilo of PETN in the dirt track? Who had placed a trigger mechanism inside a dead fox? Who had blipped the button on a car-door zapper and killed three people? Who had coolly stared at Ned through binoculars? Who had vanished into thin air. She couldn't, could she?

A bit of him didn't want to see inside, not without Kate's express invitation. He knew she'd told them where the key was, so that was like an invitation, but it was as if she were throwing a party and he was just one of the horde. Not someone special. Not like they'd been out to dinner and then she'd said, 'Would you like to come and see where I live?' And then he'd learn what sort of mugs she used, and how she made coffee. And whether she was good at keeping the pink crust from building up on the shoulder of the electric toothbrush where the head went in. Which he wasn't. And what sort of music she had. And her bed . . .

He could see the camera flashes in each room. Span checking behind the curtains. Opening each window, to see if Kate had hidden secret papers in the jambs. It was bollocks, all that about not having a personal invitation from her. The other bit of him – the detective chief inspector bit – knew he had to get in there. And wanted to. Wishing and hoping wouldn't get her into the clear. Only facts would do that. In a way, Kate Baker was guilty until proven innocent. And that last wasn't going to happen with him sitting outside twiddling his thumbs. He got out of the car, slammed the door and made for the flat.

It wasn't at all as he'd expected. It wasn't a sanctuary, or a hermit's cell. It wasn't barricaded or dark. It wasn't cold and impersonal. It was light, open and airy. It was modern and quite spare, but what there was in it was elegant and comfortable. Lots of white, some books, a good rug, a wood-burning stove. Extra Bilge was watering the plants, Span was going through the shelves, while Spick's guys were taking the backs off the flat-screen TV and stereo, and checking the wiring and fuse boxes. Pauline and Jammy were going through the kitchen cupboards. The usual shindig. Ned wandered into the bathroom. No electric toothbrush. She must have it with her. Medicine cupboard? A packet of aspirin. Some dental floss. A tube of antihistamine. Nothing else. Jammy suddenly brushed past him, followed by Pauline.

'Daft this is, isn't it, sir?'

'Certainly very strange, Pauline.'

'Doesn't seem at all right. An' Jammy reckons it's double daft, don't you, darling? All DT ever done wrong was being two sizes smaller than the rest of us. We could have done 'er for that, no worries. But terrorism?'

Pauline shook her head

'Still. Best get our heads down her toilet, hadn't we, Jams . . .'

Ned wandered across the hallway. It wasn't an eater's kitchen. In fact, it wasn't much of a kitchen at all. A few packet soups and quite a lot of rice. A bottle of vinegar, but no olive oil. One of those jars of chutney that are only given as presents, and no one ever eats. A cook-in sauce that would die a virgin. A packet of green tea Ned had given her. No sign of any coffee. Rather elegant grey mugs, matching the rest of the crockery. Hold on. Something funny here. Over the table. Three blobs of Blu-tack spaced as if they had held a photograph. Landscape, not portrait. The fourth blob was probably still on it. She'd taken it with her, perhaps. Wonder what it was of.

The Bilge moved in to take swabs for DNA, or dust the place for prints, or nick her chutney. Where next? Kate's bedroom. The boys were coming out. Ned waited till the room was empty – and went in. Span must have given them a strict talking-to. There wasn't a drawer open. Not a blouse off a hanger. Mind you, she didn't seem to be a great buyer of clothes. The wardrobe contained some of her trademark overalls, spare uniforms, an old waxed coat and an assortment of hats that would hide her face to her heart's content. A drawer of plain underwear. Another of t-shirts. A third of sweaters. Span put her head round the door to say she'd found the chunky jumper Kate wanted and had put it on the banisters. A string of beads and some silver earrings seemed to be the only jewellery. Ned couldn't believe that Kate had taken pearls and little silk numbers to Afghanistan, so assumed she ran a sartorially tight ship. Anyway, he thought. I'm just faffing around with this stuff to put off the moment when I turn round and look at . . .

Kate's bed. Unnervingly, it was rather large. Maybe five feet wide. It would have been reassuring to his male ego if it had been a pencil-wide cot, but it wasn't. Ditto if there had been a few cuddly toys dozing on the pillows, indicating no need for cuddly men. But there weren't. Crumpled sheets would have been reassuring in their own way, suggesting someone who knew only she would ever see the bed, and so didn't care. But, again, no. The sheets were clean and ironed. Under the bed – nothing. On the dresser – perfume? Not a sign or a scent. Ornaments from childhood? None. Bedside table – what was she reading? That's often a giveaway. *Your Dog* magazine, open at an article about some loopy couple travelling with their dog around Europe in an old boat. Ned's old edition of *Chance* which he'd lent her. And *Portnoy's Complaint*. Hmm. He hadn't lent her that. What was it doing there? There'd be a number of things he'd be asking Kate when he saw her. And not only about the Brecon Bombing.

'Mr Ned sir? Is this a good time?'

Enter Extra Bilge. Never mind that the car was almost due to take Ned to Brize Norton. Back-burner the gruesome report from Doc Bones that Ned had been trying not to read for days. Forget the email from Colonel Sillitoe detailing Kate's perfect alibi – he would read that on the plane.

'It's about your wodge.'

Extra Bilge flopped into a chair with legs and arms akimbo, like a collapsed puppet. He grinned expectantly at Ned.

'How long have you got?'

That's a new one, thought Ned. He'd never been given an option before. Didn't know the Bilge could do short versions.

'The car'll be here shortly. So make it bullet points . . .'

Extra Bilge looked crestfallen. Ned felt like a rat.

'. . . I suppose. Let's see how we go . . .'

'The wodge's principal ingredient is tobacco.'

Ned couldn't believe it. No digressions?

'But . . .'

Thank God. For one nasty moment Ned thought he was going to get to the airport in good time.

'. . . it isn't the tobacco that's going to help us pin this one down. Mind you, at first I thought it was from Gujarat, but I'll come back to that later.'

A digression deferred. Another first.

'It seemed possible, given the ash and moisture levels, that what we had here, Mr Ned, was the contents of a smoked pipe that had been knocked out in a non-destructive gesture, leaving what we call the dottle intact. Incidentally . . .'

A digression not-deferred. Had billions of those.

'. . . attempts to pin down the etymology of the word "dottle" have met with mixed success. "Dot" is the dictionary favourite, but has no obvious connection with pipe-smoking. A dotterel is of course a kind of plover or wading bird which, among other places, is found in Virginia – the key American state for tobacco production – and one particular type found there is called a piping plover. I know, Mr Ned, sir. It's neat. It's tempting. But is it *too* tempting? And, worst of all, it totally ignores the potential solution lying twenty-seven miles south-east of Aachen in Nordrhein-Westfalen.'

'Course it does, thought Ned. Any fool can see that.

'Give up? It's the little town of . . . Dottel.'

Extra Bilge sat back as if he had solved the mystery of life itself. Hold on a minute, thought Ned. He's wondering about the origins of the word 'dottle' which he's expressly said the wodge is not. That's an unlawful double digression.

'The clues came not from the tobacco but from the other ingredients. Because what we are looking at here is a compound, Mr Ned. Tobacco, yes, but also ash, slaked lime, cardamom, faint traces of menthol and juniper. Now it's the juniper that interested me. Do you know that juniper is widely used in folk remedies, for example in curing gleets? That's a morbid discharge from the urethra, by the way. I can guess what you're thinking, Mr Ned. You're wondering if we have a connection here with Dottel. Well, you'd be almost right. But the town thirty miles to the south-east of Dottel is Glees, not Gleet. But well done!'

Where's that car? thought Ned as he slid into a coma. Or an open window over a sheer drop?

'Now you can roast juniper, grind it and use it to make coffee . . . At least that's what you'd do if you lived in the Upper Kaghan Valley.'

If only wishing could make it so . . .

'Or . . . And here it gets really exciting . . . you mix it with slaked lime and tobacco to make *naswar*.'

There was a longish silence while Ned wondered if he could conceivably be expected to know what *naswar* was. He finally decided he could not.

'Extra Bilge, what's *naswar*?'

The Bilge looked thrilled. He didn't mind people not knowing things at all. In fact, you could say, he encouraged it. Because that way, he could tell them.

'*Naswar*, Mr Ned, is Afghan chewing tobacco.'

God, it took the patience of a saint but it was worth it.

'Although they don't chew it, so much as hold it in the mouth about ten to fifteen minutes. Much like *toombak* in the Sudan or *khaini* in India. And then they spit it out. Which is why we happen to have a wodge of it ten feet from where the bomber was lying.'

At which point the desk buzzed up to say Ned's car was there. He stood and grabbed his bags.

'Too much to hope for a DNA match?'

Extra Bilge shook his head sadly.

'You've done well, Bilgey Boy. Really well.'

But the flow of information wasn't exhausted, even if Ned was.

'One other thing. There's a question about whether in Islam *naswar* is *haram*. Whether it's forbidden. By and large, Hanafi scholars from the Indian subcontinent are lenient and say it's not; Arab scholars reckon it is unlawful, like other intoxicants.'

'So . . .?' asked Ned, trying to see the point and get out of the door at the same time.

'So your *naswar*-using bomber may be an Afghan Muslim, or he may – just possibly – be a Westerner who picked up the habit over there.'

Ned was in the corridor when he remembered the tobacco.

'What a memory you've got, Mr Ned. No, it wasn't Gujarati at all. I was just being silly. The veining was all wrong and the hue. No, the tobacco is from Kandahar.'

Almost exactly where I'm going, thought Ned, and flew to Afghanistan.

4

NO ONE MET HIM AT the airport. There was no message left with the RMP. Colonel Sillitoe was away paying a social call on his Texan opposite number at Camp Leatherneck. The only occupant of the glasshouse was a sunburnt lad sleeping something off. Kate's tent – empty.

So he left the chunky blue sweater – too clean to give him a buzz – on the end of the bed together with the next issue of her favourite dog magazine and a bag of biscuits for Jiffy, and went off to find some food for himself. A plate of compo carbonara later, and Ned was in the Ops Room where he should have gone first. WPC Baker was on a shout.

A kid from Intelligence found Ned a seat at the back. It was a richly incomprehensible scene. Staff officers bashing away at computers seemed simultaneously to be trying to follow and to run the war, rattling off acronyms into phones, and occasionally at one another. Ned presumed they were only able to run the bit of the war they could follow, and hoped it was a big enough chunk. Flat-screen monitors showed a mix of the public and the private: rolling news on some, and feeds from cameras in observation posts, spy planes and radio-controlled drones on others. Speakers relayed radio traffic between base and patrols, between helicopters and forward air controllers, occasionally between soldiers under fire.

Not that Ned could make head or tail of it. It looked and sounded like a highly controlled mess.

The Intelligence Kid returned with a pair of headphones.

'Your WPC Baker is with Easy Patrol. If we get anything from them it'll come through on here. They're in the triangle, in Gholamdastagir Kalay. The guys call it Gollum. Suspected car bomb. The ATO is Lieutenant Tom Ellison. Their escort is from 1 Para.'

At first there was nothing. So much nothing Ned wondered if the cans were broken. He was just hoping the Intelligence Kid had kept the receipt when he heard a crackle and a short beep. Then a man's voice.

'. . . 500 metre cordon. Could be looking at 400 kilos plus in there.'

'Roger, boss . . .'

Silence again. Funny – the voices were remarkably clear. Ned scanned the screens to see if any of the pictures matched the dialogue. A view across a ramshackle town. A grey blur. A huge dam. Helicopters lifting off. A polar bear with two cubs ambling across an iceberg. Nothing obvious. Another beep.

'. . . finish up your 20 metre check ASAP . . . we're all a bit exposed out here . . .'

'Nearly there, boss . . .'

More silence.

The polar bears had been succeeded by two cricket commentators in shirtsleeves silently chewing over an LBW decision. Ned guessed that, because they kept replaying a projection of the ball bouncing just over the stumps. The town view was now panning across ramshackle rooftops. The blur had coalesced into focus, but the image was still unreadable. A white band across grey fuzz.

Beep. New voice.

'Area secure, sir.'

'Thanks, Midge. Deploy Lassie.'

Silence.

73

Lassie. Is that Kate and/or Jiffy? Ned's throat went a little dry. Beep.

'Talk to me, Lassie.'

'Woof woof.'

Unmistakably her voice.

'Loud and clear, Lassie. Have a sniff around the vehicle, but watch out for other nasties. A wire'd come in handy.'

'See what I can rustle up.'

Ned now managed to feel frightened for her and mildly jealous. Other blokes, other jokes.

Beep.

'Easy Patrol, this is the Coop. SR wants to know your exact location.'

'Easy to Coop. ICP is at Grid Papa November 3145 6426. 250 metres north-west of Gollum Gate 1. Suspected VBIED is 500 metres our north. Tell SR they're nosy buggers.'

'Roger that, Easy.'

The Intelligence Kid was on the phone with his back to Ned. Was that him asking where they were?

Beep.

'Lassie 200 metres to go.'

'Looking good, Lassie'

Click. Crackle. Silence.

Ned wasn't sure how much more anxiety he could take. Would it be easier being the person walking towards a car laden with explosives?

Beep.

'Boss, movement in the field your 4 o'clock. Looks like Terry times two in dishdashas. Do we drop 'em?'

'Go firm, Lassie. Hold fire, Midge. Have the Javelin boys check it out on the CLU.'

Silence.

Ned needed some distraction. He scanned the screens. The cricket had given way to the lunchtime news. Whose lunchtime? Not Ned's. It was late-afternoon in Afghanistan. Then he noticed the Intelligence

Kid waving at him. Pointing at the screen which had once been a grey blur and was now sharp: lines, squares, dark blobs. Suddenly the Intelligence Kid's voice was in his cans.

'This is the road to Gereshk running past Gollum, sir. And this is Easy Patrol here. These are their vehicles. And this is Lassie – your WPC Baker – with her dog, stopped halfway between the Incident Command Post and the dodgy car, which is here. The possible insurgents Sergeant Midge Murray spotted are . . . let me see . . . 4 o'clock . . . could be these two dark blobs. Hold hard . . . more comms . . .'

Beep.

The Intelligence Kid waved his hand across the screen and then pointed his finger straight upwards. Spy satellite pictures. Ned nodded, looking suitably impressed. Didn't take much acting.

'Regret inform we are being dicked by two goats. One brown, one black. Brown one's rather dishy.'

'Crack on, Lassie.'

'Woof woof.'

'Ask the brown one if she's free this evening, please, Midge.'

'Roger that, boss.'

'Later, Midge, later.'

Dirty laugh from someone, then silence. On the screen he could see Kate and Jiffy gently weaving towards the car. They stopped for a moment, then moved on.

Beep.

'Lassie 100 metres to go.'

Ned found himself scanning the image to see if he could spot any trouble brewing. What was this dark patch? And this one? Is that a person on the top of this building? It was so hard to read. He then saw two officers staring intently at the screen and conferring. Of course. The Intelligence Kid hadn't laid on the bird's-eye view to impress a visitor. They too were scouting for threats to Easy Patrol – and they'd know the difference between a gunman on a roof and a rack of drying chilli peppers.

Beep.

'Lassie has reached the VBIED. Heavy nose twitching around the boot . . . and . . . he's sat down. That's a definite . . . No obvious wire. Just going to have a peek through the window . . .'

Her voice was even, matter-of-fact. How did she manage that?

'Not too close, Lassie.'

Silence.

The little blobs crept almost imperceptibly around the grey rectangle. The Intelligence Kid caught Ned's eye and made the gesture of wiping sweat from his forehead. Ned nodded fast back at him.

Beep.

'Uh oh!'

Silence.

Come on, Kate. Don't do this to me. The figures on the screen were motionless. Pause. Then they started to move from the car. Compared with how they had approached it, they were positively racing away.

Beep.

'Wotcha seen, Lassie?'

'Front seat, passenger side. Mobile phone on a small plastic box gaffer-taped to a motorcycle battery. Black and red wires running back into a slash in the rear seat cushion. Green and black wires to all doors.'

'All units take cover! Could be a bunch of rockets in the boot. If anyone sees anyone on a mobile phone – drop 'em!'

Silence. Kate passed the 100 metre mark. Then the 200 metre. She now seemed painfully slow. Evidently Ned wasn't the only person who thought that.

Beep.

'Lassie come home . . .'

Ellison spoke almost to himself. He sounded worried. She didn't reply. Moving in body armour in that heat must be eating up her energy.

300 metres.

Doesn't make sense. Why would anyone prepared to risk her

life like this in the service of her country, knowingly abet the terrorists who murdered the Defence Secretary? The answer is, she wouldn't.

400 metres.

Beep.

'On the roof above the Zam Zam sign! Northside. Saw a flash. Again!'

'He's got a phone in his . . .'

It took Ned a moment to twig that the popping sounds in his headphones were gunfire. That the bullets must be flying around Kate. That the expanding jaggedy blur in the centre of the screen was the car bomb exploding. People in the Ops Room were now standing, transfixed by the satellite image. Within a few seconds Kate had disappeared.

'Coop to Easy. Do you want air cover? Repeat, do you want air cover?'

Silence.

'Coop to Easy Patrol – come in, please.'

Silence. The faces in the Ops Room looked grim. Someone started talking to the Joint Tactical Air Controller. A senior officer slipped in from a side door and was given a quick briefing. Ned didn't know what to do or what to do with himself. The screen slowly cleared as the image was refreshed. Where the car had been, there was now a dark patch. Where Kate and Jiffy had been, there was nothing.

And then, out of the silence . . .

Beep.

'Easy Patrol to Coop. Air cover not needed. No incoming. Lone triggerman dealt with – a gnat's late.'

'Coop to Easy Patrol. Is Lassie home?'

There was an agonising pause, then crackle, then silence. It was one of those moments described by the crappy cliché: time stood still.

Beep.

'Woof.'

Her voice was as calm as ever, but the Ops Room broke into cheers. The senior officer gave a grin and returned to his office. Flap over.

The Intelligence Kid walked Ned across the camp to wait for the patrol. He reassured Ned that as it was a Friday, Easy Patrol would probably have an uneventful return journey. Fridays were days of prayer. Probably the reason why the patrol hadn't run into fire in Gollum: the locals were all busy on their knees. Except for the unfortunate gentleman who'd drawn the short straw and won the job of button-man. The insurgents went back to work on Saturdays, but that was their day for planning attacks. Then on Sunday, everything would go belly up. 'Holy Shit Sunday' some of the guys called it.

They stopped to grab some bottled water from the fridge at the gym. The shadows were lengthening, but the heat had still slammed into them when they left the cool of the Ops Room. Now Ned was wondering how he could avoid having to greet Kate after so long with an uncouth display of sweaty armpit patches. Slip back to his tent, grab a fresh shirt, wait till she appears then dive behind a burly squaddie, effect a quick change and pop out cool as a cucumber? Hardly a lasting solution. Anyway, he shouldn't be thinking about what impression he'd be making on her. She was the one in trouble. She was . . .

'Your WPC Baker, sir. Is she really mixed up in the Brecon Bombing?'

'That's rather why I'm here. To find out.'

Ned was curt, but the Kid sounded more incredulous than he had a right to. Yet another smitten youth, Ned supposed. On the other hand, he too was finding it difficult to see Kate as a terrorist. And he too was pretty smitten.

'How much do you lot out here know?'

The Intelligence Kid shook his head.

'Just the fingerprint. Colonel Sillitoe told us in case she didn't stack up and we had to move fast. I have seen her once.'

Ned nodded and finished his water. Once is all it takes, son. Although, if he was being honest with himself – and he'd learned that was generally a good idea – if Totally Smitten was ten and Absolutely Indifferent was zero, he'd have to admit to being down to about eight. Or maybe seven. It was partly a tactic – to allow himself enough margin of distance to give her the old third degree. But it was also involuntary. Like that initial moment when you wonder if the milk's off. Desperate uphill struggle for the milk to get back in your good books, no matter how cool and creamy.

A distant cloud of dust resolved into a convoy of six vehicles. The Paras turned off amid a volley of beeping horns; the disposers of ordnance continued to where Ned sat waiting in the shade of the shipping containers, known as ISOs, which housed EOD Base. Explosives Ordnance Disposal. Flurry of more dust as they pulled up. Moment of silence, then the lead truck's rear door swung open. Dog out first, then girl.

She was wearing baggy combat trousers and boots. A tight khaki sweatshirt, dust-caked with huge sweat patches. Hair tumbling down thick with sand and grime. Her bare arms encrusted with dirt and streaks of dried blood. Then she turned as a jolly-looking young officer bounced out from the passenger side and gave the dog a cuddle. Turned, so Ned got the full force of that face, the forehead, those cheekbones – all whitened with dust as fine as talcum powder. The eyes dark and dancing. The blanched lips parted in laughter.

Lassie had come home.

Eight, going on seven? Bollocks. More like ten going on fifty. Sour milk? Double bollocks. More like the freshest clotted cream. Ned stood, and literally felt weak at the knees. Who was he fooling? Not himself. Dispassionate investigator my arse, as Fatso would say. Personal considerations? It would take all his self-control just to say hullo to her, let alone ask her what her alibi was for the twenty-fifth. And he wasn't going to be saying hullo yet. The EOD team was decompressing with disparaging in-jokes thinly masking mutual adoration – and Kate and Jiffy were at the centre of it.

It reminded Ned of going backstage early on in his career to arrest the leading lady after a hit performance. So high was the cast on its group adrenalin-rush, so absorbed in its own tribal world of private language and rituals, that Hedda Gabler couldn't grasp who Ned was even as he was charging her, cautioning her, handcuffing her. He didn't exist, or perhaps he was an Ibsen afterthought. It took until the next morning before she remembered she was in fact a horrid little poisoner – and she still tried to send the warder out to gather in her reviews.

Kate turned away from the group and saw Ned. He looked vulnerable. Slimmer than she remembered. More worry in his eyes, more tension in his body. And then he smiled, his eyes crinkled, the corners of his mouth turned up and a bit of her crumpled inside. A big bit. She wanted to run into his arms. Wanted to lose herself in his neck. Wanted to breathe him in and not let him out. But she couldn't. Not with all these others around. Not with him suspecting her, or else why had he come all this way? Typical of him, not to trust Sillitoe. But she knew he'd come. Knew he'd ask her tougher questions. Knew she wouldn't be given the benefit of the doubt. But giving her a hard time over Ridley's murder wasn't the only reason he'd come. He had to. He'd given her his word he would.

They had come together during a complex case involving a dead body and a dear dog. Before that, Kate had registered him as a decent man in a world of scabby alley-cats, and Ned had fancied her rotten. But both kept their distance. Neither was a coward at work, but they both had some demon-slaying to do where relationships were concerned. The doggy case hadn't simply pushed them together; it had also gradually removed the obstacles between them. His infatuation-led tongue-tiedness was eroded by the need to talk over the case. Kate's fear of men's company – emotional and sexual – gave way to an overwhelming sense of safety in Ned's company. Till then he had no idea what she was really like because she was so private, and anyway he couldn't see past her looks. The more protective layers their time together stripped away, the more they liked what they saw.

There were two additional factors, one on her side and one on his. Dog behaviour was pivotal to the case and she knew more about that than anyone. Indeed, she knew more about that than she knew about anything else. Hence Fatso's nickname for her. Far from being a passenger, the Dog Tart was much more than an expert witness; she had driven the case forward. So she and Ned came together as equals. He needed her. Needed to understand her ideas and thoughts. This was great for her fragile self-esteem and essential in allowing him to see beyond her beauty and tantalising remoteness.

For his part, Ned had had the good sense not to jump on her. He could only claim partial credit for this. Solving tough cases became almost an out-of-body experience for him. The hoover, the telly and the washing-up sulked, unloved. Birthdays were forgotten, his bloody mother ignored. Span and Extra Bilge occasionally even had to remind him to eat. It was only as the case wound up that he came to his senses and started to see Kate as a sex object again. And that suited her, because that's how she saw him. The great brain was OK in its way, although it was odd how dense he could be at times, and at his wittiest he was almost amusing. But the crinkly eyes and the gentle smile, the long fingers and fit body . . .

The other reason why he hadn't jumped her bones was because in some tiny way he was a little afraid of her. He knew she had been hit on all her life, and when it wasn't other people running her ragged, she had done a pretty good job of it herself. Given how independent, how resolute she now was, he had no doubt he was the supplicant in the relationship. An old phrase of his late dad's came back to him: '*avec l'amour il y'a toujours celui qui aime, et celle qui se laisse être aimée.*'

It was telling that Dad made the one doing the loving the man and the one allowing herself to be loved the woman. His father had always given the impression of not quite measuring up to

Ned's mother. Not quite able to catch up with her. A worker to her queen, an altar-boy to her goddess, a swain. Never mind how little she deserved his upward gaze, how unjustified her downward disdain. Only when Dad was dying did he let slip something that suggested how he really felt: 'Don't be tough on your mother, Ned. She's doing her best.' This crystallised for Ned his suspicion that the skewed differential between them was a construct of his dad's making. Like the way he'd turn on the stairs and hug her so she was above him, could look out over him. Like the unstinting praise of her appearance. Like the way he deferred to her when it was obvious she was wrong: 'If you say so, my dear.' No one who was 'doing her best' could be perfect. She had to have allowances made for her. She had limits. She had to be humoured.

Had Dad in fact been the Jeeves to her Wooster? Masking actual domination with assumed deference? Ned didn't know, and assumed the dynamics of his parents' marriage would no longer matter. The funeral would put the lid on them. He couldn't have been more wrong. They buried Dad in one of those ghastly cemeteries beyond the most depressing fringe of suburbs. You wouldn't want to spend a moment there, let alone eternity or however long it was till the Messiah pitched up and blew the final whistle. Ned was a hopeless Jew. He knew little and believed less. He sweated out to this rain-soaked vale of tears because he had to. The last time he'd been there was for June's stone-setting. She was one of his parents' oldest friends, and Ned had been very fond of her. June had ruined so many pairs of shoes trekking through the orange clay to bury loved ones that she had bought herself a plot right by the tarmac road so no more footwear would have to suffer on her account. How unlike Ned's mother she was.

He had got through the service, survived the walk behind the coffin-bearing handcart that was identical to one he'd seen in a film of the Warsaw ghetto having rag doll corpses tossed on to it. He had steeled himself and taken the shovel to that livid, cloying soil June had so rightly detested. He didn't toss it into the grave. It wasn't an act of cavalier detachment. He gingerly let the clump of clay slide down the blade and thud – it seemed seconds later – on to the coffin lid. It was so very much not what he wanted to do to his father that, as the tears welled in his eyes, Ned felt ashamed of himself. He should have sprinkled a bottle from his father's tiny but classy wine cellar. Or scattered the contents of Dad's tobacco pouch on to the unvarnished pine. Except he would always be relieved he had not, whenever he felt such need for his father that he would put his nose deep into the soft leather and breathe in the man's wit and his smile and his unconditional love.

He reluctantly handed the spade to his nephew and turned to embrace his mother. And what she whispered in his ear told him that the dynamics of his parents' marriage would end only with her death:

'Ah, Ned, you'll have to be the man in my life now.'

As if that weren't spine-chilling enough, he was fairly certain she tried to kiss him on the mouth as he was saying goodbye to her through the window of his uncle's car. It may just have been a contorted near-miss, but you never know.

His father buried, the doggy case solved, Ned fell in love with Kate. But he couldn't shrug off the notion that he was doing the loving, and she was allowing herself to be loved. And it scared him, because he felt he had placed his happiness in her hands. So when she told him that she was thinking of joining an inter-service pool of sniffer-dog handlers to go out at little or no notice to hotspots around the globe, he didn't stand in her way. It was up to her what she did with his happiness. If she didn't want to stay with him, so be it. Could one inherit a tendency to supplicancy, along with a pouch-full of St. Bruno?

The irony, of course, was that she felt he didn't love her enough. She had heard about the Combined Dog Force before they had kissed, and after they kissed he never tried to talk her out of going. They had had a quiet but sticky scene in their favourite little restaurant a week before he was due to drive Kate and Jiffy to Brize Norton to fly out to Afghanistan.

'All you have to do is tell me not to go,' she said, 'and I won't.'

'But I can't,' he replied. 'You want to go. It isn't for me to stand in your way.'

Kate frowned in a way that he interpreted as her thinking he was being obtuse, but in fact was her looking for the right words to get her meaning across to him.

'But I might want you to stand in my way. Why not just stand in my way?'

'What – and save you having to make a decision about us for yourself?'

She shook her head.

'I can't make a decision for us. We should be making decisions together.'

'Which,' said Ned, 'is exactly why I can't put out my hand and stop you dead in your tracks. I'm not a caveman, and I don't want you resenting me for screwing up your career.'

No one said anything, and no food got finished either. Kate had no yen for a caveman, but she didn't want someone without a care if she stayed or went. She thought about mentioning the dangers, but stopped herself. She wasn't looking for a let-out or sympathy. What she really wanted was to love Ned so much that she didn't want to leave his side, whatever he felt about it. And adore him as she did, fancy him rotten, pine when apart, rejoice when together, she did not hear herself saying: 'Don't care what you have to say about it, Ned of my life, I just ain't going.'

He too kept quiet. It would be easy, wouldn't it, to say two little words: 'Don't go.' But the fact she needs me to say them proves I mustn't. So, they sat there together, obdurately apart. He got the bill. She got the car. They drove in silence. She dropped him off. They kissed fleetingly on the cheek, both knowing their lips had brushed tears. He lay in bed nearly picking up the phone and saying the words, to save their love, and maybe her life. She kept her phone by the bed and did not sleep till 4 a.m. in case she missed its ring. When she awoke with a start and checked it and there was no missed call, she knew she was doing the right thing in going. Because their relationship clearly did not have the will or the critical mass to sort this one out. It didn't mean it wouldn't have at some time in the future, but she would go out to Afghanistan without ties.

She spent the next few days packing and repacking. There were visits to the vet with Jiffy, and a drink at the Dog and Vomit with Large Sarge and the gang. Even Fatso pitched up and made a silly speech. Ned looked in, but they hardly spoke, except for her to tell him that she'd arranged with Pauline to drive her to Brize Norton. He looked deep into her eyes and nodded. 'Good idea,' he said. 'Pauline'll keep your mind off it.' Off what? she wondered. Off him? Off getting blown up by a roadside bomb amongst strangers? What was he on about?

And then, the night before she left, she found herself driving round to his house. Found herself knocking on his door. Found herself in his arms. Found herself in his bed, found themselves fucking with a pleasure and a passion they had never known in their entire lives, found themselves lying in one another's arms closer than ever, and still he did not say, 'Don't go.' Still she did not say, 'I'm not going.'

But she did say this.

'You have to promise me now that you'll come out and see me. You don't have to tell me anything else, but you have to promise me that.'

A dog had brought them together and now another dog patched them up. Enough to overcome the unease of a public meeting. Before Kate left, they had taken Jiffy on marathon walks to get him mega-fit for the heat and exhaustion. Ned too had used it as a way to regain strength after nearly drowning on their previous case. Jiffy had inherited his mother's ability to work hard and long with little panting – essential attribute for an explosives dog. The more panting, the less sniffing and the lower the level of concentration. Every half hour on those walks Ned had played ball intensively with Jiffy to push his stamina to the limit. Even so, Kate was surprised to see him bounce over and lick Ned's hands and face. Striding across wintry fields felt a distant memory and battalions of soldiers had made a fuss of him since then. But Jiffy seeming very pleased to see Ned made it easier for Kate to feel the same. She squeezed his hand and gave him a dusty kiss on the cheek.

'Your arms OK?'

'They're fine.'

'You didn't get hit by anything when that car bomb went off?'

She smiled and shook her head. They started to walk. How did he know about the car bomb?

'I was in the Ops Room, listening on headphones.'

'The Ops Room? There's posh.'

Funny. The expression hadn't entered her head for years. It was something her Nan used to say about unsalted butter and wearing tights and taking taxis.

'It sounded pretty hairy.'

'It wasn't hairy. Just noisy. If you want hairy, this is hairy!'

And she wooffled Jiffy's tummy and pulled his ears up over his head so it looked as if he was wearing a deerstalker hat.

They met in the queue outside the long beige dining tent. They exchanged tiny bows of the head and Ned passed her a tray. Kate's hair was wet, and her neck and the hints of her back and shoulders glistened. He had watched her walk down the row of tents towards him. The setting sun was so low beyond that, for a moment, the shadow of her body tantalisingly settled on his long before she reached him. He could see heads turn as she passed. The two middle-aged men in front – seemingly buried in an arcane discussion of Apache pilots' retina movements – lost the thread and simply stared. When she slipped behind them, they clearly wanted to turn round, clearly didn't dare and clunkily switched to the weather.

Ned and Kate stood in silence for a while, and then he asked her about the other women on the base. There were hundreds, and in every sort of job. There had been another sniffer-dog handler

– she and Kate had got on really well – but her tour ended last week and she and her black Lab had flown back to Sennelager in Germany.

But it wasn't easy for women. Kate had read about a Danish machine-gunner in Musa Qaleh – the only woman in the platoon house, right in the thick of the fighting. She was brave as hell and a deadly shot. Her trick for coping with all these men was apparently never to make eye contact with them. That's where the real danger lay out there. It was a tactic Kate used. Not, of course, when she was on a shout – you have to communicate with the guys – but the rest of the time. Otherwise . . . well, expectant mums weren't allowed on the front line. Did Ned know, they regularly flew pregnant girls out? Loads of them. Any of these could be the fathers. The two chaps ahead of them in the queue had been ear-wigging and in the yawning silence hastily struck up a conversation about whether to go for Chinese Night or steak garni. Kate caught Ned's eye and winked.

The food thing was a bit odd. Kate went for Thai-style salmon and pak choi off the Chinese Night menu, but Ned had compo carbonara again. It was OK, a bit gluey but edible. Why have it twice, though? They had just sat down when an echoing voice came over the tannoy.

'Standby for broadcast, standby for broadcast . . . Op Minimise, Op Minimise is on.'

The dining tent fell silent. Ned frowned questioningly at her.

'Someone's been wounded,' she whispered. 'Or killed. They've cut all communication with the outside world. No emailing, no Internet. They put tape across the phone booths. The lockdown'll last till they've told the next-of-kin.'

Ned shook his head and poked the pasta around his plate a bit. The only sound seemed to be other people doing the same thing. Then talk gradually resumed, but it was very subdued. The school canteen banter, the raucous, affectionate joking that was as much a part of winding down in a war zone as a square meal – was gone. The lockdown was internal as well as external.

Ned told Kate about a memory from college: of being in breakfast when the word went round that someone had hanged himself the night before. Who? No one knew. He was apparently in their year, but the name meant nothing to anyone. Everyone fell silent. Only the muffled clatter of cutlery. A face came into Ned's mind, the face of someone he'd seen around from time to time. Who sat alone at meals. In the library. At lectures. Not in the bar . . . he never went in the bar. Someone no one spoke to, Ned included. The face was pleasant enough, but empty. Or maybe it was simply featureless like armour-plating, annealed into dull self-protection by a short lifetime of being blanked.

The face loomed larger and larger, and the bigger it got the worse Ned felt about himself. He had known the man was totally isolated and yet had never addressed a single word to him. And now, in desperation, the man had strung up a rope, built a stack of books, put the noose tight round his neck and then kicked the books away. It was appalling. Ned had loads of friends, lots going for him, was full of compassionate talk. How much would it have cost him to smile at the man without friends, without a reason to live?

On the verge of tears, Ned gave up on his breakfast and was just leaving, when who should he see coming towards him but the blank-faced nobody. He hadn't topped himself at all. He walked straight past Ned with a fried egg on toast plus sausages and toma-toes. Bloody cheek! Ned didn't rush over to him. Didn't have a cup of coffee with him. Didn't want to connect with someone who had made Ned feel so bad about himself. Anyway, the face wasn't so much empty as. . . . slightly smug.

The odd thing was, that when Ned and his pals talked about this later, it turned out they each had a Mr Nobody whom they assidu-ously ignored, and whom they automatically assumed was the hanged man. And when they pointed out their Mr Nobodies to one another, it turned out they each had different ones. And, worst of all, it turned out that the hanged man was no one's Mr Nobody. They could never work out who was, he'd been so absolutely alone.

That evening's casualty wouldn't be like the hanged man, Kate said after a long pause. That was the great thing about the forces: the bond with mates. There'd be people worrying – or grieving. He or she wouldn't be alone.

It was dark as they left the dining tent. Kate had brought the chunky blue sweater with her, and she put it on. Around the back the chefs were baking bread for the morning and the smell mingled with a mix of diesel, aviation fuel and chemical toilets. Generators hummed on all sides. The night sky was pin-sharp though, and awesome. Then a Chinook came over low, and blew away the drains and breakfast rolls, and they were left with the aromas of the eastern country they were in, not the bubble the West had constructed to keep out the foreignness. So they smelled sheep and woodsmoke, borne on warm, dusty air up from the Helmand River.

He walked her to her tent and kissed her on her spotless cheek and, besotted but no fool, did not try to invite himself in. He walked back along the perimeter wall, passing several patrols with fierce-looking dogs, being overtaken by joggers exploiting the cool. The stars were gone now, covered by cloud. Ned stopped for a moment to stare through a gap in the wired-rubble Hesco wall, as a pair of Apaches flew out ablaze with lights below. For a moment he could see the flatness of the sand stretching out beyond the camp, until the pilots flicked out the lights and wheeled north. Then he just stared into blackness. Dasht-e Margo, it was called. The Desert of Death.

This was an odd one, he thought, as he walked across the base the next morning. Colonel Sillitoe had said Ned could use his office, so the scene he'd been dreading – Ned the Yid grills Dog Tart – would be staged at one end of the RMP's ISO. At 10 a.m. sharp. He hadn't seen Kate at breakfast. She might have gone in early, having exercised Jiffy before the day got hot. Or maybe she had some nuts and raisins in her tent. It was only since she'd become close to Ned that she'd eaten in public at all, and she didn't have much at the best of times. He couldn't think that the day he was going to question her about her involvement with terrorist bombers qualified as the best of times. So he grabbed a bowl of porridge and some orange juice in the dining tent and wondered if he'd been right to turn down Sillitoe's offer of his sergeant as a temporary No. 2.

Ned had done so because Kate had already had a formal interview with the colonel, which she'd cleared – Ned was meeting her to get information, not to wring out a confession. The reason he was having the beginnings of second thoughts was because something about it all wasn't quite right. 'That's why you're here, Ned, innit? To sort it.' 'Yeah, Fatso. It'll be on your desk by morning.' Except Ned knew it wouldn't.

The redundant sergeant was bashing a computer keyboard when Ned showed up. Carrot-topped, forearms like Popeye with accompanying tattoos.

'That Op Minimise last night,' Ned asked him. 'Do we know anything?'

The sergeant nodded. 'Effing Tali-Tubbies jumped a patrol on Route 611, on their way up to Kajaki Dam. Second Battalion the Yorkshire Regiment – the Green Howards. One P1, two P2s, two P4s. Do you know our categories, sir? P1 is acute injuries down to P3: light wounds. P4 is dead.' The sergeant shook his head, then remembered something that cheered him up a bit. Apparently the Chinook pilot who casevacced them out had seen dead insurgents scattered all around. Must have been twelve, fifteen Tali-Tubby P4s.

Each one somebody's little boy, Ned thought. Ours and theirs.

'To be fair to them, sir, they are very good about recovering their own and giving them a proper burial. You could fly over there now and not see a thing, except effing sand. Oh, and our lads' families have been told. Op Minimise is cancelled. You can speak to the wife now, sir.'

You're a proper little mind-reader, Popeye, Ned said to himself as he opened the door into the Sillitoe sanctum. That's exactly what I'm going to do.

None of Ned's guesses about WPC Kate Baker's breakfast arrangements were anywhere near the penalty area, let alone the goal. She hadn't skipped, she hadn't skimped and she hadn't scoffed alone. She'd run the perimeter with Jiffy before the sun came up, then fed him, had a shower and made her way to the camp laundry. There she joined Jamila, her brother Zabiullah and some of his co-workers, male and female. They sat out under the awning at the back and had nan bread with sesame seeds, still warm from the *tandoor*. Fried eggs. Fresh dates. Pomegranate. Yoghurt. Custardy *firni* and syrupy *jalebi*. They drank mint tea. Then Zabiullah and the others went off to feed the insatiable appetite of the laundry monster with sweaty soldiers' kit, leaving Jamila and Kate topping up their glasses. Watching the livid green leaves swirl. Talking about dogs and men.

On the dot of ten she slipped into the almost icy cool of the air-conditioned container, dazzled Sillitoe's Sergeant Fishpool for the second time in his life – he'd done a shift in the glasshouse the night she was there – and tapped on the door to the inner office. She felt sorry for Ned when she saw the expression on his face: small boy about to sit big exam. Sergeant Fishpool to the rescue.

''Ere, can I make either of you a cuppa?'

Ned said yes please, Kate said plain water would be lovely, and they made restorative small talk until the sergeant brought the drinks in and closed the door behind him.

Then she looked straight into his eyes.

'Don't be so worried, Ned. I promise you, I am not a terrorist.'

'I know you're not.'

'Well . . .?'

'Tell me how your fingerprint came to be on the casing of the mechanism which triggered the bomb.'

'You know I told Silly Toes – Colonel Sillitoe – all this.'

Ned nodded. He told her he'd read the colonel's report, but he and Sillitoe weren't doing the same job. Sillitoe had been trying to work out if she was to any degree responsible for killing the Minister of Defence, as principal or accomplice. He'd quickly worked out she wasn't. Job done. You're free to go, Miss Baker. It wasn't like that for Ned. He was tasked with solving the murder. It wasn't binary for him: on/off, yes/no. Innocent/guilty.

Yes, she knew.

'Just bear with me . . .' He had to stop himself from adding the word 'darling'. 'Just answer my questions if you can. If you can't, it doesn't matter.'

Kate nodded. Fine. No problem.

'How did the fingerprint come to be on that casing?'

So she told him. They had found a bomb factory. It was in Nad 'Ali, in a narrow street off the bazaar. The back room was fitted out with work-benches and soldering irons and stuff. Everywhere you looked there were printed circuit boards, spools of command wire, circuit testers, crocodile clips, connectors, rolls of sticky tape. In a corner was a pile of weapons – she didn't go near them, but they looked like AK-47s. The EOD guys were almost jumping up and down, there was so much gear. Except they couldn't see any explosives. Jiffy was pretty interested in the workbenches because they must have had traces, but no lumps of anything. Then he got stuck into an old carpet. The floor was compacted earth, really solid, covered with rugs. Jiffy sat down on this one by the door into the front room. He looked like the dog in the *Thief of Baghdad*, riding on the magic carpet.

Ned smiled, remembering a happy evening with Kate at the Picture Palace, before Afghanistan, before the Brecon Bombing, before all this having to interrogate your beloved.

'The boys rolled it back, scraped away the earth, lifted a hatch . . . and below it was all hollowed out. There was C4 down there – American military plastic explosive – and British PE4. Some ANFO – ammonium nitrate fuel oil. A pile of Iraqi or Chinese PMNs, maybe a dozen 107mm rockets plus some fuses, detonators and a few remote firing mechs and TPUs – timing and power units. It was a good find. I grabbed the triggers and TPUs while they were fetching some slings, then they removed the bangers while I stripped the rest of the bomb-making kit out of the factory. So that's why my fingerprint was on that casing. Assuming it was part of the Nad 'Ali haul.'

Ned thumbed through a file while Kate had a sip of water. Then he handed her a photograph. She stared at the twisted casing. At the electrical connector with its red-and-white plastic-covered wire. At the fragment of printed circuit board. So this was it. X-3, it said on the label on the back, with a GPS reference underneath, a date, a time, and Ned's initials. Funny. First she'd found X-3 in Afghanistan, and then Ned found it in Wales. Funny.

'It could be one of the ones I found — what's left of it.'

How many were there? She couldn't remember exactly. Perhaps two or three like that. With wires like that. And what happened then? Well, when they got back to Camp Bastion she gave them . . .

'No. You've skipped a bit. You've grabbed the electronics stuff and the boys have got the stash of explosives, and then what?'

Colonel Sillitoe hadn't asked her about that. Hmm. Let me see. Well, as far as she could remember, they dashed out of the house into the vehicles and raced off home. 'Drive it like you stole it,' was what the ATO said to the driver.

'And you weren't fired on?'

Kate shook her head.

'You had an escort?'

'The lovely Gurkhas.'

'But you weren't fired on coming or going?'

Kate shook her head. Definitely not. Was the bazaar busy? No, they hardly saw anyone. Did they catch any bomb-makers? Well, someone ran off as they pulled up. A few of the guys chased him for a bit, but he got away. Ned spoke as he scribbled in his notebook.

'I interrupted you before, as you were telling me what you did with the stuff you personally found . . .'

'I put it into plastic bags, labelled it and handed it over to the Weapons Intelligence Section. Don't know what happened to the explosives. If it had been an IED along a road, they'd have blown it up there and then, but this was in the middle of Nad 'Ali. Apparently the guys used to destroy everything – detonators, TPUs, whatever – but then WIS came along and said: "We want to see as much as you can safely get us." They target the bomb-makers; try to build up a picture of them, recognise their handiwork.'

Ned was still writing. And did Kate see anyone else touch the timers and triggers? No, she didn't. She thought she was the only one. And she didn't wear gloves? No. Far too hot. And they had to move fast. He nodded. Of course. Were there any lit cigarettes in ashtrays? Any glasses of steaming mint tea? No there weren't. Were the soldering irons warm? No. And between handing over the timers and triggers in their labelled bags that day, and now when he'd shown her the photograph of X-3, she hadn't seen hide nor hair of the things? She had not. He closed the notebook and looked up, open-faced and relaxed. Ah, thank God, she thought. Finished at last.

'Kate, have you had any direct, personal contact with any Afghans since you've been out here? I don't count people by the roadside or standing around in the market.'

Another question over Sillitoe's head. And right between her eyes. Beat.

'I have, yes.'

'Do you mind telling me who?'

Another beat.

'I can do better than that. You can meet her yourself. Come with me . . . to the laundry!'

Ned smiled, and said he'd be delighted. They stood and he put his arms around her oh-so-slender waist, and they kissed. At last. Then she broke away, a quizzical expression creasing the glorious face, a question remembered.

'You actually found it yourself? My X-3?'

Ned nodded.

'How odd. So there were still things to be found by the time you finally showed up?'

'Cheeky Dog Person! I was there when the bloody thing went off. I saw the three men blown apart . . . and then I had the oddest sensation of almost seeing the bomber staring at me.'

'What did he look like?'

'I don't know. Too far away. Only saw the flash of his binoculars.'

Kate shook her head. How very strange.

Ned really liked Jamila. She was warm, smart, self-possessed. It wasn't hard to see why she and Kate had become friends. They talked about the war, about mines, about dogs. The three of them walked across the base to the Barma Training Area, stopping to meet Jiffy on the way. Jamila was very honoured to meet the famous Jiffy, who licked her face and generally flirted disgracefully. Jamila had come into the camp not only to have breakfast with Kate, but at the unofficial invitation of the officer commanding the EOD detachment. Kate's idea was to see – without breaching the strict barrier between military anti-IED ops and civilian de-mining – if there were techniques that could be quietly passed on. Waiting for them in the training area was a balding boffin with a remarkable experimental contraption which could somehow detect mines under the ground using radar. When the conversation turned to stepped-frequency continuous-waves and caesium magnetometers, Ned made his polite excuses and left. He had a rendezvous for lunch at Pizza Hut with Captain Crispin.

In fact, Ned realised, although the Pizza Hut in Camp Bastion made a surprisingly good fist of being what it said it was, Captain Crispin was neither a captain nor called Crispin. He looked military enough: his desert fatigues were spotless. He had bags of cool: his brow bore not a bead of sweat. His accent was unplaceable, class-less. But it was his handshake that 'Captain Crispin' needed to work on. It was the softest, limpest Ned had ever encountered. He told Ned he was from Inter-Service Liaison, which – as cover – was no less flimsy. 'Captain Crispin' screamed spook.

To give the man his due, he did little to conceal it – but then how could he, since the purpose of the lunch was to pass on an intelligence tip-off? There was a little small-talk at first. No, Ned had never been to Afghanistan before. Yes, wasn't it hot during the day? Yes, Ned had heard the nights could be rather chilly. And how, Ned asked, were the winters? Very very short, and very, very bitter. Fancy that, said Ned. Yes, he was getting bags of help from Colonel Sillitoe. Yes, the food in Camp Bastion was very varied. All except the compo carbonara, thought Ned, who'd idly scanned the pizza menu wondering if it was available as a *calzone* filling.

'I've been asked to pass something on to you.'

'Captain Crispin' was so bald about it that Ned half expected him to reach under the table and pull out a parcel tied up with string. Some Aertex shirts and a sun hat from Ned's beloved Auntie Sheila perhaps – it being so hot out there.

'We've been told that the Brecon bomber is not a member of al-Qaeda, nor is he a Taliban or an international Jihadist. He's not a Middle Eastern terrorist at all, in fact. He is white, he's British and he's an ex-soldier. He has served out here, he's disaffected, he's angry.'

And what was he so angry about? Being asked to do the lethally impossible against a fanatical enemy with shoddy, inadequate equipment. The way ex-servicemen are treated, particularly the wounded. The whole attitude of the MoD. Hence the murderous attack on its Minister. And did their informant have a name? No, he didn't. But 'Captain Crispin' thought there were probably not that many chaps with the IED know-how to pull it off, who also bore a monster grudge. And how reliable was their source? At this, 'Captain Crispin' nodded his head meaningfully and leaned in.

'He's of the highest grade. He doesn't tell us much, but what he does is solid gold. He's never led us astray. He's never wasted our time. He's never let us down. His information can be trusted absolutely.'

And was this, Ned wanted to know, an unusually important level of information for your source? Had he boxed at this weight before? 'Captain Crispin' nodded. Yes, he had. A number of times.

'He sounds great,' said Ned, finishing his crusts. 'When can I meet him?'

To his credit, 'Captain Crispin' roared with laughter. Then he resolutely switched the conversation back to small-talk.

It doesn't matter how high-tech or air-conditioned they are, thought Ned. A tent is a tent, and sleeping in one – like sleeping on a boat – is always a little exciting. And this tent was more than a little exciting, given whose tent it was. Kate had pulled the two camp beds together and lit night-lights. Ned lay, propped on one elbow and watched her pottering about in a white T-shirt and not much else. People talk about 'leaving nothing to the imagination'; it didn't begin to apply. The sight of her slipping around the tent, ducking, stretching up, hunkering down, fed the imagination. Gorged it. Overloaded it. And what made it all sexier still was her seriousness. The absorption in those huge green eyes. She seemed at those times to have zero self-awareness. She had no real idea how beautiful she was. How that beauty was not dependent on the light, or eye shadow, or sucking her stomach in. It was there all the time, but it could also sneak up on you when you weren't concentrating. Then it would shake you and leave you a little breathless, suddenly aware of your pulse.

It happened a hell of a lot when she got dressed – on paper an unflattering, grey-lit, morning-breath event. Not with Kate. Back home, Ned had found every excuse to lie in bed and watch her. Her putting stuff on was as tantalising as her taking it off. And she had become a great one for not liking a match, and taking off her bra, or trousers and trying a different combination. Welcome signs of self-worth. Two steps forward, a delightful step back. Flimsy things, opaque things. Tiny buttons. Zips. Poppers, hooks and eyes. Arms up, arms round the back, arms down and leg lifted. There was a lovely moment when she would bend over to let her breasts take their natural, perfect shape in the bra. Then the hair. The clip hunt. Clips caught. Some thrown back, some kept. The brush. The glorious burnished gold mane tamed. She never once caught his eye. It was, he liked to imagine, just as it would be if he were not there. He wasn't really there. Not even a witness. Then, head turn at the door. You coming? You don't want to be late. Yes, Kate, I am. No, Kate, I don't. And Ned would throw the covers back and do his chilly, dull bloke dressing, thinking, come back. Start again. Encore. I missed a bit. You were right about that first bra. And I'm sure the blue knickers with the tiny frill would look better. Or the black jeans? Or breakfast in bed? Or phone in sick? Or . . .?

Somehow, during his reverie, she'd sorted stuff for the morning and found a spare collar for Jiffy and the letters he said he'd take home for her. She was sitting up in the next bed, setting her alarm, head bowed, still-wet hair masking her face. Then she straightened her back, pulled the T-shirt off and turned towards him. He shook his head a little, as he always did when he saw her. And then reached out his arms and stopped being a witness.

His flight was at dawn. As the Hercules lumbered into the air and banked he looked down, trying to spot the EOD trucks rolling out on the shout that had stopped her coming with him to the airport. So much movement, so many dust clouds kicked up by vehicles on the move. She could be anywhere down there. She and Jiffy. Jiffy in the black Swiss collar studded with tiny brass cows which they'd bought in Wengen. She in white cotton knickers and bra with lace roses at the nipple, red T-shirt with a New Yorker dog cartoon on the back, red socks, two tortoiseshell hair clips and one blue scrunchy, the chronometer watch he'd bought her as a leaving present, her tags: ID, blood group etc., then full combat gear. That's what she was wearing on the outside. He knew that for sure. Inside was another question.

The plane suddenly banked the other way, tipping Camp Bastion out of sight and blinding Ned with a sun spoiling for trouble. He settled back into the seat, baking and itchy in body armour and helmet. Maybe the case would now fall into place thanks to 'Captain

Into Dust

Crispin's' secret informant. But that wasn't what was eating away at Ned.

After a night of exquisite sex, he couldn't rid himself of the suspicion that Kate was having an affair – and not with him.

5

'HULLO, COCK. WHERE'VE YOU BEEN?'

Ah, Fatso. How I've missed you and your simple, answerable questions.

'So who did the Minister in then?'

Well, Fatso, funny you should ask that. I haven't the foggiest, but there's this bloke who calls himself Captain Crispin . . .

'Where's the Dog Tart?'

Here, Fatso. You feeling OK? That's normally your first question.

'She got that mutt Jaffa with her?'

Yes, Fatso. Jiffy is out there with her.

'How's it like the bleeding heat?'

Not a lot, Fatso. No one does much.

'So where does it kip at night? Does it bunk up with her?'

I gather it does, Fatso, some nights.

'Lucky fucking mutt.'

As you say, Fatso. As you say.

'They do duty frees, the RAF?'

If they do, Fatso, I missed them. Sorry.

'No matter, cock. Lot on your mind, I expect. We're seeing Lady Ridley at two sharp. Her place. Leave at half one.'

Ned nodded and escaped into the main office, filling his lungs with fresh air. One of these days he'd get the bends, holding his breath in Fatso's office and then rushing into the world of oxygen too fast. Probably better to spend five minutes in Fatso's doorway. Must ask Doc Bones, not that he'd know. He'd be great at diagnosing the bends in the dead, but hopeless at advising the living how to avoid them. Anyway. Enough of that. Lots to do. Lots to take in. There were new guidelines for requisitioning stationery. Something to do with his firearms permit needing renewing. Possibly his firearms permit itself. They'd changed the office recycling procedure. Paper cups now had to be wiped dry before going into the blue bins, and the soggy paper then had to go in the orange buckets. Ned was home all right.

The Ridleys had a fancy apartment within easy reach – given a chauffeured battle-wagon plus outriders – of the Ministry of Defence, the Mother of Parliaments and a host of expensive frock shops and nosheries. Security was indeed tight, with over-muscled doormen, desk clerks, lift attendants and loads of panning, blinking cameras. Bit less of that here, thought Ned, and a bit more at the country love-nest might have come in handy. Might also have saved the sight of Fatso in a black tie. Why had he done that? Wasn't that for funerals? It's armbands for mourning, isn't it? And Ridley's been dead for weeks. Who's Fatso think he is, Queen Victoria? Ned had done a number of these visits to the high-profile bereaved with Fatso, and couldn't remember him once sporting a black tie. He must have just put it on, because when Ned was in his office the superintendent was wearing the tie the team called Fatso Frittata. It succinctly explained who owned the tie, and what it was made of.

Ned started to worry that there was some ancient etiquette he knew nothing about, to do with visiting the widows of the Sovereign's Secretary of State for Defence. He checked his own in the lift mirror: dark red paisley. He'd be mouldering in the Tower before nightfall. He was about to quiz his shambles of a boss on this obscure point of protocol when the lift door suddenly opened, straight into the apartment. And there was Lady Ridley whom Ned had last seen, the scent of her husband's burning corpse filling her nostrils, having hysterics in his arms. Being led away to an ambulance, eyes streaming with tears, hands stretching towards the smoking ruins of the 4x4.

She was now wearing a dark blue silk dress to below the knee with a diamond brooch and matching earrings. Slim calves. Plain dark shoes with low heels. Hair pulled back from her face. A little make-up. A lot of class. And not a glance at the DCI who'd lain on top of her to take the bomber's bullets. She had eyes only for Fatso. Eyes which lit up as she raced into his arms.

'Oh, Benjy . . . Benjy darling. It's so lovely to see you . . . I've been so . . .'

And Ned never found out what she'd been so, because Lady Ridley burst into tears and buried her face in Fatso's neck. Gosh, thought Ned. That's very brave of her. If she knew him, she wouldn't do that. On the other hand, she must know him or she wouldn't do that. And 'Benjy'?

For his part, Fatso wrapped his arms around her and held her tight. He tenderly stroked her head. He murmured in her ear.

'I know, Janey darling. I know.'

Ned wasn't sure what he was meant to do. The lift had gone down, and his bloody phone – for once – wouldn't ring. So he stood there for a long couple of minutes trying to be invisible. He needn't have bothered. They were utterly oblivious to anything except her grief. Ned had never seen the Mighty Porker dealing with emotions in others, and, from the look of the corner of his eye, in himself. Extraordinary. He seemed almost human.

Eventually Lady Ridley broke away to reach into her bag for a handkerchief. When she turned back, she looked at Fatso and started to smile. Then the smile became a giggle.

'Oh, Benj. Your tie. I hadn't noticed. How sweet of you!'

And she gave him a fond kiss of gratitude on the cheek. He smiled back, in a brotherly way. But being so close to him she got a good look at the tie.

'Benjamin! That's a clip-on! Isn't it? A cheap, nasty, waiter's tie! Mike would have pissed himself laughing.'

He waddled a little sheepishly from one foot to the other and then he brightened up.

'You've got a choice for the memorial service, Janey. Between a bow tie that lights up, or one that spins.'

She let out a peal of laughter, and grabbing him by the arm, led him into the next room.

'You do know how to cheer a poor widow woman, Benjy. How's Esme? She sent me such a sweet note . . .'

Lady Ridley really only noticed Ned when they were seated with coffee. She looked at him hard. Her eyes were large and blue, with orange flecks. She shook her head.

'Do you know, it's terrible, but I don't recognise you at all. I remember someone running towards me, stopping me from steaming into that bloody hole. Probably saved my life – I never put my seat-belt on till I reach the road. And I've got a memory of writhing around on the ground with a weight on me, but . . . was that you?'

'Doesn't matter, Lady Ridley. It's entirely natural. It was a truly awful shock.'

'Anyway. Thanks for what you did. And I gather the bomber was still there when I showed up. If he'd opened fire, you'd have saved my life again.'

Ned said that luckily, they'd never had to find that out. They still didn't know when the bomber had left, or how he'd got away. There were lots of things they didn't know. That's how these things go at first, added Fatso. Then, bit by bit, they learn stuff. And young Ned here puts it all together. Lady Ridley nodded and smiled at them both. Then her face straightened. She was, she said, slightly surprised it was being treated as a murder investigation. Not that it was anything *but* murder. But she had been afraid it would simply be put down to terrorists and Mike would become like poor WPC Fletcher who was shot dead in the Libyan Embassy siege. Or most of the people killed on both sides in Northern Ireland. No one caught, held responsible for the specific slaughter. That was the problem, in a way. That terrorism turned murder into a group political act which was totally justified by the motives. It was upside down. The motives were normally part of the proof of guilt. With terrorism, they seemed to let you off.

So did Ned actually hope to catch the man who'd blown up Mike and Terry and Len? Yes, he replied. That was his job. That's what he intended to do. Lady Ridley seemed reassured. Would she mind, Ned asked, if he asked her a couple of questions? Not at all. He wanted to pick up on exactly what she had just said. Motives. He agreed absolutely with her about terrorist killings. It was easy for us to see them as intrinsically anonymous crimes, needing no explanation other than some blanket notion involving hatred, race, religion, east vs west and so on. But the bombing which killed Sir Michael and Sergeant Terry Sullivan and Len Kinnear must have been intensely complex to plan and execute. You might expect this to need no more explanation than that Sir Michael was the British Minister of Defence. There was a war on. He was the senior politician in charge of our armed services. He, more than anyone called the shots in Britain's 'War on Terror'. Why look any further for a motive for murdering him and those with him?

But there was a problem with this explanation. No terrorist group had credibly claimed credit for it. You'd think they'd be proud of what they'd done. Picking off so high-profile a target, on his home ground, so heavily protected. (Ned forgave himself this last white lie.) In the macho world of global terrorism this was something to brag about. Osama Bin Laden would have made a tape slapping himself on the back and issuing a bunch of threats we'd have to take seriously because of what his men had just pulled off. But here? Dead silence. So if all that wasn't the motive, what was? And that's where, Lady Ridley, you might be able to help us.

Lady Ridley took a sip of coffee. Then she crossed her legs with that almost subliminal sound of sheer, silky friction. You shouldn't be noticing these things, Ned told himself. She's in mourning and you're a caring police professional. And then there's Kate . . . Hold, don't go there now, Ned. Concentrate, Lady Ridley's speaking.

'. . . only basis on which we could avoid ugly questions in the Commons and the press. Particularly after all the fuss when we first got together. So we agreed: he wouldn't tell me a thing about what was going on at the MoD or what was in his mind about the armed forces or whatever. It probably put a greater strain on him, because he'd come home shattered and couldn't tell me why. Perhaps it meant he leaned on his staff a bit more, but it was a small price to pay for our marriage not getting wrenched apart by accusations of leaks and security breaches. Anyway, I present a little-watched arts programme, not the news. I was never very curious about where defence cuts were going to fall, or Military Intelligence's latest screw-up. So I'm not going to be very much help to you . . .'

Ned knew a 'but' was coming.

'. . . but I'm not blind and I'm not deaf.'

She got up and walked around the room. Proof of Ned's avid anticipation of what she was about to say was that he did not once look at her legs. Mind you, there was a sofa between them.

'That weekend was meant to be just for us. For a cabinet minister, and barring emergencies, Mike was pretty good at not bringing work home. If he did, it was important. He had his boxes, of course, but he'd do them on the way if he could. I can't read in a car, but it didn't bother Mike a jot. And he was a really fast reader . . . But that weekend, he had something important to do, and it involved writing not reading.'

Did Lady Ridley know what he was writing? No, she didn't. Not even the faintest clue? She shook her head. Was he a pen and paper person, or did he use a computer? Laptop. She didn't have it though; Clive took it away with him. Clive Hawkins. She rather thought Mike had printed something out, but she couldn't be sure. Did Sir Michael get in touch with anyone while he was doing this writing? As if he wanted something verified, or run past someone? Lady Ridley leaned against the back of the sofa and raised her eyebrows in thought.

'Mark Collet. He rang Mark on Sunday morning. While he was holding on he asked me if he could possibly have a cup of coffee. So tactful of him . . .'

She successfully headed off a tear, and resumed.

'. . . by the time I came back into the room the conversation was petering out. No way of knowing what they'd talked about.'

General Sir Mark Collet. Chief of the General Staff and head of the British Army. Hmm. Still, this was pretty tenuous stuff. A terrorist operation like this takes months to plan. Couldn't have been triggered by a phone chat that morning.

'I'm sorry. I wish I could give you a motive that points unerringly to one particular terrorist group. But I can't.'

They stood up. The lift was summoned. Lady Ridley and Fatso had another tender hug. She told him she was definitely selling the place in the Brecon Beacons. Couldn't bear staying there again, let alone going up that lane. Fatso passed on an invitation from Esme to stay with her in their cottage in the Forest of Bowland. And if she could stand it, he'd pop up and make 'em both laugh at the weekend. She said she'd really love to, as soon as she'd got the memorial service behind her. Then she turned to Ned and shook his hand.

'One last question, Lady Ridley.'

'Sorry, Janey,' said Fatso. 'He always has one last question.'

She gave a gracious little dip of the head.

'From what you could tell of the little you heard of their conversation, were Sir Michael and General Collet in agreement?'

She didn't have to think hard about this one. Yes, they were. The last thing Mike said was something about how it was going to be difficult, but it had to be done. Whatever 'it' was. Ned thanked her. A last kiss for Fatso and they were out of there.

Ned couldn't stop himself from looking sideways at his boss in the lift, a whole new side to the man revealed. Fatso unclipped the black tie, stuffing it into his saggy jacket pocket. Then he scratched an ear ruminatively.

'You know what, Ned? I reckon she must have mistaken me for someone else.'

For the first time ever, Ned was dreading a team meeting. Because, of course, of Kate. He didn't know what to tell them. He could say he was certain she was no terrorist, but he wasn't about to divulge his doubts about her fidelity – not least because what had alerted his suspicions was a bowl of army-issue compo carbonara. Or rather, four bowls of the same.

Over the years he had come to recognise certain signs in himself. Talking to his reflection in a mirror always meant he was drunk. And compulsive, repetitive eating meant that his current relationship was going pear-shaped. It was infallible. It had been non-dairy vanilla ice-cream with chocolate sauce when Sultry Saffron was quietly falling for that buffoon from Traffic. And a particularly indigestible brand of frozen savoury crêpe when he was drifting away from that French girl whose name he'd told himself he'd forgotten. And now it was pasta with reconstituted egg, freeze-dried hydrogenated vegetable-oil cream substitute and bacon-flavoured protein morsels made with mechanically recovered products from several countries. It was the very inedibility of the food he couldn't get enough of at such times that gave the game away. Can't have been pleasure that prompted his serial re-ordering of tasteless rubbish. So it had to be something else.

The closest he could get to understanding the phenomenon was to see it as his body irrationally cleaving to something unwanted and unlovable: what Doc Bones would call a *reductio ad absurdum*. Look how silly I'm being, body was telling heart. Bet you aren't so stupid that you'd do something like this, all the while tossing sugary shmoo or cardboardy starch or glutinous gloop down his gullet. Preferably yellow or beige in colour. Or maybe that wasn't it at all. Didn't matter. They were signs, and Ned ignored them at his peril. Compo carbonara x 4 = relationship dysfunction. Since he still adored Kate and, apart from the occasional minimum-intensity glances at a calf here, a long neck there – purely to confirm that Kate's calves, Kate's neck etc., etc., were the best on the planet – he was a practising monogamist, so it must be down to her. Best not share this with the team. They prefer a boss who's on top of his game, not a raving nutter love-loser with none-too-hidden carbonara cravings.

'Good to see you all.'

On the other hand, Ned thought as they were finding places to perch in his office, repetitive crap consumption was only an indicator. What about their actual relationship? Come back to that later.

Paper plate of rock cakes plonked on top of latest Home Office Guidelines Supplement. Span on radiator. Spick looking for something to write with. Extra Bilge's muzzle deep in coffee cup. Usual Thursday stuff. Spick opened the batting: for a Defence Secretary, Ridley didn't seem to have more than his fair share of enemies. He'd made no public statements smearing Muslims. In fact he had good relations with those in his constituency, a fair chunk of whom had voted for him. He'd attended the opening of a new mosque and over-shot his schedule apparently sitting cross-legged in the *madrassa*, listening and joining in. That's apparently a school where they study the Koran. Watch out, Bilge, thought Ned, you have a rival. And it wasn't a photo-op – no press allowed. He did indeed give evidence to the Presidential Threats Commission, but that was about drugs – something to do with controlling the international drugs traffic.

It seemed as good a time as any for Ned to tell them about 'Captain Crispin's' tip-off. They were surprised. And a little shocked. One thing for fanatical foreign extremists to go around planting bombs; quite another for one of our own blokes. So what do we know about him? Ned listed the menu items.

'He is apparently a white, British ex-soldier with IED experience who has served in Afghanistan and is harbouring a mighty grudge. We don't know why. It could be because of shortcomings in gear or training, or MoD policy, or its attitude to ex-servicemen. Maybe wounded ex-servicemen. We don't know. To which we should add what we already know about the bomber. He is pretty fit, given how he snuck away unnoticed. He has gone native enough to use *naswar*. He or someone he knows has access to the locked trophy store in the Weapons Intelligence Section in Camp Bastion.'

The locked trophy store. Ned remembered going from the blinding heat of an Afghanistan early afternoon into the WIS ISO.

Like smashing into an igloo. The morbidly eccentric lance corporal said he kept the storage container that cold in case the Camp Bastion morgue ever became overloaded. Their collection of bits of IED kit was stored at the far end. It had no windows, a double-padlocked door and an alarm. Inside was metal-racked with a rogue's gallery of DIY bomb parts. Some verged on the weird, like a timing and power unit concealed in a pile of donkey dung. They kept this in a Bart Simpson lunchbox. There was a trigger device which used the transmitter from a radio-controlled car, and key fobs, and a bunch of adapted mobile phones. There was even an electronic cat collar and the receiver which unlocks the flap, letting the cat in. Occupying an entire shelf of its own was the haul from the Nad 'Ali bomb factory labelled with the date, location and recovering unit. Fuses, printed circuit boards, command wire . . . And there, sitting in polystyrene trays like the ones takeaways come in, were the triggers and TPUs Kate had gathered up out of the earthen hidey-hole. All except one.

Of course. That explained X-3. If the bomber had been a local insurgent, he'd just have knocked up a new trigger mechanism. By stealing one from the store, the angry ex-squaddie presumably hoped – if any fragment of it happened to survive – to throw suspicion on the usual Middle Eastern suspects. He wasn't to know Kate's fingerprint was on it. Pure chance.

'No need to knock Kate off my Christmas card list, then,' remarked Span.

No, Jan Span. WPC Baker was in the clear. Flat clean. Cast-iron alibi. Zero evidence of collusion with person or persons unknown.

'So we don't have to cross-check any angry white ex-squaddies against her? I mean, we're not confined to people whose time out there overlapped with hers?'

No, Spick, we aren't. Except the trigger mech X-3 with her fingerprint had to get here somehow. That means, if the angry white squaddie served pre-Kate, he needs an accomplice to deliver X-3 to him.

Next on the agenda, Lady Ridley. Not her improbably draping

herself around Fatso, which Ned kept to himself. But something she said needs checking out. We need to know what her late husband was writing that weekend. What he rang General Sir Mark Collet about on Sunday morning, the day he died. Span took that one. She'd book the Chief of the General Staff for an early Ned toasting plus she'd read that bugger Hawkins his fortune. What time Spick would round up all and everyone who fitted the angry white ex-squaddie bill.

So that's that, then.

Except for Extra Bilge. He seemed awfully quiet,

'I've had a bit of a thought, Mr Ned sir. Shall I . . .?'

Everyone in the room froze. If Ned said, 'Fire away', not a tap of work would get done for the rest of the day. Plus the weaker brethren might die of boredom. On the other hand, Ned had been meaning to allow – or force – his subordinates to sit in on a Bilge briefing session. That way, they'd know what he had to go through . . .

Ned came to from his reverie to find the room empty except for Extra Bilge. He had advanced to the chair right in front of Ned and was about to bring his molars down on the last rock cake.

'How much, Mr Ned sir, do you know about Charles Mochet?'

Crunch!

Never heard of him.

'Doesn't matter. We'll come back to him later.'

That must be the record for subject postponement. Extra Bilge finished chomping the rock cake and started again.

'If I told you there was a car that ran on kitchen and garden waste, would you be interested? Be honest, Mr Ned. You wouldn't, would you?'

All right, dammit. No, I wouldn't. There, you've wrung it out of me.

'But supposing I told you there was a car that ran on kitchen and garden waste . . . and was only ninety-seven centimetres high?'

That, Ned agreed, would be an altogether different thing.

'It's a Swiss design with a 1.8 litre four-cylinder engine producing

120 bhp at 5,500 rpm, although you get maximum torque of 160Nm at 2,500 rpm less. And the beauty of it, Mr Ned, is that it's entirely carbon neutral; you can travel 62 miles on just 220 pounds of organic kitchen and garden waste with a top speed of 127.38 miles an hour.'

Extra Bilge sat back, hugely pleased with himself.

'Thanks for that, Extra Bilge. Just a couple of tiny snags. Firstly, why didn't I hear the engine? And, secondly, do you have any idea of the volume of grass cuttings and egg-shells you'd need? We'd have to assume the bomber stopped every five minutes to raid the compost heaps of South Wales to fuel his getaway.'

And then, fearing he'd been a bit harsh . . .

'A really clever thought, all the same. Thanks.'

But Extra Bilge had no qualms about abandoning ideas. He had a million of them, and could afford a little profligacy.

'I agree absolutely. And I'd go further. There's only one of these cars in existence, and it's in Switzerland. Anyway . . .'

He switched to a callously dismissive tone.

'. . . it's not as if it's the lowest car in the world.'

Well why, Ned wondered, are we even considering it?

'. . . that honour goes to a heavily adapted Hillman Imp, a mere twenty-six and a half inches high.'

And where, dear Bilge, is that car?

'Safe in a museum in Roscoe, Illinois, Mr Ned. And there's an interesting assassination connection here, sir, because this museum also houses a broad collection of artefacts relating to the killing of JFK.'

Ned stood up, stepped over to the window, took a couple of deep breaths, and had a think. He had to find a way of cutting through the digressions. Then it came to him. If years of dealing with Extra Bilge had taught him anything, the answer to the mystery of how the bomber had silently escaped would have something to do with . . .

'I've got just two words to say to you, Extra Bilge: Charles Mochet.'

Extra Bilge gazed admiringly at his boss. Imagine, him coming up with Charles Mochet.

'Exactly, Mr Ned! I mean, you only have to go back to the seventh of July 1933, don't you? When Francis Faure rode Mochet's Velocar for one hour in a Paris velodrome, covering 27.9 miles and smashing the record that had been set by Oscar Egg almost twenty years before. I believe, though I know you'll correct me if I'm wrong, that it was that event which, nine months later, made the *Union Cycliste Internationale* define racing bikes in a way which would rule out Mochet's invention. Rule out what we now call recumbents: low bicycles with a huge speed advantage.'

A bicycle! That's why Ned never heard him. A low bicycle! That's why Ned never saw him. A fast bicycle! That's why the bomber got well away before the cordons went up. Ned grinned at the Bilge and rushed out of the office. They'd redo the test he'd done with Jan Span. Only using a recumbent bike this time, not a car. And they were a little tricky to handle, so that might narrow Spick's field down a bit. And then there was the surveillance tape he'd watched with Span. Weren't there cycle races going on that weekend? Supposing the bomber was dressed in all the right gear, and slipped down the hill on to a route along which a race was being held? That'd give his getaway a boost. You hide in a crowd, not trying to leg it across wide open spaces. Good old Charlie Mochet. Always knew he'd come good, despite the shaky start.

Three thousand, four hundred and sixty one miles away, Kate was desperate. Desperate to hear Ned's voice, to talk to him, to tell him two banal, vital things: that he was the one she loved, and that he was the only one. But she couldn't. Not because there was an Op Minimise on; they passed in time, leaving sadness, and guilt from relief at an inconvenience ended. No, she had hovered by the phone booths for perhaps twenty minutes before a youth from Intelligence popped out with the sticky tape and sealed the doors. She was halfway back to her tent before the loudspeakers echoed their ghastly message around the camp. That was twenty minutes during which she could have spoken to Ned, and didn't. And her reason for not doing so was, she knew, shameful.

She couldn't say she loved him without saying she loved only him. And if she said that, then he'd know there was – or had been – someone else. Fine as confessions go, but supposing he had no suspicions in that direction? How daft was it to confess to a crime for which the confession is the only source of evidence? Why drag them both through the guilt and recriminations? Supposing Ned stopped loving her? Didn't want her back – sullied goods and all that? A bit of her said if he thought that, he wasn't worthy of her: best shot of him. But it wasn't her only bit. She had another bit which couldn't stand the thought of him despising her. Another bit reckoned she richly deserved his disgust. And then there was the bit which just wanted him passionately.

She changed into running gear and took Jiffy on a jog round the perimeter. To forestall conversations with strangers she ran anticlockwise, which few others did. Her headphones put off the exceptions. It was early evening. The heat was dying, and as it did so it blanketed the desert beyond the camp in red haze, visible through rare breaks in the Hesco barrier wall. Someone was smoking a sheesha; she could smell the apple tobacco. Curry Night tonight with the guys. They'd all found a few more IEDs that day without getting atomised in the process. Another result. Things should have been OK. Even good. But how could they be?

And then, as she and Jiffy pounded along, as they got into their stride, her brain steadily emptied. She was aware of the dwindling light and the smokiness, but nothing beyond and nothing closer. Not her own footfall, not her breathing, not even her own feelings.

Ned checked emails when he got home. Nothing from her. What time was it out there? Around nine thirty in the evening. Maybe the camp was in a communications shut down. Some poor sod dead or wounded. What did they call that? Op Minimise. Could ring the MoD and find out. Maybe not. What if they weren't shut down? Better not to know.

He sat in the flat as it got dark outside. Hadn't switched the lights on. Didn't know what there was for dinner. Didn't care. His post-Bilge enthusiasm had evaporated. There were signs of Kate everywhere. Scarf on the back of the sofa. Jiffy's water bowl on the hearth. Photo on the hatch into the kitchen of her and Suzy, the dog that had brought them together. What a dear old dog she'd been. Before he knew it Ned was feeling damp around the eyes. Kate. Jiffy. Suzy. Where were the buggers when you needed them?

It took him a while to realise the phone was ringing. Op Minimise must be over, thank God!

'Hullo?' he said, his voice brimming with hope.

There was a little pause.

'Ned? Ned? It's your mother.'

Oh no. Last person he wanted to talk to.

'How are you, Mother?'

'Not too good, but I don't want to worry you . . .'

'What's the problem?'

'Well, where are you? That's one problem. You said you'd pick me up at seven.'

Pick her up? Why? When had he said that?

'I've only just got back from Afghanistan, Mother. Just walked in the door.'

'They give you a lot of holidays, don't they? Well, you'll be nicely rested then. Do you want me to stand outside or will you ring the bell? Only we mustn't be late.'

Late? For what? Ned didn't think his heart had any further to sink, but it obligingly found the dearest little trough . . .

'. . . out to dinner. I'm not at all hungry, but we have to go. Promise me you'll leave straight away? I'm not going to wait outside; my left leg's swollen again. If I could get to the doctor's that'd be a start. And don't jab the bell. It only works now if you press it very gently. I've been hoping someone would come round and fix it for me . . .'

Ned knew he wasn't good with her. His patience, his skills at playing a long game, his trick of becoming calmer in the face of hostility and danger – these ace qualities left him for dead at the approach of his dear mama. Thinking he had been in Afghanistan on holiday was the sort of thing people who didn't know her, like his friends, would just laugh at and put down to her age; Ned knew better. He knew she'd never cared enough about him or his sister Louise to be honestly interested in what they were doing, or feeling, or going through.

He often thought that what would have suited her really well would have been to be a mistress or maybe a courtesan. A *Grande Horizontale*. She'd have had the bubbly and the dancing and the clothes, and no responsibilities. She'd never have tried to get the man to leave his wife, or hope her handsomest customer would make a decent woman of her. In a way, this was her tragedy: she'd never realised her potential as a flirter-bolter. She'd allowed herself to be respectable – and had never been able to handle it.

Anyway. When Ned had stayed with Lou before that fateful drive over the Brecon Beacons, they'd talked about 'handling Mother' and he'd resolved to follow Lou's example and bite his tongue. Apart from anything else, it would save all that guilt after she was dead.

'I'll get a new one, Mother. It's the button that's on the blink. Not worth mending. I'm sure the bell bit is fine. I'll be there in fifteen minutes. Where are we going?'

'Your Uncle Morris. He's cooking . . .'

'Fine. You ring Uncle Morris and tell him not to worry. Tell him we're famished. It'll mean a lot to him, and I'll eat yours when he's not looking.'

Uncle Morris. He was a totally different kettle of fish. *Gefilte*, of course. For a start, he was unashamedly Jewish. Except in her reflex deployment of guilt, Morris's kid sister couldn't even bother to behave like a Jewish mother: no autocracy; no aspirational protectiveness; no use of food as a weapon; no unhealthy interest in her children's sex lives. Morris Milton, however, was Ned's Jewish uncle. He'd been in the timber trade. He was schmaltzy, noisy, colourful. He wore bow-ties like an architect. He spoke

Yiddish. He shrugged his shoulders, and clapped his hand to his forehead, and waved his arms about. He couldn't pronounce his 'r's. He hated arguments. He never talked about religion or politics. He had an irrepressible sense of humour. When Ned was little and had to attend some wretched family do, he always found himself standing near Uncle Morris, who'd take his mind off it.

Once they'd stood at the back at a circumcision. As far back as they could get, and facing the wall. Uncle Morris pointed out to Ned the way the grain went in the panelling. He explained that, when laying veneers one had the choice of 'book' or 'slip'. With 'book' you opened out the veneers so the pattern met in the middle; with 'slip' you slid the veneer strip and placed it alongside the previous one so the pattern repeated. By the time Ned had grasped the difference – the room they were in was definitely 'slip' – the ghastly stuff had been and gone unnoticed by him. It took another circumcision and a funeral or two for Ned to realise that Uncle Morris wasn't at his side distracting him by accident.

As often happened his mother wasn't as whingey as she'd been on the phone. She had dressed herself up, and looked well. A little bit heavier since Ned's father had died but still tall and striking. And being told so put her in a better mood still. Ned didn't have to worry about the bell; she was used to it now. It was the people pressing the button who'd need to get used to it, Ned thought, and bit his tongue. Lights left on for the burglars, into the car and away.

Morris was no longer in the wood business. He had bought a boat and reinvented himself as a modestly successful author of humorous handbooks supposedly for Jews taking to the water. The first was called *Boating in Socks*, and the second *Berth with Mirth*. Single all his life and possibly gay – though whether Uncle Morris knew it, Ned couldn't be sure – Morris knocked out a fair dinner. The one drawback was he hadn't bought a cookbook for forty years. So they sat down to avocado prawn, Chicken Kiev with duchesse potatoes and peas, followed by a dark chocolate mousse.

Ned had devised a little plan for the dinner. He prized the bollocks moments in films and TV programmes in which the detective, stumped by an impossible murder mystery, bumps into someone totally unconnected with the case who artlessly says something which immediately sets the detective's mind racing. Of course, that's the key to it! And off he races to nab the culprit, leaving a bemused pal thinking, 'What did I say?' Who better than Uncle Morris to light unwittingly on the solution to the Brecon Bombing?

The consequence of this game was that Ned spent the evening trying to be sociable and participate while desperately cross-checking everything Morris said against Ned's data bank of Ridley murder facts. In it all went: the pigeon joke (Morris knew no others, thank goodness); the choice of possible titles for the new book: *Sink Schmink* or *Water Daughter!* or *Oy Vay, Under Way* or *How Come There Are No Great Jewish Admirals* (which wasn't, Morris stressed, a question); what the French word for 'innit' was (Morris said it was obviously 'nespa'); the secret of Chicken Kiev (which, after forty years of explaining it every time he served it was not much of a secret). No eureka moment to be had unless Ned was missing something. And then, because Morris was a generous and lovely chap, he asked his younger sister and Ned loads of questions and for some reason Ned had not envisaged the possibility that his mother might inadvertently finger the killer. So then he had to process everything she said as well. All in vain. Unless, of course, Chicken Kiev was itself the key: Ridley the victim of a hit by a rogue unit of the old KGB . . . which had served in Afghanistan! Hence the *naswar*. Yes! . . . On second thoughts, it was probably past Ned's bedtime.

He hadn't drunk at Uncle Morris's. When he got home he opened a half bottle of good St-Émilion, put on some jazz Kate had really liked and relaxed on the sofa. This was a bit more like it. They'd had a good steer thanks to 'Captain Crispin'; there couldn't be that many angry ex-squaddies who'd fit the bill. Give the devil her due, his mother was on reasonable form. Morris was a delight as ever. And Kate? Ah, Kate. Kate was Kate. Kate was just . . . glorious. On reflection, and helped by a delicate balance of Cabernet Sauvignon and Merlot from limestone slopes, he'd probably got it all round his ear. She hadn't been seeing anyone else. That repetitive food thing was probably what Morris would call '*bollockim*'. Pure coincidence with the crêpes and ice-cream. Plus he'd always had a weakness for spaghetti carbonara. The closer he got to the *voleur*, the more certain he became that he'd imagined the whole thing.

Something had changed during Kate's run. Something settled. It was really odd. By the time she took her shower, with Jiffy fed and snuggled down, she no longer felt any shame. She'd done nothing wrong. She belonged to herself. Comfort zones were there to be left, and regained. She could have tea and toast for breakfast, then go out and look for hidden bombs down wild, dusty roads, and then come back and darn socks. It might not suit everyone to live like that, but so what? Self-determining adults make choices.

Anyway, she was sure Ned knew – saucy pun intended – someone had come between them. She could tell from how he'd been the only time they'd made love out there. It was as if he was starting over from the beginning, assuming nothing, taking no intimacy for granted. And although there'd been a thoroughly delightful conclusion, she'd felt a slight formality between them on the way there. Like lustful strangers. As though, she being unknown to him, he wasn't sure of himself. And that translated as meaning he wasn't sure of her. And he was right not to be.

She hadn't meant to eavesdrop, still less fall in love.

It was a few weeks after she arrived in Camp Bastion. So much stuff was flying at her – bombs, bullets, jargon, acronyms, rules – that she could barely get a sense of the enemy. She had talked to the officer commanding the EOD detachment and he, not expecting such curiosity and initiative from a dog-handler, suggested she take a look at the IED Intelligence files. He told her that since roadside bombs had become such a killer in Iraq, the army had started to draw on police intelligence methods to build up a picture of the insurgents: their methods, aims, command structures. They used to find a bomb, blow it up and move on to the next. Now, when an IED was found, they'd fill out a report on it including date, time, map refs, photographs and details of the device. How it was constructed, wired, placed, triggered, controlled. Gradually they were turning clues into patterns and patterns into profiles, and then extrapolating signatures from those profiles. And your signature can hang you.

So late one afternoon she took herself to the maze of interconnecting containers which housed Intelligence. There she stumbled on the Intelligence Kid who recovered well and took her to the section marked WPNS INT. He showed her the lever-arch box files, got her on to the computer system and left her alone. It was that, or make an utter twit of himself. She soon became absorbed by the IED Intelligence reports. At first she just tried to learn more about the different techniques for planting and detonating roadside bombs. Gradually she started to see under the dodgy little mounds which Jiffy would sniff and then sit alongside. She started to get beneath the dust.

Time passed. Other people came and left. She went on to the computer, studying analyses of similarities between incidents. One IED gang was clearly working its way through a stash of the Portuguese plastic explosive PE4-A which had been brought in from Iraq. Another bunch of charmers were big fans of the Type 72 anti-personnel mine and its lethal variants. One of these was so sensitive that a magnetic mine detector would set it off. Some bombers specialised in attacks on arterial roads like Highway 1, the strategic route to Kandahar City. Others favoured built-up areas – markets, health centres, schools – where there was a good chance of pro-government locals getting killed.

And then there were the occasional personal touches. Particular bomb disposal specialists targeted with multiple booby traps and non-tamper devices. Scenarios designed to draw patrols into ambushes. Fake trigger devices filled with human excrement. There were the skilled, evolving new techniques to stay one jump ahead of their highly trained opponents. And the hopeless, desperately trying not to blow themselves up before they could dish out death to others. Yet for all the data and cross-referencing, the actual people behind the bombs remained in the shadows. She was looking for photographs, but all she could see were black silhouettes.

The Intelligence Kid came back to check on her, then went off somewhere to eat his supper. Alone in the office, Kate went back to the box files; that's when she started to hear voices. She didn't distinguish them at first. But then the IED reports started to feel samey and the voices became intriguing. Three, maybe four men, and a woman. Speaking English, except one of the men had an accent. He wasn't native English. The woman was too quiet to hear, but she seemed to be asking the questions. And the person doing most of the answering was the man with the accent. Judging by the tone and rhythm, it was a rather serious conversation. About what? And where were they?

Kate had come into the Weapons Intelligence Section through a door some way behind her, but to her right was another door and it was ajar. It opened on to an unlit corridor and directly opposite was another door. That too was ajar. There must be two containers with a passageway between them. She looked across. No one visible, but the lights were on and she could see the corner of a desk and a small suitcase. There was a sign on the door but it was too dark to read. She could hear someone moving about, then a lull in the conversation. The sound of a filing cabinet drawer opening, then the chink of glasses. Then quiet. Then laughter. Then things grew serious again, and one of the men spoke a lot. Then there was another silence and what sounded like heavy paper being unrolled. A map perhaps? They all seemed to speak at once, then they started to listen to the man with the accent and Kate caught some words at last: Kandahar . . . Zhari . . . Sangsar village . . . Panjva'i . . . Must be a map. Then one of the other men said something about Operation Hedgerow. After which the woman asked a question, in which Kate could definitely make out the words 'IED' and 'bombers'. She buried her head in the box files so that she'd look innocently absorbed if anyone noticed her.

In films, she thought, this was the point at which the eavesdropper gets a coughing fit, and then they find her and take her into the next room and handcuff her to the radiator and say that they are going to have to kill her because of what she knows. Except she didn't think they had radiators in Camp Bastion and her throat wasn't ticklish. So she listened some more. The man with the accent was now in full flow, though Kate couldn't make out what he was saying. But it was obvious from the tone of the voices and the occasional laughter, that he was giving information willingly and that he was not deferring to them. When he spoke, they listened. The next sound she became aware of was the map being rolled up again. A chair scraped. One or two of them stood up. The woman asked something which contained the words 'scramble' and 'London'. One of the other men answered and there was the sound of people moving about. Then the woman spoke as if into a phone.

Something made Kate look up. She saw a figure passing through the doorway into the gloom of the corridor. She scrutinised a report she'd already read and hoped she was invisible. Whoever it was in the corridor hadn't gone far, because she heard a match being struck. She was so quiet and alert it sounded deafening. Someone had slipped out for a fag. Silence. Then the smell of a local cigarette. Accent Man? She turned a page of the report. Then silence again, broken by a soft voice very close to her.

'Hullo.'

Kate looked up into the most beautiful black eyes she had ever seen. In fact the whole face was unbelievably handsome and she didn't normally like beards. This beard wasn't weedy, but it wasn't extreme either. And it looked very clean. He stood in the door smiling down at her with enough twinkle to light up the night sky. She was lost for words, so she made do with a smile back. The bolt of lightning which had just struck her bounced straight back and floored him. They looked into one another's eyes and said nothing. Something was happening, but neither had the foggiest what to do about it. It was a very odd moment in both of their lives.

After a while, how long Kate couldn't tell, the man gave a tiny nod and slipped back across the corridor into the other room. She felt paralysed. Her instincts told her to get out of there and go straight off and bury her head in Jiffy's neck and think about home. But if she did that she wouldn't see that extraordinary, beautiful man ever again and she didn't think she could stand that. So she stayed.

The sounds next door became difficult to read. More walking about and talking. Then Kate saw movement out of the corner of her eye, and angling her head towards the computer screen, saw a woman bending down and picking up the suitcase. She placed it on the desk, back to Kate, opened it and started rummaging inside. She had a good figure. Indeterminate age. She snapped the case shut and moved out of sight. Kate next heard a crackling sound, as if they were trying out a radio. Or maybe some sort of walkie-talkie. That went on for some time. Then there was more conversation. Kate was tired now, and couldn't make sense of it at all, except that the man with the accent and much more besides wasn't saying much. She should have left, and still she didn't. Then without a sound, he was suddenly by her side again. He pressed a slip of paper into her hand, touched her on the shoulder and vanished. So very, very strange. She could smell him still. An exotic, lemony smell. So very, very exciting.

And then something even more bizarre happened. From the room next door came the sound of scuffling. Someone being beaten up. Someone hurt. Oh God! She'd misread the whole thing. It wasn't a benign question and answer session at all. It was a full-on inter-rogation which had turned into torture. She couldn't just sit there and listen to it. She jumped up and dashed across the corridor. What she saw defied understanding. Someone she hadn't seen before, a young Afghan man, was indeed being beaten up. His face was covered in blood, and he was doubled over in pain. Another man was idly putting some papers away. The woman was not to be seen. Kate screamed at them to stop. The men doing the beating up looked at her, not angrily or guiltily but uncomprehending. As if they didn't know what to do. She couldn't, at first, see the beautiful man but then he suddenly appeared from somewhere behind the door and seemed to take charge. He interposed himself between the victim and his attackers, raising the bleeding man up with a brotherly hand under each arm and looking into his eyes. He said something in Pashto which sounded as if he was making sure the man was OK, then he turned the full force of those eyes on Kate. He really was very commanding.

'He is fine – don't worry. It isn't like you think. Please don't worry.'

6

NED WAS TREATING HIMSELF TO a bit of *déjà vu*. He lay in his old spot on the rise by the parapet with his binoculars to his eyes, staring up at the vantage point. It was strange being back. The hole was still there. They'd had a request from the farmers to fill it in, but Ned hadn't agreed. He wasn't sure why precisely, but he knew he wasn't ready to have the crime scene bulldozed.

In some related way, he probably hadn't needed to go on this jaunt – he could have left it to the Bilge – but he wanted to. Besides, he didn't trust anyone else to find his exact, original position. A few inches up or down the slope could make all the difference. It felt very different today. Light, smells, mood. Then it was bright, acrid, sharp. Now: drizzly, dank, hazy. Lucky he'd brought a ground-sheet and umbrella. Plus a thermos and a tub of chocolate flapjacks.

Up on the hill Extra Bilge was measuring the height of the recumbent, the height of the seat, the height of the rider, the mean height of the gorse, the height of the vantage point above sea level . . . It was always a toss-up whether to involve Extra Bilge in practical research operations like this one. He didn't really have any powers of self-restraint. He'd already spent an age fussing over the cycling kit he insisted the rider should wear.

High-visibility, of course, but should it be the orange or the yellow or the mauve or the red? He even tried measuring the light refracted from them with a light meter, but plumped in the end for the orange on the basis that the bike shop assistant's brother who worked on the railways had a vest in the identical colour. If it kept Dafydd from being mown down by the local train from Gower it would probably do fine. Funny, thought Ned, how that had suddenly come back to him. It was one of his dad's driving songs:

> *Oh the local train from Gower*
> *It go forty mile an hour.*
> *As it steam into the station*
> *It do frighten all the nation . . .*

There was every chance that Recumbent Rhodri would frighten all the nation. He was beefy with mad eyebrows. Bike, rider and running mechanic came courtesy of the Brecon Bikers – the local force's cycling club. They were pals of the abseilers who'd found the wodge. Ned couldn't help wondering how much coppering got done in this part of the world. Police work can so easily put a crimp in your hobby time if you aren't careful. Anyway, they were tickled pink to be of help. Well, livid orange.

Rhodri manfully donned Extra Bilge's choice of biking wardrobe, while Emrys went round with the bike oil and grease and tightened some things up and slackened other things off. The bike apparently had one of the lowest profiles on the market, with the seat a shade under a foot off the road. Extra Bilge scribbled furious notes as Emrys described its turning circle – wider than other recumbent types – and its ride – smoother than virtually any other bike. This all wafted down to Ned via an open-circuit walkie-talkie.

He decided to let the Bilge direct the show. At least for now. Eventually the faffing stopped and Rhodri lay down over the edge of the vantage point, dayglo almost pulsing through the drizzle.

Then Ned heard Extra Bilge shout a cue and Rhodri crawled back, mounted the bike and cycled off to the west as fast as he could. The only problem was that he never once went totally out of sight. After he'd gone half a mile they stopped him and pulled him back. There were enough other problems with the experiment for Ned to relinquish his cosy dry patch and drive up to the vantage point for a rethink.

When he and Span had tried this, going east had provided better cover. That's how they'd arrived at the maximum height for the bomber's profile of 36 inches. So not much point in testing the westerly exit route, Ned told the bike crew and Extra Bilge, not least because to stay on the left-hand side of the road, in case he met a car, Rhodri would have to travel along the open edge, not the side tucked into the hill. Ned also suggested that at the start the bike be placed as far from the edge as possible to minimise the chances of the rider being seen during the mount. The other change was to ask Extra Bilge and Emrys to stay out of sight themselves; having them standing around staring after the cyclist was distracting. Oh, and could Rhodri not be so visible looking over the edge? He should lie only as far forward as was necessary for him to see Ned through the vegetation and rocks. Fine. Swigs of coffee and flapjacks all round. Take two.

While the DCI was driving back to the bridge, Extra Bilge rehearsed Rhodri's Le Mans start a few times, applying some limbo-dancer techniques. Then with Mr Ned back on his ground-sheet, binoculars trained on the vantage point ready and waiting, Extra Bilge squatted out of sight behind a boulder next to Emrys. Rhodri lay down peering through a gorse bush at the umbrella in the valley below; the Bilge waited a minute and then gave Rhodri the off. Rhodri wiggled back, hugging the ground, across the road to the recumbent. He slipped agilely on to the seat, and kicking away with his feet, teetered for a second along the hill-side edge of the road. Emrys and Extra Bilge held their breath until Rhodri managed to get a purchase on the pedals and then accelerated away. The bike really was fast. They soon lost sight of him round the first left-hand bend. Then picked him up as the road swung back to the right. Then they lost him again and never got him back.

Down below, Ned saw Rhodri peeping through the gorse. Then, suddenly, he wasn't there. He panned the binoculars to the right . . . no sign of him. Had he in fact started? He must have done. Ned scanned the hill as far right as he could see. Nothing. Not a flicker of movement anywhere. Not a smudge of dayglo orange against the darkening hillside. And then the walkie-talkie crackled and he heard Extra Bilge's excited tones.

'Did you see him, Mr Ned sir? He'll be halfway to Aberdare if we don't stop him!'

To make doubly sure, they did the experiment twice more. On the last, Extra Bilge and Emrys joined Ned on the slope by the bridge, each armed with binoculars. None of them saw Rhodri once he pulled back from the vantage point. None of them saw him mount the recumbent. And none of them saw his escape from the hill. He gave Aberdare a miss and went straight to the pub. He was on his second pint when the others trooped in, soaking wet and jubilant.

The presence of two cycling experts was too much for Ned to resist, and he made them sing for their supper. Recumbents, according to Rhodri, were not quite the equal of conventional bikes at coping with steep ascents. You couldn't stand up on the pedals; you had to use low gears and pedal fast. Supposing, Ned asked, someone had driven the bomber and his bike up to the vantage point? In that case the worst would be behind him, Emrys reckoned. From the end of that valley where the bomb had gone off, it was mostly downhill all the way. A couple of nasty sharp rises, but they were short. And once he'd cleared the valley, no one would have given him a second glance. There were bikes all over the Brecon Beacons that Sunday. He'd have had a fast, easy getaway.

'But given the recumbent isn't great on hills, wouldn't he have stood out among a load of conventional bikes?'

Rhodri shook his head. There had been a big Fun Ride on Sunday. There were all sorts out: recumbents, racers, trail bikes, mountain bikes – you name it. He could easily have slipped in amongst them.

Interesting, thought Ned. Let's go back a bit.

'When I asked you to dodge out of sight, where you then hid, was there room for a recumbent?'

Extra Bilge and Emrys nodded. There was a run of boulders, Emrys said, with a drainage ditch between them and the sharp rise of the hill. No problem hiding the bike.

So, Ned mused, a van drops him off, then rendezvous with him somewhere the next day. Wonder if anyone saw two guys stuffing a recumbent into the back of a van? Big ask, that one, given the huge geographical spread. He'd have wanted to leg it as far and as fast as he could, before we got the cordon in place. How fast are they? An easy twenty miles an hour down these roads. So by the time the road blocks were established . . . Emrys and Rhodri nodded – they'd both been drafted in when the balloon went up. Turned out forty-five minutes had elapsed after the explosion before they managed to close their roads. The bomber could have got well clear.

'Then again,' Rhodri added, 'he'd probably have worn dark cycling gear, not the dayglo togs you made me wear so I'd stand out – and maybe he slipped on a bike number for the getaway. Easy enough to get hold of one . . .'

Ned wasn't really sure how likely the Sunday biker bluff was. He was increasingly certain that the bomber would have chosen invisibility over camouflage. He might well have become a temporary Fun Rider to get clear, but he wasn't about to finish the race and receive a participant's sash and drink the free can of lurid sports drink and compare punctures or grazes or whatever. Too much contact, too many cameras. Boom, as Major Butterman would say, and into thin air. That's his style.

Just as the Brecon Bikers were venturing into the deluge, something occurred to the DCI.

'How easy is it to ride one of those recumbents?'

Emrys looked to Rhodri for an answer.

'Not easy. You can't leap on to one and hope. Initially you find yourself planning everything: starts, stops, turns. And steering is a different game. On a conventional bike, you steer to balance. You can't really do that on a recumbent. And if you're used to a bike, you'll find you can't lean the opposite way out of a fall. You have to steer into it. Takes a week or two to get by on one. Longer to get good.'

'And to use one as a getaway vehicle in difficult terrain?'

'He'd have to be really good. Almost certainly turn out, sir, when you catch the bugger, that he's got one.'

Thank you, Rhodri. Thank you, Emrys. As soon as we find some suspects we must have a look in their garden sheds. See you in the morning, O Bilge.

Up the rickety stairs. Same room as last time. Same blend of must and mothballs. Same lumpy mattress. Unfortunately Ned had clean forgotten the lie of the land, tried lying right down the middle of the valley and barely got a wink till the small hours.

After breakfast, he went for a purposeful stroll leaving Extra Bilge behind. The rain had lost interest overnight, leaving the valley sodden. He could see the sheep high on Lesseps' hill, munching their way from the shelter of beetling crags and arthritic trees. About halfway down the road a rusty old pickup truck drove past him, then braked hard and backed up. The window wound down and who should lean out with a cheery greeting but the lovelorn swain Edward Tamblin. Apparently it had all been pretty quiet round there since Ned's lot had cleared out. Though, having said that, old man Lesseps hadn't been quiet at all. He was well worked up about that hole. He'd told Edward that he was going to put in a mileage claim to the police for having to drive the extra miles round . . .

'And how do you and . . .'

'Jackie.'

'. . . Jackie manage, only having the one road up there?'

'He don't care no more, now we're on a proper basis.'

Ned congratulated them both on their proper basis and told him to tell Mr Lesseps that it wouldn't be long before he could fill the hole in. They'd let him know. Tamblin offered Ned a lift which was politely declined. He drove off and Ned walked on.

In any bollocks cop show on the telly, he mused, if the detective went back to the scene of the crime and bumped into a colourful local again, the colourful local would have some vital clue for him. Jackie's been thinking about that night, he'd have said, and she now recalls seeing a white Renault van parked opposite the farm track with these two chaps in it. She doesn't know if this is important, but one of them was holding a metal box with wires coming out of it. They looked to her like a couple of disgruntled ex-squaddies back from a tour in Afghanistan. Weighed down, they seemed, by a ton of personal resentment against the Minister of Defence. She only had the quick glance, mind. She's not sure how useful this is, but she did jot down the van's registration, on the off-chance her hunch was proved correct by some later wrong-doing in the vicinity . . .

He stood on the track, back to the road, facing the hole. To his left: the open field where the 4x4 and most of the bits had landed. To his right: the embankment where the bomb had been buried, the adjacent trees helping to channel the blast, all but the biggest partially uprooted. After all that rain, he'd have expected the hole to have become a pond, but no. Must be all that red sandstone Extra Bilge was boring on about on the way down. Nothing obvious about the hole he'd missed. He walked slowly round. The skid marks from where Lady Ridley had brought the BMW to a halt were still visible. Somewhere here was where he'd wrestled the widow to the ground and – unmemorably for her – had lain upon her, awaiting the bomber's bullet.

Also around here was where the handsome Wilton had found him, after so many years. Had he ever lain upon Wilton? Or vice versa? Why couldn't he remember? Was Wilton beautiful? It was a question he'd long pondered when they were flirt friends. The answer was probably no. She had a boot face. It had something to do with the tightly rounded forehead, the set of the mouth and chin, and the way the skin made a less than tenacious leap from jaw-line to neck. Boot faces could be attractive, even sexy, but never beautiful. What made her handsome was her figure, which had lost no tautness with the passing of time . . .

Ned awoke from his schoolboy reverie about the MI6 officer's bottom, to find himself on the spot where he had found the remains of the trigger mechanism, X-3. The marker was still in the ground. Ned looked up from it to the tree that had just managed to withstand the blast. And then he started to realise why he hadn't given the farmers the OK to repossess the bomb site. Something about where things were wasn't right. Let the evidence speak to you, his old governor used to say, and you might notice something whose significance you've missed. Stay open.

Ned found a long branch, removed the twigs and stuck it in the ground by X-3's marker. Then he draped his red scarf over and around it, to make sure he could see it from a distance. And then he slowly walked to the track, keeping the same distance from the centre of the hole. What was it Major Butterman had said? The thing that was hammered into them during their bomb disposal training? By now Ned was back where he'd started on the track, and he could still see the scarf. Out now into the field where the 4x4 had wound up. The further he walked round, the more he, the hole and the tree came into alignment. But at the point where they were exactly in line, the scarf was no longer visible. Ah, that was it! Major Butterman had said: look for the absence of the normal and the presence of the abnormal. Well, hullo, abnormal! How, with the explosion directed away from the trees towards the field, had X-3 – adorned with Kate's perfect fingerprint – managed to land directly behind the one tree which had remained intact?

Poetry had always made Kate cringe. Part of the problem was the breathy way it was recited by teachers at school and poets on the radio. Listen to my soul, they were saying. Marvel at its depth. Wonder at the uncanny way my words express your most secret feelings – feelings you could never describe, let alone in metre and rhyme. She hated those horridly soft, self-important voices. As if they were inside your head. Invasive, intrusive. Like being burgled or worse. She had been at a huge team meeting the day someone had stolen a Modigliani nude from a major gallery. It was on loan from the French, was worth a fortune, a guard had been killed and Fatso was in full flow: the arrogance of the Garlics, as he called the French; the toffee-nosed idiocy of the gallery; the crap security arrangements; the stupidity of the Home Office in winding down the Art Squad, etc., etc. Spick had come in late and, during a Fatso pause for breath, asked the detective superintendent what it was a picture of, this painting that had been brutally nicked.

'Naked girl on a sofa,' said Fatso. Adding airily: 'I mean, that's the whole point of art – so painters can get women to take their kit off.'

Whereas this fell short of explaining all those dull landscapes Kate had been trotted past on a school visit to the National Gallery, it struck a chord with her over the poetry. She didn't want those sighing, yearning voices burrowing into her. They always sounded as if they expected to be repaid for their empathy and emotional acumen with sex. On yer bike, poet. And then she heard her first landay:

> *You watch an old man lead me to bed*
> *Then, cruel people, wonder why I weep and tear my hair.*

Afghan poems with just two lines, with nine syllables in the first and thirteen in the second. Poems of love, passion, sorrow, exile, rejection, war. And, best of all, poems written mostly by women, for one another. Landays were shared while cutting the fabric for a wedding dress, or drawing water from the well, or at *nazar* – when women met weekly to pray, eat and gossip. Kate was at

Jamila's house when they started reciting them. Some were traditional, like the lines spoken by Malalai, a patriotic young Afghan woman who led her country's soldiers in battle against the British in 1880:

> *If, young love, war spares you at Maiwand,*
> *It must be because you are needed as shame's symbol.*

Most were written not by warrior-heroines or great poets, but by ordinary women. Landays provided them with a secret outlet which would make other women nod in recognition but which, heard by a man, might lead to a thrashing or even being stoned to death. It mattered less whether the poem expressed an aching wish or described its passionate fulfilment. Its strength lay in the fact that a woman had put her emotions into words and passed them on. This is what I feel, she was saying; it's OK to feel like this:

> *I will give my mouth to you gladly*
> *But why stir up my pitcher? Here I am now, all wet.*

At first Kate was shocked by the explicitness, and by the seizure of the sexual initiative. It was partly because she was herself a latecomer to the idea that women could want and expect sex on their terms and should enjoy it without guilt. Only since Ned, really, and some nights were easier than others. She didn't know why this was. It wasn't his fault. He was sweet. It was how she felt about it that mattered. That was what she was working on. It was going fine, really. And then here she was, sitting curled up on a rug with a glass of mint tea, listening to Fatima and Hossai and Jamila's sister Parween broaching the most intimate secrets via these mini poems.

Kate realised that the burqas had fooled her into seeing the women as asexual and repressed. She had thought of them as downtrodden and inarticulate, accepting their lot like the donkeys braying outside. But Hossai, forced into marriage with her father's oldest cousin, had taken a lover – a man her age she had met at a wedding. He was a handsome teacher who hated the authority of bigots and misogynists. Her husband was stupid and cruel, with foul breath and an eye for Hossai's twelve-year-old sister. The tradition in landays was apparently to refer to these ghastly husbands of forced marriages as 'little horrors'. Hossai whispered the poem she had written to her lover into Parween's ear, for her to translate. Whispered as if her husband were in the next room, not in Qalat on business.

> *Tonight we will lie locked in embrace*
> *You safe from enemies, I from the 'little horror'.*

As soon as Parween fell silent, Hossai started to apologise. It was, Hossai said, the only landay she had written. It was clumsy. Her own mother's were beautiful . . .

'No, no,' said Kate. 'It's good. Really good. So what did he say? When you recited it to him?'

Hossai looked into Kate's eyes for a moment, and then down. She shook her head.

'I haven't. I have never said it to him . . .'

When Hossai looked up, she was crying. Kate stretched out and gripped her shoulder. Hossai rested her head tenderly against the back of Kate's hand.

'He knows,' said Parween. 'She doesn't need to tell him. Anyway, the big thing is that she has written it.'

Yes, thought Kate. It's how we feel about it that matters. Time enough after that to worry about the guys.

Then it was Fatima's turn. She was in her fifties, and reasonably happily married, but in the 1980s during the Soviet occupation her husband had started doing little jobs for the invaders. A bit of fetching and carrying at first, then showing them around, which would have led to fully paid-up collaboration had Fatima not written a landay on a slip of paper she tucked into his wallet. He was in the queue outside the local base, about to show his ID card to the Soviet guard, when he noticed it:

> *Consider well what you really love*
> *If you are false to my country you are false to me.*

He pretended he'd left his ID behind, turned on his heel, went home and never returned. The women all laughed and clapped when Fatima told the story, though they had heard it before. A landay with a result! Then they turned to Parween. She is the best poet of all of us. The bravest. The most forward. Parween shook her head, hating the attention and praise. She rose and went into the kitchen to boil water for more tea. Parween, Jamila said when she had gone, takes no shit from anyone. This is one of hers, written to get rid of a hopeless lover:

> *You left my body unsatisfied*
> *And it has told my heart, which can never forgive you.*

The women did not clap and laugh, but nodded and whispered to one another. These were things that few women were in a position to think, still fewer could express so cleverly, and only a handful dared utter. When she came back into the room the women couldn't help staring at her, leading Parween to frown at her sister and shake her head.

As Jamila was seeing the women to the door her brother Zabiullah arrived to drive Kate to the base. He kindly agreed to take the others home first and then return for Kate. When Jamila got back into the room she found Kate scribbling on a scrap of paper. Words were written and scratched out. Jamila smiled to herself and waited. Syllables were counted on fingers. Then Kate stopped and looked up at her friend. It was almost as if she had thought she was alone.

'Well?' asked Jamila. 'Is it a landay?'

Kate shrugged, a little embarrassed.

'Not really . . . sort of . . .'

But she handed the paper over to Jamila. Jamila read it and nodded, impressed, before returning it to Kate with a smile. The man Ned was lucky indeed, she thought.

'. . . *by a roadside bomb in Helmand Province. The dead have now been named as Staff Sergeant Edmund Corbett of The Royal Logistic Corps, Sapper Richard Belton of the Corps of Royal Engineers, Rifleman Tom Leighton of The Rifles, and Rifleman James Haslam also of The Rifles. Their next of kin have been informed. Just before we came on air we spoke to Lieutenant-Colonel Mike Gatiss of The Grenadier Guards in Helmand Province.*

'*These four men are a huge loss to us out here; I don't want to say irreplaceable, but in a sense each individual is exactly that: irreplaceable. Our hearts and sympathies go out to their families back home, and all I can say to them is that their loved ones died serving their country with great bravery and distinction.*'

'*You had actually met them recently, hadn't you? Weren't you . . .?*'

'*Yes, absolutely . . . What makes this particularly sad for me was that, by chance, I was on patrol with the four of them only the day before, and was struck by their utter professionalism, coupled with a great sense of team-working, and no small amount of humour. The troops out here do an incredibly complex and dangerous job, which is difficult to understand even for us at HQ unless you actually see it at first hand. Well, I went out with them and saw it for myself, and all I can say is I am proud to have known them, even for such a brief time . . .*'

Ned switched off the car radio. The country must be divided, he thought, into those who listen to news items like this with tears pouring down their cheeks, and the rest of us – the vast majority – for whom it is as remote as a Sumatran tsunami. Sad, sure, but something happening to other people. The rest of us slip easily on from such heart-breaking announcements to a cosily indignant rant: . . . the situation out there is unwinnable . . . even the Soviets wound up getting out . . . why do we always get bounced into these things by the Americans? We're going to have to bring the troops home in the end – why not cut our losses now?

And all the while there are families for whom our presence in Afghanistan is not simply an academic accident of history or the result of national self-aggrandisement. Families with fathers, sons, daughters, brothers, sisters, husbands, wives, lovers driving through the dust, sweltering in the heat, palms damp with fear, joke cracking, hearts beating. Next-of-kin dreading the call from the MoD. Next-of kin who 'have been informed' so the radio can name the names. It's always bad news, being 'next-of-kin'. And we hear the list of regiments and think: Royal Logistic Corps – how come pen-pushers are getting blown up by roadside bombs? Crazy! The Rifles – we need a bit more than rifles out there, surely? Grenadier Guards – how quaint! Isn't there an old song about them? And we listen to the names of the dead and they mean even less to us.

Spick parked the car some way short down the row of identical army homes and they walked to number 36a. The place was in turmoil. This was the family's penultimate day in the house. Since Will had been killed, they none of them wanted to live there. Wanted to get as far from the army as they could. They were moving to be up near his sister. Tea or coffee?

Ned and Spick sat among the boxes while Mrs Marcham went into the kitchen to put the kettle on. She was in her late twenties. Slender, in grey tracksuit bottoms and a white T-shirt. Cloud of black hair scraped off an exhausted face. From Spick's notes, Will Marcham had been blown up in a Snatch Land Rover six months before. From her eyes, Jill Marcham had been crying ever since.

A boy of about nine clutching a sports bag overflowing with gaming gear appeared in the doorway. He ignored the detectives' greeting, dropped the bag in the hall and sidled into the kitchen. They could hear the sounds of a surly, uncooperative son being yanked into line by a mother who had had it up to here. Then, after a while, they heard the sounds of a lad who had recently lost his father being comforted by his recently bereaved mother. Par for the course round at number 36a, thought Ned. The door from the kitchen opened and she came out with red eyes and the coffees, and he came out with red eyes and a plate of chocolate digestives.

'This is Micky. Say hullo to the policemen, Micky.'

The hullo was almost a whisper, but he said it and his mum ruffled his hair. Spick had a son of the same age and after a faltering start, Micky started replying to him. Ned let them talk for a bit, and then asked Mrs Marcham when she was expecting her father-in-law home. Any moment. He'd popped up to the adjutant's office. Wouldn't be long, she was sure. And then Micky took Spick outside to show him something, and Ned asked her if Will had been anything like his father. Mrs Marcham gave the glimmerings of a smile for the first time, and shook her head. No, she didn't think she could've stood it, having him in the house if he'd reminded her of Will. No, Will had a kind word for everyone. He was, for a soldier, really gentle. She could never see how he managed to kill people. Which he did have to, because he talked about it his first time back. Said how sick he'd felt afterwards. Spoke the once, and then never referred to it. She didn't know if he stopped feeling sick after killing and that's why he never said anything about it again, or if he didn't want to trouble her. Or himself. She didn't ask him, because she didn't want to know the answer. No, he was dead gentle.

She reached forward to a box of tissues on the table, but it was empty. She went into the kitchen and returned, dabbing her eyes with kitchen paper.

'Trouble was, me and Will got on so well. Otherwise it'd be easier. There are some girls on the base who've lost their husbands and they aren't doing so bad with it. Extreme case: there's one girl – lived near here – her husband used to knock her around. A real hard nut he was. She'd only just got back from seeing the solicitor about getting a divorce when she got the call: killed in a rocket attack. Friendly fire. She always reckoned it was his mates couldn't take any more of the horrible bastard. She's got a new life now, with a man she'd known before. His wife had left him and they got together. Like I say, an extreme case, but a whole lot easier than when you loved 'em to pieces. Ah, here he is. Here's Grandad.'

A bear of a man of about fifty pushed his way into the room. He patted his daughter-in-law affectionately and hugged his grandson who raced in from the back, followed by Spick.

'Mr Marcham? I'm Detective Chief Inspector Bale, and this is Detective Sergeant Pick. I believe DS Pick spoke to you on the phone. We're investigating the Brecon Bombing. Could we have a quiet couple of words with you, sir?'

To get on Spick's hit list you had to tick three boxes. You had to know how to handle explosives. You had to have been in the country that weekend. You had to be disaffected. 'Disaffected' was not the word Spick used, but it meant the same thing. You had to have a grudge against the MoD and/or the Minister. Other factors would whittle the possibles down further – lack of a sound alibi, ability to ride a recumbent, traces of plastic explosive found in your garden shed, sketch-maps of the target zone pinned to the wall, huge photo of Ridley above your bed with 'This man must die!' scrawled across it by you in red, signed confession . . . you name it. But that would come later. In Malcolm Marcham's case, later meant now. He'd already ticked the first three boxes bigtime. He had served in the Falklands and Northern Ireland in bomb disposal, receiving the Queen's Commendation for Bravery after a sticky few hours in Ballygawley. He was, by his own admission, in the country the weekend of the Brecon Bombing. He was a major thorn in the MoD's flesh for his virulent and informed public attacks upon the lethal inadequacy of the equipment provided for front-line troops.

'My son, Lance Corporal William Marcham, was the thirty-third soldier to be killed in a Snatch Land Rover. I mean, you'd think they'd get the message after, what, the third at a pinch? Fourth if they're half-awake? Fifth? Sixth? Given how thick they are, let's give 'em ten. There. Ten lads die in Snatches and any halfway bright person would think, "Hold on! Something not right here."

Not our top brass. Brass Wallies, I call 'em. Fucking blood on their hands, that's what they've got.'

He reached into a folder and handed Ned and Spick a sheaf of photos of bare, twisted metal, almost unrecognisable as having once been vehicles. Thumbing through them, Ned saw one that had appeared in a newspaper campaign to have the Snatch Land Rover taken out of service. A tangle of jagged, bloody aluminium.

'If the kit can't handle the mission, you've either got to modify the kit or the mission. If the replacement for the kit is a year away, then it's the mission you go for. But that's not how the Brass Wallies think. They've continued to send the lads out in vehicles that weren't designed to cope with an IED. Not designed for front-line service. We had 'em in Ulster, where the big worry was the IRA rolling barrels under 'cm, so they fitted them with skirts. It was a different world. Loads of ways of getting killed in Northern Ireland, make no mistake, but the roads are basically tarmac. In Iraq and Afghanistan you can dig a hole anywhere with your bare hands. Neat packet of plastic, simple trembler or pressure pad, and goodnight Vienna! Mobile coffins, the lads call them. Murder, I call it.'

In one of the photographs, a torso sat behind the remains of a steering wheel. A torso without clothes, skin flayed, flesh scorched. Marcham saw Ned wince.

'That the one with half a body? He was a pal of Will's. Corporal Joseph Nkosi CGC. That's the Conspicuous Gallantry Cross to you. Lovely bloke was Joe. You can't tell from the photo.'

'May I ask, Mr Marcham, how you got hold of these photographs? They don't look like the sort the MoD Press Office dishes out . . .'

Malcolm Marcham's reply wasn't even boasting. It was guileless.

'No. Well. You got to know people. It's impossible to campaign for something when you're in the forces, but it's different for us that's out of it. And there's always someone somewhere who doesn't want his mates to get slaughtered needlessly.'

Marcham handed over a sheaf of newspaper clippings: 'War Hero says Scrap the Snatch!' read a typical headline. There was a photograph of ex-Colour Sergeant Malcolm Marcham QCB and the picture Ned had recognised of the twisted, bloody metal that had carried three men to their deaths.

So, Ned replied, there are connections between the guys out there and people like you back home. Malcolm Marcham shrugged, and said there was no law against soldiers talking to their families. Or texting or whatever. That was not, Ned said gently, exactly what he had in mind. He rather meant the sort of connections that could get back photographs such as the ones Marcham had shown them. A sort of network of like-minded individuals. Marcham thought about it a moment and replied that he supposed you could call it that. Not an organised thing, but . . . And could you get other things from there? Well, some of the guys bring back souvenirs.

'And what about parts to make a bomb?'

'Why bring one back? Easier to make one here. Less trouble.'

Again, guileless. But that didn't mean guiltless.

'You now talking about Ridley, Chief Inspector? Should I have my solicitor here?'

'It's entirely up to you, Mr Marcham,' said Spick, quick as a flash. 'You know best if you need him. What do you reckon?'

Marcham rested his elbows on his knees, and his chin in his palms. Angry bear thinking. He shook his head. No, he did not need his solicitor.

'I didn't do it, if that's what you're asking.'

'Would you like to have done it?' asked Ned, genuinely curious.

Marcham started to laugh. It wasn't the sodding politicians he was after. They don't know any better. Always looking to cut the defence budget, without a clue that some arsehole can be sitting in Whitehall one minute rubbing out figures on a budget, and next thing you know some poor bastard's being zipped into a body bag in Helmand. But Michael Ridley was different, Ned ventured. He had been a soldier himself. Served in Ireland, the First Gulf War . . . Mentioned in Despatches. He'd have had more than a clue.

Maybe, replied Marcham, but it's the Brass Wallies who have to carry the can. It's their job to tell the politicians when the kit's crap. When a job can't be done. It's the Brass Wallies who should look out for the lads. If they don't, who will?

'Is that why you do what you do?' Ned asked.

'Campaigning, yes. Talking to the newspapers, organising veterans and bereaved families. That's one of the reasons I'm glad to be moving out of an army house. That's why I was up at the adjutant's when you arrived. Another bollocking for an interview I gave to local radio last week. But killing the Minister of Defence?'

He shook his head.

Ned often wondered how he would respond if accused of murder. Would he give all the reasons why he wouldn't have done it? Or the reasons why he couldn't have done it? Or would he just stick to saying he simply hadn't? He had often wondered if there was a pattern to which of these options the guilty chose. How would Marcham jump?

'. . . apart from anything else, if I had wanted to bump Ridley off, last thing I'd have wanted was the deaths of those other two – what were they, his driver and minder? – on my conscience.'

Ah. That's why he wouldn't have done it. But hold on . . .

'. . . then again, it's been so bloody long since I defused a bomb, I don't know as I'd remember how to do it. We used to say in Northern Ireland that the most dangerous time was when you came back off leave, because you're a tiny bit out of it and things move on, really quick. You could only be away a week and some bastard's worked out how to fiddle the wires round so it looks exactly like the last one you disabled, except now it's negative earthed. So you snip the black wire and . . .'

And that's 'he couldn't have done it'. Except . . .

'. . . except, Mr Marcham, we're not talking about defusing a bomb. We're talking about making and setting one. And if you were feeling a little rusty, you could always ask the guys you're in touch with out in Helmand Province.'

Marcham said he could see what the Chief Inspector was driving at, but he couldn't help. He didn't do it.

And that's the hat-trick: wouldn't; couldn't; didn't.

So where was he over that weekend? The 24/25 July? Right here. The whole time? The whole time; he remembered seeing the newsflash on the Sunday. Were his daughter-in-law and grandson with him? No, they'd taken the car up to see his daughter. The one they're moving near. Anyone see him or visit him? Nope. Go out to get the Sunday papers? Nope. What did he do all weekend? On the Internet, mostly. Did he speak to Jill? Yes. She rang on the Friday to say they'd got there. When? Around half-six in the evening. And then again on the Sunday to say they were leaving and not to wait up. But he did wait up. When did she ring? Just as the rerun of that series about the First World War was starting on the telly. Did she phone the landline here or his mobile? The landline. Shit awful reception for mobiles here.

Ned thanked him. They'd check the phone records. And they may well want to take a look at his computer – to verify that he was online at this address over that weekend. Marcham wasn't happy about that. He would need to talk to his solicitor. Not that he had a problem with clearing himself if that's what the computer could do for him, but he didn't want anyone poking around his files. People told him stuff in strict confidence. He couldn't betray them. Ned was sure they could work something out; it was in Mr Marcham's interests. Marcham could see that, but he was worried. He'd have to talk to his solicitor.

In the meantime did Mr Marcham have any objection to giving a DNA sample? No, he supposed he didn't. That wasn't going to stitch anyone else up but him, was it? While Spick fiddled about with swabs, jars, bags and labels, Ned had another flick through Marcham's clippings folders.

'Looks from this as if your campaign may have succeeded, Mr Marcham. It says here ". . . the army will be introducing the latest generation light protected patrol vehicle at the end of next year to replace the Snatch. The Ocelot weighs in at seven and a half tons and is designed with a V-shaped hull to withstand Improvised Explosive Devices – responsible for more than three quarters of British casualties in Afghanistan . . ."'

The inside of his cheek having been resoundingly swabbed, Marcham wiped his mouth on his sleeve and pulled a face.

'Wasn't down to me. Even the Brass Wallies finally realised they couldn't take the losses. In fact it was your Ridley signed off on the deal, as I remember. But it's a ways off, isn't it, the end of next year? How many guys will get pulverised in Snatches between now and then? Still, better late than never, I suppose. What'll really make the difference is they're scaling back on the FOBs – the Forward Operating Bases. Less chance of the lads getting caught in one of those rabbit runs with only a bit of tin between bomb and bollock.'

'So,' said Ned. 'Mission modified as well as kit?'

Marcham nodded with a concessionary grin.

'But,' he went on, 'there'll be something else. There always is. Do you know about the Type 40 Personal Communicators? They're Type 40 because that's the IQ of the twit that invented them, and they call 'em personal because the only person you can talk to on them is yourself. Don't get me started . . .'

Ned smiled and shook his hand.

'I'm racking me brains for anything from my ancient past might help you, Chief Inspector. Only thing comes to mind is to say that the man who makes the explosive device is rarely the man who sticks it in the ground. And the man who sets it off it may well be someone else again. If it isn't triggered automatically.'

Ned thanked him. He'd bear it in mind. Spick put his bits and pieces away and they stood to leave. Then Ned did one of his 'Just one more' questions.

'Mr Marcham, you know you said you can get stuff sent back from Camp Bastion, like those photographs?'

Marcham nodded.

'Could you get some *naswar*?'

Marcham looked genuinely puzzled.

'What's that?'

'It's chewing tobacco. Afghan chewing tobacco.'

Marcham shook his head blankly.

'Why would anyone want that?'

Ned popped into the kitchen to say goodbye to Jill Marcham. No sign of Micky. She seemed faintly pleased to see him.

'You know what I was saying before? Well, I was thinking. There's the widow of the lad who won that VC for taking on a whole bunch of them in that truck – posthumous, they call it – she only lives round the corner. They used to row something terrible. We used to say we didn't know why he bothered going out to Helmand – he was getting enough war at home. Now he's gone, some days she's worse than me. There's no sense to it.'

She started shoving a drawer-full of carrier bags into a refuse sack.

'He didn't do it you know – Grandad. He's that angry, but he can't keep anything in these days. He'd have had to say something. Blurt it out.'

'Thanks,' said Ned. 'And thanks for the coffee. Good luck with the move.'

He wanted to say more, but there wasn't anything.

'No recumbent bike then?' asked Ned when they were back in the car.

Spick shook his head and started the engine.

'Naa. I got Micky to show me his racer, and asked if his mum or his grandad rode a bike. He laughed and said no. His mum jogs alongside him sometimes. His grandad's got that blue Fiesta.'

'And what about the timings? Could he have got there and back between the two calls, assuming they check out? And given Mrs Marcham and Micky had the car, assuming he had alternative transport or an accomplice.'

Spick thought for a moment.

'He could have got there to place it. He's got all Saturday night for that. It's worse getting back. When did you see the second flash from the binoculars, sir?'

'Eleven-oh-four, Sunday morning.'

'That First World War series is on at four on Sundays. Three hundred miles cross-country in five hours . . . Very tight, I'd say.

Though as he sort of says himself, he could've rigged up the bomb and left it to an accomplice to light the blue touchpaper – that'd be Accomplice Number Two since Number One's got to get him back in time for his daughter's phone call around four. Which case, us not getting a DNA match with the wodge wouldn't let Marcham off the hook.'

Spick's learning, thought Ned. Using his noddle instead of rampaging about scaring the horses. But Ned wasn't at all sure about Marcham's offering about the maker and the placer and the trigger being three different people. Why did he say it? A cheap self-incriminating blind, designed to make us lose the scent? Or is what you see with the sergeant what you get?

'Check with security at the gatehouse if he came and went at all that weekend. Have them check the security cameras. And are there any ways to get on and off the base without anyone knowing? And get a warrant for his hard drive.'

As they drove past the house, Ned saw Jill Marcham dump the refuse sack with a pile of others at the foot of the path. Then she turned back towards the unsettled house, with its furious father-in-law and distressed son. She looked like a waif.

The day before Kate wrote her first landay she had been invited in to have a little chat with a Captain Crispin. As this was some six weeks before the Brecon Bombing, Kate met Captain Crispin before Ned did, and not being of Ned's suspicious turn of mind did not immediately have him down as a spook, although she too noted that he had the handshake of a dead jellyfish.

He asked her to meet him in the padre's office, of all places, leading her to wonder if the Camp Bastion chapel choir was short one tone-deaf mezzo soprano. She got there early, and whiled away the minutes staring at a document pinned to the noticeboard entitled 'Strategic Prayer Diary'. She noted that Friday was the day for asking God's help in the safe detection and removal of improvised explosive devices and the removal of IED factories. Kate wasn't sure, if so, who was covering the rest of the week.

Saturday prayers went a little close to the bone. That was apparently when one asked for the protection of all forces' marriages and the preservation from temptation of those tempted to be unfaithful. Hmmm. Moving swiftly on . . . This was a bit more like it: Tuesday – prayers for all Afghan nationals and security services undergoing treatment at Bastion Hospital. And what about those poor Afghan nationals beaten to a pulp by *our* security services? Did they have their own prayer day? Their dedicated ward in Bastion Hospital? Right on cue, up popped Captain Crispin who wanted to talk about precisely that sort of thing. But only after beating about the bush a bit.

'You're doing a simply grand job out here, Miss Baker. Everyone says so.'

'Thanks. Are you the padre?'

Crispin laughed. No he wasn't, but they were servicing the aircon unit in his ISO and he knew the chaplain was at Lash today, so . . .

No singing audition, then. Kate relaxed.

'I want to talk to you about those rather odd events you might have glimpsed the other night. In the Intell ISO.'

That bloodbath. Kate tensed.

'I know they must have seemed really difficult to understand. But before we get on to that, I just need you to tell me why you were in Intell that evening.'

Kate told him. That the officer commanding the EOD detachment had encouraged her to look at the Intelligence files so she could get a better, bigger picture of how the insurgents' IED teams were working. Apparently a lot of the EOD guys had been in there to read up on it all, though she thought she was the first dog-handler. Captain Crispin nodded. And how long had she been in there before she became aware that there were people across the corridor? A couple of hours. She couldn't be sure. And how long did she stay on after that? Not that long, she didn't think. Maybe ten minutes. Captain Crispin nodded again. And could she make out what they were saying, these people over the way? No. The occasional word maybe. Do any particular words stick in your mind? Take your time.

It was difficult. Some of the words were foreign. There were some place names . . . Kandahar was one, she thought. And she remembered a village . . . Sangar village. Or Sangsar. That was it: Sangsar village. Then another voice talked about an Operation . . . Hedgerow. And someone mentioned the words 'bombings' and 'IED'.

Captain Crispin made a note. When he looked up, Kate saw he had one of those little smiles which are meant to reassure, but in fact just make you think the person smiling is really shitting himself. And his voice started to sound as if he was talking to a child.

'Now, this Operation Hedgerow. Had you ever heard of it?'

Kate had not.

'Have you heard it mentioned by anyone since that evening?'

No, she hadn't.

'Do you know what it is?'

Not the foggiest.

Captain Crispin held her look for a beat, and then did the little smile again.

'Actually, between you and me, Miss Baker, this particular operation was more of a twinkle in the eye than anything else. So we've no need to dwell on it, have we?'

Kate made a little shrugging gesture designed to leave Captain Crispin in no doubt that it was as good as forgotten.

'Now. These people . . . were they all men?'

Kate shook her head. One was a woman.

Captain Crispin looked as if he wished she hadn't said that.

'And, this woman, did you see her face?'

No, she did not.

'Do you think, nevertheless, that you might be able to recognise her if you saw her again?'

Kate half wondered if she should tell Captain Crispin exactly what the woman had been wearing and about her hair and that she had a very good figure, but guessed that this might worry him. The less Kate remembered, probably the happier Captain Crispin would be. So she told him about how dark it was and how she was barely aware of any of these people and no, she would not be able to recognise this woman again if she saw her. Captain Crispin seemed to relax ever so slightly. And then he consulted his notebook and the little uneasy smile came back.

'Now up till then, Miss Baker, these voices and people you could scarcely make out were all on the far side of the corridor. But did one of them then cross that corridor?'

Yes. One did.

'And did you . . . see him at all? Given it was so dark?'

Yes. The lights were on where she was working. And he came right up to her.

'And – same question as before – would you be able to recognise him again if you saw him?'

Oh yes. Absolutely.

Captain Crispin looked like the driving test examiner does straight after you've gone into the back of the bus in front. And Kate had been doing so well! They sat there in silence. Funny, she thought. Why hadn't she fudged the beautiful man's visit across the corridor, the way she'd done with the curvy woman? Because she didn't care about the curvy woman, whoever she was, and she did care about the beautiful man. She hadn't been able to put him out of her mind ever since. She was blowed if she was going to fib about him.

'Miss Baker, have you ever signed the Official Secrets Act?'

Yes.

'Good, good. Then you'll remember that Section 2 of the Act makes it a criminal offence for Crown servants – like you and me, Miss Baker – to make a damaging disclosure. And that anyone who receives information which has been obtained unlawfully and whose disclosure may be damaging, may also be guilty under Section 5 of the Act. It's pretty catch-all stuff, isn't it?'

Kate presumed it was pretty catch-all, yes.

'Good.'

They sat again in silence. Kate wasn't about to fill any of the gaps in his discourse.

'Now, just before your mind goes a total blank about this man – whoever he was – I need to know if he said anything to you when he came across the corridor.'

Kate said she wondered whether, in the light of Sections 2 and 5, she really ought to tell him anything more.

Captain Crispin gave another of his not very real laughs.

'It's fine to tell me. In fact – you have to.'

She thought for a moment.

He said 'hullo'.

'I see. And what did you say back?'

Nothing. She didn't reply.

'Better and better.'

Captain Crispin made some more notes.

'And what happened next?'

Kate said she heard the sound of someone being beaten up, and went across the corridor to the other room to see . . .

'To see what was happening. Perfectly natural.'

No. To see if she could do anything to help the victim.

'Of course, of course.'

More scribbling.

And then she actually saw someone being beaten up. Punched. There was a lot of blood. And one of the men was sorting through his papers and not lifting a finger.

'". . . not lifting a finger . . ." And was the man – the victim as you call him – was he resisting in any way, or trying to defend himself?'

No, he wasn't. He was doubled over in agony. And then the other man intervened – the one who had said hullo.

Captain Crispin stopped writing and sat back, staring at her, then up at the ceiling.

'Now look I know there's an awful lot of talk in the papers about the use of torture and so on. Let me reassure you that, regardless of what anyone else may suggest, we simply do not do torture. Full stop. So I need you to be absolutely clear in your own mind that whatever you think you saw or didn't see over there, it wasn't torture. I think the man who had already come across the corridor to say hullo to you reassured you along those lines, didn't he?'

Yes. He said something of the kind.

'Exactly. What you saw was a little pretence going on. To make it look, to people out there . . .' Captain Crispin waved his hand beyond the camp perimeter '. . . as though this chap you saw with a little blood on him *was* a victim.'

As though we do, in fact, do torture. Odd that. The little pretence only really works if we are known on occasion to beat people to a pulp.

'Now, I just want to talk to you a little bit about the man who came over to say hullo to you. Who, as you say, intervened when he saw the chap being "beaten up" . . .'

At which point Captain Crispin made the irritating inverted commas sign with his fingers.

'. . . well, that's him all over. Concern for others. He is an absolute hero, doing one of the most dangerous jobs imaginable. He is simply critical to our effort out here and it's vital that no one ever finds out that you saw him inside Camp Bastion. Vital that you never breathe a word about his existence to anybody. His life depends upon it, and the lives of countless others. I can't say anything more, but . . . you get the picture?'

Kate supposed she did, when it was put like that.

'Good, good. And even as we speak, you're forgetting the whole thing, aren't you?'

He laughed, and Kate decided to keep him company by laughing as well.

'What did you say your name was?' Kate asked Captain Crispin. 'And why are we in the padre's office?'

'Exactly!' he said, standing up, interview over, job cracked.

It was the very next day that Kate painstakingly wrote her first landay, showed it to Jamila and made her smile. Then Kate dug out the slip of paper the beautiful hero had handed to her just before helping the man being beaten up, and texted the two lines of nine syllables and thirteen to the mobile number scrawled on it:

> *Map me from above, hills and valley,*
> *Then come down to earth and explore the hidden places.*

7

THE ROAD AHEAD WAS CLOSED, and the men who had closed it looked very scary. They had long beards and eyes dark with kohl. They were heavily armed. Kate recognised Kalashnikovs, Heckler & Koch G3s and a Steyr 9mm. She started to feel frightened. Then the man in charge, who had been peering at the jeep, gave an order, and the others immediately started to pull the barriers aside. Hamid barely had to stop the jeep, but accelerated through the gap with utter confidence. The man in command of the road block raised a hand in salute, which Hamid returned with the tiniest inclination of his head. When this had happened twice more, Kate started to relax.

At first Hamid hardly said a word. She sat beside him, staring at the muscles in his forearm and drinking in the lemony smell of clean skin. He seemed oblivious to her until they had been travelling for a good ten minutes and then he turned to her with a smile and asked if she was OK. Thereafter it wasn't that old cliché about feeling they had known one another for years. The more they spoke, the clearer it became that they were strangers and that was part of what made it so exciting. Everything to play for. Everything to find out. And then there was the fact that they were on the same side and were risking their lives for the same cause. Exciting and dangerous.

Kate expected to feel unnerved by the strangeness of what she was doing, but she didn't. Since coming to Afghanistan she had surprised herself by embracing the unfamiliar. The whole setup out there was so weird and dangerous that there was no point in looking for the safe to cling on to. Not that her job back home had been a risk-less breeze. It was far from that. But it was daily life that had scared her, not the moments of danger involving sniffer dogs and bombs. Perhaps that was why she had volunteered. Why she had been prepared to leave the Dog Unit, with its familiar routines and faces. To leave Ned. Because when she was shakier within herself she had needed the comfort of the familiar. The protection of routines. The sameness of the faces. And now she was stronger she seemed to want to shed the rituals which had cushioned her. She wanted the unfamiliar. New places. New faces. Hamid's face, with eyes like burning black coals, and arching cheekbones and slightly furrowed brow and its look of absolute confidence.

He kept his eyes on the road. She increasingly kept hers on him. She had no history of fancying a stranger and then making a play for him. She supposed, given her looks, she could have done this any time since she was a teenager. Perhaps that's why she had been so bullied at school: to ensure she didn't. To make sure, if she ever showed up at a party which she did very rarely, she looked as plain as possible. Plain enough to be no competition. No make-up, and clothes that covered her legs and muffled her body. So what had changed? Why was she hurtling across the desert with a total stranger? Because she was totally turned on by him.

She imagined him between her legs with his tongue, licking her clitoris. Before, it had always come as a surprise whenever that happened. A generally nice surprise, but not one that crossed her mind from one day to the next. Now she imagined his head glimpsed between her breasts down the length of her body, with her fingers in the curls of his hair. And then she imagined other things. Her desire surprised her, and that heightened it further.

Where were they? She didn't know. The road was long and dusty and wound uphill. It was almost dusk when they arrived somewhere high and hidden in the mountains. Hamid's refuge. It was a turreted hunting lodge built of stone and earth the colour and texture of the crags on which it was perched. Hamid came round and opened the door for her. She jumped down from the jeep and followed him into a small courtyard. They were met by smiling faces and warm greeting hands. Baba Nazar was in his seventies; he had a straggly grey beard and a maroon skullcap. He kept house there with his wife, old Khalida. She wore a smock with baggy trousers in washed-out colours. They seemed as discreet as they were devoted.

Kate and Hamid sat on the balcony sipping fresh lemonade, eating pistachios and olives, and watched the sun sink behind the saw blade of distant mountains. It was very still. Magical.

Then Hamid suddenly remembered something and called down into the tiny courtyard below. He had a short exchange with Baba which made Hamid laugh and led to a flurry of barks and the sound of paws on wooden stairs. A very handsome Afghan Hound bounded on to the balcony and smothered Hamid in licks and love. Then Hamid spoke to him and the dog sat in front of Kate and offered a paw which Kate took and held. She was delighted to meet a real Afghan Hound; she had kept an eye out for one ever since she'd arrived in the country, but had come to the reluctant conclusion they had all gone for export, or that the name had become meaningless, a bit like Swiss Roll.

'What made you laugh?' Kate wanted to know.

'I asked Baba Nazar where is Ustad my dog, and he said he keeps Ustad in the kitchen in case the English lady is frightened with dogs. I told him: she is the world expert of dogs.'

And he laughed again and shelled some more pistachios for her. Ustad lay down at Kate's feet while the first stars peeked out and the scent of woodsmoke and spice wafted up from below.

She might have expected to feel petrified at the prospect of intimacy with a stranger, yet she felt the opposite. The old Kate would have sat on the balcony watching the sun go down in dread, throat dry with fear, hearing nothing the man said, refusing the pistachios, sipping no lemonade, racking her brains for ways to sleep alone. To escape. Hold on. That was all rubbish. The old Kate would never have been on that balcony in the first place. That's exactly why the new Kate was there, eyes aglow from the dying rays, body on fire.

The idyll was broken by something that summed up how far she'd come, and not just in air-miles. Baba Nazar led them up a spiral staircase to a round, wood-panelled room in the tower, lit by oil-lamps. The table was set for dinner, and Khalida set a dish between them of a shoulder of barbecued lamb on a bed of rice.

'I'm sorry. I didn't say – I'm a vegetarian. I don't eat meat or fish.'

Hamid bowed his head to her and apologised for not asking her first. An elaborate discussion followed in which it seemed as if Hamid was pointing out that it wasn't simply a question of removing the meat, as the *pulao* was now soaked in meat juices. Khalida took it all in her stride, and whisked the dish off the table.

'There's no reason why you can't eat it. It's just me.'

Hamid wouldn't dream of it. They would eat the same or nothing. There would be a little wait. Khalida had more *pulao* in the kitchen – the tastiest crispy bit – which had never touched meat, and a dish of peppers and tomatoes with aubergine and parsley which she and Baba were going to eat, but now they would have the unwanted lamb *pulao*. Khalida would quickly make some *borani* – fried vegetables in yoghurt – and Baba Nazar wanted to grill some special cheese for the English lady . . .

Kate thanked them both and smiled her glorious smile, and they bustled away. Funny, she thought as Hamid started to show her some of the objects in the room. Food had always been such a threatening and vulnerable part of her life, and here she was, a million miles from home among strangers and it hadn't occurred to her to wonder what she would eat. Good.

The tower was full of treasures. Pride of place went to a highly decorated fourteenth-century illuminated copy of the Koran sitting on a simple lectern. Dotted around the walls were exquisite miniature paintings, some by the master Bihzad, showing scenes of hunting and feasting, dogs and horses, wise men and prophets. Above the door was a scimitar belonging to Abdur Rahman Khan – the Iron Amir. A sixteenth-century Ardabil rug depicted the plan of a Persian garden in muted pastels that looked as if it had been woven the week before. On its own shelf was a brass and copper helmet chased with silver which had apparently belonged to Genghis Khan himself. Well, said Hamid, smiling at his own gullibility, so Sotheby's in New York had said.

Kate had never heard of Bihzad, or Ardabil. She vaguely knew Genghis Khan was an ancient barbarian ruler. But she could see how beautiful these things were. She assumed they cost shedloads of money. Money meant little to her, but she was struck by the fact that it didn't seem to mean much to Hamid either, except maybe in terms of the lovely things he could buy with it. His jeep wasn't particularly flashy, and neither were his clothes. Then again, some of the stuff had been handed down in his family.

'. . . belonging to my great-great-grandfather. He was a diplomat working sort of between the lines. Look, what is written.'

Hamid handed Kate a mint red and gold copy of *Kim*, inscribed by the author: 'To my old friend Akbar Hassani, in memory of great games played, whisky drunk, stories spun – Rudyard Kipling.'

'Is this where the British connection began? With your great-great-grandfather?'

'Yes,' replied Hamid. 'But not where it ends.'

She stood under the shower, tight with desire. He had been attentive and animated throughout dinner, but still seemed sexually uninterested. She wished she had asked Jamila about sex with Afghan men. Or, better, Parween – she seemed to have no inhibitions. But Kate had told no one about Hamid. How passive was she expected to be? She remembered the landays at Jamila's that day. They seemed to suggest – not very. She sat on a low, tiled ledge, leaning back against marble, legs apart, water running cool over her. She thought back to that moment in the Intelligence ISO when she and Hamid had looked into one another's eyes and said nothing. Was that what her friend Pauline would call a spiritual moment? Or was it simply a mutual realisation that they really wanted one another? She certainly fancied him rotten. But what about Hamid? He was a little difficult to read. She might have to take the initiative.

She carried the thought with her as she dried. As she slipped a fine shirt over her head. She lay down on the crisp sheets and ran her hand between her legs. A sudden creak of the door. He was standing there. She felt a tide of embarrassment rush up her neck and face. What would he – a Muslim – make of a woman stroking herself? But she didn't stop. He watched her for a while, and she held his eye. Then she reached out to him, drawing herself into a kneeling position as she did so. His beautiful olive skin was still wet from his shower. Slowly, slowly, they kissed, her mouth over his, her tongue seeking him out. She drew one hand over his shoulders and down his back; the other caressed his balls. He sighed as if he were releasing his last breath, and in that moment she knew she could take the lead. Easing him gently from her she rolled him on to his stomach and lifted his hips into the air. Her eyes, accustomed to the dark, could see the curve of his bottom and his smooth erect penis below.

Afterwards, as they lay back, he had thrown the sheet off and simply stared at her. The shutters were closed, and anyway there was no moon, but hanging on either side of the bed were two copper lanterns drilled with star and crescent-shaped holes. The pinpricks of light played like a miniature night sky across her. You are, he told her, the most beautiful woman in the world. He stroked her, ever so slowly, with one fingertip, from her toes to the crown of her head. She didn't reply. What could she say? You're wrong, there's this unbelievable-looking girl in the pet shop in Hendon? Silence was best. He seemed almost in awe of her. As if he could not believe his luck. By the time he finally pulled the sheet over her peerless body, followed by the blanket that smelled of the rare Karakul lamb from whose coat it was woven, she was asleep.

'Can you ride a horse?'

Kate nodded, without opening her eyes. Without really waking.

'Good. I put your breakfast here. *Assalam u alaikum*.'

She vaguely heard the door close and the footsteps fade before falling back into a doze. It seemed very early. A sound woke her – she couldn't say how much later: a burst of sharp squawking in the distance. A bird, but not like any she'd ever heard. She sat up a little, drawing the woollen blanket around her bare shoulders. It smelled of sheep. The pillows of duck. And there were other, more edible aromas. What had the voice said? Something about breakfast. She opened her eyes. It was a beautiful room, with ancient beams and faded colours. The filigree shutters were open a crack, revealing the bluest of skies and admitting a shaft of light in which dust swirled. On the side table was an array of interlocking blue and white dishes. There were dates, grapes, pomegranate and melon, set yoghurt with honey and toasted pistachios and pumpkin seeds, a chopped soft-boiled egg with flecks of pink peppercorn and chives. There was a chilled glass of something straw-yellow, which tasted of banana and cream and more honey with a drop of lemon. A polished copper-bound glass of mint tea. And wrapped in a cloth, two miniature freshly baked sesame nan breads. Such a pretty sight. Such exotic smells and tastes and feels.

The voice had said something else. What was it? Ah yes: *Assalam u alaikum* – peace be on you. *Wa alaikum u ssalam*. And upon you peace, Hamid.

She picked a little at the egg and the bread and sipped the tea. And then Hamid slipped back into the room with a selection of riding boots and clothes. Would she like this *pirhan tumban* to wear? It would be hot and dusty out there. He placed the long white shirt and loose cotton trousers on the end of the bed. He was very considerate and very, very handsome, and she told him so, reaching up and kissing him. He slipped an arm around her, stroking her shoulder blades, her arching back. Yes, please, she breathed, but then he patted her on the swell of her bottom and whispered that, unfortunately, they really ought to go, before the sun rose any higher. Besides, Shukria was ready to go. They couldn't keep her waiting.

Shukria? Who the hell was Shukria? His mother? His daughter? His wife? One of his wives? Oh God – she really knew nothing about the man. What had he told her on the drive while she was busy feeling more and more aroused? She'd have remembered if he'd mentioned having a wife, but a subtle hint in that direction could well have passed her by . . . She got up and pushed him out of the room with cursory tenderness. Ten minutes, he called out as she slipped into the shower. It was probably Shukria's clothes that were waiting for her on the end of the bed. Kate thought they'd look pretty good on her, but that was bound to make things worse. The water was deliciously cool. If only she could stay in there until Shukria had grown tired of waiting, by which time Kate would look like a wrinkly prune. Perhaps not. It sounded as if this Shukria had a short fuse.

Kate stepped into the light. She knew she looked stunning: long white shirt with an old belt tight around her waist; baggy white cotton trousers tucked into riding boots; hair flowing from under a scarlet scarf. OK Shukria, I'm ready for you. Two horses stood in the courtyard. Baba Nazar was putting water bottles into their saddlebags. Apparently Amir was Hamid's, Kate would ride Nasima. Khalida was feeding the chickens. No sign of Hamid. Handsome horses. Grey, with arched necks and high tails. Arabs, of course. Hamid was clearly the kind of guy who only has the best. Shukria must be quite something.

The first Kate saw of Hamid was his back, coming out of a small door off the courtyard, right arm outstretched – so the last thing she saw was what was perched on his wrist.

'Kate, meet Shukria!'

He turned, and there she was: gold-framed feathers such a light grey they were almost white. Pale, mottled brown underbelly.

Round, piercing black eyes. Rim of bright yellow around the beak. The most beautiful falcon imaginable. The source, presumably, of the earlier squawking.

'Some people put hoods on their falcons. Burqas, they even call them.' Hamid shook his head in distaste. 'I can't. Look at her. How lovely she is.'

On cue, Shukria turned and stared at Kate. The falcon blinked first, then looked away. Kate went closer.

'She's gorgeous. What is she?'

'A Saker falcon. The female is bigger than the male. Huge wing-span; over a hundred and thirty centimetres. They are endangered species. Not only bigger than the male: more aggressive. Other falcons sit on the wrist; you see the prey and let her go. Then she comes back like a well-behaved boomerang. Not the Saker. You will see. We let Shukria go, and she climbs high, high. Several thousands of metres in the air. She hovers, she circles, she waits. Then we send Ustad the dog away. This is traditional Afghan hunting. He is a courser, do you say? He hunts by sight. Finds the prey: Houbara bustard, grey hare, desert squirrel. Only then she will dive. They say two hundred miles an hour. Down, down . . . then if it is the bustard, up and underneath. Bam! It is over. If she is in a good mood, she brings it to me. If not, she gets no supper from Baba Nazar.'

After that, Kate half expected Shukria to shrug as if to say, 'What do you expect – I'm a Saker falcon.' But she dipped her beak into her breast and scratched an itch or snaffled a flea or something. If falcons have fleas.

'OK,' said Hamid. 'We go.'

The next two hours were utterly exhilarating. They rode a cascade of sand and stones down the mountain on which Hamid's house was hidden. Then across the desert at a gallop, Ustad to the side, Shukria a mile above them. Hamid was a superb rider, and luckily Kate was pretty good. Scarves streamed in the wind, hooves flew and Ustad kept a steady pace. Behind them, clouds of dust; ahead, a range of hills in the distance, getting ever closer. And whenever Kate looked up, there was Shukria: the most elegant of dots in the sky, like a guardian angel. The hills were distinct now: a tight shuffle of peaks. At the foot of the closest was a full drinking trough for the horses and dog and, tucked in the shade between rocks, a flagon of chilled lemonade for Kate and Hamid, together with bags of dried mulberries and Bamiyan apples. Baba Nazar wakes early on hunting days, Hamid explained. And then they were away again. Now climbing mountain tracks. Higher. Higher. At one point Kate looked up and Shukria was not to be seen. She was about to call out to Hamid, but he wouldn't have heard her and, anyway, suddenly there she was: soaring in a lazy spiral above the loftiest peak. Heels in, catch Hamid.

They stopped at a place where the clutch of hills diverged into separate peaks. Between the ridges was a long, wide, straight belt of hard sand. It looked for all the world like an airstrip.

'It is. It is, exactly,' replied Hamid, offering Kate water from a hip flask while trying to stop his horse from pirouetting.

'Once, years ago, rich Saudi sheikhs would fly here for hunting falcons. To kill the Houbara bustard was their dream. They believe its flesh makes them into these great men in bed. I don't know. I never talked to their girls to find if it is true . . . I don't think so. But they came here, in their transport planes, with their Porsche Cayennes and Lamborghini SUVs and servants and falcons they said were worth maybe a million dollars.'

Hamid laughed at the stupidity of it.

'They would meet with all kinds of people to hunt the Houbara – tribal warlords, Taliban leaders, bad men. Men who drank their whisky and flattered them and took their money and their SUVs – the sheikhs would leave them like tips. Everyone went away happy, except the Houbara bustards. That's why I hope we don't meet one. Hope Shukria doesn't meet one. They become rare. Better they turn their mates on, not fat Saudi sheikhs.'

They galloped down the runway. Halfway along, Ustad saw

something ahead, and halted. Hamid slowed and made a tight circle before stopping by Kate's side.

'Look – a hare! There!'

Nothing, then a grey streak shot across the runway five hundred yards ahead of them. Ustad tensed, eyes glued. Kate looked up. Way above the peaks Shukria was already making her dive. She must have seen the hare even before the dog. Kate watched, amazed. In that seemingly tiny bird-brain, immense calculations of speed and angle and descent were being made in fractions of a second. The falcon could not simply aim for the hare even allowing for lead, like a marksman trying to hit a moving target. She would hit the ground at two hundred miles an hour with only a puny desert hare for crash helmet. No, her sums were infinitely more complex. She had to swoop down in an arc which would bring her almost to ground level right behind that fluffy white tail. Then what? The hare would be carried into the air, dead from the talons' grip on its neck if not from shock. Wheeled around the peaks, and then dropped for Ustad to recover? Or landed in an eyrie – Shukria's brunch?

Oh, no. Poor hare. Poor hare. It had dived back diagonally across the runway. Shukria was coming down behind them, her arc flattening out, moving almost too fast to be seen. In a moment she would pass the two horses and the waiting dog. The hare twisted back the other way. Shukria skimmed past them, talons lowered like undercarriage. The hare was only yards from her. Then, suddenly, she snatched it up, beak high, wings beating, climbing, climbing, climbing. The hare twitched for a moment, then went limp.

Kate slumped in the saddle, tears welling in her eyes. Hamid brought his horse alongside hers and leaned across to her, gently lifting her chin.

'What did you expect, Kate? She is a falcon. We are hunting.'

He kissed her eyelids, then held her tight.

The jeep was parked alongside a mud shack tucked into the rock at the far end of the runway. Smoke curled from its squat chimney, a table was set under a shade of palm leaves, overlooking the desert that stretched all the way to Baluchistan. Baba Nazar greeted them at the door with cold towels and icy pomegranate juice, and pointed to a perch under the eaves of the hut. Shukria didn't glance up. She had her beak buried in dead hare.

They sat with the extraordinary view before them, all golds and pinks and greys – starting sharp, and ending in haze. They held hands, and talked of landays and love. Her poem, he said. It was as if she knew all about Shukria already: '*Map me from above, hills and valley* . . .' Then he leaned across and kissed her. First on the forehead, then on the lips. It was quite the most romantic moment in her entire life.

Then, behind them, Baba Nazar made a clumsy show of clattering enamel plates, and Hamid smiled at Kate before asking him something.

'He says you have to go, my darling. Your clothes are in the jeep; Khalida has packed them. Baba Nazar will drive you, while I will take Shukria home on Amir with your Nasima and Ustad.'

Kate got back to Camp Bastion with twenty minutes to go before her pass expired. She had told them she was with Jamila, a friendship now officially blessed by the Provincial Reconstruction Team as part of their aim to build bridges with Afghan women. It felt like Sunday, with school the next day. She wasn't one for moping, but it was going to be tough slipping back into the old routines after the last two days. Jiffy . . . He was the answer. She went straight to the tent, changed into running gear and raced over to the kennels to pick up her beloved dog.

He was delirious to see her, and she virtually had to carry him the first few hundred yards, so desperate was he to be in her arms. They jogged round the perimeter, anticlockwise as usual. It was dusk now. Charcoal greys, the colour of the unlucky hare. Streaks of orange and gold in the sky at the start, and then, by the time they were running along the barrier wall bordering the Dasht-e Margo, the stars had come out. She remembered the two lanterns in the tower room, and Hamid's finger tracing her starlit body from south to north. Khalida and Baba Nazar would be in the little kitchen below, cooking up marvels, and Hamid? Sitting on his balcony, with Ustad at his feet, thinking of her?

'You'd like him, Jiffs,' she whispered to the dog by her side. 'You'd love them both.'

'We were on the A926. Then we turned off at Kirriemur on the B951. Then there was the T-junction, by the old garage. We went right. Then second left. Didn't we?'

Ned was lost. On the rare occasions this happened it was because the road he was looking for was newer than his in-car navigation system. This one was clearly so much older it had never made the digital leap. Bother. He reached into the rear seat pocket and found a UK atlas. Spick stopped the car and got out for a fag. It was the first time the rain had stopped drizzling for days. While Ned was struggling to find their destination somewhere in square C3 on page 144, a tractor lumbered up the road behind them. A few moments later Spick stuck his head into the car.

'We passed it, sir. Two miles back. It was that turning to the right after the second left. Or whatever it was.'

The Hermit didn't have a dead son or a red-eyed daughter-in-law or anybody. He lived alone in the Cairngorms and he *was* alone. Which was why Spick called him the Hermit.

'Another bloody dirt track in wild, Celtic country, sir. Are we starting to see a pattern in this bloody case?'

'Takes three things for a pattern, Spick. Two things is sod's luck.'

Spick nodded and concentrated on the ruts.

Major James McCullough CGC of the Royal Regiment of Scotland didn't look like a hermit. Hermits should look like the picture of Ben Gunn in Ned's dad's copy of *Treasure Island*. Rake-thin, mad white hair, rags for clothes, bandy-legged with arms in the air. That's your hermit. This one looked a bit like a newsreader. He was Action-Man handsome; wore a smart suit; his greying hair was short and tidy; he had shaved. And yet Ned couldn't believe he'd put on a suit to see them, let alone that he'd wear one around his cottage.

'Sorry we're a bit late, sir.'

'Good thing you are. Only just got back from a memorial service. My favourite sergeant. Stepped on an IED, poor sod. Tea?'

Major McCullough certainly ticked Spick's three boxes. He was an ordnance disposal expert, he was in the country when the Minister was killed, and he was cheesed off. He'd shot his mouth off during a Staff College lecture, and – none of his doing – some of his rant had popped up on Twitter. Unlike Colour Sergeant Marcham, he wasn't at all fussed about the kit. According to him, the army fought every war with the kit that had arrived too late for the last one.

'It's traditional. We'd probably all die of shock if we were given the right gear from the off. No, what gets my goat is the war itself. Why are we in Afghanistan? We all know you don't win wars of insurgency. We all know in the end you have to sit down with terrorists. We all know there's no model for beating the Afghan on his own ground.'

He reached a volume off the shelf behind him and opened it at a bookmark.

'Read you something: "Tribe wars with tribe. Every man's hand is against the other and all are against the stranger. The state of continual tumult has produced a habit of mind which holds life cheap and embarks on war with careless levity." Know who wrote that?'

Ned and Spick shook their heads.

'Winston Churchill. Over a hundred years ago. He'd served with the Malakand Field Force on the North-West Frontier – he knew. He said the British only had three options: run the place tight as a drum at the point of a gun, or get the local tribes to work with you and gradually take over, or clear out sharpish. Well, we are pretending we're doing Option One, without either the military resources or the political nerve. At the same time, we're having a desultory go at sliding sideways into Option Two, but seem to have forgotten the old North-West Frontier adage: "You can't buy an Afghan. You just rent him for a while." The sensible option – and the only one of the three we are sure to pull off – is Number Three. None of which would matter a damn if we had the wit to learn by our experience. But, oh, no. I was observing the niceties after the service for poor old Sergeant Neil, and the colonel whispered in my ear: "It'll be the Yemen next, Jimmy. Fancy topping up your tan?"'

The kettle was boiling, and the Hermit went off into the kitchen. He didn't sound nearly cheesed off enough to blow the Minister of Defence to smithereens. Clearly his own colonel didn't think he'd entirely turned his back on soldiering. Ned and Spick exchanged puzzled glances, and then Ned got up and stood in the kitchen doorway.

'So how long have you been out, Major?'

'I'm back, Chief Inspector, not out. After my third tour ended in June, I spent my leave here getting the place shipshape, then I started on the education side. I go around the country, talking to chaps going to Afghanistan for the first time. Giving them a few practical tips about how to keep their bollocks attached for as long as possible. You see, when they get to Bastion, it's pretty much death by PowerPoint at first. Granted they then get a few days of live-firing practice in the heat and dust, but current thinking is to beef up the preparation process at the UK end.'

And would he, Ned wanted to know, go back to the sharp end? In the Yemen, say? The Hermit laughed and started pouring the tea.

'Probably would. Probably would at that. You see, what a lot of soldiers really like doing isn't training, or peacekeeping, or even being home on leave. No, what we like best is fighting. Having a crack at the Boche, as they used to say. You remember old John Glubb's words on Armistice Day 1918? "Pity," he said, "just when I was really starting to enjoy it." My grandfather had had the devil of a time in destroyers on the Murmansk run in the '39–'45 war, and the instant the bells rang out on VE Day, he was pestering everyone he knew to get a billet on a warship going out to the Far

East. "I didn't want to miss the show," was how he put it. Obviously most conscripts are gagging to get home, but by and large chaps in regular armies are there because they want to fight.'

Ned carried a plate of oatcakes into the sitting room, giving Spick a tiny shake of his head. No, this is not our man.

'So,' said the Hermit, sitting down with smile, 'you chaps must be a bit stuck if you think I bumped Mike Ridley off.'

Spick looked a bit taken aback but Ned couldn't suppress a laugh.

'What I can't fathom, is why you're poking around for the killer over here. From what I read in the papers this was a classic insurgent IED attack. Al-Qaeda, Taliban, Hezb-i Islami, Al-Shabaab, Hezbollah . . .'

Ned replied that he was sure the major would see that he couldn't tell him anything about the case that would answer his excellent points. The Hermit said he quite understood. For a moment the three men drank their tea and munched oatcakes. Then Spick took the Hermit through his movements that weekend, just – as Spick put it – so we can cross you off the list in ink rather than pencil. The Hermit had no alibi for the Saturday; he was trying a bit of scorched-earth on the garden. And on Sunday? On Sunday he was reading the lesson in church about twelve miles away. Witnesses? The minister and a dozen stalwarts. What was the lesson? *Luke* 7, Verses 36 to 50. Spick nodded, which surprised Ned. Ned looked impassive, which didn't surprise Spick at all.

'Would you mind, sir, submitting to a DNA test? It won't take a second and you can keep all your clothes on.'

'How could I refuse an offer like that, Sergeant?'

Spick got his stuff out, while Ned took down the minister's contact details. With the Hermit safely post-swab, Ned asked him if, while he was out there, he'd ever used *naswar*?

'Not on your life, Chief Inspector. I was once on a NATO jolly in Copenhagen and tried that *snus* stuff. All went well until I swallowed some of the juice . . . Never again. Funnily enough, I have yet to see any of our chaps with *naswar*.'

'So how do you know about it, Major?'

'It came up years ago on a tracking course I was sent on, run by a real tough case – an ex-Selous Scout. "Know your enemy's presence from his spoor" and all that. Cigarette butts, shit of course, ration wrappers, bubble gum and chewing tobacco. He reckoned it could save our lives. Well, he may have been right. They all seem to chew the stuff in Afghanistan. National pastime. They spit it out; if you find it wet and warm – best slip off that safety catch.'

Spick dashed out to start the car, while Ned thanked the Hermit.

'Major, you said you teach the lads how to keep their bollocks on in Afghanistan. What do you say to the women?'

'I say they must have bollocks, or they wouldn't be going. Have you ever met a woman who's served out there, Chief Inspector? A most impressive breed.'

Ah, thought Ned. A hermit's hermit. He nodded before diving through the deluge to reach the car.

Span met Ned off the night sleeper.

'Hullo, Jan Span. Good to see you.'

'Hullo, sir. Good to see you too. Car's over here. There's a double macchiato in the bag and a sesame pretzel. We can't stop; the Lord High Gopher says the general can only give us ten minutes between bangs.'

Seems fair enough, thought Ned. Mustn't keep a general from his bangs. He tucked into breakfast while Span drove east. The rain had finally stopped, thank God. He had slept well on the train, but only after a turbulent hour thinking about Kate. He hadn't spoken to her since getting back from Afghanistan. They had exchanged texts and emails, but hers were fairly reticent. He wasn't quite at the stage of wishing the pretzel was a bowl of compo carbonara, but he could sense it was only a matter of time. Something *was* wrong. Maybe badly wrong. If only he knew, one way or the other. He wasn't sure he'd be able to stand it if she were having an affair.

Affair be blowed. Supposing she'd fallen in love? After all, she was surrounded by fit, handsome heroes. The Intelligence Kid seemed pretty taken with her. And Lieutenant Ellison. But who wouldn't be? It didn't bear thinking about. Ned should ask her, point-blank. But given what she was having to go through every day, the dangers she was running, did he have the right to put her under more pressure? He should trust her. She'd tell him if there was anything. She was straight as a die. Painfully honest. She'd just have come out with it that night in the tent. The fact that he was in her tent itself suggested there wasn't anyone else. He couldn't see Kate as a two-timer. But there was something. He knew it.

Did she know he adored her? He'd email her when he got back and try to arrange a phone call for tomorrow, early evening her time. He'd tell her then that he adored her. The evening in the restaurant before she left, when he'd told her he wasn't a caveman and wasn't going to screw up her career by standing in her way and stopping her from going to Afghanistan. . . . it was very non-sexist and right on and made him sound great. All New Man with a fully developed feminine side.

But what he should have said was: 'No, you are not going. You are staying here with me because I adore you and fancy you and can't stand a day when I don't see you and, anyway, you are MINE. I may not look like a caveman, but there must have been Jewish cavemen. Else where did we come from? Anyway, you'll have to take it from me that I'm from the caveman side. Forget everything you associate me with so far: cosmopolitan charm, silly ideas, crappy jokes. It's all going to be different from here on in. I'm going to drag you by the scruff of the neck from this restaurant all the way to my cave. Then I'm going to . . .'

'You all right, sir?'

He hadn't been speaking aloud, had he? Oh God, he hoped not. He couldn't stand Jan Span knowing his feelings for Kate. Bloody awful caveman he'd make.

'Fine, Jan Span. Just working out my questions for the General. So. What do you know that I don't?'

'Ah ha! Dying for you to ask me that. I've been talking to my new best friend Hawkins. You remember? From the MoD. The one who was tiptoeing around the crime scene picking up all the Minister's papers?'

It felt like a decade ago.

Jan Span, sharp of face and resolute of mind, had not for one minute accepted Clive Hawkins's refusal to take her calls. She had remained unfailingly polite, of course, but she was unstoppable. She sent letters. She left voice messages. She emailed him. She texted him. Then she phoned his flat and who should pick up but his girlfriend Amanda? Jan Span asked her if the next time she happened to bump into Clive, she could possibly pass on this message? That the police needed to talk to him about a murder. It did the trick. Hawkins rang her back almost immediately after putting down the receiver from an irate Amanda.

Did he seriously think, Mands had asked him, that she'd be going to Glyndebourne with someone who was wanted by the police for murder? Given Amanda's leggy charms, to say nothing of the fact that the mighty hamper he'd ordered from Fortnum's couldn't be cancelled, he'd said it was simply a misunderstanding over a parking ticket and he'd pick Amanda up at ten as planned.

'You damn' near sabotaged my entire life,' he whined to Span.

'That's the thing we've noticed so often about murder cases, sir. The ripples catch so many people sideways.'

He hadn't been avoiding her, Hawkins insisted when they met at his office in the MoD the next day. He'd had been waiting for the appropriate security clearance before sharing with her the remains of the late Sir Michael Ridley's briefcase and despatch boxes. It had landed in his intray a few minutes before DS Span had phoned Amanda.

'Of course, Mr Hawkins,' said Jan Span without the slightest hint of irony.

'Just so we understand one another . . .' added Hawkins as if he had any vestige of dignity to salvage.

He led her down corridors to a locked door with an MoD security guard outside. Hawkins had the key on a chain attached to his belt.

The door opened into a meeting room for perhaps forty people. Laid out on the long table were one hundred and thirty-seven fragments of paper. Most were singed. Some were tiny scraps. A few were almost complete pages.

'This is absolutely everything the Minister had with him in the car, Mr Hawkins? I am asking you formally.'

Hawkins manfully suppressed further annoyance.

'It is, apart from the laptop which is with our specialists. According to them, it's a write-off. The hard drive has been destroyed. You're welcome to have your technical people come here and work on it, but I'm told categorically there is nothing recoverable from it. His diary and address book are on the side-table by the window, with the remains of the despatch-boxes, his pens, calculator, etc. I hope you don't mind, but I've been asked not to leave anyone alone in the room with all this stuff.'

'Fine by me.'

Span put down her things and set up shop on an unused writing-desk. Notebook, pencil, portable miniature rostrum stand with lights, digital camera.

'Didn't think you'd bring a camera.' Hawkins sounded as if he was racking his brains for an MoD by-law.

'Really? It was specifically mentioned in the request from our Chief Superintendent Larribee, which your Permanent Secretary agreed to. That we'd be copying the documents. I find photocopiers a bit bulky on the Tube, don't you?'

Hawkins grunted. After DS Jan Span, Mands was a positive breeze. He hadn't realised it before.

'Right then, Mr Hawkins, all set. Hope you've brought a good book.'

He lasted about half an hour, then slipped out for five minutes. Soon he was out of the room more than he was in it. Span spent the afternoon alone. As she photographed each page she checked it against the log she had compiled with Hawkins that day in the Brecon Beacons after the DCI had wrung him dry. Everything was there. And one fragment stood out.

It had caught her eye while she was photographing it: five or six inches across, with blackened edges, burn holes and tears. Judging by the font, there were no other surviving bits from this document. Nothing else in the same font. Which might fit with Ridley having printed out something at the cottage that weekend.

Back at the office she went through all the photos she had taken at the MoD, and Fragment 56 was the only one which seemed possibly relevant to the sort of conversation Ridley might have had with General Sir Mark Collet that Sunday. It was about some policy, but what exactly, the fragment didn't say. They'd stop at the next garage, she said, and Ned could take a look at it while she filled up.

. . . given PD's breakthrough formula . . . [illegible] . . . ppy crop with no apparent long-ter . . . [illegible] . . . timate up to £1b in subs . . . [illegible] . . . However a lasting solution would . . . [illegible] . . . cursor chemic . . . [illegible] . . . iquid for . . . [illegible] . . . destroy the labor . . . [illegible] . . . going to be dangerous and highly unpopular . . . [illegible] . . . has to be done.

This, Ned thought, was a textbook clue if ever he'd seen one. If only he knew what the hell it meant . . . Jan Span handed him some mints and started the engine.

'Do you know what PD is, sir?'

Ned didn't.

'Neither did I. I asked Extra Bilge. He said it could be 'per diem', which would fit if the note were about the Minister's expenses. Or it might be Porton Down.'

Porton Down. The Chemical and Biological Defence Establishment. What had they discovered? No good asking them. Could Hawkins shed any light? No. Span had asked him but he'd said he didn't know. Didn't have the clearance, or something.

Ned carefully put the photograph of Fragment 56 back into its protective sleeve.

'How did you leave it with Hawkins?'

Jan Span couldn't help giggling at the memory. She was packing up when he'd wandered back in, trying to look as if he'd been interrupted from running the nation by the need to see her off the premises. So she tried a little small talk.

'Your friend Amanda said you were going to Glyndebourne tomorrow.'

'Fiancée. She's my fiancée,' Hawkins replied quickly. 'And we are. We're going to see *Salome*.'

'That's the one about the girl who chops the man's head off, and serves it up on a platter, isn't it? Lovely! Just a shame about the weather forecast. All that rain! Still. Best be off. Thanks for everything.'

Ned had a giggle too. Well done, Jan Span. He slipped his seat back a couple of notches. Wasn't as bad as it looked, really. He hadn't much more than an inkling what Fragment 56 meant, but they were on their way to see a man who almost certainly did. Something would start making sense soon. Bound to. Next Christmas party they'd all be saying they couldn't see why it had taken them so long to crack the case. Yes . . . first he'd bring the Brecon Bomber to justice. Then he'd win back Kate and never let her go.

He had another, longer look at Fragment 56, an exchange of texts with Extra Bilge, and then fell asleep. He didn't wake up until Jan Span drove the car across the lifting bridge on to Foulness Island, with the great tidal estuary shimmering beyond.

Her Majesty's Gunnery Range at Shoeburyness was a jolly odd place. It wouldn't have done at all, for example, if you'd had a headache. Or suffered from nerves. The place was shaken by explosions which came in waves. Through the window of the guardhouse, Ned watched a burst of explosions on the distant flats of the Maplin Sands. Bang! Whizz! Crump! Mud and flame tangoed into the sky. The security guy had a sixth sense as to when an explosion would take place, and spoke in an odd stagger as he straddled words on either side of bangs, and then crammed a whole sentence into a staccato between crumps. It took quite a long time to get their identities and passes sorted out. We can't be late for the general, Span tried telling him.

'Can't help - - - - - that, ma'am - - - - - Thegeneralisrunning-latetodayplusyoumaygethelduponthewaytohim- - - - - 'orrible mess.'

Can you tell him we're here? Span asked during the course of a particularly long whizz.

'Noneed - - - - - here's Corporal Simmonds for you now - - - - - Thesearethetwopolicevisitorstoseethegeneral.'

Half a mile away down a muddy metalled road, past a huge army low-loader at an ugly angle with an overturned self-propelled howitzer alongside it, past a row of bunkers and Nissen huts, past batteries of killing machines under test, past soldiers and scientists, was the man in charge of it and them all: General Sir Mark Collet, Chief of the General Staff. He was sitting under a strange domed shelter eating a bacon sandwich, drinking tea from an enamel mug and reading a railway magazine.

He didn't seem too rushed off his feet. The particular bang he had come to see, hear and bless was evidently still being prised from the sticky hands of the boffins. No, not the muddy mess they'd passed on the way in. That had nothing to do with him, thank heavens. Before they started, did they fancy something to eat or drink? No? Fine, fire away. By the way. Meant to ask. Was Ned any relation of Lieutenant General Bobby Bale? Late of 40 Commando and now doing a first-rate job for us in Washington? Ned thought of his CND badge-wearing, Aldermaston-marching father, and of his grandfather who'd spent most of the Second World War in the Western Desert, never rising above Leading Aircraftman (Acting). No, said Ned. No relation.

'Firstly, sir, thank you for sparing us your time. As you know, we are investigating the deaths of Sir Michael Ridley, Sergeant Terry Sullivan and Len Kinnear.'

The general nodded approvingly.

'Glad you mention Sullivan and Kinnear. Papers always seem to leave them out.'

'We believe Sir Michael was the target, and that, hidden within the broad terrorist aim of sowing fear and disruption, this was murder with a narrow intent. We are therefore looking for a motive that could help lead us to the perpetrators. So the question is: what was Sir Michael doing or planning which his killers wished to frustrate, and of which they could somehow have received sufficient notice?'

The general nodded approvingly, rather than answering. Ned carried on as if his question had been rhetorical.

'We understand from Lady Ridley that Sir Michael spent some time that last weekend writing something important on his laptop. And that he had a possibly related phone conversation with you on Sunday morning, discussing something Sir Michael was reluctant to let even his wife hear. May we ask you what you talked about?'

The general had a small, thin face that creased up endearingly when he smiled. It went pretty creasy for a moment. But only a moment.

'Before we get on to that, have you seen what he was writing? I gather some papers survived . . .'

'How could we tell which of the remains had been part of the document?'

Span glanced at her boss. His expression was disingenuous, however sharp his question. And the general? Not a crease in sight.

Before the meeting, General Sir Mark Collet had his Intelligence chaps send him half a page on Mr Policeman Bale. They said he was very bright, very brave, distinguished record blah blah . . . all the necessary security clearances blah blah . . . and then they used a really odd phrase. If DCI Ned Bale rang any alarm bells, they said, it was because he was 'dangerously dogged'. The general wasn't at all sure this could be counted a fault. But it could be a worry, if he were outside the tent pissing in.

'Good point, Chief Inspector. But my guess is, you've taken a look at the debris and something's caught your eye.'

No, sir, thought Span. That's not a guess. Hawkins has told his boss who's told the general's Lord High Gopher who's told the general that she had asked about Fragment 56.

'Well, there is something . . .'

Ned reached into his briefcase and pulled the photograph of Fragment 56 out of its sleeve. He took a brief glance at it again, before passing it over to the general. He slid his glasses down his nose and peered at it. Ned always had to think what that meant. Ah, yes. Short-sighted. Not an ideal quality in a Chief of the General Staff.

'So, Chief Inspector. What do *you* make of it?'

I see, thought Ned. I show you mine, but you keep yours well hidden . . . All right then; here's mine.

'I think it's all about poppies.'

The silence that followed would have done a library proud. In the middle of a gunnery range it was positively anechoic. Almost painful. Like wearing noise-cancelling headphones without switching the music on. Span looked even more surprised than the general. A rattle of machine-gun fire surprisingly close by failed to make any of them jump. The general hid his face in his enamel mug, and then asked Ned to go on.

'I think the late Minister was putting forward a combination of initiatives. Porton Down has come up with a systemic herbicide that will kill the opium poppy stone dead, but with a sufficiently abbreviated half-life not to kill the soil or pollute the water-table and aquifers. This would allow a safe, rapid turnaround for replanting with other, legal, crops. But his main proposal was to target the laboratories in Afghanistan that actually make the heroin.'

The general sat motionless for a moment, then gently waved the photo of Fragment 56 in the air.

'You got all that – from this?'

Ned nodded.

The general put the photo on the table and brought his fingers together in a tiny, silent clap. Span, amazed by her boss's deductions, took it as a patronising gesture. Ned didn't care. He'd taken a mighty leap, and had just landed on firm ground.

The general slipped off his glasses. This was a cut above 'dangerously dogged'. Time to get this Bale in the tent, pissing out.

'It was more Mike's idea than mine, I have to say. I was worried for our soldiers in Helmand. There was every possibility that the farmers there would be so angry about the loss of their livelihood that they'd throw their lot in with the other side and the whole province would become a no-go area.'

'What was Sir Michael's answer to that?'

'Oh, he said he'd been talking to the PM and the Americans and the IMF and UNODC and God knows who else, to raise billions in subsidies to the opium farmers. To soften the blow. Heavily structured, of course, with a tapering-off year on year as we reduced our role towards 2015.'

'And can you, sir, explain to us the reference to chemicals?'

The general wrinkled his nose.

'That was more of a side issue for the drug enforcement people, to do with controlling the chemicals used in the processing. No, the main thing was the eradication policy and doing something about the labs.'

Ned made a note, and then carried on.

'If we can go back, sir, to that Sunday morning. I assume Mike Ridley emailed the plan to you, and then followed it up with a phone-call – to get your final sign-off.'

The general allowed that it was a reasonable assumption.

'And did you give it him?'

The general nodded, and suddenly looked rather sad.

'Will the plan still go ahead?'

General Collet shook his head. He had no idea. He'd heard nothing.

'How long had Sir Michael and you been talking about this, and who else knew about the plan?'

A huge explosion rocked the ground and brought the general back to life.

'You're wondering if PALEP – the Poppy and Lab Eradication Plan – could be your motive? Must take a while to mount an attack like that . . .'

The general had a think, then reached into his pocket and pulled out a BlackBerry. Half a minute of thumbing and the general looked up.

'We first talked about it in February of this year. Porton Down had just given him the green light. Apparently they'd been growing acres of poppies on Salisbury Plain under plastic, pumping in heat and all that. Well, they whipped the covers off and sprayed sometime late summer last year, and by mid-February this, they were getting perfectly healthy barley, sugar beet and tobacco on those same fields. He told me about it while we were watching HMS *Astute* make her first dive. That was on the eighteenth of February.'

The general slipped the BlackBerry into his pocket and moved on to Ned's second question.

'Which leaves us with, who knew?'

He tugged at his chin.

'Well. My closest chaps for starters, Mike's people ditto. The team at Porton Down knew, of course. Military Intelligence knew, as they'd prepared the assessments. Air Chief Marshal Sir Richard Forrest knew, along with a handful of his brightest sparks; the RAF was tasked with the spraying and the air-strikes against the heroin labs. The Foreign Secretary and the Chancellor knew. Our ambassador in Kabul knew. The heads of MI6 and MI5 knew. The chairman of the Joint Intelligence Committee knew.

'People always know, Chief Inspector. It's useless to pretend they don't. I mean, you assume no one who knows will tell anyone who shouldn't know – and it *was* a deadly bloody secret. But . . . it's like ground elder. Secrets creep out under things. And if your enemy is smart, he'll piece stuff together from candle-ends.'

The general passed the photo of Fragment 56 back to Ned.

'Just as you did, Chief Inspector.'

A senior officer peered round a pillar, saluted and gave the general the thumbs-up.

'I'll have our counter-intelligence chaps take a look at it. You should get a call from a Brigadier Mossman. Can't promise anything. Still . . . not sure you need that much help, Chief Inspector. You seem to be doing rather well on your own.'

'Nevertheless, sir, we'd very much appreciate a copy of the complete document Sir Mike emailed you. To see what we missed . . .'

'Not a lot, I'd have to say. See what I can do.'

They stood and shook hands. General Sir Mark Collet removed his glasses presumably so as not to miss any of the forthcoming bang, while Ned and Jan Span trudged through the mud to the waiting jeep. They did not see the general's creasy smile switch off the second their backs were turned, nor did they see him watch them go. He wasn't at all confident that DCI Ned Bale was safely in the tent, let alone facing out.

8

THE MINUTE FATSO HEARD THE word 'drugs' in the same breath as the phrase 'Brecon Bombing', it was clear to Ned that Fatso knew something that he did not. A back-story. The whereabouts of a buried body. Fatso was a hopeless actor. And he'd looked so up, as he trotted into the meeting room and plonked himself down on the table in front of them. And then Ned mentioned the 'd' word, and Fatso looked as if someone had let his air out. He listened to the briefing without pleasure.

It wasn't as if there was a whole lot of good news to tell him apart from the fact that, thanks to Fragment 56, they might now have a possible motive. Spick said he'd checked security at the army base; there was no indication that Marcham had gone anywhere that weekend. He'd had no visitors either. According to the phone records, Jill Marcham had telephoned the house at 18.26 on the Friday, and at 16.04 on the Sunday. Exactly as he had told them. It turned out that, as a result of his rabble-rousing, Colour Sergeant Malcolm Marcham was currently starring on Special Branch's bad boy list, and his landline, cell phone and email traffic were firmly attached by bell wire and crocodile clips to the earwiggers at GCHQ. No high-threat activity. Just the usual griping with veterans and their families over crappy kit, wrong-sized boots, etc.

The threat of a warrant had been enough to jolt Marcham into letting Extra Bilge shine a torch into his hard drive. Again, nothing too worrying. The Bilge had checked all his recent file deletions. Evidently Marcham had tried to protect his informants' identities by wiping a number of emails and addresses off his system, but the Bilge had found them all – the way he always did. File Marcham under Awkward Squad, not Guy Fawkes.

Spick had also checked with the Reverend Hamish Finch who confirmed that on Sunday 25th July Major James McCullough did indeed read a chunk of *Luke* 7 at St Andrews-by-the-Burn. And to make matters worse for hard-working coppers trying to nail a cold-blooded killer, Reverend Finch had happened past McCullough's cottage the day before and seen him burning a pile of garden waste. McCullough hadn't noticed him, but had thereby acquired a heaven-backed alibi for the entire weekend. Extra Bilge then said the DNA tests they had done on Marcham and the Hermit had not tied either of them in to the wodge of *naswar*.

Fatso frowned.

'Who told us to look in the British Army for the bomber?'

The others turned to Ned.

'A Captain Crispin. That's what he calls himself. I believe he's the MI6 guy at Camp Bastion. Or one of them.'

Ned checked his notebook.

'He asked to see me. Told me they'd had a tip-off from a trusted source that the Brecon Bomber is not a member of al-Qaeda, nor is he a Taliban nor an international Jihadist. He's a white, British ex-soldier who has served in Afghanistan and is harbouring a grudge.'

Ned shut the notebook.

'Spick has sifted through all the people who in any way fitted the bill, including instructors in Improvised Explosive Device Disposal, who have the necessary bomb-making expertise and had the opportunity. It boils down to precious few, all of whom we've checked out thoroughly. Marcham and McCullough were top of the list. As Spick and Extra Bilge say, they are in the clear. So either Crispin was misinformed, or – for some unknown reason – he was trying to throw me off the scent. Hard to say which.'

Fatso shifted his weight; the tabletop bowed – and held.

'Sod him. What else have we got?'

'Well,' replied Ned, 'we should start afresh on the basis that the bomber is almost certainly of Middle Eastern origin – the chewing tobacco strongly points to that – with close links to Afghanistan's drug lords.'

And maybe Chief Superintendent Larribee's late-night exhortation wasn't senseless drivel.

'We need to think bigger than we have been. Let's remember, no plausibly capable terrorist organisation has stuck its hand up. This was almost certainly a killing motivated by drugs, not Jihad. We need to recalibrate our investigations accordingly.'

Fatso nodded, swung his legs to and then fro and sprung off the table.

'When you've set them their homework, put your head round the door.'

And off he darted with his usual surprising speed.

'I'll tell you, Ned, why Mike Ridley might've wanted to spray the poppy crop. Didn't think the others needed to know.'

On a personal level, Ned reckoned, this was shaping up to be an odd case. He had witnessed the crime himself. Kate's fingerprint was on the key piece of evidence. And Fatso had known the victim.

'Go on, sir. All ears.'

'Mike Ridley had a daughter. By his first wife, Mildred. Anna was seventeen. One Saturday night she went to a party with friends. Mike was at the House of Commons for some do, and swung by to fetch her. Finds the street's full of police cars and closed off. They see who it is, and wave him through. He gets to the address, and there's this ambulance outside. Before he knows it, someone's grabbed his arm and said, "She's in here, sir, but I think you're too late." He climbs in, and there's his daughter stretched out dead – neck broken. Apparently there was a balcony in the house and she was off her face. Went straight over. They kept it out of the papers somehow.'

Apparently Mike and Mildred hadn't a clue about Anna and drugs . . . Their marriage hadn't been in great shape, but Anna's death did for it. And then Mike met Jane.

It was starting to make sense. Early on Spick had said that Ridley had given evidence to the Presidential Threats Commission about controlling the international drugs traffic. Ned hadn't thought any more about it because he was looking for a terrorism connection. But that wasn't the link. Drugs were the link. The father was murdered trying to stop the thing that had killed his daughter.

'How well did you know them, sir? What's the connection?'

'My wife Esme – her elder sister is Jane Ridley's mum. Esme is Jane's favourite aunt . . .'

Fatso's voice tailed off. Ned didn't think he'd ever seen him sad. Pig pleased, petulant, puzzled, pissed – even pensive. But not sad.

'It's a terrible story, sir,' said Ned sympathetically.

'Yeah,' replied Fatso. 'But that's what we do, Ned. No terrible stories, and we've had it. Thing is, we never run out of 'em, do we?'

He brightened at the thought.

'Anyway, cock. When you seeing Carrie Anne?'

Ah! Carrie Anne.

Ned always had a spring in his step on his way to see Carrie Anne.

> *Hey Carrie Anne!*
> *What's your game now?*
> *Can anybody play?*

It was a song Ned's dad used to play on the Dansette in his attic bolt-hole. It was bone-dry up there and smelled of hardboard and old carpet underfelt. Little Ned used to love climbing the rickety fold-down ladder to say goodnight to his father. Dad had started to put up an old train-set under the eaves, but had not gone more than a few yards. Ned would push the trucks up and down while his father read essays or marked papers. His mother never twigged how Ned always managed to avoid a telling-off by coming down in time for his bath. Dad had learned how to read the activity in the house from what the water tanks were doing. It kept them both out of trouble.

When the bath was being filled below, the roar of cold water replenishing the tank in the attic drowned the sound of hot water going down the lagged pipes. But if you rested a foot on them, as Ned and his Dad did conspiratorially, you could feel the pipes judder slightly. It was Ned's introduction to detective work. It didn't matter if the Dansette was blaring out the Hollies, or Unit 4 + 2, or the Moody Blues. When the judder stopped, that would be the cue for a quick hug and kiss goodnight, and then Ned would dive through the trapdoor to a world of transparent brown bars of soap that made your eyes sting, and pyjamas with all the give of cardboard.

> *You're so . . . so like a woman to me . . .*
> So *like a woman to me . . .*

They always met in the same restaurant. Small and old-fashioned, with tables tucked safely into alcoves and ancient waiters who never made a show of remembering either Carrie Anne or Ned. None of that 'Your usual, Madam?' bollocks. It was anonymous. Utterly relaxing. The food was good, rather than very good, but that wasn't the point. Carrie Anne was the point, and as usual, she was there before him. Glass of champagne in one hand, menu in the other, spectacles on the end of her *mignon* nose.

'Hullo, Carrie Anne.'

Her face lit up.

'Ned . . . darling.'

She adored him. He was just the dearest, gentlest, handsomest man. And of all the young officers she'd met in over forty years in the force, Ned was the smartest by far. He sat, and they talked and sipped champagne and peered at the menu they knew by heart. Then they ordered what they always ordered: steamed turbot with hollandaise and spinach and new potatoes. They ordered a bottle of very good Chablis, and then they talked some more.

When he first met Carrie Anne, Ned fleetingly wondered if he stood a chance with her. Never mind she was a superintendent, even then. Never mind she was twenty-four years his senior – she was a very svelte, very sassy forty-something. Never mind she was said to be married. It was just a bit of wondering, what it would be like. She was so chic, so worldly, so very fearless. It was as well, he thought, that he kept his wonderings to himself. Better to be Carrie Anne's friend for twenty years than her lover for an afternoon. Or maybe not, but it was too late to find out. She was, after all, old enough to be Kate's grandmother.

For her part, Carrie Anne had been a little surprised that she and Ned had not become lovers twenty years ago. And she could see no incompatibility between Ned starting as her lover and then graduating to friend. She had done that a number of times, rather successfully. In time, she had come to regard their affair – the one they hadn't had – as something that might simply happen at any moment. Their lunches together were opportunities to savour the period before a relationship becomes sexual. Nothing to do with flirting. She and Ned did not flirt. Strangers flirt. If lovers flirt it is unutterably coy. Carrie Anne had always relished those precious, heady meetings between pre-lovers, and no matter how sublime the later sex, no matter how uxorious and long-lasting the marriage, she knew she could never have those particular feelings again with that person. It was perhaps that which she valued above all in her relationship with Ned. Two decades of devoted pre-intimacy.

No one in the country knew more about the international drugs trade than Chief Superintendent Dame Carrie Anne Pollard. She was nearing the close of a dazzling career she had begun with a bang. A fast-track graduate and fluent in Spanish and Portuguese, she had been sent on secondment to the US Department of Justice

Bureau of Narcotics and Dangerous Drugs, supposedly for a month's fact-finding. In the event the Bureau was in the process of being merged into the DEA and in the confusion Carrie Anne got sent down to the field office in Panama City. Or had herself sent there. Anyway, within a fortnight she had managed to infiltrate the Berrio cartel in Medellín.

It wasn't difficult, she later told Ned. All she had to do was to be in the Café Ibagué near the Botanical Gardens, wearing not much more than a knotted blouse, a short skirt and a smile, when César Berrio came in for his thimble-sized *tinto* from Tolima and *buñuelos*. Subsequent survival in the cartel took a great deal more than a skimpy wardrobe and a taste for fine coffee. Carrie Anne didn't get back to the UK for almost a year, by which time she had secretly passed enough information and evidence to the DEA to enable the Colombians to smash one of the nastiest cocaine families in South America. And the clever trick was, Berrio went to the firing squad thinking of Carrie Anne as his loyal and tantalisingly delicious interpreter. Not surprisingly, with all that was on his mind, he failed to see her observing from a distance as the DEA agents abseiled into his compound from helicopters. It was apparently something she had insisted on – being in at the kill. If anyone could help Ned understand about drugs and Afghanistan, it was Carrie Anne.

'Do you remember *The Wizard of Oz*, Ned? The Judy Garland film?'

He smiled and nodded. Their local cinema used to run it at Christmas. His dad had taken him and his sister Lou. Ned had been scared witless. Violent cyclones that turn your life upside down, wicked witches, munchkins diving between your legs, everyone you love in permanent jeopardy – horrific! He'd probably only watched one minute in ten.

'Do you remember when Dorothy steps off the Yellow Brick Road and falls asleep in the field of poppies?'

Of course. Watched via closed-circuit crystal ball by the Wicked Witch of the West.

'"Poppies . . ."' said Ned in the Witch's quavery, croaky voice. '"Poppies will put them to sleep!"'

Carrie Anne grinned at him.

'Exactly. *Papaver somniferum.*'

That's one for Doc Bones, thought Ned, with his love of Latin. Carrie Anne unfolded her napkin and placed it across her lap.

'The opium poppy. Source of heroin, with its attendant misery, poverty, crime, war, death. Afghanistan makes it; the world buys it. And the *Appellation d'Origine Contrôlée* of most of this heroin is Helmand Province.'

The Montée de Tonnerre arrived on cue. Even given the restaurant's considerable discretion, Carrie Anne did not carry on until the wine waiter was safely away.

'Do you know, Ned, the UNODC says the opium situation in the southern provinces of Afghanistan is "out of control"!'

She gave a tiny dismissive snort, wrinkling her perfect nose.

'It isn't out of control; it's just out of *our* control. This isn't a sideshow run by mavericks, Ned. It's a core Afghan national activity. It goes with bloody tribal feuds and the subjugation of women. And, of course, drugs go perfectly with terrorism. They thrive in the same climate: lawlessness, instability, violence, fear. Helmand Province is ideal. A bomb goes off, there's a body in the alley, armed men load packets of white powder into a lorry at night – who's going to say a thing?'

Ned thought of that agonising session in the Ops Room at Camp Bastion, eyes riveted to the screens as Kate and Jiffy inched across the deserted street in Gollum. Deserted except for the armed triggerman behind the Zam Zam sign. How far in advance had mothers made sure their children were in off the streets? What was it like to live in a place where survival depended on seeing everything and registering nothing?

'Do you know, darling, perhaps half a billion dollars flow into insurgents' coffers from the Afghan opium trade every year? The Taliban, al-Qaeda and the other terror organisations in Afghanistan and beyond, all need and pray for a good poppy crop. And they get it! Poppies are resistant to drought, and anyway, the police and Taliban in Helmand make sure the poppy fields get the water first, not the wheat. Nothing interferes with the harvest – not even war. From December foot-soldiers start returning to their farms, and the fighting only resumes fully after they've got the crop in.

'It isn't only the Taliban and the police. Warlords, government officials – they're all in it together, and it's remarkably difficult to tell one from the other. Like the men who are fighters one month, farmers the next, a regional Afghan governor can also be a devout Muslim, a tribal leader *and* a drug baron. Plus a CIA or MI6 asset in the bargain.'

Waiters arrived with the turbot. Another break in the conversation.

'Looked at one way, the Afghan drug lords are pulling off a considerable feat. Not only are they meeting over ninety per cent of entire world demand. For the last few years they've been manufacturing twice as much heroin as the world uses, without any related drop in the street price.'

Ned frowned. Where was it going?

'I think it's being stashed away, against a rainy day. Maybe twelve thousand tons to date.'

'And what constitutes a rainy day? A poor harvest?'

'Yes, that. Or if Mike Ridley had lived to implement his package of policies . . .'

Ned looked up quickly.

'You knew about that?'

Carrie Anne nodded.

'We talked about it a number of times. You know, Ned, people have this awfully silly – almost romantic – notion that heroin production in Afghanistan is all about simple peasants with hoes, and donkeys carrying little packets out of the country hidden in their colourful saddlebags. It isn't. It's an industrial operation, with profit levels multinationals would kill for. Mike Ridley had worked out that the way to stop it was to triangulate the solution. Destroy the heroin labs which process opium into heroin via morphine. Prevent the import of the chemical acetic anhydride used to dissolve the morphine. It's absolutely essential to the heroin process, and it comes in unchecked by the tanker-load. And, lastly, destroy the poppy crop itself. That's important, because otherwise they'll simply carry on selling the opium as resin. The Porton Down breakthrough meant the soil wouldn't be dead for ever after, and it provided a framework for compensation and cooperation with the farmers. But Mike was certain that the secret of long-term success was to target the labs and the precursor chemicals.'

'Precursor chemicals'. Interesting, thought Ned. So that was the phrase in Fragment 56. And what had General Collet said about them? That they were a side issue.

'I'm trying to work out, Carrie Anne, if Sir Mike was murdered to prevent him from implementing this plan. It would only make sense if, without his backing, the whole thing gets quietly dropped. But if everyone agreed with him, then we'll open the papers tomorrow and find the new Minister of Defence announcing it, and I'll have to look elsewhere for the motive.'

She gave a little shrug of golden shoulders.

'Without Mike, there may be desultory attempts to destroy the poppy crop. Or, more likely, inconclusive discussions about doing so. Without Mike, it is highly unlikely that there will be any attack on the heroin labs. And without Mike there is no chance on God's earth that a finger will be lifted to stop the flow of precursor chemicals into Afghanistan.'

'Why?'

She poured more hollandaise on to the side of her plate.

'They'll never destroy the whole poppy crop. And the drug lords have stand-by labs hidden across the country, waiting in the wings. More than enough to continue production even if all existing processing capacity were wiped out. But stopping acetic anhydride from entering the country? That's the elephant in the room. Do that, and you'll kill heroin manufacture stone dead. There is no substitute for it. Opium resin is a fraction of the value for weight and bulk. You'll slash everyone's profits.

'That's why, every time anyone has suggested hitting the flow of precursor chemicals into Afghanistan, they've been howled down. And leading the howls: senior US National Security Advisers, the CIA, SIS, Pakistan intelligence, Turkish intelligence, etcetera. They need the drugs trade; they always have. It gives them power, contacts, money, information, leverage, operating space. An old DEA friend told me in Washington last month that virtually all the targets of his international narcotics investigations over the past thirty years had turned out to be working in some guise for the CIA. The traffickers and the spooks are in bed, entwined.

'Plus no one wants to upset Afghan tribal leaders involved in the drug trade, whom they need on-side to stand up against the Taliban. It would even be potentially destabilising for some national economies, because entire banks have been kept afloat during the recession by deposits and cash flows from the heroin trade. With Mike dead, everyone will heave a sigh of relief.'

They ate for a moment in silence, broken by Ned.

'The argument I don't buy is that "it'll only go elsewhere, like shipbuilding". You know: "What's the point of shutting down opium production in Afghanistan? The bad guys will only start up again in Kyrgyzstan, or Sumatra or wherever." Isn't the point that it depends on whether you're trying to make life difficult for the bad guys or easy for yourself? One of the soldiers I've seen recently – can't remember which; I've met a ton of them – said it would be suicidal for the army in Helmand to alienate the locals by destroying the poppy crop. But if you want to disrupt the bad guys, to frustrate their knavish tricks, then you *have* to destroy their entire business in Afghanistan. And do the same wherever they go next. Bugger them, I say.'

Carrie Anne gave a tiny grin.

'That's almost, word for word, what I told Mike Ridley.'

Ned poured her the last of the Chablis.

'Presumably hoarding heroin is a bit more than an insurance policy against a Ridley popping up, or a hedge against fluctuation in world demand? It must give the drug lords huge clout with the insurgents.

After all, it effectively turns them into the Taliban's bankers. If no poppy were ever to grow in Afghanistan ever again, they could still afford to fund the Taliban for years to come. And how do the Mullahs square that with the Koran's injunctions against intoxication?'

Carrie Anne nodded. He really was the sharpest arrow in the quiver.

'Some of the devout are horrified and want nothing to do with drugs. The Taliban, after all, had a desultory go at banning opium production when they were last in power. But others don't care. "Jihad by needle" was the phrase I heard, Ned. Heroin is fine for the infidel, they said. It's what the infidel deserves. But the trouble is now, one and a half million of the faithful in Afghanistan are addicts . . .'

The maître d' glided over with the dessert menus. It was the only moment in the lunches with Carrie Anne in which either side acknowledged familiarity. He was an old-style Austrian. He bowed. He kissed her hand. He gave Ned to understand he had won the lottery of life to be having lunch with the *gnädige Frau*. Ned beamed. Carrie Anne asked him how the *Heuriger* was this year. Marvellous. His brother-in-law was bringing it over next week. He would keep some for her. She smiled and handed him back the menu unopened.

'One *crème brûlée*,' Carrie Anne ordered. 'With two spoons.'

'And two *caffè lungo macchiato* please,' added Ned, not to be outdone in the pre-intimate mutual food-ordering stakes.

Another bow, and the maître d' glided away.

'Of course,' Carrie Anne went on, 'it's perfect country for wickedness. Most tribesmen don't give a hang for national boundaries and aren't members of Neighbourhood Watch. That Afghan-Pakistan frontier is probably the leakiest in the world. A free trade zone a thousand miles long: drugs, chemicals, weapons, people. In *and* out. No problem whatsoever. When you were in Camp Bastion, did you ever peek through the barrier on the south side?'

Ned thought back to walking the perimeter in the dark after seeing Kate for the first time in ages. To seeing the beams from the two helicopters fleetingly light up the Dasht-e Margo. He nodded.

'Slip through the wire, keep going a hundred and eighty miles or so and you're in Baluchistan. Beautiful, wild, bandit country. All sorts of surprising things happen there.'

The *crème brûlée* and coffees arrived.

'Which leads, rather neatly, to my punchline. It's highly likely that the inevitable talks between the West and the Afghan terrorists – and they are absolutely inevitable, Ned, whatever you hear to the contrary – will be brokered by men who are used to working both with Muslim insurgents and regional leadership, with top government officials and tribal warlords. One group stands out, with the contacts and the power: the drug lords. Of course, they won't look like drug lords. They'll seem like businessmen, or elected democrats or men of the cloth or someone important's brother . . . or a combination of those things. But only they will have the address book and the enduring muscle, the wealth and know-how to deliver the names in it. Enduring – courtesy of Mike Ridley's killers.'

One more dip into the *crème brûlée* and their spoons would touch. They both stopped and set them down, with just a tiny, fragile border of brittle toffee and golden cream between them.

They stood on the pavement waiting for her taxi, talking about Fatso/Benjamin, Large Sarge and the old Vice Squad Gaffer. Remembering stake-outs, leaving lunches and funerals. Then the taxi came, and Carrie Anne reached up and kissed him not in the air but on the cheek, and only the one cheek. She held him to her for a beat longer than kissing protocols required, and he smelled man's perfume in her hair, and found himself hoping it was indeed man's, and not a man's.

'How's Kate?' she asked as they slipped apart.

Dame Carrie Anne's legendary powers of intuition and deduction, her ability to read character and mood, her eye for the gesture and ear for the inflection, her perfect timing – were they what lay behind the question? Did she know? Could she tell? Was that a longer kiss than usual?

'Fine, I think.'

Carrie Anne squeezed her eyes shut in a tiny 'I'm glad for you' expression and the taxi took her away – bliss averted for another few months.

When Ned checked his phone there were three missed calls and two text messages from Fatso, telling him to skip pudding and coffee with Carrie Anne and get his arse over to an address near Admiralty Arch. So he did.

It was impossible to tell from the outside what the place was. Under pressure, the reception desk conceded that Ned was in the office of the Joint Intelligence Committee. Security was as tight as security gets. He eventually passed muster and was taken to a grand office at the top of the building with a good view of the places from which wars and empire had once been won and run. The people in the room looked more like the sort who lose them. Blimey, thought Ned, I've fallen among thieves. There was the head of the Security Service – MI5. And the rat-like man he was talking to ran MI6. Fatso, looking particularly dishevelled, was with a scholarly looking cove and a senior officer in the US Air Force. Where was the elderly gentleman who had been so pleased to see Julia in the pub? Didn't he chair the JIC? Ned felt a tap on the shoulder, turned and there was Chief Superintendent Larribee. Desiccated-croissant face herself. This was looking serious.

'There you are, Bale, in the nick of time. They're getting the feed any minute.'

What feed? He couldn't eat another thing. No. Couldn't mean that. A lackey was lowering a screen; another was closing blinds. Fatso had now been cornered by someone vaguely familiar. Who was she? Ned remembered an article he'd seen in one of the Sundays about the ten most important British Asians. She was definitely one of them. Baroness . . . Baroness Rajani . . . Nasreen. That was it. But what was she doing here? And what was going on? There was nowhere to sit near anyone he liked enough to ask. He plonked himself next to a man with a beard and bow-tie who shook his hand without introducing himself. His breath smelled of wintergreen gum. Like lavatory cleanser.

'Looks like this kinda closes your case for you, don't it?' whispered the man – clearly American – waving an arm towards the projection screen.

Ned was about to ask why and how, when the screen came to life and the lights went out. A USAF officer wearing an earpiece stood to one side and explained that this was not real-time. Meteorology had warned of severe sandstorms by 1300 hours at the launch field in the northern Chāgal Hills, so they'd pulled the operation forward three hours. The screen was split into a gallery of images: the view looking forward from some sort of aircraft flying high over a desert; a view from the top of the craft's tailplane; an instrument panel; a moving map with an icon of an aeroplane at the centre; a static view of foothills with a ridge of mountains beyond; looking over the shoulders of a row of men and women in T-shirts with headphones in front of a rack of monitors showing some of the same images. Then the sound started to come through. A confusing cross between Air Traffic Control and flightdeck. The USAF officer spoke again.

'The delivery platform is the MQ-9 Reaper. The payload is mission-customised. In this case the hunter-killer pack: Hellfire P lazer-guided missiles. Just to remind you, the voices you hear are coming from the pilot, flight crew and mission controllers at Creech Air Force Base, Nevada. That's the River Indus over there to the east. As you see from the clock, we are one hour fifty-six minutes in with six minutes to target. Do not change your watches; these operations run on local time Afghanistan. It avoids confusion on handovers between Creech AFB and ground crew in theatre.'

The bow-tie man next to Ned wafted more lavatory cleanser into his ear.

'Crazy or what? The UAV's over Pakistan, the pilot's in Nevada. He flies the mission, jogs home, shoots some hoops, grills some steaks, fucks the neighbour's wife . . .'

Charming.

So there was no one on board the aircraft. UAV?

'Unmanned Aerial Vehicle. Drone.'

Oh.

The UAV had been flying north, parallel with the Indus. It now started to bank westwards towards a range of low mountains. It took Ned a moment to realise that the mountains were the same as in the static shot. They must also have a spy plane up there.

'The Reaper crossed into Pakistan forty miles south-west of Quetta, so we've been in Pakistan airspace for one hour nine minutes.'

We? Ned asked himself. Speak for yourself.

'That's Taunsa village you can see there. Then Magrotha, Koro, Basti Buzdar.'

Ned saw the line of tiny villages, made from the same earth on which they had been built. A few houses, some animals. Children, bound to be. Oh, God what was about to happen?

'Our friends in Islamabad know all about this mission. If you don't believe me, just ask my old buddy Colonel Jinnah of ISI who's here in the room somewhere. Where are ya, Zulfikar? OK, gotcha!'

Knowing chuckles from the intelligence professionals. Puzzled glance round from Ned. Bow-tie man raced to his aid with a whisper that would remove stubborn stains.

'Pakistan Intelligence's London guy.'

'Four minutes to target.'

What target? Was it in sight yet? A voice from Nevada pronounced it twelve miles away. A minute later, another languid voice described the weapons as armed and locked on. He sounded like someone out of a cowboy film. The ice-cool gunman.

'Two minutes to target.'

The Reaper was now losing height. Ned could see fields. Crops. Cattle. People. A group of houses appeared dead ahead. They looked like any others in the area, except this one had a flashing red cross superimposed over it and a heavily armed UAV bearing down on it. Children were playing in the dust outside.

'One minute to target.'

Someone, somewhere, started counting down. And then the Reaper shivered as two plumes of smoke shot away towards the buildings.

'Missiles away.'

The Reaper leaped into the air.

Ned realised no one in the room was breathing, foreshadowing what would soon be happening in and around the clutch of doomed mud-houses.

They were watching a snuff movie.

The view from the on-board cameras now showed sky and dazzling sun as the Reaper banked away home, but Ned was not going to be spared the sight of the target's fate. Someone in the spy plane or Nevada had tweaked the zoom. The static view of the foothills and mountains had closed in to a close-up of the mud-houses. Here one moment . . . a succession of fireballs . . . all gone.

A mighty dust cloud stacked up into the air, the kind you expected to see a genie emerge from. The kind of genie who can be teased into showing off his powers by sucking himself back into the bottle. Except this genie wasn't going anywhere. The pall of dust and smoke hung over the tranquil landscape. Silence, and then a strange sound, like the crackling of fire. Did they have microphones there as well as cameras? It took a while before Ned realised the sound was coming from the room he was in, and that it was the sound of clapping.

The lackeys raised the screen and the blinds. Light poured into the room sending the spooks scurrying for corner seats like beetles under an upturned stone. When they had finished checking their smart-phones and the lackeys and USAF officers had left, Baroness Rajani Nasreen opened the proceedings. She was, she told them, honoured to be chairing the Joint Intelligence Committee, particularly as she had been at Pembroke during Sir Geoffrey Arthur's time. Many of them in the room would remember the previous incumbent, Sir Dudley Singleton, with respect and affection, and would want to join with her in wishing him a very happy retirement.

'. . . out on his ass . . .' came the whisper in Ned's ear. So Bow-tie was still there. He was proving rather helpful. Who was he? Then Ned heard his own name mentioned, and realised the Baroness was introducing rough coppers to smooth spooks.

'. . . joining us, together with Colonel Jinnah of Pakistan's ISI, on a one-off basis for this extraordinary meeting of the JIC. The sole topic on our agenda is the so-called Brecon Bombing, which resulted in the deaths of Sir Michael Ridley and two others. These murders are, as you know, the subject of a criminal investigation being conducted by our police colleagues in Chief Superintendent Larribee's specialist unit. A jurisdictional authority agreed on by all interested parties, I should remind you, at a meeting convened *in situ* by my predecessor.'

A stitch-up in a boozer was another way of describing it, thought Ned, catching Fatso's eye. Fatso looked totally deadpan. And what did that 'I should remind you' mean? That some in the room might be less than thrilled at Ned & Co. investigating the bombing? The Baroness rolled on.

'Now . . . We have just seen our American friends rather effectively destroy a vital objective in the foothills of the Sulaiman Range in Western Pakistan, about a hundred miles from the Afghan border. As you saw, there might have been some civilian collateral damage. However unfortunate, this is of course unavoidable in these operations. The targets within the buildings were, we can assure you, anything but civilian. As usual, we have the Chief of the London station, Central Intelligence Agency, with us . . . Jerry Wald, for those who haven't met him. May we ask him to explain? Jerry?'

No wonder Bow-tie was so well-informed. Ned's whisperer was Mr CIA. Jerry didn't waste time on preliminaries. The CIA had received information from their colleagues in ISI that the Brecon Bombing had been planned and executed by an ultra-devout, ultra-fanatic group called Jibrail. It was named after the Archangel Gabriel who had acted as the intermediary between God and Mohammed, passing down the divine revelations which became the Koran. The leader of Jibrail, Muhammad Ali Nizari, was known to the CIA and ISI for a series of violent and successful bomb attacks. One, on a Sunni mosque in Faisalabad, killed seventy-three people. Another, on a hostel for female medical students and nurses at a hospital in Multan, killed forty-seven.

Jerry shrugged with a 'What kind of people are these?' roll of his eyes skywards.

'ISI has a guy inside Jibrail. He was training at the safe house near Taunsa when news came through that the British Defence Minister had been assassinated in Southern Wales. All the guys went ape, and there was much talk about Nizari – who was absent. Nizari this, Nizari that. He's a hero . . . he's a god . . . yadda yadda. A week later and Nizari suddenly arrived. It was the middle of the night, but they all went ape again, and wanted to party and hoist him on their shoulders and crown him king or whatever. And this Nizari gets real mad with them, and tells them that they have no discipline, and they're thinking of what they're doing like they're in a Hollywood movie when they should be living the life of devout martyrs, not looking for praise or reward. They all get whipped and put on bread and water for a week. And Ali Nizari insists they have to whip him as well, to drive out any vestiges of pride. Crazy or what?

'Then our informant learns that there's going to be this big deal meeting at the safe house for all the Jibrail leadership – maybe ten, fifteen of them – so Nizari can map out the future struggle. Our guy's a very brave guy. He gets a message to his ISI handlers with the time and exact location. They tell us, and you saw our response.'

There was silence. Then the Baroness turned to Colonel Jinnah to ask if there was anything he wanted to add. Had their man managed to escape? The colonel, who was rather handsome in a caddish way, did not know yet. He hoped so, but . . . It was as Mr Wald had said. These were very bad men. It was good for Pakistan and for the West, what they had all just seen happen.

'Detective Chief Inspector Bale – you must feel a little torn? On the one hand cheated of an arrest. On the other hand, case successfully closed.'

Never let them know what you're thinking. That's what Ned's first governor had dinned into him.

'Absolutely, ma'am.'

'You've been pursuing your investigations for, what, seven weeks? Is anything you've learned in that time at odds with Ali Nizari being the Brecon Bomber?'

Ned worked his mind faster than he could ever remember doing. How to play this? The only person in the room he trusted one hundred per cent was Fatso, and Ned hadn't even told him yet where his suspicions lay. Mustn't give anything away. What to say, though? Everyone's looking at me. Let's try . . . the truth.

'I had never heard of Nizari and Jibrail before today, so I can't say, I'm afraid, whether we have in fact been chasing Colonel Jinnah's target all along without realising it. If we haven't, then we'd better find out whether it's me that's up a gum tree.'

Larribee's rheumy eyes widened. The scholarly gentleman, who ran GCHQ, allowed himself the ghost of a smile. Colonel Jinnah was impassive. Ned went straight on, with about the most devastating smile he could muster aimed straight at Baroness Rajani Nasreen.

'May I just ask a couple of questions? To see if we are all on the same tack?'

'Of course, Chief Inspector.'

'Thanks. Colonel Jinnah, do you have any record of Nizari ever operating in Afghanistan?'

Jinnah frowned and thought. Then he shook his head. No. Not as far as they knew. Nizari did not concern himself with other people's fights. He made his own. Against those he considered had offended against Islam. Who scorned the word of Allah.

'And did your informant say why Nizari had murdered Sir Michael Ridley?'

The response in the room to this question was split. The police and security contingents wanted to hear the answer; the intelligence community clearly didn't think it a question that needed to be asked. In the event it was someone from the latter group who replied: Jerry Wald.

'He was the British Minister of Defence. What other reason do you need? He was a powerful enemy infidel, waging aggressive war on terror, for Chrissakes. He ticked all their boxes.'

'And,' added Jinnah, 'he put aside his wife, did he not? Nizari was very, very strict about these things.'

Ned successfully avoided catching Fatso's eye.

'So no involvement, for example, in the drugs trade?'

Jinnah reserved a special barking laugh for moments like this.

'Drugs are what are called *haram*, Chief Inspector. This means forbidden under Islam. I am telling you, this Nizari was a very religious man.'

'And was he a planner from afar or did he take part in the actual operations?'

'Nizari was the brains and the brawn as you would say, Chief Inspector.'

'So he was in the Brecon Beacons?'

'Undoubtedly.'

'And do you have any information as to how he got away after triggering the bomb?'

This was clearly a question Colonel Jinnah had been praying someone would ask. He looked like a man holding the winning lottery ticket.

'Very interesting question, Chief Inspector. Our man on the inside reported that Nizari had spent many hours practising on a special bicycle . . . very low, with small wheels. They are called recumbents? Up and down the track to the safe house he went. Up and down, up and down. No one there knew why. But, perhaps, you do?'

An electric tremor went right up Ned's neck. Not a figure of speech, but real. He half expected to smell singed hair. Oh dear, he thought. I am up against someone very, very clever. He'd known the bomber was all the things you don't want your enemy to be:

dangerous, ruthless, ice-cool, lucky. But Ned was counting on being cleverer. The way you knew Clint Eastwood could take on anyone who might swing a punch at him in a bar. Doesn't matter, everyone had said all Ned's life, he's clever. He'll work it out. But supposing the other guy in the bar is Arnold Schwarzenegger?

'How interesting – yes, that ties in absolutely. It's exactly what we worked out. That a recumbent bike would ensure a silent, inconspicuous getaway from the crime scene.'

Much relief in the room. The nodding of heads reminded Ned of the fuzzy dog on the rear ledge of his father's Cortina. He made sure his tone was that of someone trying to keep up, not someone laying a trap.

'And will your men be able to examine the target location? Go through the rubble and remains?'

'They are there already.'

No need to fret, silly Englishman, Colonel Jinnah's face said. We have it all under control. And Jerry Wald sported a supercilious grin.

'Excellent.' Ned looked relieved. 'So can we rely on them to send us DNA samples from any human remains they find? To match against the bomber's from the Brecon murder scene.'

No one spoke. No one breathed. No one moved.

Unfortunately for Colonel Jinnah, it took a moment to achieve the requisite level of facial impassiveness, and in that moment he resembled the god of thunder. Jerry Wald looked totally vacant, as if he had just nipped out for a lobotomy. What Ned couldn't see and Fatso could, were the very serious expressions on the faces of the heads of MI5 and GCHQ. The person who broke the silence was the boss of MI6.

'You've got some DNA from the bomber? For definite?'

'Yes,' replied Ned, making sure he gave no impression he was taking pleasure from the room's surprise and discomfiture. 'Absolutely.'

The nation's top spook had the wit and skill to respond without pause.

'Didn't know that. Good.'

But he didn't look hugely pleased. And neither did anyone else, except for Fatso who barely controlled his instinct to holler 'Gotcha – you bastards'. The Baroness stepped in to sweep away the bad karma that had suddenly amassed in her first special meeting of the JIC.

'I am sure anything they find they will pass on, although it is hard to see anything surviving intact from that.'

She waved her hand vaguely towards where the screen had been.

'Either way, I'm glad we're now able to close the tragic Ridley case so satisfactorily. The coincidence of two Middle Eastern terrorists both using low bikes as getaway vehicles does rather challenge the laws of probability.'

Everyone looked relieved at this insight, and Ned had the sense to keep his lip buttoned. Papers away. Briefcases snapped shut. Panic over. The noble lady hadn't quite finished though. Time for a platitude.

'This has been a textbook case, if I may say, of inter-service cooperation, both here at home and abroad. Thank you all. Case closed.'

So that was it. Nations could sleep easier in their beds. Fatso shook hands with the Baroness and hurried out of the room followed by Chief Superintendent Larribee. Ned gave Colonel Jinnah and Jerry Wald his contacts so they'd know where to send any DNA samples they found in the rubble. Both men pretended to take the notion very seriously. Of course, the colonel reassured Ned, he would make it his particular business to let Ned know what his people found at the Jibrail safe house. Indeed, it might speed things up if the detective could give him some of the Brecon bomber's DNA so they could make the comparisons for themselves. Ned thanked him very politely and said that, regrettably, it would not be possible to split the sample, but he greatly looked forward to receiving whatever they turned up. Colonel Jinnah had a really nifty switch-on/switch-off smile which he tested out there and then on Ned. No worries, Zulfikar, thought Ned, it works a treat.

'See ya around,' Jerry Wald said with his face in Ned's but

without conviction. He turned and walked away, leaving behind a
faint sickly smell.

'So, the cowboys got the wrong man,' declared Fatso when they
were safely in the car.

'I'm not at all sure that's what I took away from that meeting,'
said Chief Superintendent Larribee, miraculously finding space on
her forehead for a few more wrinkles. 'Bale?'

'Well, ma'am. I'm with the Superintendent. The Americans might
have just destroyed a terrorist cell. Or, more likely, some unfortunate Pakistan farmer and his family. But they've certainly not got
the killers of Ridley, Sullivan and Kinnear.'

Fatso looked out of the window with a blithe 'told you so'
expression. The chief superintendent wanted to know how Bale
could be so sure. Ned had to think very fast for the second time
in the day. His boss's boss was rather stupid, and she went off at
terrible tangents. Give her one thing. Not the drugs bit – she'd
never get it. Something really simple.

'You remember that at the crime scene we found the remains of
the trigger mechanism? And that it bore the fingerprint of WPC
Kate Baker?'

Larribee nodded.

'Why would this Nizari, who is not known ever to have visited
Afghanistan, risk sneaking – or getting someone else to sneak – into
the locked-down depths of the most secure section of a heavily
guarded British military base in Helmand Province to steal a trigger
unit an alpha terrorist like him could knock up in his sleep?'

'Well, when you put it like that . . .'

Larribee racked her brain for the counter-argument, failed to find
it, and on backing out, bumped into the evidence the Baroness had
held up as the clincher.

'The bike, Bale! What about the bike? Low – with small wheels,
he said – that Colonel Jinnah.'

Fatso glanced confidently at Ned. Go on, son. What's the answer
to that?

'What,' Ned asked by way of reply, 'was the result of Colonel Jinnah telling us Ali Nizari had been practising with a recumbent bike?'

'Well . . .'

Chief Superintendent Larribee was going to have to think about this one. Fatso didn't need to.

'It allowed the Baroness to say the target of those missiles was definitely the Brecon Bomber. Because it tallied with what Ned here had worked out for himself about how the bomber had got away.'

'Exactly. It did exactly what the real bomber – who is still very much alive – wanted. And it's given us some rather useful information in the process.'

Larribee tried to look as if she were keeping up, an illusion Ned and Fatso did nothing to destroy.

'Till now,' Ned went on, 'we'd only suspected he used a recumbent bike. Now we not only know he did – we know he's guessed that we'd be puzzled by how he got away. Because he knows there were witnesses. He wouldn't have known who I was, but he certainly saw me through his binoculars, and probably Lady Ridley too. So, using his active contacts with Western Intelligence agencies, he let out a piece of conclusive information supposedly via a mole in Jibrail which he knew would reach us. After all, we have never made public that there was any mystery about the getaway. He knew that when Jinnah mentioned the recumbent bike we'd know the source was absolutely authentic. And that we would then be convinced that Ali Nizari was the bomber, and that he'd been killed in the drone attack.'

Chief Superintendent Larribee suddenly caught up.

'Which is why, when you asked Jinnah about the getaway, he looked like the cat that had got the cream!'

Ned nodded.

'It's possible,' he added, almost to himself, 'that Jibrail, Nizari and the mole were a pure construct. That the bomber created a terrorist alter-ego he could get rid of when it suited him. God knows who those poor people were sacrificed to the drone attack.'

There was silence in the car for a moment or two. Ned felt sure the trigger-happy team at the airforce base in Nevada should share some of the responsibility for the slaughter of innocents. How callously disengaged would you have to be to kill by remote control, thousands of miles from your victims, and on the dubious say-so of Colonel Jinnah?

Larribee suddenly stirred.

'And you say the real bomber is in active contact with Western intelligence agencies. Can you be sure of that?'

'Firstly, there's the information about the recumbent bike. Only the bomber knew how he got away, and he communicated it to us via Colonel Jinnah of ISI. But that's not all. This is the second time my investigation has been given categorical information about the identity of the bomber. In Camp Bastion I was told by the MI6 man there that we should look for a disgruntled white ex-squaddie who has served in Afghanistan. Today, according to the CIA and ISI, our man is – or was – a Pakistani religious fanatic über-terrorist who has yet to visit Afghanistan. He's playing with us, through them.'

'He's trying to,' Fatso snorted. 'Not succeeding.'

Larribee had another question.

'You also said something about him giving us some rather useful information. What did you have in mind exactly?'

This was, Ned had been thinking to himself, possibly the most intriguing and dangerous aspect of the whole thing. In some way he couldn't yet put his finger on, the bomber seemed to be taking what he'd done very seriously, almost personally, instead of just getting on with the next atrocity. Ned was reminded of what Lady Ridley had said. That she was almost surprised they were going to try to catch her husband's killers. The way the bomber was acting, he didn't seem to be at all surprised.

'By spilling the beans about the recumbent bike, the bomber's engaging with us. He's trying to put us off the scent. First he tried steering us up blind alleys. Now he's trying to persuade us that he's just been killed in a rocket attack. It shows he isn't just some fire-and-forget fanatic. He's thinking himself into our minds, working out our thought-processes.'

'And he nearly got away with it,' Fatso added. 'His low bike tip-off certainly shut the Baroness up. As she said, case closed.'

Whether Chief Superintendent Larribee grasped all the nuances was suddenly neither here nor there. Fatso had unwittingly struck a winning blow. No one closed *her* cases. The only person who did that was the redoubtable croissant herself.

'And I'm a long way off doing that, Ned, I can tell you.'

Ned. Not Bale, or DCI Bale, or Chief Inspector, but Ned. Must be love.

'I told you when we started this to think big. Well, it's an order I have not rescinded. You have carte blanche to pursue your investigations without prejudice. I don't want you fettering your discretion. Ah – excellent! Drop me off right here, driver.'

They pulled up outside a department store. Ned sprang out to hold the door open for her. She had a go at a smile which came out exactly like an inverted grimace, grunted and steamed in to terrorise the haberdashery department.

'Creep,' said Fatso when Ned got back into the car.

They were almost back at the office when Fatso scratched his belly and popped the question that had been nagging at him.

'Go on then, Ned. You haven't answered your own question. Why did the bomber sneak into the most secure bit of a British Army base in Afghanistan to nick the Dog Tart's trigger mech? Eh?'

'Can I answer that tomorrow, sir? I need to look at something first . . .'

'Whenever you're ready, Ned. No rush . . .'

Ned nodded his thanks, sat back and wondered about the bomber for the millionth time since clocking the flash of his binoculars. If he wasn't an aggy ex-squaddie or the devout Ali Nizari, then who the hell was he? Ned had barely any spare brain cells to think about Kate, so absorbed was he by the bomber. Probably owed his nemesis a beer for taking his mind off worrying himself witless over her. Funny. He'd never ever used the word nemesis. He'd never had one before. He'd had criminals he was trying to catch. He'd had some he'd had to understand fairly intimately in order to catch them. But he'd never thought of them as his arch-enemy. Perhaps because they weren't . . . reactive, like this one. This was shaping up more like Sherlock Holmes and Professor Moriarty. And look what happened there – Holmes lured to his death at the Reichenbach Falls . . .

9

THE SOMETHING NED WANTED TO look at was X-3.

It was no coincidence, Fatso wondering why the bomber would nick the trigger mech X-3 which Kate had found. Fatso was nobody's fool and it was – it had always been – the key question. Ned went straight down to the basement to the cage where the Brecon Bombing evidence was stored. He put on gloves, took it out of its bag and stuck it in the middle of the table between two anglepoise lights: the remains of a metal box with jaggedy edges with a length of wire coming off it with part of a printed circuit board at the end. And on that board were some diodes or transistors or whatever they were: tiny coloured cylinders with wires at both ends. He hadn't looked at them closely before.

He stared at it for twenty minutes and then Jan Span found him. She had something to say to him, but then he started to talk to her about X-3, and she pulled up a chair, and pretty soon she was staring at it too – the thing she wanted to tell or ask the DCI quite forgotten.

Next thing they did was hare up to Extra Bilge's cubbyhole, and drag out the map the Bilge had compiled showing the GPS location of evidence and landmarks at the crime scene. It was a nit-pickingly accurate version of the whiteboard he'd had up on the side of his van. Here was the patch of undergrowth where Ned had found X-3, just after Wilton pitched up. There on the verge was where he'd spotted the fox on the surveillance tape. That was the epicentre of the explosion. These are the trees. The biggest is the one that remained intact.

'Have you got a long ruler, Extra Bilge?'

Ten minutes later, Ned and Jan and the Bilge raced down to the basement and had a three-way stare at X-3. And then they rang Doc Bones who was sitting on the fire escape outside his charnel-house, smoking his pipe and wondering how to tell Mrs Bones that he hated light opera and did they really have to go to *Die Fledermaus* that evening? And lo and behold, prayers do get answered because here was the admirable young Nedicus on the blower wanting him to give X-3 an urgent going-over. Whatever X-3 was. Didn't matter. It was clearly going to take time, this X-3 thingy. That's old Strauss out the window. Sorry, old girl – bit of a flap on . . . shame to waste the ticket . . . you could always try Jo next door . . . such jolly tunes, too.

And then there were four of them sitting in the gloom of the basement around X-3 lit like a diva. Wagons in a hollow circle, batten down the hatches, all leave cancelled. Doc Bones said he'd let Extra Bilge go first, in case Mrs Bones suggested he join her at the interval. Extra Bilge raced away, Jan Span went off to ring Major Butterman and Colonel Sillitoe, while Ned raided the canteen for vital sustenance for the troops. And while he was up there he had a cup of coffee in peace, to think through the extraordinary implications if the explanation for X-3 was as he feared.

When everyone had reported back – Extra Bilge and Doc Bones after they'd each had their turn with X-3, and Jan Span after she'd picked the experts' brains – Ned slept on what they all told him.

The next day, he went down to see Fatso as promised, bearing tea, lardy cake, Extra Bilge's map and a worried expression that gave his boss sudden hope.

'You know who did it, don't you, Ned the Yid?'

'I don't have a name. But I think I know who we're looking for.

And I think I know how to find him. This is a complex one, sir. I'm going to have to take you back to before the explosion.'

Fatso was a great listener, and he liked nothing more than to listen to Ned's explanation of a crime. He poured a shedload of sugar into his tea, made sure the lardy cake was within easy reach – and listened.

Ned began with the fable of the fox.

'According to the surveillance tapes, at dawn on the day of the bombing there was a dead fox by the side of the track up to Ridley's cottage. A dead fox that hadn't been there at dusk the night before. Theoretically, it could have been run over by a car during the intervening hours, but we can't tell what happened overnight because the bomber had stuck black foil over the floodlight on the telephone pole. He didn't disable the motion sensor because if he had, an alarm would have rung in the old lambing shed where the Minister's personal protection officers supposedly watched the screens in shifts 24/7 when the Minister was in residence. The bomber had done his homework.

'As a matter of fact, we know someone did drive up the track that night, and did not appear on the screens. He was a local lad taking his girlfriend back to one of the farms, and they noticed that the security light didn't come on. She thought the bulb might have gone. He used to switch off his own vehicle lights anyway, so her dad couldn't find out from Ridley's security guys if the lovers had broken curfew by returning after midnight. So, with no moon, no lights and the vehicle dark blue, the camera didn't pick up a thing.'

Fatso was gripped.

'As it happens,' Ned went on, 'we know that the fox was not run over that night by the wayward lovers because, according to Doc Bones, it had been dead for several days. The likeliest explanation for its presence is that the bomber used it the way they use dead dogs in Iraq and Afghanistan. He placed it on the verge close to where he'd buried the PETN charge, hiding inside it the electronic bits needed to trigger the bomb. Major Butterman believes this would have consisted of a number of components linked by radio signal to the bomber in line of sight a few hundred yards away. First, the bomber had a key fob – the kind that locks and unlocks car doors remotely. It might have had some sort of booster, to ensure the signal would reach the dead fox. Then, inside the fox itself, there would have been a receiver for the key fob, linked by wire to the trigger mechanism for the bomb itself, with its own power-pack.

'As you know, I found part of the trigger mechanism myself at the crime scene, which turned out to have WPC Kate Baker's fingerprint on the twisted metal housing. Great, we thought. Bombs need triggers. There's a bomb, here's a trigger, problem solved. Except it wasn't, sir. The mechanism I found, logged as X-3, did not trigger the bomb that killed Ridley, Sullivan and Kinnear.'

Fatso shook his head in wonder.

'We didn't look much further, I'm afraid sir. Not for ages. It seemed to fit so well, we thought it did fit. It wasn't the forensics that led us to think again, but the logic. The forensics came later.'

Ned moved on to the saga of X-3.

Fatso had to understand that the devices that set off bombs are often made out of stuff that's to hand, or is easy to get or steal. Bits you could pick up in a garage, a mobile phone shop, an electrical goods supplier. So it was odd from the start that the bomber had used X-3 rather than just made himself another ninepenny trigger. X-3 had, after all, been found along with a load of other gear in a raid on a bomb factory. It had been taken back to Camp Bastion and locked away in a secure store. So what made X-3 so special?

'The Dog Tart,' said Fatso, chiming in like a kid at a Punch and Judy show. 'The Dog Tart made it special.'

'Exactly. Her fingerprint was on it. And the bomber had to know her fingerprint was on it. How could he be sure of that? He would have to have been there when she touched it. Or she had to tell him she'd touched it. Or someone else had to tell him she'd touched it. Or he had to have access to X-3 and the other finds from the raid so he could check for himself which one bore her fingerprint, and then take that one. Or maybe all the bomber needed to know was that WPC Baker was the one who had recovered the electronics bits and pieces, and knowing she wouldn't have been wearing gloves in the heat, could gamble that they would all bear at least one of her fingerprints.'

'Did Extra Bilge check to see if the print had been transferred?'

Ned nodded. He had. No trace of Sellotape or adhesive. It was an absolutely genuine print. The bomber's next challenge was to steal the trigger mechanism from the locked store. So he had to have had access to some pretty secret places within Camp Bastion . . .

'Now the bomber's got X-3,' Ned continued, 'his problems aren't over. He has to ensure that we will stumble on it sufficiently intact to find the fingerprint. This is where the forensics comes in. If X-3 had been inside the dead fox, you'd have expected some minute trace of it somewhere on the casing. Sure, it would have been wrapped in plastic to keep it nice and dry in there, but the minute the bomb blew, chances are some bit of fox or blood would make contact with the aluminium housing.'

Ned shook his head.

'Doc Bones gave it a thorough going-over, and it was as clean as a whistle. Then Extra Bilge started to look at the inside of X-3 in a way we hadn't done up till now. As I said, I'd assumed we'd found the trigger . . . Now. When WPC Baker found it, X-3 hadn't been used. It was completely intact. So the bomber had a challenge. He had to make it look as if it had played its part in the explosion but had – by chance – partly survived. So it had to look as if it had suffered bomb damage. Extra Bilge discovered it had indeed been blown up, but – from the inside! The bomber had used a minuscule charge of PETN to rip it open. Now all the bomber had to do was place it not simply where we'd find it, but where he could be sure it would suffer no further damage from the real bomb. So it had to be close, but shielded.'

Ned took Fatso through Extra Bilge's map, showing him the key elements. He pointed out where he had found X-3: with a battered but still standing tree between it and the explosion. Jan Span had talked it through with Major Butterman. Although it hadn't rung alarm bells for him when he was at the crime scene any more than it had for Ned, he could now see that it was a very odd place for the trigger mechanism to have wound up. The force of the blast was, after all, channelled by the embankment towards the field where the 4x4 had landed. Not back over its own shoulder and then swerving around a tenacious old oak.

Fatso squinted at the map, turning it round so as to see X-3 from the centre of the explosion and then vice versa. When he was satisfied, he nodded at Ned to continue.

'Of course, it might have suited the bomber better if the tree hadn't put up such a stout defence. He couldn't have guessed that it would be left standing, drawing attention to the fact that it lay between the blast and the supposed trigger mech.'

And what, Fatso wanted to know, was the motive for all this? Why did the bomber want to stitch up the Dog Tart?

This was the bit of the story that was least susceptible to forensic verification. The simplest explanation was that one of the bombers was in love with her, and that she had not reciprocated and he was angry. And resentful.

'So he blows up the Minister of Defence? If he's really that pissed off, he'd do better blowing *her* up, wouldn't he?'

'The target was always the Minister of Defence,' Ned argued. 'His murder was almost certainly planned long before any falling in love. It had to be recce'd. The Minister's movements studied. It will have taken time, resources, manpower. Mike Ridley was killed because of his drugs policy. That was the main thing I took away from my lunch with Carrie Anne.'

He waited a beat for a dirty Fatso scoff but none came.

'Ridley's proposals would, if successfully implemented, have ended heroin production in Afghanistan. Proposals which are now being shredded. Given that so many people, groups, factions and nationalities stood to gain from his death, I don't know where we'd start. But the connection to WPC Baker puts us way ahead, sir. The killers may have seen this thing with X-3 as an afterthought, tacked on to the main event. A way of getting her into trouble. Diverting suspicion. But it gives us a priceless lead.'

'So who are you looking for? Someone she's served with out there? Ties in with the tip-off that our guy was an arsey squaddie.'

'Yes, it does. He'd certainly have to know about bomb-making and he'd have to have had access to the secure bit in Camp Bastion where the evidence was stored.'

'And he'd have to be gutted over the Dog Tart giving him the heave-ho . . .'

'There was someone,' Ned said tentatively. It was a long shot. But there was an explosives expert who'd served with her. Who really liked her. Colonel Sillitoe, the senior Royal Military Police officer in Camp Bastion had told Ned that this man had proposed to WPC Baker. They had just got away with their lives from some hairy incident with booby-trap bombs.

Fatso's eyes narrowed.

'How did they know where this bomb factory was?'

Ned said they'd had a tip-off.

'So where is this bloke who wanted to marry the Dog Tart?'

Fatso spoke as if his permission would be needed before anyone could marry the Dog Tart. Our Dog Tart.

'In hospital, here in the UK. He was wounded the other day and they flew him back. We've checked with Colonel Sillitoe, and there's no way this man Ellison could have been the man in the Brecon Beacons who placed or triggered the bomb. He has a rock-solid alibi. But he could have known and sympathised with the bombers sufficiently to supply them with X-3. Sympathised with their aim of killing Mike Ridley and his poppy and lab eradication plan stone dead. And they'd need to have trusted him. It's a long shot, but Tom Ellison does tick some of the boxes. He knows all about bombs. He was in charge of the raid on the bomb factory. He knew which things WPC Baker had touched. He could have gained access to the secure store. And he really liked her.'

'When you seeing him?'

'Today, sir. On my way to Afghanistan to ask Kate Baker in person who it is who's got such a grudge against her that they'd go to these lengths. She must know . . .'

There was a long pause. Fatso was looking very serious. No longer like a little boy listening to a bedtime story, but a wise old boar. Wise, and worried.

'I reckon you've done brilliantly, Ned the Yid, working that lot out. I don't know if this Ellison is your man, or if it's someone else. You'll find that out. But remember me saying about you bonking the bomber?'

Ned smiled and nodded ruefully.

'Well I was wrong about that. But I wasn't all wrong. I don't mean to upset you, Ned, talking about this but we've got to face the facts. Of course, the Dog Tart may not have slept with him. She may have told him where to get off. But, either way, someone dangerous has got it bad. Got it very bad.'

Fatso was now doing the thinking and the talking. Ned was doing the listening.

'Don't assume, Ned, all this jerking around with X-3 is just to shaft the Dog Tart. Because it only took her seconds to prove to us that she had nothing to do with the bombing. As innocent as she is gutsy, our Dog Tart. Except she's got someone all worked up and wild. And she may not now be his only target. Given that, him blowing X-3 up from inside and then carefully placing it behind a tree where it makes you come over all sussy, starts looking less like a cock-up and more like a plan.'

Ned started to see where Fatso was going.

'Supposing, Ned, he comes on to her and she tells him straight out she isn't interested . . . that there's this bloke back home she's got the major hots for, blah blah blah? What then? Who's he going to have it in for now, eh? It may be this fellow you're off to see in hospital, but it may not. You watch your back out in Afghanistan, Ned. Could be a trap to get you out there. Watch your bleeding back.'

*   *   *

It had taken a little while to find him. It helped to know he was now Captain Tom Ellison, not Lieutenant. It was a hospital for civilians as well as soldiers, but the deeper Ned went, the more military it became. More uniforms. Fewer and fewer patients over forty. Greater sense of order and discipline. Less lounging about. Ned passed a packed day room – lecture in progress. Down one corridor, brave men with limbs missing were getting used to prosthetics, crutches and wheelchairs. Down another, Ned was overtaken by a miniature radio-controlled helicopter, followed by a son on his way to see Dad. Ned watched as he flew it into a ward, forcing the nurses to duck but landing it neatly on the end of his RAF father's bed. Much laughter and clapping.

For a while two mothers with babies in strollers walked ahead of Ned. Women who had evidently got to know one another because their husbands were in adjacent beds. Smartly dressed, hair shining, an effort made. They turned off into a ward where things seemed fairly hushed and serious, with bleepy machines and closed curtains. In a side corridor, a young woman and a young man, both in dressing-gowns, kissed like lovers in a film. Coming towards Ned, a couple in their fifties, in tears, holding on to one another. Parents of a patient in a poor way? Oh dear, thought Ned. Bugger this for a game of soldiers.

Sister said Captain Ellison was doing very well. They'd spent a while taking bomb fragments out of him, and sorting out the burns on his arms and face, but nothing terrible. He'd been very lucky. Amazing, really. They'd probably discharge him next week. You'll find him in the bed in the far left corner. By the window.

He didn't look bad at all. His arms were bandaged, and there were dressings on his neck and left cheek, but Ned recognised him instantly as the sunny-faced man he'd seen jump out of the truck and pet Jiffy when Kate returned from Gollum with Easy Patrol. Ellison didn't know Ned from Adam.

'Remember getting back that day – but didn't notice you there, sir. Sorry. It's sort of hard to see anyone else when you're near her.'

Tell me about it, Tom.

'She wasn't with you the day this happened to you, I gather?'

When Jan Span had phoned Sillitoe to find out where Ellison was, and heard he'd caught a side swipe from an IED, the first question she'd asked was not how Ellison was, but if WPC Kate Baker was OK? The colonel had said he'd ring round and get back to her. Jan made sure she did not see Ned while Sillitoe was checking. Knew he'd tell instantly that something was up. She didn't know what she'd do if she had to tell him anything had happened to Kate. Sillitoe called back within ten minutes. Baker was fine. She'd been assigned to Charlie Patrol. They hadn't gone out that day. Jan Span nearly broke into song.

'No. In fact I didn't see very much of her after that yukky day in Gollum. Not for want of trying, but some pen-pusher re-jigged the dog teams – the way they do when things are going well. Charlie Patrol got Kate and Jiffy, and I got this lot.'

Ned asked what exactly had happened to him. Ellison shrugged. He didn't much want to talk about it, not because it was upsetting, but because he was the sort of person who likes to look forward. No good living in the past in my racket, he said. Otherwise, you go through life with a hundred near-misses sitting on your shoulder. Bad for business, doing that. Fine to remember the lessons from the past. They're often what saves your life, but best forget the fear and the grief. If you can. Anyway . . .

'We were on a shout near Shuga patrol base. Three clicks from FOB Jackson. The path went through a clutch of dead-looking trees. All eyes were on the undergrowth for tripwires and nasties. Well, there was a tripwire, but it was in the air, slung between branches.

'The dishdashas had rigged it up so we'd swipe it with our antennae. You know, these days we're all bristling with them. And swipe it I did. It was the first one of these we'd met. Patrols now have someone looking up as well as down if there are buildings or trees about . . .

'Well, we were jammy sods. They'd placed the IED about five metres before the tripwire – maybe they expected us to come the other way – and we reckon it was slack. Maybe a branch had got dislodged. Because by the time I'd snagged it, I was maybe eight metres from the blast, was half-turned and it wasn't a big bang anyway, thank God . . . My backpack got the worst of it, plus I had full body armour on, and a day sack over my shoulder. Midge Murray was twenty paces behind me and he must've sensed something because I heard him yell out, and the boys all hit the deck. They were fine; Midge took some frags, but he's OK. They patched him up out there. So . . . How can I help you, Chief Inspector?'

Ned explained that he was investigating the so-called Brecon Bombing and that what he wanted to discuss was subject to the Official Secrets Act. Captain Ellison said he understood. He suddenly looked a little pained, which confused Ned until he realised Ellison's pillows needed some adjustment. That done, Ned went on.

'I want to ask you about the Nad 'Ali bomb factory.'

Ellison thought and nodded. What did he want to know?

'What were you told about the operation beforehand?'

'I was briefed early that morning by Intelligence. They'd had a tip-off about a suspected bomb-factory in Nad 'Ali, that the Royal Gurkha Rifles would be providing our escort and that we should expect to be opposed. I was also told that the fact we were acting on a tip-off had to remain a secret. It was no good steaming straight in there. We had to make it look as arbitrary as possible. It was left to me how.'

'And how did you?'

'Midge and I stood in the street and put on an "eeny, meeny, miney, mo" show. Then we hit the factory.'

'Did someone from Intelligence go with you?'

Ellison shook his head and smiled.

'No. No takers there. Apparently they reckoned it would give the game away if one of them was recognised. I said to Midge and Kate that if there was a danger of that then the jig was up – I mean, if the Taliban were recognising individual Intelligence officers . . .'

And he shook his head again.

'What's Nad 'Ali like?'

'It's meant to be a bit of a showcase. You know, look what we've done for the Afghan people: a new bazaar, a big push by DFID to support local farmers, and the PRT – the Provincial Reconstruction Team – backing a community council, cash-for-work programmes and all that. But the truth is, Nad 'Ali is a tip. A deeply unhealthy tip. West Belfast with minarets on. We nicked the old livestock market and built a fortress there to give ourselves some defensible space – and the Tali-Tubbies kick the shit out of it on a regular basis. Nowhere's safe in Nad 'Ali. We hate going in to places like that. Snipers. Car bombs. Ambushes up side alleys. Rocket attacks from rooftops. And none of the locals thank us. The Army put us all through a "Pashto for Beginners" class. You can guess the kind of thing: "Hullo – I am a British soldier, I am your friend. We are here to help you." And then Midge Murray pipes up from the back: "Sir, what's the Pashto for 'Please could you stop trying to kill us'?"'

Ned couldn't help smiling.

'And how was Nad 'Ali that day?'

'Here's the thing. It was dead quiet. There was one lad who legged it as we pulled up. He'd been standing in the doorway of the shop opposite where the bomb factory was. A grocer's or something. The Gurkhas chased him for a bit, but he got clear. Might have been totally innocent; after all, often we show up and bullets fly. It's sensible to make yourself scarce even if you've done nothing. After that, we kept expecting the shit to hit the fan. But no. No shit. No fan.'

A nurse put her head round the door. Did they want a cup of tea? Yes please. Bit of a delay while that was sorted out. Then, back to that dream holiday destination, Nad 'Ali.

'How do you generally read it when you arrive somewhere and the place is deserted?'

'That the locals have been tipped off. That we are about to get some incoming.'

Ned told Ellison he'd been in the Ops Room when Easy Patrol

went into Gollum. Ah, yes, said Ellison, sipping his tea, the *Marie Celeste*-car bomb combo.

'How unusual is it for you to pitch up somewhere, find there's no one about, but *nothing* happens?'

Ellison raised his eyebrows and thought hard. He couldn't actually remember it ever happening – apart from that time in Nad 'Ali with Kate and Jiffy. They sat and drank their tea for a bit. Then Ned asked if Ellison knew anything about how these tip-offs came in? No, he didn't. Did it necessarily mean there were informers or moles in the insurgents' ranks? No, it could mean that they'd bugged a phone or read an email or intercepted a radio message. There was a lot of that going on. Stuff being monitored all the time. They often had an Afghan interpreter with them to give a running translation of Taliban radio traffic. The chief inspector would have to ask Intelligence how they got the bomb factory address. Though he probably wouldn't get an answer . . .

'So then you grabbed the stuff and left?'

Ellison finished his tea and nodded.

'WPC Kate Baker said you told the driver to "drive it like you stole it".'

Ellison laughed. He didn't remember his exact words. But that would have been the gist. They'd got what they'd come for. Best to foxtrot oscar sharpish after that.

'Is it true, Chief Inspector, that the only fingerprints found on the electronics from the bomb factory were Kate's?'

Something like that, said Ned, unimpressed by security within Camp Bastion. Intrigued by Ellison raising the subject himself.

'Really odd, isn't it? I mean, you'd expect them to wipe everything clear of prints before using them – though they don't always – but apparently these were all absolutely clean. Even bits and pieces lying around on the workbenches . . .'

Yes, Ned agreed. It was a bit odd.

Either Ellison was clean, or he was dangerous.

'How much do you know, Captain Ellison, about WPC Baker?'

'Enough to know she can't have had a thing to do with the

bombing of the Defence Minister. For starters, she was with us that day. On a particularly grotty shout at the village of Kariz south of Lash . . . Lashkar Gāh. The RMP quizzed us about all this. Don't know what they thought – that Kate had dodged back home for the weekend to bump off the Minister? Well, she hadn't. And the idea of her doing anything to harm her country . . . whoever could suggest that plainly doesn't know her. She and Jiffy played an absolute blinder in Kariz. A claymore had just killed one Welsh Guardsman and smashed up another. Plus – it turned out – there were three IEDs that the Vallon didn't pick up on at all, but which Jiffy and Kate found, one after the other. Under sporadic fire, in the dust and heat. And she found time in the middle of it all to get the wounded man to safety. I told the Provost Marshal, I asked her there and then to marry me . . .'

So . . . The day Ellison proposed to Kate was the day the Minister was killed. No time, then, for rejection to fester into revenge.

'And what did she say?'

'She said she couldn't. She said there was someone else. And then she picked Jiffy up and gave him a great big hug. Well, I didn't feel so bad after that.'

Captain Ellison laughed self-deprecatingly. Then looked into Ned's eyes.

'She was only being kind. There must be someone. Couldn't not be, really. Could there . . .?'

Best dodge that question, Ned reckoned. Not least because he no longer knew the answer to it himself.

The two men, total strangers really, sat for a while in silence with their cold tea. In a corner of a drab ward, connected by a visceral ache for the same woman. A woman neither could quite grasp.

Ned broke the silence. Anything to get the last image of *Casablanca* out of his mind, in which he and Ellison as Humphrey Bogart and Claude Rains walk across the runway after watching Kate fly off with Paul Henreid.

'Who would have known that the only person on the spot to handle the Nad 'Ali electronics haul was WPC Baker?'

Ellison snapped to it, grateful for the question.

'All of us in Easy Patrol. The Gurkhas who were covering us. The Weapons Intelligence Section guys who took the stuff off us, and whoever dusted it for fingerprints. That's about it, I'd have thought.'

'Could someone have been watching you in Nad 'Ali? And seen WPC Baker carrying out the triggers and things in her hands?'

Ellison raised his eyebrows. That hadn't occurred to him. Possibly. Like he'd said, it was dead quiet. Suspiciously so. The Gurkhas hadn't spotted anyone dicking them; they're all very alert to attack from above. But there were buildings on all sides, and if someone was dressed dark and standing well back from the window . . . maybe. It was possible.

Could Ned ask one more favour? Given that he had a captive IED expert there? Would Captain Ellison take a look at a sketch map of a crime scene where an IED had been used to blow up a car? Ned wasn't going to tell him which incident this was, or when. It could be theoretical. Sure. Ellison would be happy to. Ned showed him the map with the position of the explosives, the trees, the road, the fox and where the trigger unit X-3 was found. Did Captain Ellison see anything wrong?

Ned knew from Major Butterman what the professional's answer to this was, but he wanted to know how Ellison would handle the question. If he was guilty, would his face give anything away? Would he try to throw Ned off by saying it looks wrong at first sight, but stuff lands in some strange places when bombs go off?

Captain Ellison looked at it for a while before answering.

'This looks really unlikely, Chief Inspector. I don't know who drew your sketch-map for you, but they must have made a mistake . . .'

And he explained why, exactly as Butterman had done. And did it in a totally guileless way. It was looking more and more likely that Ellison was innocent. Ned thanked him for his time, and hoped he'd make a swift recovery.

'Bloody better, Chief Inspector. I've got to be back in Helmand before the end of the month. My sort are a bit thin on the ground. No excuse for skiving accepted. Besides. I miss the guys. By the way, have you heard anything about Kate, sir? Is she OK? And Jiffy?'

'I have heard, and they're both fine.'

Captain Tom Ellison QGM smiled his sunny face, and Ned couldn't think of a better note to leave him on.

The driver looked relieved to see him. Ned had stayed longer with Ellison than planned, and it was getting late. Brize Norton was a good hour away, and Ned had a plane to catch.

He felt, without much justification, like an old hand on the flight to Kandahar. He'd only done it once before, but that was once more than the three hundred and twenty men and women of the Royal Anglian Regiment and the Royal Army Medical Corps on the Tristar with him. Their fresh, unscarred faces were a shock after the tanned, the battle-worn and the bandaged he'd just seen. On his way out of the hospital, Ned had stopped for a chat with a lad who had lost both legs to an IED in Sangin. He was having a rest after pounding up and down the Physio corridor on titanium limbs.

'You been out there, sir? I don't know what you reckon, but we think they're getting more necky, the Taliban. Pisses us off a bit, fighting people who bury crap where you're going to walk and won't face you. Won't look you in the eye. Still, if the Afghans waltzed into Dagenham, we'd do the same to them. And worse.

'I'm a lucky sod, I am. My mate Stevo was killed in the blast. He'd just heard he'd become a dad for the second time. And look at these chancers. There's six of us been doing our exercises down this corridor, and all we got between us is . . . four legs and – how many arms you got exactly, Squawker? – eight and a half arms. The British Army's going to cream the world at the next Paralympics . . .'

After that, Ned almost didn't want to catch the eyes of the soldiers on the plane. A lance corporal smiled nervously as she sat down next to him. Face full of freckles, close-cropped ginger hair, Medical Corps flashes. Forget feeling jumpy about going to war; it turned out she'd never flown before. Her mum had put together a pack for her. There was another one for the flight back which her dad had provided: full of sweeties, perfume and a forbidden miniature of vodka. Her mum's had moisturiser, a rehydrating spray, tissues, wet wipes, a bottle of Rescue Remedy – in case she felt anxious, a herbal antidote to reduce the effects of jet-lag, some socks and an eye-mask. 'Bit of a fusser, my mum,' she said, and proceeded to apply/swallow/wear the entire contents before take-off. Apart from the tissues. She slept like a log, unlike Ned.

For the first time since he had clapped eyes on her, Ned was dreading seeing Kate. With what he knew now, there were questions he was going to have to ask her he wouldn't have much cared to ask a stranger. Hard to see a happy ending for their relationship on the far side of that conversation. In normal circumstances he'd have taken Jan Span with him, but Helmand Province wasn't normal. She'd offered to go with him, of course. That was the sort of brave and considerate person she was. He'd mulled it over for a moment or two, but didn't want Kate to think the interview was any more formal than the one they'd had on his first visit to Camp Bastion. And there was something else: he didn't want Kate to think he'd brought Jan along so he didn't have to face her alone. He had to see her alone. For the two of them, never mind the case.

The case. The case was something else, beyond the way circumstances and chance had conspired to muddle up the Brecon Bombing with the most important relationship of his life. Or, if Fatso turned out to be right, the relationship *and* his life.

Early hours of the morning. Ned had barely slept. The engine note changed and the Tristar started to bank. The tannoy blared. Helmet and body armour time. Kandahar here we come. The freckly medic grinned at Ned as they struggled. He grinned back in a fatherly way. Then the descent and its accompanying pitch-darkness, with triple engines roaring behind them. He felt his forearm gripped. Then gripped tighter. Freckles must be petrified. He thought for a moment, then put his free hand over hers. What did it matter? It was dark. No one could see. Her fingers relaxed a little below his, until a clunky touchdown made her lock on tight again until the plane taxied for long enough for it to be obvious it was down for good. Then she eased her hand out from under his. He made a decision not to catch her eye, but when the lights came on she tapped his shoulder and mouthed 'thank you' at him. She had done a pretty good job with the tissues, but he could tell she'd been crying.

An hour or so milling about and Ned caught the Hercules to Camp Bastion.

Ned spent the one hour flight thinking about when and how he'd make contact with Kate.

Of course, he'd first have to find his billet, and grab some breakfast. And there'd be Colonel Sillitoe to check in with. Then there was some stuff about Nad 'Ali he wanted to sort out. And he hadn't had much of a sleep. He'd want to get an early night. Perhaps he'd leave seeing her till tomorrow. Apart from anything else, it would give him a chance to work out how to put it all to her. That he knew there was someone else. That he believed this someone else was directly tied in to the bombing in the Brecon Beacons. That it seemed to him that she was in a vulnerable position, as a result of rebuffing this person's attentions. That Fatso thought the man might even have it in for Ned. And they'd have to be able to talk about all this as two professionals, and put everything else behind them. Whatever their relationship had been, and whatever it had presumably become . . . reduced to, now wasn't the time to go into all that. They'd have to park their personal feelings until he'd done his job. And what she had to do was not to get emotional but answer his questions as dispassionately as possible, because that was the only way he'd be able to get through this and solve the crime. That they'd both be able to get through this.

There. Bit pompous in places, but it made sense. It was a plan.

Always good to have a plan. But he mustn't appear to be judgemental. Or jealous. Or angry. And he didn't have rights. He had duties, sure, as a detective investigating a triple murder, but he had no rights. Not where Kate was concerned. He must remember not to say this in a way that made it sound as if he thought he did. He knew he sometimes did this. Was very clever in working out what his position ought to be, but in explaining it somehow let slip that really he felt a load of other stuff as well. Or perhaps that should be instead.

Maybe the answer was just to be totally professional. He could do that. He was good at that. Being detached. Cool. Not letting his work get to him. Simply a job. That was it. He had come to Afghanistan purely in the exercise of his job. Anything he had to ask WPC Kate Baker was in direct consequence of his professional responsibilities. That was the start and end of it. Calm. Collected. Mature. Focussed. Totally focussed. Good.

The burly Marines on either side of Ned did not grip his forearms as the great transport plane executed a slack corkscrew out of the heavens down on to the third busiest British airport after Heathrow and Gatwick. Then again, Ned made sure he crossed his arms before the descent began. The heat hit him even harder than it had done on disembarking at Kandahar. The distant hills rippled out of the haze hanging over the Dasht-e Margo. It was the view Carrie Anne had asked him if he'd seen, stretching from military order in the foreground into the lawless distance.

He was carried along in the herd of Marines crossing the runway. Huge, hollow clatter of boots. No talking. Then orders bellowed. Forming up. Muster. Away. Ned was alone by the time he saw in the distance the ISO where he'd reported the first time he arrived in Camp Bastion. Ah. Someone's come to meet me, he thought. Through the dust mirage shimmer he saw a slight figure step forward from the shade of the converted container as he drew nearer. One of Sillitoe's lot? Probably. Then the figure started to walk towards him. And he saw who it was and quickened his step. And soon he was running. Into

Kate's arms. He forgot the plan. He forgot everything except that he adored her.

They stood entwined, in blinding heat, in the middle of an army base at war and the only thing he lacked was one of Freckles's tissues.

10

THE FIRST THING KATE TOLD Ned, as they sat facing one another on camp beds in his tent, was that she had fallen in love with someone. His name was Hamid Hassani. She didn't feel sorry. She didn't feel foolish. She didn't feel bad. She did feel very sad because she knew it would hurt Ned. But there it was.

She didn't tell Ned that Hamid was very beautiful, very sexy and very exciting. That the instant she saw him, she felt a strange thing, very hard to describe. Like the most intense sensation of circuits switching on with huge force. She had never felt it before.

She did say that the first time they met, they barely spoke. Moments later, he was gone. She felt devastated. Exhausted. She got in touch with him. Sent him a message. They met, and she spent two days with him. She said to Ned she was not going to talk to him about those two days, because they had nothing to do with him.

Privately, she thought that in some way she had been very slightly mad during those two days. Mad to go with Hamid Hassani. Mad with desire for Hamid Hassani. She might talk to Ned about it at some point in the future. When she could look back on it more clearly. And when – and if – she and Ned were really together again.

Kate stopped talking, and Ned didn't start. He thought about his first trip to Camp Bastion. Making love to her. Wading through all

229

that compo carbonara. And she thought about when she'd first told Jamila about Hamid.

'Not Ned . . . I don't mean Ned. It's someone else. Someone new.'
    Jamila hid her surprise successfully.
'So? And who is the gentleman?'
They were in the training area, exercising Jiffy with a tennis racquet and ball, so the conversation was more fragmented than it might have been. Frustrating for Jamila, agreeable for Kate who was in love and was taking pleasure in choosing the words to talk about it. And being careful not to say anything old Sillitoe would send her to the Tower of London for revealing.
'He's . . . good, Jiffy. Good dog . . . stay . . . fetch! He's called . . . Hamid. He's gorgeous, Jamila, and very gentle. Very considerate. Very romantic. He thinks about me. And I think about him. Most of the time!'
Jiffy bounded back and dropped the ball at Kate's feet and sat. Kate gave him a pat and then smashed the ball away again. Her eyes were dancing when she looked back at Jamila.
'He is not married, in case you are wondering. He has his own business. And a really lovely house out in the desert. An old hunting lodge, full of beautiful things. And he's got horses and a dog and an amazing falcon.'
Jamila looked impressed.
'What's his name?'
'Hamid Hassani.'
Jamila shook her head. The name meant nothing to her. And did he speak English? Could they have a proper conversation? It was always the abstract things that were hard to talk about in another language. Or weren't they talking abstracts yet? Kate giggled and said they were. They talked about all sorts of things. His English was good. He had been to Britain. She thought he'd studied there for a bit. And America. So, Jamila wondered, it was for Hamid that Kate had written the landay? Not Ned? No. Not Ned. Hamid. And Kate whacked the ball into the distance.

They walked back to the kennels in silence. Then on to the laundry. Kate was lost in her happiness; Jamila was worried. She waited until they were sitting alone out the back with glasses of mint tea before trying to talk to Kate about it. Jamila obviously didn't know this man, but . . . the trouble was, so many men were not very nice. And it was difficult for foreigners to read the signs. She was sure that even with her own good English, if she and Kate were in the UK, Jamila might meet someone she thought was great, but Kate would have the instincts to see beyond. There'd be warning bells only someone local would hear. She didn't want to pour cold water over Kate. She only wanted to make sure Hamid was as lovely as Kate said he was. As lovely as she deserved.

Kate felt herself redden. A little with anger, a little with embarrassment. It was a bit like a grown-up offering to go to the lavatory with you when you've been going by yourself for years. She liked Jamila a lot. Loved her, really. But Kate knew what she was doing. Apart from anything else, she knew – but couldn't tell anyone – that Hamid was a super-brave secret agent risking his own life and saving the lives of others for Britain. For Kate's own country. So she couldn't tell Jamila that he had been checked out thoroughly by the best in the business and had passed with flying colours.

And then there were Kate's own instincts. Her personal bullshit detectors. How he treated animals – a critical test for everyone she came into contact with. How Hamid was with Baba Nazar and Khalida. How he was with her. In bed. Things, looks, touches that can't be faked. After they had made love. The next morning. How he had held her after Shukria snatched the hare. How they fitted together, as equals. How he had said goodbye to her. The landay he had written for her on a scrap of ancient parchment:

> *To live twin lives of danger apart*
> *Or be together: safe, alive and aglow – you choose!*

It was a hell of an offer. Kate hadn't thought through its practical implications. No need to yet. There was plenty of time for that. The point was, Hamid had recognised that something had come along for both of them that seemed to trump the amazing, risky, fulfilling lives they already had. Being with him seemed a whole lot less dangerous than what she did every time she left the gates of Camp Bastion with Jiffy and the guys. And a whole lot more exciting. And he was asking her, not telling her. *You choose!*

His landay made sense of what she had felt when they had first met. Made sense of the landay she had texted him. It was an outrageous thing to tell a stranger, to explore her hidden places. But it wasn't outrageous to tell Hamid. It was an honest, necessary thing, because it was what she felt about him. It reminded Kate of an old film from the war she'd watched with her Nan years ago. When a beautiful WAAF takes a brave Spitfire pilot in her arms – and presumably into her bed, although they didn't show that in those days – because he could be dead tomorrow and so could she. The threat of death could make you do something you shouldn't because it muffles your doubts. Or it could be like taking the lift rather than climbing the stairs. You know you're going to the top floor. Why waste time walking? Cut the crap. Get where you both want to be, quick.

Kate grinned. What did she have to lose? Hamid would pass any test, she knew it. There was nothing to worry about. What information did Jamila need? Jamila looked relieved, and patted Kate's arm. Anything more she knew about him. An address? Kate thought hard. The place she went to with him was in the hills, about two or three hours away. She didn't know where it was exactly. But due south of here. She was sure of that.

'And did you have an escort? That's . . . what is the word? In America, they say . . . badlands.'

Kate shook her head. They just went. In an old jeep. That's how they were, she thought to herself. They just did things. Stuff the rest of the world.

Strange, thought Jamila. You don't go down there unless you are crazy. Or untouchable. But she didn't say anything.

'Anything else you remember?'

'He has these two servants. They've been with him forever. He's called Baba Nazar, and she's Khalida. They're married. And devoted to Hamid.'

Jamila nodded. The names meant nothing to her, but she'd ask Parween. And Hossai's lover, the schoolteacher Saleh. He knew lots of people. And of course her brother Zabiullah, who was coming to drop off some laundry-workers and pick her up. If the car was empty on the way back she'd ask him if he knew anything about this Hamid. They finished their tea. Time to go. And then after Kate and Jamila kissed goodbye, Kate held on to her hand for a fraction.

'You *are* right, Jamila. If it were the other way round, and we were in the UK in the middle of a horrible war and you'd fallen in love, I'd think someone has to watch your back. Particularly if I thought you weren't in a fit state to. Thank you.'

And Kate kissed her again and went back to the kennels to feed Jiffy.

There were other people in the car with them, and Zabiullah dropped her off first, so Jamila didn't get a chance to ask him about Hamid Hassani. The house was empty apart from Fazl who was back from school with his cousin, Parween's son Mohad. Jamila went into the kitchen and started to prepare the evening meal. She sat at the table chopping onions and grating carrot, thinking. It wasn't a good sign, this long drive south with only the two of them in a jeep. How long had it taken? Two or three hours, Kate had said. Say, thirty, forty miles an hour. They must have gone perhaps a hundred miles. Jamila knew that road from years ago, when she was young. She'd never take it today unless she had to. Along the Helmand River, through 'Aynak and Baykhan Khalay, down to Kartakah. Her father's family came from Kartakah. But that couldn't be more than fifty miles away.

They went twice as far. The river curves right . . . where is that? . . . at Alimardan Khan-e Bagat. But there is a track which continues south, into the Chāgal Hills. That's almost on the Baluchistan border. Who has a house there? Hamid Hassani, that's who. But who *is* he?

She started cutting red peppers in half and removing the seeds. That thought of hers before, that you'd have to be crazy or untouchable to do that drive without an escort, how true was it? The crazy bit was, obviously. But was anyone so untouchable to everyone? Not likely. It wasn't something you'd gamble your life and your beloved's on. Then the dogs barked in the yard and her sister Parween and Hossai came in with their little daughters. For a moment all was forgotten in cuddles and lemonade and sugar almonds. Then the girls went off to play and Jamila asked Parween and Hossai the question that was troubling her, without mentioning Kate.

Neither woman knew of Hamid Hassani. Hossai said it was probably a good thing. Meant he wasn't notorious, but Parween wasn't sure. She too was surprised by the hunting lodge and the drive there through wild, bandit country. And when would Hossai be seeing her lover, the handsome Saleh? Ah. The Little Horror was going away tomorrow. To Kabul. He'd be gone several days. So she hoped she might see Saleh tomorrow night. If Parween could have Sharifa to stay over. Parween would be delighted to. And then there were peppers to stuff and *pulao* to make and Hamid Hassani was forgotten. For two whole days.

Saleh knew something. The others drew a blank. But Hossai talked to Saleh, and he said he'd had been to university with a Hamid Hassani who came from somewhere down south. He had remembered him, because his family had been royal falconers. From way back. This Hassani had once asked Saleh to spend a weekend with him in their home, which apparently had been one of the King's hunting lodges. He hadn't gone. It was too far, and the journey wasn't safe. The fighting was pretty intense then.

Kabul University closed down not long after and Saleh didn't see Hassani again. He had heard something about him going to Britain. After that, nothing. One lost touch with so many people.

It's a start, thought Jamila. But it doesn't add up to much. Could she talk to Saleh herself? This wasn't going to be easy for Hossai to arrange. The Little Horror was due back that same day, and she didn't know when she'd be seeing Saleh again. Was it very urgent? Would it keep? No, it wouldn't. Jamila told Hossai not to worry. She knew another way to get in touch with Saleh.

It wasn't appropriate for single women to meet single men in public, and Jamila – although she cared little for misogynist convention – did not want to draw any attention. Especially given his affair with Hossai; she didn't want it to look as if she were acting as Hossai's go-between. And then there was Hamid Hassani. Best proceed fearing the worst. But Saleh was a schoolteacher, and Jamila had been into his school to talk to the children about landmines. What was more natural than that she should visit the headmaster before break to discuss another visit?

The head had long since given up being surprised by anything, and was pleased to see Jamila. Yes, it was high time she came back. There was a new class since she'd last been, and it wouldn't hurt the older years to hear it again. Apparently two children had been killed in Wazirian three days ago on the bare ground between the irrigation channels. Had Jamila heard? Yes. She had . . .

The head droned on, with Jamila desperate not to let Saleh slip away. She could see down the main school corridor through the pane of glass in the head's door, and the bell had already sounded. A tidal wave of children was cascading towards the far exit, sweeping up teachers in the rush. Had Saleh come out of his class yet? No, headmaster, I agree. It is the sports that are suffering most . . . Is that Saleh? Yes, headmaster, there is a campaign to clear the sports fields, but it all takes time – oh! Sorry. Must run! Just seen someone I need to speak to about getting some overhead slides made . . . Jamila dived into the tumult as Saleh bobbed away into the distance, leaving the headmaster unfazed. He was as used to hasty departures as to unexpected arrivals.

The next bit was daring, but quite clever. They could have gone into a classroom to talk like teacher and parent, except that Fazl went to another school. It would look suspicious. So they went outside in plain sight and sat on the bench a discreet distance apart surrounded by children playing, eating, arguing. From time to time he broke up a fight, and from time to time she'd pass him a piece of paper which he would study and then hand back. To an observer it would look as if Saleh was on playground duty, and Jamila was getting his help in planning a new talk about the danger of landmines. In fact, he was telling her a worrying story, and she was doing her damnedest not to look worried.

Ever since Jamila's friend – he didn't use Hossai's name – had asked him about a certain person, Saleh had been thinking. At the time, he couldn't remember what the person had studied at Kabul. One of the sciences. Then it came to him. Chemistry. He was studying chemistry and he was one of the top students. Saleh had looked at home and found his university year book, with a little piece about each of them – and a photo. The one of this man showed him with a falcon on his wrist and an older man standing behind. His father Nazar.

'You're sure it was his father, this Nazar?'

That was what the caption said.

Hmm. Why, Jamila wondered to herself, would he pretend that Baba Nazar was his servant, not his father?

Saleh had become intrigued. What had happened to him, this rather brilliant, dashing, intriguing man he'd once known slightly? There was someone he could ask. A friend who had been at Kabul University with them, who then went into the police. He was quietly doing well, in the reptile pit of Helmand Province's police authority. They met now and again anyway. What more natural than to have lunch with his old pal and talk about old times?

As so often in Afghanistan, Jamila thought, it all depended on knowing people. And getting the answer to an important – maybe subversive – question often required a number of people to go 'undercover'. To tell a little lie. To take a little chance. Jamila handed Saleh another innocent piece of paper.

'I talked about loads of people to my old pal,' Saleh went on. 'Taking another look at that yearbook put a bunch of names into my mind. I had to make sure I didn't appear to remember too much. I hope I did OK. About halfway through, I dropped the name of a certain person. Big response. Not like any of the others. My old pal raised his eyes and touched his finger to his lips. I thought he was going to look over both shoulders, like in a spy movie. He certainly looked uneasy. But he also looked a bit excited. Like you do when you're about to spill a secret. "Didn't I know?" he asked. "Hadn't I heard? Where had I been that I didn't know about Ha . . . about this certain person?"

'If they don't have children in my school, I replied, then I don't know anything. I didn't press him for an answer to my question, but he went straight on. Like I said, excited.'

'"Well," my pal the policeman said. "You remember that this certain person was brilliant at chemistry? After Kabul he went to Birmingham University in England and then to Southern California. To San Diego, on the border with Mexico. Then there's a time gap of about three, four years. A blank. And then we start to hear things. About someone who's cornered the market in importing certain chemicals into Afghanistan. Someone now very, very rich. Someone with such powerful friends that no one will lay a finger on him, because his supplies are always on time, guaranteed quality, good price – even though he barely has any competition."'

Saleh had to get up at this point to separate two gangs of boys fighting around, and maybe over, the drinking fountain. Importing chemicals? Jamila asked herself. Sounds pretty innocent. So what?

The answer to that came when Saleh sat down.

'My old pal told me that this certain person turns out to be the major supplier of chemicals to Afghanistan's drug lords. The most important and valuable is something called acetic anhydride. Thanks to him, these drug lords don't have to sell the opium cheap at the resin stage, letting foreigners do the processing and make the big profits. They can produce the finished heroin, here in Afghanistan. He has made a lot of very evil people a great deal richer, as well as himself. In addition to the old hunting lodge he invited me to, he now has houses in Switzerland and America. There's also a huge mansion in Kabul – in Sherpur, of course – and one here in Lashkar Gāh. At the end of Bost Sarak. One trusted source told my pal that Hamid also smuggles in materials to make explosives, for particular client groups. To make bombs that can't be detected. But my pal said nothing more was known about that, and his source was now dead.

'So,' I asked my pal, 'how does he do it, this guaranteed importing?' 'Easy,' he said. 'The person knows the latest science, has the necessary contacts outside the country, plus he has special ways of moving the chemicals in. Old routes through the mountains. Overland, and also by air, using hidden airstrips no one knows about. They say he doesn't touch the narcotics once they are made. He doesn't do exports. But then, he doesn't need to. He'll never be able to spend the money he's made, if he lives to be a hundred. Which, my old pal the policeman says, is quite likely. He has a very few people who work for him, but no associates to betray him or steal the business away. It's really just this person and his father and mother. They're the only people he trusts in the whole world: his father who taught him all the old tracks and hiding places, and his mother who keeps his house and adores him. It isn't simply that he won't trust others . . . he likes doing things himself. It gives him a kick. He might drive the tanker, or fly the plane, or slit a throat. That's why the drug lords he deals with trust him. Because he takes care of the whole package.

'Now,' said my pal. 'Best never mention this person ever again, Saleh. Safest for you and for me. He has the scariest friends in Afghanistan. But none as scary and as clever as he is. You know the source I mentioned? The one who is now dead? He was killed outside his home in broad daylight. Many people saw the knifeman, but strangely no one could remember anything about him. Except, according to one woman, he was handsome like a movie star.'

Jamila noticed that, as he related all this to her, Saleh often spoke with his hand in front of his mouth, his fingers rolled into a loose fist as if he had a cough. He did it so discreetly that it was only later she realised he was doing it to thwart lip readers. And she also realised that, as Saleh had handed her back a couple of the lecture sheets she had passed to him, he'd managed to slip between them a page from his university yearbook. With the picture of the great untouchable chemicals king in his golden youth, with his falcon and his loyal retainer-father, Baba Nazar.

Jamila told no one what Saleh had said about Hamid Hassani. Not even Parween. In fact, she and Saleh agreed that, if asked, they'd say they'd just talked about Jamila's lecture, and the slides she'd need. Hamid Hassani was a dangerous man to know of. Even more dangerous to ask questions about. And to fall in love with? It didn't bear imagining.

But she had to tell Kate.

Jamila thought it would be easier to tell her that Hamid was dead. She even considered saying exactly that. No need to go into his character. No having to persuade Kate that her lover was not at all he seemed. That he was evil. That he dealt in death, and did so in a cultivated, elegant way. As if, like one of his own falcons, he were flying over it at such a great height that its stench did not reach his nostrils. It would have been easier. But Jamila had to tell her the truth.

It was a week or so before she had the chance. Kate came into Lashkar Gāh with a PRT team and a group of servicewomen from different branches: a pilot, a doctor, a firefighter, a driver, an electrician. They met a group of Afghan women in rather artificial circumstances. Security was a big issue, and women prepared to attend were thin on the ground. But Kate shone. Jamila watched her, pouring tea and making sure everyone had some. Talking to the quietest. Involving them. Smiling that smile. Making others smile as she tried her phrases of Pashto. Looking calm and happy. Glowing with it, really, so that the people talking to her became more relaxed than any other group in the room.

When it came time for the British women to leave, Jamila almost had to tear Kate away from a cluster of local women. And what made it even more difficult was that Jamila knew what she was about to put her through. Kate had an overnight pass to stay with Jamila, and would return with the early morning shift of laundry-workers. That was another thing. Jamila knew Kate would go on duty soon after getting back to Bastion. How safe for her would it be to go out with Jiffy looking for roadside bombs, knowing what Jamila was about to tell her? Her stomach would be churning. Her mind elsewhere.

Kate did not stay all bubbly after she got into the car, much to Jamila's relief. She was dreading having to wipe that smile away. But it was gone before Jamila had even started the engine.

'You know something about Hamid, don't you?' she asked Jamila. 'I could tell, from the way you were looking at me in there. I can't bear it. Please just say it.'

'I can't stop here. It isn't safe. And I don't think I can tell you and drive. Please, Kate, please.'

And she reached out her hand and held Kate's arm, and – for all the heat – felt her shiver. They drove in silence. Like the silence when you've heard horrible news, and are going to the hospital. Or to a patch of waste ground where your husband is lying incomplete and yet finished. Jamila couldn't remember returning with Sadhar's body. Someone must have driven them back. And changed her dress, because she was covered with his blood. And washed her. Parween, perhaps. Not the least because no one else she knew could have resisted returning to it at some point in the future, albeit as self-effacingly as possible. But nevertheless reminding Jamila of the service she had done for her: the comforting, the undressing, the washing, the getting her dressed and into bed. Because that's the first thing Jamila remembered. Waking up, spotless and husbandless. Yes, it must have been Parween.

The only other person Jamila knew who'd be there for her like that, was Kate. And here was Jamila, driving like a mad thing through Lashkar Gāh, nearly cutting-up a black Toyota bristling with kohl-eyed, bearded, scary men, refusing to tell Kate what she needed to know more than anything in the world. The two women sat tight-lipped until they reached Jamila's house. They went straight up to her bedroom and closed the door.

First, Jamila passed Kate the page from the University of Kabul yearbook.

'Is this him, Kate? To make absolutely sure we are talking about the same . . .'

Kate looked at it. She ran the edge of her thumb across Hamid's face as if she were clearing enough to see her eyes in a steamed-up mirror. Then she looked up at Jamila and nodded.

Jamila told Kate everything Saleh had told her. Everything his policeman friend had told him. What the source had told the policeman friend before he was killed. The tears welled up in Kate's huge eyes, making them glisten brighter than ever, before running down her cheeks. Bigger tears than Jamila had ever seen. Jamila's grandmother once told her that it was the greatest test of a beautiful woman, if she looked beautiful when she cried.

Jamila had never really understood what her grandmother meant till then.

Ned, too, got a sense of what Jamila's grandmother was on about by the time Kate had told him all this. He reached out a hand across the divide between the two camp beds and stroked her heaving shoulder. Then he stood up and stepped outside.

241

It was dusk already. A great pink, hazy, dusty dusk, filled with the din of generators. How to handle this? Not the case, which was making a bit more sense, but Kate. Had she broken it off with Hassani? She hadn't yet said that she had. If so, how did he take it? If not, how should Ned take it? It was easy being the copper – impossible being the lover. But if this affair took place before the Brecon Bombing, then Ned and Kate had slept together since Hassani appeared on the scene. Odd. On his first trip to Camp Bastion, she had acted as if she and Ned were still a couple, carrying on where they'd left off when he drove her to Brize Norton. So either she hadn't yet met Hassani, or she had and was keeping mighty quiet about it. Except you can't fool compo carbonara. Given the first scenario, Hassani was not Ned's man for the Ridley murders. Second scenario: he was Ned's man, and Kate had no idea of it yet. Ned's man, Kate's man. Damn the man. What were the timings?

'I met him around the twelfth or thirteenth of June, Ned. Whichever the Sunday was.'

Kate looked a bit better. A bit stronger. She'd put the chunky sweater he'd brought out to her last time around her shoulders, and turned the aircon low. The tent felt warmer. Thirteenth of June? So she had met him six weeks before the bombing. Three weeks before the raid on Nad 'Ali. Was that time enough for it all to happen and turn nasty?

'The two days I spent with him at his house was a week after we first met. It was only about a week after that, that Jamila told me everything I've told you. I broke it off the next day, I think.'

She got rid of him, thought Ned. Thank fuck. Stay cool. No rowdy rejoicing.

Funny, Kate thought. I've only seen Hamid twice, ever. He was like a tsunami. Came out of nowhere, tore my life inside out, and vanished.

'And can you remember the actual date when you broke it off?'

Do the maths, girl. Think straight. When did she text Hamid the landay? Not the first one when she was on fire, but the second when she was so empty:

> *You are not the man I thought you were,*
> *So I am not a woman you'll ever see again*

It was Jamila who persuaded her to end it with a landay. She said it would strike home harder, as that was a traditional theme of landays: the rejection of men by women. Particularly for their failure to come up to the mark. It would be more powerful for Kate to stay in the Afghan idiom, rather than suddenly kissing him off like a Western woman. Kate had, after all, opened the affair with a landay; it seemed right to end it the same way. Short, sharp, unanswerable. She didn't repeat the landay to Ned. Either of the landays. Any of the landays. She had written a third she did not send, because although it said exactly what she wanted to tell him, it felt too intimate – because it referred to something Hamid had said to her in the early hours of the morning.

> *My breasts are no longer your refuge*
> *A poisoned well is no more safe for the poisoner.*

'I told him I would never see him again about ten days later. Around the end of June. By text.'

There was a silence. She looked at Ned who was sitting with eyes closed, fingertips to forehead. Bloody hell. He's working out if I was still sleeping with Hamid when he and I made love that night in my tent. Great!

But he wasn't. He was working out the chronology.

'I've got the raid on the bomb factory in Nad 'Ali as happening on the fifth of July, three weeks before the Minister was killed. Do you have any idea when the tip-off came in? It doesn't matter if not. I can always ask Sillitoe.'

Kate was about to answer when something suddenly occurred to her. She had sensed that his questions were those of a detective, not a scorned lover, but had thought that was Ned managing his own distress. Slipping into autopilot. May I ask you where you were that night, madam and all that. But that's not actually how he was sounding. He wasn't distracted. He was in lock-on. He was piecing it together. Like he did for work. Why go on about the dates? A lover would be asking how she felt about Hamid now. How she felt about the lover. A lover might be upset. Might shout. But would he want to know the dates of things? Only . . . if he was wondering if Hamid had had something to do with the Brecon Bombing. Oh, God! Was it possible . . .? The fingerprint! As if things weren't grim enough already . . .

And then, just when she was fearing he was about to tell her something really appalling, maybe that Hamid himself was the murderer, Ned did something unexpected but oddly soothing. He lay on his back on the camp bed and started to talk to her. She loved the sound of his voice. He told her about how no one had seemed to want to touch the case. About the resistance his investigation had met from the start. How Hawkins had given them the runaround. How General Collet still hadn't shown him Ridley's original document. How Collet's intelligence guy Mossman hadn't been in touch. How MI6 in the person of Captain Crispin had sent him down a blind alley by saying he should be looking for a disgruntled ex-squaddie. How a whole bunch of international Intelligence agencies had laid on a show designed to persuade him that the killer was some Pakistani religious fanatic – a show in which innocent children had probably lost their lives.

Ned then told Kate about X-3. Told her what Extra Bilge and Doc Bones had discovered. Told her where it had been found, and what Ellison and Butterman had deduced from that. He told her about Mike Ridley and the death of his daughter. About Porton Down's breakthrough, and Ridley's plan to eradicate the poppy crop, destroy the heroin laboratories and prevent precursor chemicals from entering the country. About the possibility that someone who stood to lose a great deal if Ridley did all this, had decided to stop him. And, at the last moment, decided to kill two more birds with the same stone. To embroil in the murder the woman who had rejected him, and – if Fatso was right – to lure Ned himself out to Afghanistan.

And so he didn't need to tell her that Hamid was the killer. As for the very last bit, the luring of Ned, it would have seemed like mad conspiracy theorist fantasy to her a few hours ago. But not now. She knew, after all, what she had told Hamid about Ned. Because while they were stopped on their ride for the chilled lemonade and fruit Baba Nazar had left for them, Hamid had asked her if she loved anyone else. And she told him 'there had been someone'.

When she told Ned this, Kate took care to say 'there is someone', partly because she didn't want to hurt him any more, and partly because she hoped it would become true again. But when she and Hamid were talking about it, she put Ned firmly in the past tense – so fully did Hamid occupy her present.

Yes, she had told Hamid. There had been someone. Someone she worked with. His name was Ned Bale and he was very nice, and gentle. And very clever. What did he do? Hamid wanted to know. He was a Detective Chief Inspector in a special unit that only worked on the most serious crimes. Murders, mostly. He was brilliant at working things out. Seeing hidden connections. When there was a big mystery in the UK, one no one else could solve, they got him in. Ah, said Hamid. Ned. A policeman. And then they rode away with Shukria hovering over them.

'I'm sorry, Ned. I'm really sorry.'

'It isn't any kind of problem. We don't own one another. That's why I didn't tell you not to go to Afghanistan. You have nothing to be sorry for.'

'I have. I should never have talked about you to him. The thought that he might now be gunning for you . . . it's horrible. It makes me feel so frightened . . .'

Her voice tailed away. In trying to take her mind off having put Ned in jeopardy, she remembered the other reason for apology.

'And I'm sorry because I should have told you about him when you came over. Before you and I slept together again. You had a right to know, and I carried on as if nothing had changed. I tried to treat it as if I'd had a spot, which went away before you showed up. No need to tell you: there was a spot here but now it's gone.'

Some spot, he thought, but had the wit to keep it to himself.

'In fact,' she went on, 'it was worse than that. I actually lied to you. When you were questioning me that morning in Silly Toes' office, you asked if I'd had any contacts with any Afghans. It was a horrible moment. And I only mentioned Jamila. I'm really, really sorry . . .'

Ned leaned forward across the camp bed gulf, accepted the apology with a kiss and lay back again. The lover bit of him was so bloody relieved that this Hassani bloke was no longer in her life that, inside, his heart was leaping. He adored her, and it was once again all to play for. If they could pull off the trick of getting home in one piece. Kate got up and put the kettle on.

'You haven't actually told me how you met him. It can't have been through Jamila because you said she knew nothing about him.'

No, she said. It had nothing to do with Jamila. She'd met him one night here in Camp Bastion. And she added, not by way of justification, that she had been threatened with the full force of the Official Secrets Act if she ever breathed a word to anyone about seeing him.

Ned sat bolt upright. Here in the camp? Who exactly had waved the Act under her nose?

Captain Crispin.

'Tell me, Kate, as much as you can remember about what happened that night, and about the conversation you then had with "Captain Crispin".'

So she told him what she could remember. Something about what she had seen and heard across the corridor rang an alarm bell and Ned asked her to go back over it.

'I heard voices. Maybe two or three men and a woman. One of the men had an accent. Him, I suppose.'

'And can you remember hearing anything that was said?'

Kate had to think hard. It had been fresh in her mind when she'd seen Crispin and a lot had happened since. Perhaps Crispin telling her to forget it all had had its effect.

'Something, Kate. Anything.'

She sat for a while, staring into space. The trick was to remember not what she'd told Crispin, but what she had heard that actual night.

'OK. "Operation Hedgerow" was mentioned, and "Sangsar village". Plus the words "IED" and "bombers". And the woman asked a question about "having a scramble to London" or something. Could she get one, or did they have one? Something like that. I don't remember.'

'And what sort of voice did this woman have? Any accent?'

'Posh. Head Girl.'

'And you saw her . . .'

'Yes. She bent over and picked up a small suitcase. She wasn't in uniform, but she was smartly dressed. She had a very good figure. One of those bottoms some men drool over.'

One of those bottoms . . . It couldn't be, could it? Wilton? Her of the superb rump? What had Wilton said to Ned at the crime scene? That she was there because everyone else in MI6 was glued to the tennis and she was duty muggins? Duty muggins my arse. Her arse.

'Did you talk to Hassani subsequently about what you'd seen that evening?'

Yes, she did. They hadn't dwelt on it, but it came up on the long drive to the hunting lodge. She'd asked him about the beating up. He said that someone from London had flown over at short notice to see him. He described her as 'a senior secret lady'. They hadn't had time to arrange an invisible pick-up, so an Army patrol snatched him off a street corner in Lashkar Gāh along with another man who happened to be standing around – Hassani didn't know who the man was. It was entirely random. Happened all the time. The man was only being beaten up for his own protection. So that when he was turfed out at a street corner that night he wouldn't be mistaken for an informer. It was just a bit of blood.

Or, wondered Ned, was the poor man going to pay with his life for the misfortune of seeing Hassani picked up by his British pals? No point in sharing this bleak thought with Kate . . .

'Presumably he didn't say what the reason was for the visit of this "senior secret lady"?'

No. And it hadn't occurred to Kate to ask.

'And did he say anything about the sort of things he does for Queen and country?'

'He said he provides information. Tip-offs, things like that. He said he "points out bad people".'

Hmm, Ned thought. Bad people who are then hauled away on rendition flights for interrogation, torture and incarceration in places like Guantánamo? Or like 'Ali Nizari' and his family – death by drone? And he wondered what it was that was so urgent that a senior secret lady with a drool-worthy bottom would dash out to Afghanistan at short notice? What did Hassani know that was so vital for her to hear?

Or was it the other way round?

He recalled Carrie Anne's words in the restaurant – words whose import was just starting to sink in: 'the traffickers and the spooks are in bed, entwined.' Could the woman possibly have come to tip Hassani off that the British Minister of Defence was about to scupper the precursor chemicals business in Afghanistan?

Kate could see the drained expression on Ned's face.

'I meant what I said, Ned, about being sorry.'

Desperate for anything to take his mind off the enormity of this last thought and the realisation that he'd been played for a fool on all fronts, Ned focussed on Kate's last words. He couldn't remember her ever apologising before. He tended to throw out sorries the way French kings tossed coins at beggars from their carriage windows. It had little to do with the way he'd been brought up. His mother never apologised for anything, and his father had been hopelessly permissive. No, it was like touching wood. You don't have to believe in it. You just do it to cover yourself. Sooner or later, one of the sorries would find their mark. Maybe it was more like spermatozoa than touching wood. Talking of which . . . how does one ask one's beloved if she might have anything in her possession still . . . something Extra Bilge could get a DNA sample off? Not the sort of conversation it would be easy to row away from: 'By the way, darling, have any of your undies got Hamid's semen on? They have, great! Stick them in this evidence bag and we'll go and grab a bite of supper.'

Hell's bells, Ned thought. We're never going to eat tonight, and it's got to be asked. How much worse can things get between us? So he asked.

Kate shook her head. He was hopeless at second-guessing the way she'd react.

'I've been thinking about that. The answer's no. Nothing. After Jamila told me, I put everything I wore over those two days in the camp incinerator. I didn't want any of it around. That's why I needed this chunky sweater. Sorry. Look, I'm really hungry. Do you mind if we get something to eat?'

After dinner – salad bar for her and fish, chips and mushy peas for him – they walked across the camp to Jiffy's kennel. Sometimes nothing else in life will do but a dog, and this was one of those times. And to balance out the confessions, Ned admitted that the last time he had come to Bastion he made sure he'd fingered some dog biscuits before seeing Jiffy. So he'd get a warm welcome, which he knew would stand him in good stead with the mistress. Kate said she had guessed that, because Ned had stroked her cheek and she'd smelled it. Let's see, she said, how he treats you this time. No problem, thought Ned, what with me eating chips with my fingers. And then Kate handed him a wet-wipe, and made sure he was thorough. Didn't matter a damn. Jiffy bounded out of his cage and leaped up at Ned and licked his face several times. Thank you, Jiffy, thought Ned. I need all the help I can get.

It was a clear night. They walked round the perimeter, stopping when there was any kind of gap in the Hesco barrier to peer out across the desert. Something took off from Camp Leatherhead, and then all was still and the blackness rolled back, smothering the lights on the airstrip. Kate seemed more relaxed than he had seen her for ages, and it was lovely walking Jiffy again. Which was why Ned wished one more question had not occurred to him – something he should have asked in the tent before supper, when it would simply have got lost in the general misery. Now, it would look like he was shoving her back into the swamp. Could he leave it till morning? Yes, the lover told the detective firmly. He could. And then, as they were nearing her tent, where they'd agreed platonically she would spend the night with Jiffy while Ned slept in his own tent, she sort of answered the query herself. It started with a question of her own.

'Did you guys manage to get a sample of the bomber's DNA?'

'We did. Some abseiling Welsh coppers played a blinder. And the Bilge was no slouch. Odd, really. It's a wad of chewing tobacco. *Naswar* they call it in Afghanistan. He must have been chewing it while waiting on the hillside for Ridley to show.'

Because it was night, he couldn't see the expression on her face. The worry return to her eyes. The memory of the only uncouth thing she had ever seen Hamid do.

'Hamid Hassani chewed something. He spat it out of the jeep window as we pulled up at the hunting lodge. Same again when we were riding, before we reached the shack in the hills by the old airstrip. And the way he spat, it wasn't chewing gum.'

Small wodge. Big desert. Best of luck, Chief Inspector.

Kate and Jiffy left before dawn with Charlie Patrol, leaving Ned free to ask elusive people inconvenient questions. Top of his target list was 'Captain Crispin'. First time round, the spook with the limpest handshake in history had found him. But how do you find a spook? You use a sprat to catch mackerel. Ned made his way to the Ops Room. Their day was just warming up. Patrols out. A chopper reported damaged over Yakhchal, but limping home. A shoot and scoot outside Tall Kala. Dragon Company of the US 101st Airborne in a full-on firefight in Panjva'i.

'Welcome back to the war, sir.'

The Intelligence Kid was almost unrecognisable. He looked ten years older than Ned remembered. Pale, thin. Like those undiscovered prehistoric fish they're forever discovering at the bottom of the sea that need no oxygen or light or heat or food or sex or holidays.

'Any chance of inveigling you out for a cup of coffee?'

The Kid glanced at the clock on the wall, and then at the screens before replying.

'No problem. But I must see this chopper thing through first. I've been on it since 0620. It was me who asked the Joint Tactical Air Controller for help evacuating an ambushed patrol.'

They sat like expectant fathers in the waiting room. It turned out the Sea King pilot had managed to set his machine down in a farmyard to pick up three P1s – acute wounds, and two P3s – walking wounded, which he probably shouldn't have tried. Except there was no other way of getting the men out. Plus he had medics on board. They had an Apache as escort which didn't set down but circled and kept the dishdashas' heads down during the rescue. The first reports suggested the Sea King had been hit, but no. It had tipped slightly on take-off, and clipped a low wall. They're slow and old. Luckily the sun wasn't fully up, because the hotter it gets, the more sluggishly the Sea King performs. And there was a 'Heat Stress Alert State Red' on. That could mean temperatures of 55°.

The Intelligence Kid broke off the explanations as one of the screens pixillated out of nothing into a shot of the Sea King itself shuddering along worryingly low, presumably coming from a camera on the escorting Apache. Two or three people got up to peer at the screen, shake their heads and then return to their own mayhems. A voice from the speakers crackled out.

'Looking good, Foxy Two.'

The door gunner in the Sea King raised a thumbs-up towards the camera, then pointed up at the rotor blades.

'Most of it's still there, Foxy Two . . . though they'll probably want you to go back for the missing bits.'

The gunner looked inside towards the cockpit, then turned back and made a grandiose V-sign. A long pause, and then Ned heard the voice of the Air Controller telling the Sea King pilot he had a clear field. All other traffic held. Nothing in their way. Ambulances standing by for the wounded. In your own time. From the view he had of Foxy Two, they should be fine to land, assuming Squadron Leader Vaughan had remembered to knock off the same amount from each rotor arm. A few laughs, but not that many. It would only be funny when and if they landed safely.

Ned stuck the extreme tension for a bit, then told the Intelligence Kid he'd see him outside. Unfortunately for Ned, as he got into the open air, what should he see but the two helicopters hovering about a thousand feet above Camp Bastion? He couldn't not look. The Apache stood off, while Foxy Two held, and then started to judder down. Ned knew nothing about helicopters, but it sounded distinctly unwell. Down, down, until he could no longer see it behind the adjacent ISOs. No ball of fire, please. We don't want any balls of fire. It must be down by now. Must be. Then the ugly noise stopped, and even above the noise of the Apache Ned heard the distant cheering. When the Intelligence Kid emerged, dazzled by the light, he looked more relieved than happy.

'Good idea, sir, coming out to see it land. One of the P1s didn't make it, I'm afraid. The vibration onboard was apparently fearsome . . . Right, sir. Sorry to hold you up. I'm all yours. Bit surprised to see you, actually. Heard the Yanks had got your bomber – somewhere in Western Pakistan, wasn't it?'

Ned put him straight, and then they grabbed some coffee and sat in the shade. Ned didn't waste time.

'I need to see Captain Crispin rather urgently.'

'No chance, sir. He's in the Yemen . . .'

The Kid's voice tailed off.

'I'd be grateful, sir, if you could forget what I just said.'

No problem at all, Ned reassured him. Didn't hear a thing. The Kid looked relieved and swigged his coffee. So, the Yemen already. What was it the Hermit's CO had said to him? 'It'll be the Yemen next, Jimmy. Fancy topping up your tan?' Al-Qaeda's base in the Arab Peninsula, home of the least-guarded nuclear materials on the planet, unstable and unpredictable: the Yemen was clearly *the* place to be. Ned felt so last year, still hanging out in Helmand. OMG – it was like . . . so Gonesville! The Kid looked as if he had zero sense of humour, so Ned kept his fashionista terrorista thoughts to himself.

'So who's taken over from him? And is he also called "Captain Crispin"?'

'No,' replied the Intelligence Kid looking puzzled. 'We don't know who the new person is . . . or what he'll be . . . what he's called.'

So who, Ned wanted to know, is holding the fort?

The Kid looked around as if hoping to find someone drifting by to palm Ned off on to.

'I suppose . . . that would . . . possibly be me.'

Bingo! The next bit took rather more time and wheedling. Ned had to remind him that he was investigating the murder of a British Government Minister plus two other members of MoD staff. Eventually the Kid admitted that he knew MI6 was running a major asset, an Afghan national codenamed 'Sunshine'. The kid had been briefed by Captain Crispin in case there was any delay with his replacement. And in case anything cropped up. But he couldn't tell Ned a thing about him. No, of course not.

Then again, Ned pretty much knew all about him, including his real name, his exact description, his various addresses, his background, his profession, his make of vehicle, his hobby, his London case-officer's name, etc., etc. And to frighten the Kid into a tiddly bit of cooperation, he told him the name of 'Sunshine's' pet falcon and his father, Baba Nazar's recipe for grilled cheese. With a hint of dried mint and slivers of garlic tucked into tiny slits. And – because of the three it would probably be the only one the Kid could check easily – his mobile phone number.

The Kid looked rather less than poker-faced. It sounds, he told Ned, as though you know more about him than we do. What more can you possibly want?

Silly boy for asking, thought Ned. But thanks.

'Were you party to London's questionnaire about possible Afghan responses to PALEP?'

There was a pause. Ned had no idea if there had been any such request for information. But it was a low-risk query. Because if London had not shown any interest in knowing what the Afghan people would make of Ridley's plan to spray the poppies, kill the chemical imports and smash the labs, then the Kid would simply answer no. But he didn't.

'We all were. It wasn't only Camp Bastion's Intelligence community that was asked. The Provincial Reconstruction Team, the agricultural guys who work with the farmers, the medical outreach teams – anyone in touch with local Afghan people was quietly asked for feedback on what they thought would happen were the plan to be put in place.'

Blimey. It's so secret that Mike Ridley won't speak about it in front of his wife, but over here it's the subject of an opinion poll. Ned just needed to make absolutely sure.

'The full, three-pronged plan: crops, chemicals, labs?'

Yes, said the Intelligence Kid. The three-pronged plan.

'And "Sunshine"? Was he asked?'

Long, long pause.

'Look, sir. I can't say. I never saw his name on the raw responses to the questionnaire. And there are no names in the final report.'

'That could mean "Sunshine's" product was called something else.'

The Kid reluctantly conceded it was possible.

And was it?

Yes, he supposed it might have been. That was how it was generally done . . .

So had 'Sunshine' given any answer to the questionnaire?

The Intelligence Kid nodded his head, and said that he ought to be getting back to the Ops Room. Ned assumed he'd pushed him as far as he would go and the two men shook hands rather seriously.

Then, as Ned was about to reassure the Kid that none of this would go any further, the Kid said that someone – he couldn't, of course, say who – had said that the farmers might not like it. Having their fields sprayed. Never mind the loss of cash crops . . . money could soften that blow to some extent. No, it was more to do with ownership. Farmers don't like being told what to do. One thing to have foreign troops on your soil. Another thing to have them spray poison on it. It was, this source said, more an issue of sovereignty. All he said about the labs and chemicals was something about there not being much point in interfering with any of that – the drugs men would immediately work round it.

'Thank you very much,' Ned said.

'Don't mention it,' replied the Intelligence Kid, and then looked a little bashful as he realised he had just made a little joke.

So. Proof positive that Hassani knew that his precursor chemicals business was about to go down the tubes. And his response was perfect. As the Afghan patriot worried about the little farmers, and as the realist. But not as the dealer in death worried about profits.

Next!

Next was Colonel Sillitoe. Sillitoe seemed quite pleased to see him again. Although he too thought Ned's case was all wound up. Oh, it wasn't? The rags had got it round their ear as usual? Typical,

typical. Oh, by the way, Ned's WPC Baker was doing really rather well. Don't breathe a word to a soul, least of all her, but she was about to get a rather good nod in the next Operational Honours List for that business at Kariz. The chaps all absolutely doted on her. He'd sat next to the CO of the Coldstream Guards at dinner last night, and he didn't know her name, but even he had heard about this extraordinary girl and her dog. Reckoned the sight of them walking fearlessly into danger was worth an extra division in terms of morale. And Lord knows how many lives they'd saved . . . Just a shame her tour would be up soon. Not a shame for Baker and Jiffy, Sillitoe conceded, but they'd leave a yawning gap.

Anyway. What could he do for Ned? Yes, he'd certainly be able to introduce Ned to the kind of chaps who could facilitate his arresting someone. He'd convene the 'Snatch Committee'. It had his own people on it, plus one or two from Intelligence and some of the Hereford lot. If it was a high-profile arrest that might be contested by the person in question, then having the SAS along made a lot of sense. A very can-do man from RAF Intelligence handled the travel arrangements if they were going in by chopper. Whom did Ned have it in mind to arrest, exactly? Ned said he'd be in a better position to talk about that in a few days. Thereafter, the sooner they could move the better. Fine. Colonel Sillitoe would ring around and see how everyone was fixed for the end of the week.

Kate had said she'd knock on Ned's tent flap on her way to the kennels to feed Jiffy. He was starting to get anxious, wondering whether to go round to the Ops Room and see how Charlie Patrol was doing, when she and Jiffy put their heads through the flap. Heads covered in dust.

'Good day?'

'Yes, good day. Charlie Patrol still in one piece. Amazing sand storms out there.'

They set out for the kennels. Sun dropping, but still a hell of a heat punch the second Ned stepped outside the tent. How was he going to nail this bastard Hassani? A bit of DNA proof would be nice. A bit of wodge on wodge action. Though Ned hardly dared think it likely that Hassani had pitched up in Brecon himself.

'He's got a house in Lashkar Gāh, you said. At the end of . . . Bost Sarak?'

Kate nodded. She too had spent some time thinking about this. Hamid Hassani had spat out his chewing tobacco just short of the hunting lodge and shack. He'd do the same at his house; he wouldn't want to sully his hand-polished gravel. According to Jamila this Bost Sarak was a very expensive area. Full of what she called 'poppy palaccs'. Big, ornate mansions set back from the road behind high fences and electric gates. Inside: swimming pools, jacuzzis, safe play areas for the children of drug lords. The style known as 'narcotecture'. Not to be confused with the war-torn mud huts of the unfortunate masses who weren't coining it from drugs, graft or siphoned international aid.

She found it hard to see Hamid with a place like that, but then everything about him was getting hard to see. As he evermore receded from her, Kate was becoming increasingly determined to help Ned get him. It wasn't simply because he had so misrepresented himself to her. That was the least of it. It was his total disregard for the lives he was ruining. The death and havoc he was causing. And it just so happened WPC Kate Baker was particularly well-equipped to find a wad of chewing tobacco in the street outside his poppy palace.

'Jiffy.'

The dog in question, still wet from his shower, stayed snout down in his dinner. But Ned looked up at her.

'I've been thinking, Ned. I could borrow a burqa from Jamila and take Jiffy for a walk to Hassani's mansion. If I prepare him beforehand, Jiffy should be able to find some of this chewing tobacco stuff outside the gate. As long as there's a bit there. Then we come home and it's dog biscuits all round.'

In all the years Kate had known Ned, she had never seen him react so badly. She'd thought he'd be all excited and pleased. He wasn't. He was appalled. He read her the riot act. He used phrases like 'on no account' and 'I absolutely forbid you'. It was suicide, nothing less. Hassani was utterly ruthless. The area would be watched. There'd be guards and cameras everywhere. And the dog was hopeless. It screamed police. It might as well be wearing big black boots and saying, 'Right, Sunshine. You're nicked!' Or have a flashing blue light on its bonce. Did she really think civilian dogs sniffed like that? Using systematic search patterns? And then sat down good as gold alongside the 'find'? Ned made Kate swear on Jiffy's life she and the dog would do no such thing. She smiled and agreed. And he said, no – she had to swear on Jiffy's life. So she swore on Jiffy's life.

And then, in the middle of her shower, she thought of another way to get the wodge. Not involving Jiffy at all. Only this time she wouldn't tell Ned about it till afterwards.

11

THIS WOULD MAKE THINGS A little easier. Hamid Hassani no longer had the last house in Bost Sarak. It was four or five from the end, and beyond it the road rose towards open ground awaiting the planting of more poppy palaces. Kate wasn't sure whose side the weather was on. They were in the period of the '120-day wind', which went with baking heat and whirlwinds. If it blew any harder, they'd have to abort. But a bit of a breeze might work. The worse the conditions, the less people notice. Not too much, though. No one would take an innocent stroll in a gale of dust. They got themselves ready – most expensive burqas, finest shoes, best children's clothes, new kite and skateboard – and they waited, getting hotter and hotter. What had been sold to the boys as an adventure was becoming a frustrating ordeal, and the grown-ups were being given dangerously long to think about what they were about to do.

Eventually, around noon, the patch of polythene sheeting on the neighbour's roof stopped its insane flapping, the smoke from the baker's chimney at last defied gravity and they left. Zabiullah drove, using a smart 4x4 with blackened windows which he'd borrowed from his dodgy cousin. No need to worry about the plates, Ajab had said, we'll change them when you get back. I have a thousand of them. They drove across the grid of streets in silence.

Then when they drew near, they went over the plan one last time. The boys looked impatient and said they understood. The women checked one another's appearance. A squirt of expensive perfume. This is it. Stop here. Let's go.

Three women and two boys got out of the 4x4. Smart and rich. The women of a drug lord's household, taking his sons to try out new toys. Fazl ran with the kite, while Mohad tried to chase him on the skateboard. Jamila next, with Parween and Kate behind. They kept up the appearance of a conversation in Pashto, while Jamila watched the boys, issuing maternal warnings to be careful, not to hurt themselves, to give one another a go. They walked past houses like none Kate had ever seen: garish, pillared, mirror-tiled. Minarets, turrets, balconies. Great gobs of colour and flash. Nods to Southfork and the fairground. Brighton Pavilion on speed. Teetering, lurid. Obscene.

'Don't stare!' Parween whispered in English. 'You see these all the time. You live in one, remember?'

Head down. Keep going. Concentrate on Parween. Remember to nod. To laugh. Mustn't trip up – I hate heels like these.

Hamid. How can he live here? How can I have got him so wrong? How can someone be so misleading? Is he like all those clichés? The men with secret families, the quiet serial killer next door, the nice old boy who turns out to have been a sadistic concentration camp guard in his blond youth? Or were the signs there? Are they always there, but we miss them? We have our doubts about so many things – why do they fail us over the big things? We so rarely find ourselves eating stale bread, how come we so often fall in love with the wrong person? What had Hamid Hassani really meant by his landay to her, the one he wrote on parchment?

> *To live twin lives of danger apart*
> *Or be together: safe, alive and aglow – you choose!*

What if he wasn't simply referring to spying, but to his drug life as well? What if he was thinking of giving it all up to be with her?

Would that make any difference? She didn't have to think about it. It made things much worse. He's amassed several fortunes, with houses around the world; then he meets me. He isn't having a moment's moral doubt. He's planning a drug-money-fuelled retirement with a besotted English girl who'll fuck his brains out 24/7. Well, he can go hang himself.

'It's this one, Kate. Just keep going.'

They were walking along beside an eight foot high concrete wall, topped with razor wire. If she'd wanted to look, she'd have seen nothing. There was a metal gate ahead, and the two boys had stopped in front of it, pretending to fiddle with their toys while in fact scanning the ground. Parween glanced back over her shoulder. No one. But two men were coming down the hill on the far side of the road. They didn't look like workmen, but they were on foot. And then there were the cameras on poles at the corners of the properties . . . Not a place to linger. Jamila had gone on ahead, stopped and turned to wait for the boys. Kate walked with Parween past the entrance, almost hurting her eyes as she squinted sideways at the edge of the wall on the driver's side. Nothing. Then on. And on past Jamila. The men across the road were staring at them. Mustn't break step. Parween is telling some sort of gossipy story. She's laughing. Laugh with her. The men turn away. The two boys dart ahead of them up the hill. Can't tell if they found anything. Doesn't look like they have. Jamila catches up with them. No, she whispers as she goes by. Nothing.

Bugger.

They took a breather at the top of the hill. The boys played around, while Kate looked at the staked-out ground plans of new monstrosities. How many heroin addicts would it take to put a flash mansion on every plot? What was the going rate? How many fixes buy a brick? Or a mirror-tile? Lives would be lost before the estate was finished. How could Hamid live with himself? How could he have been so open, so responsive with her, and so closed off to the suffering he was causing around the world? It was scary. *He* must be so scary. She'd had a really narrow escape. Imagine if she had got in deeper before finding out. Imagine if she'd been a material girl: hang the morals – give me the bling! Imagine explaining to her and Hamid's children about the chalet in St Moritz and the town house on the Upper East Side. Daddy worked hard and was lucky, darlings. Then he met me and retired.

Kate turned away in disgust from the building plots to look down the road. As casually as she could, she worked out which was his poppy palace. Fourth down, on the left. Great things burqas – if you can take the heat, the sweat and the misogyny. She didn't know if a tiny part of her would feel relieved if Hamid's house showed better taste than the others, or if it turned out to be as vulgar as its neighbours. What she hadn't counted on was it being, if anything, more grandiose. More disgusting. Maybe they'd got the wrong place. Bugger. The boys couldn't loiter in every gateway up Bost Sarak. She asked Jamila if she was sure of the address. She was positive. Kate shook her head.

It was really difficult being wrenched instantaneously from such intimacy to utter revulsion. Not simply the uninhibited passion of those few days, but that corniest sense of two hearts beating as one. Except they weren't two hearts. It was one heart – hers – and some organ she did not recognise. An organ with the ability to mimic. To camouflage itself, and pass itself off as a heart. Oh, what was the use? She was going round and round in circles. It was like when someone dies. At first you don't necessarily cry, and then the loss starts to hit you and you can't do anything else. Yet Kate didn't want him back. She didn't miss him. She felt furious with herself for the way she had opened herself to him. But most of all, she felt as if she were falling. As if those days with Hamid had taken her somewhere so high that she was soaring effortlessly and ecstatically above everything else. And then, like in the cartoons when Road Runner shoots off the top of a crag and pedals like mad in the air with his legs a-blur, she came to and realised she wasn't flying. She was falling.

'We'd better go. One more chance on the way back.'

Jamila must have sensed how upset Kate was because she

squeezed her hand before turning to round up the boys. A quiet word to them both and the little procession set off back down the road. The wind was starting to get up again. A tiny sand devil pirouetted towards them, swaying and spinning almost across Kate's path. She felt her burqa lift for a moment and then fall back. She tasted dust through the gauze in her niqāb. I'd really like to get out of here, she thought.

As on the walk up the hill, the boys were in front, then Jamila, then Parween and Kate. No one else in sight. Parween kept up the babble in Pashto, in case someone popped out of a side-gate. They had reached the first house down, when Kate saw a cloud of dust at the foot of the road. Zabiullah had been told to wait down there, not to come and pick them up. Perhaps he was worried. How long had they been? Hold on. It wasn't the dodgy cousin's 4x4. It was a jeep. And not just any jeep. A jeep Kate knew. A jeep she'd been in. Oh, God!

Hamid was coming up the road towards them. She couldn't speak. She couldn't tell Parween. Her mouth wouldn't move. Sounds wouldn't come out. He slowed as he neared his house. It *was* his house, then. The worst, most pompous pile of all. But maybe it wasn't him. Perhaps it was Baba Nazar driving alone. The window wound down as the jeep turned in towards the metal gate. No. It was Hamid. He stretched out an arm and clicked a fob to open the gate. An arm that had encircled her body. And as he waited he spat something out of the window. Kate could not believe what was happening. And then Hamid looked across at them. At her. She might have been wearing ten burqas – she would still have felt as if he could see every inch of her body. Would know it was her. Would get out and call her name. What would she do? And then the wind gusted, and she felt the burqa billow up. She slammed both hands to her sides. Had he seen her legs? Please, please not. Because they were bare beneath the burqa.

The gate was moving now, and Hamid looked away from Kate. He hadn't recognised her. The window started going up as the boys reached the jeep. Mohad, rather cleverly, bent down to tie up his shoelace. Or maybe he really needed to. Fazl fiddled with the wheels of the skateboard, spinning them to and fro. The gate was open enough, because the jeep started to move forward. And as it was halfway through the entrance, Fazl bent down and picked something up. The wad of chewing tobacco. No, Fazl! Wait! Why didn't he wait? By now, Jamila was well ahead, and Kate and Parween were drawing level with the gateway. As the two boys started to move off something terrible happened. The jeep stopped. And backed. Then the other window was wound down and Hamid shouted something to the boys. They faltered, clearly wondering whether to run for it. He shouted again. In a very commanding tone. The two boys hesitated, then turned to Hamid. Kate didn't know what to do.

Parween whispered in English to keep walking. The boys must handle it. Jamila had stopped and was looking back. And then Kate could stand it no more, and she too turned to see what was going on. The boys were by the car window listening to the man inside. To Hamid. Then Fazl reluctantly threw away the wad he had picked up. There was a bit more conversation, and Hamid fiddled out of sight and then handed the boys something each. It was done conspiratorially. And Hamid was clearly not angry, but smiling. The smile Kate had seen the very first time she had met him, that night in the Intelligence offices.

Then he gunned the jeep's engine and drove inside the walled compound. And the boys ran down the hill towards the women, grinning and swaggering a little. Like boys who've been told, don't bother with *naswar* someone has spat out. It isn't clean. Here. Have some of your own. And don't tell your mother and aunts. The dope-seller at the school gate.

They were like youths who'd scored. Reluctant to admit what had just been said to them. Reluctant to hand over what they'd just been given. And while they were arguing with their mothers, Kate waited till she heard the gate clang shut, checked the cameras were pointing the other way and then walked coolly back up the road, bent down, poo bag in hand, and picked up Hamid's shit. His still-warm wodge.

Ned didn't know where she was. He knew she wasn't on a shout or breaking her solemn promise, because he went up to the kennels and there was Jiffy. Stir-crazy, and delighted to see him. So Ned took him for a walk around the camp, and was surprised how many people knew the dog. A fearsome-looking bunch of paratroopers went all gooey over him; apparently he'd cleared their way out of a tight corner near Gereshk. So where's his missus then? they all wanted to know. Not sure, Ned replied. We're trying to track her down. You do that, the paras said. She's special.

They stopped at Colonel Sillitoe's office. The colonel wasn't in, but Sergeant Fishpool had a biscuit for Jiffy and the answer for Ned. She's got a 24 hour pass. Staying with her friend Jamila in Lash. Back in the morning with the early shift at the laundry.

Did the sergeant think it was safe for her?

'Safe. Now there's a word, sir. Hard to know what it means out here . . .'

Ned left feeling thoroughly unreassured. He took Jiffy back to the kennels and went to his tent for a think. The only thing they'd discussed which Kate thought Jamila might have the answer to was why Hassani had pretended his parents were his servants? But that wasn't important enough to take Kate to Lashkar Gāh. Only the wodge was worth that, and she'd given her word.

Ned tried lying on the bed, hoping he'd fall asleep and wouldn't wake till she was back. But he was too cold, so he fiddled with the aircon and then he was too warm. Maybe lunch was the answer, but nothing on the menu at the canteen appealed to him. He wandered around in limbo. Kate and the case. The case and Kate. How could he separate the two? Did she miss Hassani? How could Ned get proof that Hassani had masterminded the Brecon Bombing? Why had she fallen for him? Did Ned have enough grounds to arrest him? The Snatch Committee was all very well, but would they do as they were told? He was adamant he wasn't going to let this go down the rendition/torture route. But would he have a say in it, or would it be taken out of his hands on grounds of national security? Jolly clever, that Hassani, protecting his business by tucking himself in with the spooks.

Very clever and very dangerous, maybe, but he had made one mistake. An easy one to make. He'd fallen in love with WPC Kate Baker. Her kiss-off had hurt his ego, forcing a retaliation that linked him to the bombing. But, given that 'Captain Crispin' and the Intelligence Kid would never pitch up on the witness stand to shine a light into the case's darker corners, the only thing so far tying Hassani to the Brecon Bombing was his affair with Kate. So how would the case stand up in court?

Ned could almost hear the derisive tones of the best QC Hassani's limitless wealth could buy. 'Does the prosecution really expect this court to find my client guilty of murder because the trigger mechanism X-3 it alleges he supplied to the bombers was expressly NOT used to kill the Minister and two others? Guilt is not, surely, to be adduced by its absence. The prosecution has failed to produce a single piece of evidence linking this trigger mechanism to my client. What other evidence is there? A strange bicycle no one has seen, including the detective chief inspector who was, by his own admission, present while the murders were committed. No witnesses testify to my client's involvement in these crimes. There is no forensic evidence. The only fingerprint in the entire case is that of a British WPC with whom, again by his own admission, the DCI has had an affair. There is no proof that she ever met my client. And the motive? Supposedly contained in a top-secret initiative against Afghanistan's heroin trade of which the prosecution has been unable to obtain a single copy. The *in camera* testimony from senior members of the Secret Intelligence Service that my client has rendered invaluable service to Great Britain in time of war, at huge personal risk to himself, rather suggests that what my client deserves from this country is a considerable civilian honour . . .'

By this time Ned had thoroughly depressed himself. He also,

oddly, found himself at Kate's tent. So he went in, kicked off his shoes and sat on her spare camp bed. Everything neat. Nothing personal left lying around. Just her alarm clock and her clean smell. Nothing else. It was as if she expected strangers and wanted to tell them nothing about herself. He lay down and closed his eyes. Was he one of those strangers? How could he remake his relationship with her? Where do you begin?

Well, certainly not with wondering what exactly had happened during those two days. The two days she won't talk about. Probably as well – however buoyant and confident you might be, it was probably best not to know the intimate details of what your beloved had got up to with someone else. Not only deeply upsetting. Imagine how awful if, consciously or not, you found yourself trying any of it at home yourself. And another thing. No good Ned sublimating his anger and jealousy in humour, as he normally did. Not a good idea to make any gags at Hamid Hassani's expense. No threatening to buy himself a budgie, for example. And was Hassani really a spot that had cleared up? Or was he a cold sore? A virus that could come back?

Ned moved to the other bed. Her bed. He lay down and saw something only Kate could see. Something which cheered him enormously. Stuck to the inside edge of the folding table by the bed was a photograph. Was this the one that was missing from her kitchen? The one on the wall where he'd seen the blobs of Blu-tack. It was a photo of Kate with her arm around Ned, with the beloved old dog Suzy at their feet. He remembered the moment – happy and close. They were having a picnic in the park near his flat, and they asked a gardener if he was any good with a camera. So . . . She'd had the photo in her flat, and then taken it with her when she went to war. Anything on the back? He gently prised it away and turned it over. Kate had written the date, and the words 'With Ned and Suzy'. She'd underlined Suzy's name with the drawing of a bone, and around his name she'd doodled a tiny heart of flowers.

He put the photo back and fell asleep. She woke him early that evening with the two things he needed more than anything in the whole world. A kiss, and a moist, used wad of chewing tobacco.

He couldn't remember ever running so fast. First to see Colonel Sillitoe and then on to Flight Operations while Sillitoe rang ahead. Ned packed and addressed the Jiffy bag in the back of a bouncing jeep on the way out to the plane. The overnight flight to Brize Norton had been held on the end of the runway, looking like a snorting bull about to charge. The captain took the precious parcel himself and gamely swore it would be handed over in person only to someone who looked like a mad horse and would identify himself with his warrant card and the two words 'Extra Bilge'. Ned watched the plane till it clambered into the stars. Then back to Sillitoe's lair to make phone calls. Then on to Kate's tent to give her an almighty bollocking for breaking her promise to him. She said she had sworn she wouldn't go with Jiffy to find the wad, and she hadn't. So they went off to Pizza Hut for dinner instead.

Ned kept working out how soon before he could expect an answer from the Bilge, and got a different answer every time. The flight was going via Kabul and Cyprus, and Ned decided to factor in a breakdown somewhere that would take four hours to fix. There was also the time difference, but he was never sure whether that should be added on or taken away. He then gave Extra Bilge a puncture on his way to Brize Norton, plus an hour faffing about trying to find the pilot off the Afghanistan flight. Then the Bilge would have to get back to his cubbyhole and his Boys' Own Chemistry Set. That could take a while.

Then there was the question of how the mad horse would communicate the answer. Ned told Sergeant Fishpool to put a fresh ream in the fax machine because, on past form, he'd send pages of calculations, a dissertation on methodology, a thesis on DNA, a glossary of terms, a bibliography, a transcript of his exchanges with Spick and Span during the test and the Wolverhampton Bus Timetable for Christmas 1957. There was often a stray bit of the

Bilge's private obsessions which found its way into the vital mix. Ned was once making a presentation to the Home Secretary and the Justice Minister when he happened to glance at the preview window on his laptop and realised he was about to lecture the high and mighty on the use of Bakelite in 1920s telephone manufacture.

Such provision had Ned made for delay and so shoddy was his arithmetic that he was genuinely surprised when Sergeant Fishpool tapped him on the arm and told him something was coming through. He put down the two day old newspaper, switched off his iPod and ambled over to the fax machine, certain that it couldn't be for him. How many pages? he asked. The cover sheet plus one. No chance Extra Bilge then. He was about to return to the *Daily Mail* and Borodin, when he saw what was written on the sole page. One word, scrawled huge: GOTTIM!

Ned, hovering on the edge of serious elation, asked to see the cover sheet. It was from Fatso himself, getting in quick before the line got clogged by and with Bilge. By the time the fax machine started chattering with the job which would surely be the death of it, Ned was already speaking to Jan Span, being passed to Fatso and then, finally to Extra Bilge who said he'd only sent the short version – eighteen pages – and was Ned making perfect sense of it?

The only thing Ned was making sense of was that the man who'd triggered the bomb which had killed Mike Ridley, Terry Sullivan and Len Kinnear, who'd stared at Ned through glinting binoculars, who'd watched the woman he had just widowed in hysterics, who'd made his invisible escape on a recumbent bike, whose tip-off had led to the slaughter of innocents on a Pakistan hillside – this man was definitely Hamid Hassani, dealer in death and Kate Baker's former lover.

Ned found the Snatch Committee slightly uphill work. What the Special Forces guys really wanted to do was kill Hassani. 'Harvesting', they called it. It was a growth business. They had harvested hundreds of high level Taliban commanders, controlling fighting units and IED production and deployment, along with countless mid-level jokers. It was apparently a lot easier harvesting than snatching. They might consider renaming the committee then, Ned thought to himself. Make it simpler for people like him flicking through Camp Bastion's Yellow Pages. Not, a wiry, affable SAS major assured him, that they didn't do snatches – but snatches were riskier. You had to get right up to the target, and the spoilsport might have a bomb under his dishdasha. But essentially they were up for it. What did Ned have? A description? Good. An address? Great. Mobile number, hobbies, vehicle description, mother's name. More than enough. How important was the man? How well guarded? How security-minded? How likely was he to know about the way they did things?

The answers to the last four questions didn't greatly amuse the Snatch Committee. A bullet or ten in his brains wouldn't do as well? No, Ned insisted. So what are you going to do with him? What's he done, anyway?

'I intend to arrest him, take him back to the UK and put him on trial for the murder of the Minister of Defence, Sir Michael Ridley, and his driver and personal protection officer.'

There was a rewarding little silence. Sounds reasonable to us, the SAS major reckoned. Ned was about to ask if he could go with them to arrest Hassani when a new voice piped up: a beady-eyed, middle-aged man in civvies called Coulson.

'We need to check your man against the "P" list. What is his full name?'

'What's the "P" list?' Ned wanted to know.

'The Protect list. There are all sorts of characters that different agencies have their dibs on. Chaps they're running undercover. Chaps they've invested in. No good Major Wells here harvesting someone the Security Service has been nursing, whose kids they're sending through Marlborough and all that. House in Godalming waiting for them when they've Dun Talibanning. Small thanks we'd get for squishing their prize marrow. The form is, you give us your man's name, and as long as he isn't on the list, you can have him. Trussed up and good to go.'

Ned thought, but not for long. What choice did he have?

'Last name: Hassani. First name: Hamid.'

'Any aliases? *Noms de guerre*? Nicknames?'

Ned shook his head. None that he knew of. Major Wells of the SAS rolled his eyes. Clearly he too found Coulson a bit of a pill. Ned was expecting to have to come back a day later, but Coulson evidently had the 'P' list with him, because the next thing Ned knew he was taking great pleasure in telling Ned that not only was this Hassani on the 'P' list, but he was 'P**'.

'The two asterisks mean the protecting agency has to be notified at once if Hassani's name is put up before the Snatch Committee.'

'And can I guess which the protecting agency is?' Ned asked. 'SIS – MI6?'

Coulson gave a chilly little smile.

'The "P" list requires specific security clearance, I'm afraid. So I can't confirm or deny your guess.'

Major Wells had the decency to follow Ned out. He was sorry about that. Didn't like to think of the Brecon Bomber getting away with it. Least of all because he'd been covering his arse by feeding the Intelligence Service a load of bollocks. This happened a lot: absolute ruffians going scot-free because some twit was padding his list of assets to impress London. It wasn't unheard of for the SAS to knock their pipes out bagging some evil raggy bastard, only to have a spook pop up and whip him off the plane seconds before take-off. Mistake, they'd say, waving their Nectar cards under the pilot's nose. He's ours. And off he goes for a week by the pool in Dubai with a selection of bendy blondes to take away the taste. Can't be helped, the major supposed. Intelligence was pure shit. Give him war any day.

While the SAS major was talking, the rest of the Snatch Committee filed out past them and Ned's mind sprinted. Coulson would be on to London as soon as he got back to his slimy little hollow. Ned only had minutes before MI6 would know the identity of his prime suspect in the Brecon Bombing. Better watch his back then. What could he do in those minutes to throw them off the scent? Nothing. So was there anything he could do to flush them out further?

Sillitoe was settling down with a mug of tea when the door burst open. The rather decent DCI needed to make an urgent call. A bit of a sensitive one. Was there a particular phone he should use?

Yes, of course. Ned should use this one. If he held down this blue button, there would be no way of anyone at this end knowing what number Ned had dialled. And it'd simply come up as a private number at the other. Lovely. Thanks.

When Sillitoe had left the room, Ned checked the time. Around 8.45 a.m. in the UK. Fine. He opened his wallet and pulled out the folded beer mat that had been in there since the start of the case. The one Wilton had handed him a million years ago in a Brecon boozer. The one with her mobile number on it, scrawled in haste before she legged it out the door with the rest of them, leaving Ned with the poisoned chalice.

He dialled the number. Four rings, and then a pause before a cool, clear, measured 'hullo'. At first Ned thought it was going to be the start of an answerphone message. But no, it was her. In the flesh.

'Wilton?'

Tiniest of pauses.

'Bale! How are you? And how are you getting on?'

'Oh, you know. Pretty ghastly! But I'm sure it's what we all expected.'

He said it with a jolly, self-deprecating laugh.

'Poor Bale. You sound as if you need an old friend to haul you off for a large gin and tonic. Where are you? Are you free for lunch?'

'As a matter of fact, Wilton, I am. The snag is, I'm in Helmand Province.'

'Oh, Bale darling! You *have* drawn the short straw!'

'It doesn't matter – they're very good sorts here. And . . .'

At this point, Ned dropped into Jack Lemmon's girly, gossipy cadences from *Some Like It Hot*.

'. . . Hamid's an absolute poppet!'

'Isn't he just!'

She stopped suddenly for two clear seconds before continuing.

'Damn you, Ned!'

And the line went dead.

That was it, then. It *was* Wilton that Kate had seen across the corridor. Come to forewarn and forearm MI6's vital Afghan asset. It was the bottom that clenched it, so to speak. That and the fact that she had called him Ned.

And then it all came back: he had never slept with Wilton. Because he could only remember her calling him Ned once before, after some ball she had taken him to at university. They were at her place in the small hours. He had a memory of her taking her clothes off while he backed as quietly as he could towards the door. Trying to slip away without causing offence. It was a sign of how drunk he was that he thought such a thing was achievable. And as she was finally revealing her finest asset for his privileged delectation she looked up to see if he was silently overcome with desire or what, Bale? But no. He was fiddling with the lock.

'Too drunk, Wilton. Sorry. Pearls before swine . . .'

'Damn you, Ned!'

And he left. Perhaps she had never really forgiven him. Or maybe it was just business. Small wonder her lot had never wanted the case solved. How would the headlines go? Hard to see the tabloids settling for much less than 'MI6 Man Murders Minister'. There would be resignations. Maybe even the Foreign Secretary's. And the last thing MI6 would want was Hassani shooting his mouth off in custody. How will they try to stop that? Ned fleetingly wondered if – Fatso's wild scenario – there was any danger of Hassani coming after him, but that seemed unlikely. He remembered what Major Wells had said, about MI6 packing off their prize assets for poolside R&R to soothe their ruffled feathers. Hassani would probably love that, particularly with Wilton doing some of the soothing.

Ned had a shower, then lay down on his camp bed and had a think about how to arrest Hassani and get him home with no one any the wiser. And when he failed to dream up an answer, he started to think about how Wilton & Co would try to stop him from doing exactly that. They had no idea, after all, that he didn't have a plan. Anyway, perhaps second-guessing their defensive tactics would suggest an offensive course of action to him. Wilton's easiest gambit was to get her bosses to ask Baroness Rajani Nasreen to order Chief Superintendent Larribee to recall Ned on the next flight home. Would Larribee agree to that? She may be slightly thick, but she was usefully bloody-minded. But then all they needed to do was mention the 'national interest', 'national security' and the protection of vital intelligence assets, and Larribee would probably fall apart like the flaky pastry she so bizarrely resembled.

This was, Ned realised, shaping up to have the worst of all outcomes. Ned knew who did it. Ned knew how he did it. Ned knew why he did it. Ned knew how he escaped. Ned knew he'd had an affair with the person Ned loved more than anyone in the whole world. Ned knew where he lived. And Ned knew the bastard was going to walk away from this: rich, gloating and ready to do it again. The worst thing was, Ned didn't know how to stop him.

Kate returned at dusk with Charlie Patrol. She washed Jiffy down and fed him, then showered and went to find Ned. He was asleep in his tent. She saw and read the pile of papers on the side table: Fatso's message and the eighteen pages from Extra Bilge. It was the strangest feeling, knowing that Hamid Hassani was a murderer. Not fearing it or wondering, but knowing. She tried to wake Ned, but he was in the deepest of sleeps, so she put the papers back and left.

She and Jiffy were out again with Charlie Patrol before dawn. They now had only two more days left before their tour of duty was up and they'd be flying home. The following evening she again went to find Ned. This time his tent was empty, the papers gone. Colonel Sillitoe had no idea where he was and instituted a search. No one had seen him all day. He hadn't been to the canteen, and according to Security he hadn't left the camp. By midnight DCI Ned Bale was officially posted missing.

12

THE JEEP WENT SOUTH THROUGH the Dasht-e Margo. A cloud of dust behind like a bride's train caught by the wind. The road skirted the Helmand River for ninety miles, leaving it at Alimardan Khan-e Bagat to continue south towards the Chāgal Hills and Baluchistan. No one stopped the jeep, neither Afghan Army nor Taliban road blocks, and although many saw it pass, none remembered they had. The road deteriorated until there was little discernible difference between it and the desert. Navigation owed more to the sea than to land. The jeep slowed slightly; the penalties for error were severe. From here, the desert was one vast minefield. The Russians had sown it, and the mujahideen and the Americans had filled in the gaps. The jeep steered a careful course and after another hour came to a halt.

Ned had been awake for perhaps twenty minutes. He could barely breathe. His head was in a foul-smelling sack, the rope round his neck almost strangling him. He couldn't move. His wrists and ankles were tied, his arms behind his back, his legs doubled up and bound tight. He was in considerable pain. He had no clue where he was. He couldn't follow any twists and turns in the road because there weren't any, and his brain wasn't working clearly. His last memory was of waking from his camp bed as a hand closed over his face. A hand holding a pad of white cloth infused with something. Chloral hydrate in alcohol, Ned guessed, given the irritation around his mouth and nose. A potentially coma-inducing combination.

How had he been smuggled out of Camp Bastion? Ned couldn't imagine. They could have had help from inside. After all, Hassani and the other man had been driven out of the camp back to Lashkar Gāh the night Kate first met him – and Ned betted Security hadn't been given the chance to shine their torches into the back of that vehicle. There must be a whole lot of stuff going on everyone knew not to ask about . . .

What time was it? How long had they been travelling? How far would they go before someone – probably Kate – realised he was missing? What did it matter? True, he hadn't been killed in his tent, but that only suggested they had something worse planned. This wasn't a kidnap. This wasn't even about extracting information from him. What did Ned know that he could do anything about? No, this had to be personal.

It really was a bit odd: Ned and Kate. Ned and Wilton. Kate and Hamid. Hamid and Wilton. Wilton and Kate. Only Ned and Hamid to go. Maybe that was what was happening now: the final combination. Fatso had been right on the money. Ned remembered asking him at one point how he reconciled the bomber continually trying to put them off the scent, with him effectively luring Ned out to Afghanistan. The way the bomber sees it, Fatso reckoned, if you don't work it out then you're not a worthy adversary. If you do, then – game on! So. A trap had been set, which Ned had fallen straight into. He clearly wasn't quite clever enough. This, he thought, showed all the signs of something that ends badly. And then he blacked out.

When Ned came to, he was lying on the ground. Someone was taking the sack off. Someone then lifted him into a kneeling position. Someone sprinkled water over his face. Ned was groggy, and dazzled by the light. Then someone came between him and the light. And then someone spoke, in a gentle voice without apparent threat.

'Ned. The policeman.'

It wasn't a question. Someone knew exactly who he was.

'I am Hamid Hassani.'

Ned tried to look at the face. Focus on it. Hard work. The first things he saw were the eyes. Extraordinary, black, glowing. Not mad. Beautiful, really. Then the rest of the face followed. All seemed fine. Very good-looking guy. No scars. No knife between clenched teeth. Almost a benign expression. Was this the last face he would ever see?

Ned wasn't sure how long they spent staring at one another, these two men joined by so much. Nor did he know where they were with the introductions. Whose turn was it to speak? His, he thought. Stuff it. What was there to say? Nothing.

Hamid Hassani squatted down so they were on a level with one another. He looked around the horizon. The wind seemed to be getting up a bit. Then he spoke.

'Ned the policeman.'

He obviously enjoyed saying the words. He had a little smile around his mouth. And then he started to speak some more. His voice was so soft it took a while for Ned to hear the tension in it. The hatred.

'I knew there was someone. A woman like that, there must be a big queue. Maybe the biggest. Listen to her talk about the someone – this special someone – and you know if you really have her. Not just for a night or two, but you have her. So I asked, and then I listened. And she spoke to me about you.'

He was almost whispering.

'Yes, she told me. There had been someone . . . Ah ha, I thought.'

Hassani looked at Ned with eyebrows raised. His elbows were resting on his knees and he now opened his hands towards Ned. As if he were asking: Well, do you get it? No. Ned did not get it, so he kept quiet.

'She said "had been someone" like it was over. But I could hear in her voice – maybe it wasn't dead. Not nearly dead enough . . .'

Hassani pursed his lips and stared into the distance.

'Then, when she told me to go away – as if she had found out something about my business she did not like . . .'

He shrugged his shoulders as if she were mad.

'. . . then I thought, maybe she really still loves this Ned the Policeman. He is so clever, she tells me. So gentle . . . Maybe he has become my problem.'

Bad position to be in, Ned thought. To be this man's problem.

'So . . . After being so clever with understanding this and that and maybe everything, here you are in what we call the Desert of Death. And not only a desert – a minefield. You see, Ned the Policeman, I have brought you here to die.'

Hassani nodded his head at Ned, as if his words needed more emphasis. Then he airily waved an arm around.

'There are many, many mines all around. Some very old. The trembler fuses are very sensitive now . . . the chamber walls rusted away . . . the explosive charges become highly volatile. You only have to breathe on them . . . Sometimes I am driving by here and one explodes far away just with the vibration from my jeep. It's strange to see . . .'

Hassani's voice trailed away. When it came back, it was a whisper in Ned's ear.

'How you die, I don't know. Maybe you tread on something, or the heat is too great and you go mad? There is no water. No shelter. All you'll see, maybe, are the vultures who will eat you.'

Ned wasn't sure if he blacked out again. But the next thing he heard was the same repeated phrase.

'Ned the Policeman? Ned the Policeman?'

Hassani slapped his face hard.

'Why don't you say something? Or maybe ask a question, Ned the Policeman?'

Hassani stood, and as he did so, Ned felt the wind stronger on his face.

'One question, out of so many you must have. Perhaps about her? About what we did together. What she did to me in bed, what I did to her . . .'

Ned started to say something, but his lips weren't really working. He tried again, and failed. Hassani laughed a little.

'Ned the Policeman, it is so hard to understand you. Please. Take your time.'

And he squatted down so Ned's mouth was close to his ear. And then Ned started to talk, as distinctly as he could.

'Hamid Hassani, I am arresting you for the murders of Michael Ridley, Terry Sullivan and Len Kinnear. You have the right to remain silent . . .'

Ned felt himself about to black out, but he screwed together every ounce of control and carried on.

'. . . but it may harm your defence if you do not mention when questioned something you later . . . rely on in court . . . Anything you do say may be given in evidence . . . Do you understand?'

Hassani looked puzzled for a moment, then angry. And then he started to laugh.

'So, Ned the Policeman. You have arrested me. But I think in fact I have arrested you! You also can remain silent. Or you can scream. You have this choice.'

Hassani stood for the last time and took a step away.

'I too have choices, Ned the Policeman. Do I go back for Kate now? Or do I wait till she goes home to her little apartment in London? There is no hurry. Maybe when you are dead some time, and she has really forgotten you. Then I have another big choice. Do I fuck her first, or kill her? You tell me, Ned the Policeman – I will do just as you suggest – which one first?'

He gave a broad, handsome grin, as if his dear friend Ned were about to impart wonderful news which would make them both so happy. Ned's response was lost in a big gust of wind; then again, Hassani wouldn't have understood it.

Turning, Hassani took another step away, and stopped. After a while his shoulders started to sag as if, for some strange reason, the fight had gone out of him. He stood there for what seemed an age. Then he spoke. Even with his back to Ned, even against the rising wind, Ned heard him. And the words sounded as if they were coming from inside Ned's head.

'You know, I never felt like that about a woman. About anyone. Never . . . never.'

Hamid Hassani glanced back and for a crazy moment Ned thought he saw tears in his eyes. Then he turned and walked off.

Ned saw him pull something out his pocket – he couldn't see what – which he kept glancing at as he trod carefully from where he had left Ned to the distant jeep. Ned tried to memorise the route Hassani was taking, but it had too many turns. There was someone else by the jeep. Maybe an older man. Was this Baba Nazar? The father/servant? Ned's vision seemed to be returning, but the wind was now whipping up dust. He watched the two men climb into the jeep. Heard the engine start up. Saw it move away.

Then, out of the corner of Ned's eye he saw something else, way behind them. A giant whirlwind was swaying across the desert towards them. Hundreds of yards high, sucking sand into the sky. The men in the jeep didn't seem to see it at first, but after a moment they slowed and then speeded up, trying to outrun it. With minefields on either side, they couldn't veer off the track. Ned had no idea if the sand devil was big enough to lift the jeep, but evidently Hassani and Nazar thought so, because they were now racing flat out across the desert. Then, suddenly, as if it was something it could have done any time it liked, the sand devil pounced and engulfed the jeep. It was lost from sight for several seconds, and then either the driver steered off the straight and narrow or the whirlwind did it for him. There was a terrible flash, followed by a shock-wave. A ball of fire was sucked skywards and then Ned saw the remains of the jeep falling. The debris must have triggered more mines, because a succession of blasts followed, covering Ned in dust.

The sand devil itself whirled on a bit, but the life had been knocked out of it by the explosions. It staggered like a punch-drunk fighter, and collapsed.

* * *

Kate stared at the map of Afghanistan on the wall of Colonel Sillitoe's office. Sillitoe himself was in a huddle with Major Wells of the SAS and two other officers. She couldn't hear what they were saying, but she knew it wasn't good. They didn't have a clue where Ned was. He had left no traces and they had no leads. They didn't even know if he had left the camp of his own free will to find Hassani, or whether he'd somehow been forcibly taken from his tent and whisked away. Where? The country was vast and almost entirely hostile. He might not even be in the country. Or he might already be dead. Why had she ever mentioned Ned to Hamid Hassani? What good purpose had it served? How could she ever live with herself? She turned from the map and made for the door. One of them tried to say something to her as she passed, but she didn't stop. She could tell it was just some reassuring phrase and she knew there was no reassurance to be had.

She went to Ned's tent. One of Sillitoe's men was on guard outside, but he knew Kate and let her pass. She found the shirt Ned had worn the day before in a bag under his bed and sneaked it away to Jiffy's kennel. They had done their last patrol, but their work wasn't quite over.

'Here, Jiffy, smell this. It's Ned's. You have a good old sniff, and then we'll take a look around the camp. Where's that Ned? Where's he gone?'

It was probably a futile exercise but it was better than staring at the emptiness of a map, crying her eyes out.

Must. Must turn. Must turn round. Must keep the sun off the back of my neck. Must let my lunch go down before I have a swim. Must drink plenty of liquids. Must hold still and not fidget while a grown-up puts on my suntan lotion. Must do my holiday diary. Must write my thank-you letters. Must . . .

He was on his side, looking up at the sky. It was late in the day. The sun had done its damage and was leaving. The wind had dropped. The air was still. A perfect temperature. But night was not long off, and the temperature in the desert could drop to near freezing at this time of year. His head hurt, though he no longer felt quite so delirious. He had lost all feeling in his legs. He could move his wrists, but not enough to get them free. But could he reach the ropes that bound his legs? Just. Where was the knot? Or knots? Here was one. Right. Here was his plan for the evening. He wasn't going out. He was going to stay in and undo the knot.

He thought about Hamid Hassani while he felt and tugged. About how scary Hassani was. He could tell, because in the entire time Hassani had been with him, Ned hadn't thought of anything vaguely amusing. No gags, no quick ripostes, no jokes. Must have been really bad. Still is, only Hassani is dead. He's not free to find Kate, thank God.

Don't tug. Be systematic.

He felt around the knot, looking for its weak spot. A place where the rope has some slight give in it. Ah, what's this?

He worked away at the only soft loop in the knot and as he did so, Hassani came back into his mind. This time, not his viciousness, but his smile. If he wasn't trying to scare the shit out of you, he would probably have been very charming. It wasn't hard to see what Kate had seen in him. He'd be fine, as long as you didn't cross him . . . It would never be a good idea for a woman to tell a man like that to get lost. But how much worse if she had really got under his skin? If he had fallen for her so utterly that his defences – so honed and hard – had crumbled. If he had become vulnerable to love for the first time in his life. And then she told him she didn't want to know . . .

Night. Not thinking now. Too busy shivering. Colder than he could imagine. Teeth-chattering cold. Head tucked down into lap. Crash position. Already crashed. And lost. Not looking good. Feeling in fingers now gone. What's that? And that? In the sky. Shooting stars? Could be. That's nice. Not for me, though. Who's won this? Has anyone won yet? Not me. So cold. So . . . mustn't swear. No excuse for swearing, however strongly you feel. Go to your room. Yes, please. Can I? Can I please go to my room?

Kate fed the exhausted Jiffy and bedded him down before walking back to her tent. She had wondered about letting him sleep with her, but thought he'd get more rest in his kennel. It had been a hopeless day. She wasn't sure at first if, given all his explosives training, Jiffy would be any good at playing bloodhound so she handed him to Sergeant Fishpool for a walk around the block. Meanwhile she tore a sleeve off Ned's shirt and hid it in Colonel Sillitoe's wastepaper basket. Jiffy found it in seconds. But that was the only flicker of response she saw from him all day, and they scoured Camp Bastion.

They weren't alone. Word had got around that Ned was missing, and Kate and Jiffy kept bumping into people they knew. Charlie Patrol spent their precious day off hunting for Ned. Kate met two Gurkhas who warmly remembered her and Jiffy from the Nad 'Ali raid. They were recuperating from minor wounds but wouldn't listen to Kate's entreaties and insisted on joining the search. Zabiullah organised a team to turn the laundry upside down. Kate and Jiffy had a particularly unpleasant trawl through the refuse area and around the latrines. Nothing.

She was lying on her camp bed unable to sleep, when she heard a voice outside.

'Miss? It's me – Sergeant Fishpool. There's something . . .'

On their way to Colonel Sillitoe's office the sergeant made sure Kate realised this something wasn't necessarily good news. In fact, it could well be the exact opposite. She'd better brace herself . . .

She couldn't see what she was meant to be noticing. The picture on the screen in Sillitoe's office showed a flat, distant view of endless desert. It was a view from a surveillance aircraft, high in the air. It looked totally featureless – immobile except for timecode ticking away in the corner.

'Wait a sec, Miss. Any minute now.'

The sergeant pointed to near the edge of the frame. It took Kate a second or two to spot a grey dot moving ever so slowly. It then seem to flicker and vanish. Then, where it had been, she saw a blister of light swell and fade away.

'What is it? What was that?'

'An explosion.'

It was Colonel Sillitoe who answered. She hadn't noticed him when she'd entered the room. He was standing behind her.

'The chaps whose job it is to read pictures like these all day long say it was a moving vehicle being blown up. Not a big one. Smaller than a truck. Maybe a Snatch or a jeep or something. Due south of here, near the Baluchistan border'

He showed Kate a map. A cross in a circle marked the position where the explosion had occurred: on a track which ran straight through an area of red hatching, with the word 'MINEFIELD' stamped on either side. The track, she now knew from her conversations with Ned, that Hamid had driven her down, in his jeep . . .

Kate didn't really take in what Colonel Sillitoe said after that. It was something to do with it being too dark to see anything now, although they could use infra-red . . . But it would take a few hours to set this sort of thing up . . . it would probably be morning, either way. Kate hadn't a clue what 'this sort of thing' was, and didn't much care. She couldn't think past the possibility that she had just seen Ned being blown to pieces – in Hamid Hassani's jeep.

A noise. He was woken by a noise. A faint whirring sound. Was it something very, very quiet and very close? Like a cricket, near his ear? Or was it something loud a long way off? He opened his eyes. Nothing. He couldn't see the source of the sound. It was dawn. Streaky, pink and grey. Not as cold. Wiggle fingers. Not a lot going on. Come back to them. Wiggle toes. Something there, in the left foot for sure. Not certain about the right. Hold on. Where was his left foot? Felt a long way away. He looked down. His left leg was straight. And the reason he had no feeling in his right was that it was still tucked up under him. But if he could shift his weight . . . there! Both legs straight! He must have got the knot undone in the night. And now the rope around his wrists felt loose. Loose enough to . . . yes! His arms were now free. He could stand. Move around. Get away . . .

No. Hold hard. How come it was possible to get the ropes untied? Rope. Just the one, binding both legs and arms. And not binding them too tight to undo. What was that about? Presumably Hassani intended him to get free, to encourage him to stumble off to certain death in the minefield. So, don't move. Don't stray. Lie back. You may be free but you are trapped. Even so, for a while, on that warming sand, it felt wonderful.

There it was again. The sound. And now he thought he saw something. Something circling overhead. Bloody hell. A vulture. That's all he needed. If he kept moving, would it see that he was alive? Was it against their religion to eat the living? Perhaps if he stood. Mustn't move off this spot, though. On to side. Careful! Mustn't roll, not in a minefield. On to front. Knees up. Lift! One foot on ground. Up! Standing, at last. No sign of the vulture now. So where are Hassani's tracks? Could Ned see how he'd got from here to the jeep? No. The sand devil and the falling dust from the mines must have covered everything up. Bugger.

And then Ned noticed something about a hundred yards away. Something he hadn't seen when he was lying down. Something not at all nice: the body of a man. It didn't seem to have a face. Something had eaten it away. Wolves, perhaps? Or, more likely, vultures. Wolves were unlikely to have made it that far over so many hair-trigger mines. And were those bones over there, white against the sand? Ned was clearly not the first of Hassani's enemies to be given the choice of death by exposure or explosion.

As the sun started to peep over the distant mountains, Ned heard the noise again. The vulture was high. Soaring. Ned kept his eyes on it this time. It seemed to be flying in a figure of eight, at the same height, without once flapping its wings. Or was it the bloody man's pet falcon? Come to find its master and then peck Ned's eyes out? Ned knew nothing about birds, but didn't they occasionally have to flap their wings? Unless they were riding thermals,

286

but wasn't it too early in the day for them? Then, slowly, Ned put it together. The lack of wing-flap. The odd noise. The strange flight pattern. It wasn't a bird of prey up there. It was a pilot-less aircraft. A drone.

Was it one of ours? Who else had them? Was it a hunter-killer, like that Reaper, or was it for surveillance? Ned couldn't see any missiles slung under its wings, but it was a little too high to be sure. And then, as he watched, it grew bigger and bigger. It was dropping in height. A few minutes later, and the drone was circling him, perhaps five hundred yards off the ground. Ned stared at it as it pottered around him. And then he waved at it. Tentatively at first, then like a mad thing. Could it see him? There seemed to be a pod on a small arm, and there was some sort of lens in the pod because he could see the rising sun reflected in it at the point when the sun, Ned and the drone were exactly in line. So he waved some more.

Then he realised that in a few hours the temperature would be in the fifties. Shelter was the thing. He couldn't move from the spot, so all he could do was dig. He'd need to dig down and then along, to get out of the sun. But the trouble was, the sand was so fine, the hole would probably keep falling in. It would be slow going. But he knew he wouldn't survive another day in the direct sun. His body might, possibly. But he knew his mind would not. The trouble was that he didn't know how close the nearest mine was. Supposing he disturbed it? Supposing he kicked dust on top of a trembler mechanism? And how, with the sun directly above, would a hole protect him? He'd need to dig down and then along. But the trouble was, the sand was so fine, the hole would keep falling in . . .

Hold on. He'd just thought that a moment ago, hadn't he? He was going round in circles. Best sit down for a moment. Cup of coffee would work a treat. Plus? Always a problem that, croissant or brioche? Definitely brioche today. Croissants reminded him a bit too much of old Larribee. Think big, she'd said. Well, he wouldn't be in her good books now. He was thinking as small as it's possible to think. There's nothing in the world as small as your own life.

Kate never saw the man waving. But she heard about it the second she walked into the Ops Room. She had only fallen asleep in the small hours of the morning and woke late to the sound of Sergeant Fishpool again outside her tent. But she could tell from his voice that this wasn't quite the same as before. He didn't want to raise her hopes, he said, but they'd spotted someone . . .

The Ops Room was packed. The usual team on duty had been joined by more senior officers as well as by outsiders like Colonel Sillitoe. Evidently the man in the desert had waved while the sergeant was fetching Kate, because it was news to him as well. But Kate had more to catch up on. She had never been in the Ops Room before, and she couldn't see which of the many screens she should be looking at. Which of the sounds she should be listening to. Sillitoe spotted her and came over. He told her in a whisper they'd sent up a drone to search the area where the explosion had occurred. They were drawing a complete blank, and then the pilot – the drone was being controlled from Creech Air Force Base in Nevada – thought he'd seen something in a bit of desert they'd already covered. Some of the guys wondered if it was because the man had stood up that the pilot noticed him. So the drone went in closer and they saw him. That's when he waved. The trouble was, none of them knew what this Hassani looked like. Apart from Kate.

She started to go hot and cold, and then she remembered telling Silly Toes herself about that night in the Intelligence ISO. She couldn't assume he knew about her affair . . .

'So if the man who waved isn't DCI Bale,' Sillitoe went on, 'you might be able to tell us if it's Hamid Hassani.'

Kate felt sick at the thought that it might be Hamid and not Ned who had survived. Sick and so angry. And then it occurred to her that Sillitoe had no reason to know how special DCI Bale was to her, either. That, given there were two obvious candidates for the identity of the man in the desert who had waved, she had loved both of them. Had slept with both of them. Had melded her life, however briefly in Hamid's case, with both of theirs. And she didn't wish Hamid dead for all his wickedness, unless that was what it took for Ned to be the survivor . . . It was a potentially ghastly thing Sillitoe was asking her to do. He had to ask her to repeat her next words because they came out so quietly.

'Where is he? Where should I look?'

Colonel Sillitoe pointed to one of the screens. At the unsteady centre of an orbiting frame. Kate stared at it.

'Do you recognise him?'

She edged closer and stared some more. It was only a dot in the middle of nowhere. She shook her head.

'I can't see clearly enough. Can they zoom in at all?'

Sillitoe spoke to the Intelligence Kid who spoke to someone else. There was a pause, and then Kate heard a voice from one of the speakers. An American voice.

'. . . not sure how steady we are going to be able to hold it . . . still gusting in that sector . . . but stay tuned . . .'

Nothing happened for a moment. And then the camera on the drone zoomed in. Zoomed in so far it lost the dot completely. Kate felt like shouting out: zoom out! Bit to the left! Perhaps she started to, because she felt Sillitoe's hand on her arm. Wait, he said. It's circling. Let it do a complete turn. We might get a glimpse of him . . .

The image was very shaky. For an age it just seemed to be desert, and slightly out of focus desert at that. Then it zoomed out with a jerk. And then back in, but not as close as before. Kate stared at the screen. Whether the room went quiet, or whether her brain was shutting down everything in the world apart from that screen, she had no idea. But she couldn't hear anything, wasn't aware of anyone, couldn't see beyond that rectangle of dull grey plastic. She almost stopped breathing. And then she did stop. Because there, fleetingly in and out of the frame was a man – a man she knew very well. He was only on the screen for a second at most, and he looked in a poor state, but he was on his feet. He was alive.

'Well, WPC Baker? Which of them is it?'

She answered in a whisper without taking her eyes off the screen – so desperate was she not to miss a second glimpse of him.

'It's him. It's Ned.'

She could vaguely hear Sillitoe relaying her words, followed by the room erupting in cheers. And all that relief and happiness flowing around her somehow made it real for her, and she started to breathe again.

What time was it? Sun bang overhead. Where's that hole? He'd dug a hole hadn't he? Against this eventuality? What eventuality? The sun being directly overhead, silly. You are silly, Ned. No hole? That's OK, I'll just sit here. So why did Hassani tell me Kate said 'there had been someone'? That's not what she said at all. 'There is someone,' was what she said. The cheek of the man! As my grandfather would say, he's a four-letter man. Was. Tenses can be tricky things. There *is* someone. Me! And I love her. I LOVE KATE BAKER!

What's that noise? The drone. I might have got drones wrong before; they aren't all bad. Some are very good. Here, girl. Good drone. Sit! If you don't sit, you're not getting a biscuit. Drone's a bit loud today, isn't it? Sure it's feeling OK? It sounds dreadful. Never mind the drone, I don't feel well. Not feeling at all well. Such a shame, after cracking the case, to feel a bit peaky. Poor Ned. Poor old chap. You lie here, like this. It'll all go away. Better in the morning old chap. All be well in the morning . . .

The convoy stopped some way short of the vast crater to the side of the track. The Afghan guide who had led them through the minefield got out and lit a cigarette. Next out was a woman with a dog, followed by soldiers with metal detectors, ladders and a tracked robot bristling with sensors and cameras. They could see the man in the distance, deep in the minefield. Curled up, with his shirt flapped up over his head. He wasn't moving. But something was: a small, white drone circling faithfully above him.

One of the soldiers said something into a radio. And on the other side of the world in Nevada, the pilot who had refused to leave his post until the man in the desert he would never meet was rescued, dipped the drone's wings to acknowledge that he could see that the convoy had got within sight of the man. And still the drone wouldn't leave. It waited while the dog and the woman found all the mines between the road and the man, and the soldiers defused some, and bridged others. It waited until the woman and the dog reached the man, and the dog licked the man's face and the woman gave him a little water, and then something that looked suspiciously like a kiss. That was the moment when the man really seemed to come back to life. There was quite a crowd around the bank of monitors at Creech Air Force Base by this time, and when they saw that, a great roar went up. Only then did the pilot hand over the controls of the drone.

He jogged home.

He was too tired to shoot some hoops. He wasn't hungry and he didn't fancy his neighbour's wife. So he climbed into bed with his own wife whom he fancied rather a lot, and fell fast asleep.

Epilogue

NED SPENT THREE DAYS IN the hospital at Camp Bastion. He had little memory at first of what had happened to him, but bits of it started to come back. He didn't mind that. He didn't much like gaps. He had a lot of visitors. First to pitch up was the whole of Easy Patrol. Rescuing Ned was their first shout since the antenna had snagged that IED tripwire near Shuga patrol base. They were on great form: Tom Ellison and Sergeant Midge Murray and the others. They sat on his bed and ate most of his fruit and all the *baklawa* that Jamila and Zabiullah had brought over, and made him laugh till it hurt.

Colonel Sillitoe, Sergeant Fishpool and Major Wells of the SAS came to see him. Major Wells gave Ned a bit of a bollocking for hogging all the fun for himself. And reminded him that next time anything like this cropped up, Ned should come straight to the SAS. They'd be delighted to help. One-stop shop for mayhem, and no questions asked. Then who should pitch up at the foot of Ned's bed but the Intelligence Kid? Ned tried to read into the Kid's demeanour whether he was the one who had helped Hassani break into the camp and lift Ned. Didn't look like he was, but Ned decided he had nothing to lose so he asked him point-blank if he knew who it was. The Kid said he didn't know. He really didn't know. But he didn't say the whole idea was absurd, and how could Ned think such uncharitable thoughts?

And WPC Kate Baker, GC and now GM? She barely left his side. She was first in the ward in the morning and last out at night. Once, she got Midge Murray to pass Jiffy in through the window so the dog could make sure for himself that Ned was all right. That same evening she sat watching Ned after he had fallen asleep. Only a few bandages now, white against his skin. Arms by his side on top of the sheets. He was so very clever and brave. And so very, very fit. And as she watched over him, she realised she was no longer falling.

The only unresolved problem between them – the only thing that still divided them – was where they should sit on the plane going home. Ned wanted to be next to Kate. But on the C-17 there are seats facing one another, and that was how she wanted them to sit, so she never had to lose sight of him. So he'd be the first thing she saw when she woke up. And that's where they sat, except when they went to check on Jiffy, which they did rather often. Because the other good thing about the C-17 is that it's dark at the back on long night flights, and no one can see you kiss.

Acknowledgements

In the course of writing *Into Dust* I read much excellent journalism on Afghanistan, its women and its war, including pieces by Karen McVeigh, Richard Norton-Taylor, Jonathan Steele, Nafeesa Shan and Stuart Webb. The Internet provided a range of fascinating material, from the diary of the late Lieutenant Mark Evison to the News Archive of Rawa – the Revolutionary Association of the Women of Afghanistan. My reading list included *Songs of Love and War* by Sayd Bahodine Majrouh, *Raising my Voice* by Malalai Joya, *The Bookseller of Kabul* by Åsne Scierstad, *Taliban* by James Fergusson, *Eight Lives Down* by Chris Hunter and *Spoken From the Front* by Andy McNab.

But *Into Dust* is fiction.

ALSO BY JONATHAN LEWIS

INTO DARKNESS

A body half submerged in the stinking mud of a tidal river – one of the most famous men in the world has apparently fallen to his death. But Sir Tommy Best was not only a great actor. He was also completely blind.

So where is his legendary seeing dog, Suzy? Why would she lead him into danger? And why did she run?

Under mounting pressure, the police turn to two of their most idiosyncratic talents: Ned Bale, a cop with the knack of solving the unsolvable, and Kate Baker, supremely gifted police dog handler. If Sir Tommy's last walk was not what it seemed, then his brilliant guide dog is the only witness.

Unputdownable – with characters you won't forget – here is an exceptional crime novel.

'A very promising debut' *Literary Review*

'A classic detective story with an affecting romance in the mix . . . A distinctive and zestful novel' Cath Staincliffe, author of *The Kindest Thing* and creator of *Blue Murder*

arrow books

THE POWER OF READING

Visit the Random House website and get connected with
information on all our books and authors

EXTRACTS from our recently
published books and selected
backlist titles

**COMPETITIONS AND PRIZE
DRAWS** Win signed books,
audiobooks and more

AUTHOR EVENTS Find out which
of our authors are on tour and
where you can meet them

LATEST NEWS on bestsellers,
awards and new publications

MINISITES with exclusive
special features dedicated to our
authors and their titles

READING GROUPS Reading
guides, special features and all
the information you need for
your reading group

LISTEN to extracts from the
latest audiobook publications

WATCH video clips of
interviews and readings with
our authors

RANDOM HOUSE INFORMATION
including advice for writers,
job vacancies and all your
general queries answered

Come home to Random House

www.rbooks.co.uk

𝑃